EARLY PRAISE FOR NUMBERS GAME

Get ready for this in-the-moment Wisconsin based detective mystery novel with the Appleton Police Department. Features candid, raw, very human, and full characters with connections in this well researched third novel by JP Jordan. Jump in with both feet!

- Christina L. P. W. Johnson, MA-LIS, Door County Library - Sister Bay/Liberty Grove Library Branch Manager

As an avid reader of police-procedurals and crime mysteries, I was thrilled to find JP Jordan's books. His third book, *Numbers Game*, had me captivated from chapter one. The pace (and my heartbeat!) quickened with every page turn. Jordan's books always include fascinating characters. In his first book we received a glimpse of Detective Nowitzke, the second book developed his character, and this book delivers Nowitzke at his full-blown, offbeat best. While I tried to unravel where the story was headed, Jordan dropped clues but kept me guessing and in suspense to the very end. His books rival those written by the likes of James Patterson, Michael Connelly, and Stieg Larsson.

- Bob Gebhardt, Retired Insurance Professional

Cleverly layered with suspense, grit, depth, and a decent dose of Wisconsin wit. *Numbers Game* will leave you adding up the bodies and the intrigue. The unusually paired detective team of Nowitzke & Taylor push a current high-profile investigation and a series of cold cases to the very edge. Highest praise for this entire series!

- Sara Schultz

5 of 5 stars for *Numbers Game*! JP Jordan is a masterful storyteller, combining mystery, intrigue, wit, surprise, and emotion into a 'who-dun-it/who's doing it' page-turner experience!

- Elizabeth Lombard

Thoroughly enjoyable. *Numbers Game* is a real page-turner. JP Jordan's writing style presents detailed information helping with the development of characters and the explanation of specific processes and procedures. All the elements of the story are presented in a logical sequence as the story unfolds. And, there is always an element of surprise at the end of the book!

- Sally Neiderer

Jordan's best book to date. Full of action, suspense, humor, and snappy dialogue. I couldn't put it down. The development of Chuck Nowitzke's and Anissa Taylor's characters and friendship is engrossing as is the friendship with Chuck's landlady.

- Sue Menhennick

NUMBERS GAME

A Chuck Nowitzke Novel

J. P. JORDAN

Ten|16
PRESS

ten16press.com - Waukesha, WI

Also from J. P. Jordan:

MEN OF GOD

Also from J. P. Jordan:

ALL IN

Numbers Game
Copyrighted © 2022 J. P. Jordan
ISBN 9781645384632
First Edition

Numbers Game
by J. P. Jordan

For information, please contact:

www.ten16press.com
Waukesha, WI

Edited by Lauren Blue & Pam Parker
Cover design by Josh McFarlane
Art Director: Kaeley Dunteman

Dedication

Since I began my second career (or third depending upon who's counting), I have been blessed with the support of my family. My wife, Nanc, offers me all manner of encouragement regarding my small business and in life. And my MOG Marketing team (Jamie, Mila, Ivy, and Arie) are my social media stars with their relentless energy and creativity in giving me a presence that helps sell my books.

Additionally, my circle of friends in the literary field has grown exponentially including readers, authors, bookstore owners, editors, beta readers, ARC readers, and subject matter experts. Their help continues to make my work better.

Jim

CHAPTER 1

It was an uncharacteristically steamy June evening in Wisconsin, but Senator Anthony Hecht could have cared less. The climate within the mansion of his long-time friend Bradford Hawkins was perfect. With the election just five months away, his campaign team had hit the ground running, and the early polls showed him with a commanding lead over his political rival. Best of all, the fundraiser organized by Brad had infused Hecht with an additional source of energy courtesy of his newest "friends" who had lined up to make major contributions to his already full war chest. Even though Hecht believed he was ahead based on his record alone, he knew from several prior successful campaigns that cash was indeed king.

Hecht had expertly worked the room. Actually, all the rooms in Brad's sprawling home. A former district attorney, Brad was empathetic to his friend's cause, understanding the mental, physical, and financial demands on a candidate. Since moving into private practice, his aim had been to leverage the power and money of his local contacts to benefit his political allies.

Moving through Brad's home, Hecht was grateful for the strong showing of support, glad-handing those in attendance. Wherever he turned, he was surrounded by well-dressed, shiny people with smiles on their faces and drinks in their hands making light conversation. The waitstaff, outfitted in crisp white shirts, black bowties, vests, and pants, was doing its best to circulate through the crowd to keep the glasses full while offering hand-passed appetizers. Brad had obviously done well for himself. In fact, no one else Hecht knew lived in a home with a name: Ivy House, chosen by a prior owner for the ivy that covered the expansive red brick exterior walls. At some point, Hecht had lost count of the number of rooms; each was filled with well-heeled couples. Besides taking their money, he was also making vital contacts to call on when needed, whether in office or working as a lobbyist after his political career was over. CEOs. Philanthropists. Doctors. Lawyers. A veritable who's who of the local power brokers, at least those aligned to his party. Hecht had even reacquainted himself with Marcus Clark, the current Appleton police chief, who had made an appearance.

Hecht, now in his fifties, was a self-made man. Early on, he had worked a series of odd jobs before buying a business, then a second, and a third. But a dispute about a local zoning law changed his life. Fearing that the new law would negatively affect one of his companies, Tony, as he was known then, fought back against city hall. It was an old story he told often. "I went to the city fathers, spent my time and money to prepare, and presented my argument. I lost. No one was sympathetic to me. Several wouldn't even give me the time of day." Even though he no longer remembered the issue, he recalled being incensed enough to run for alderman with the idea of righting the wrong. He positioned himself as a businessman, someone who created jobs and paid taxes. A person who would listen to his constituents rather than being another "bureaucratic asshole" like the one who had ruled against him. Hecht won an alderman's seat on the city council in a landslide. More importantly, he discovered a calling. He became a man of the people who enjoyed shaking hands and kissing babies at Fourth of July picnics and holiday parades. His friends encouraged him to run for state office. Again, Hecht won on his first attempt against a long-time incumbent. After a successful term, national office called. By the age of forty, he had become Senator Hecht.

Despite his political success, the role had taken a toll on the man. Hecht maintained a relentless schedule in Washington or working in Wisconsin. Without making time for himself, he had gained some fifty pounds over the years, the result of too much steak and alcohol. The senator also suffered from hypertension and was taking medication to control his cholesterol. His doctor had warned that Hecht needed to make some serious changes in his life if he wanted to see age sixty. But he enjoyed his job, his "people," his lifestyle, and pushed on regardless. Still, even the demands of the fundraiser had taken a toll on the senator. Finding an unoccupied corner of a room, he took several deep breaths before spotting his host standing all by himself at the bar, enjoying his martini and a quiet moment. Hecht walked over and joined him. "Brad, I can't thank you enough for your help. My God, the people here blew me away with their generosity."

Brad smiled, lifting his glass toward the senator. "You've earned it. Keep doing your work from the perspective of the little guy, and the people will support you." He took a sip of his drink. "I wish Maggie could have been a part of all this."

"Me too," replied Tony, his voice tightening. "My wife would have loved it. It's been four years now since she passed."

"Well, my friend, not to be disrespectful to Maggie, but have you gotten a look at the redhead across the room?"

"That's a big yes. I'm a senator, Brad. Not a monk," Hecht said, getting back into the flow of the crowd. In fact, he had first spotted the woman earlier in the evening on his initial walk through the home. A thirty-something, willowy, auburn-haired beauty wearing a flaming-red cocktail dress. With his head on a swivel keeping a lookout for the woman, Hecht crossed paths with her several times. On their most recent pass, they made eye contact. She offered a smile. He gave her a nod with a tip of his glass in return. As far as Tony could tell, she was unattached as he studied her moving through the room, making small talk with others.

Now, with the crowd thinning as the night progressed, Hecht saw his opportunity. The woman was casually chatting with a couple at the portable bar in the library. When Hecht approached, the man and his wife turned on cue to greet him. "Senator Hecht. I don't know if you remember her, but this is my wife . . ."

"Please, call me Tony, Dr. Reardon. How could I forget Laura from our earlier meeting?" The fact that the senator had remembered her name, along with the effects of a third glass of wine, caused Laura to cackle uncontrollably. "But I have not had the pleasure of meeting this young woman," he said with a warm, gin-filled gaze at their companion.

Jeff politely interceded. "We just met ourselves. Senator, this is Savanna. But I apologize. I guess I never got your last name," he said, looking at the woman.

"Smythe. Savanna Smythe." She beamed at Hecht as she offered her hand. "I've been looking forward to this all night, Senator," she said, subtly commandeering Tony, moving him away from the couple at the bar. "Can I get you a drink?"

"Sure. Martini, please," Tony said, looking directly at the bartender, who was already within earshot. "What do you need?" he questioned Savanna.

"Nothing," she replied, holding up a half-filled glass of Chardonnay. "So, Senator," started the young woman demurely, "I hear you have somewhat of a reputation with the ladies."

"Oh, it's nothing but rumors and innuendo. Propaganda put out by the other party to try to discredit me . . . mostly," he concluded with a telling grin.

"Pity," Savanna said, playing along, looking into his eyes while rubbing her body against his. "Because I've never fucked a senator before," she whispered into his ear. She turned away, but Tony gently tugged at her hand, managing to keep her from leaving. Looking into his eyes, she quietly said, "Rather than making boring conversation all night, I scoped out the house. Did you know there's a wine cellar in the basement? Quiet. Secluded," she purred.

Tony said nothing as Savanna took his arm, and they walked silently toward an elevator in the foyer. While she avoided contact with other partygoers, it was inevitable that those they encountered would acknowledge the politician in some way. However, Tony walked with a laser focus, like he was wearing horse blinders, politely ignoring his benefactors as if they were invisible. When they arrived at the elevator, Savanna pushed the button, and the doors opened immediately. Once inside, after the doors closed, she reached up and kissed him gently, taking his hand. The lift dropped two floors, opening into a dimly lit and dank-smelling lower level. They stepped onto a stone floor as Savanna continued to lead like she knew where she was going. Aside from the echo of her heels reverberating against the stone, it was dead quiet. Then, the passageway narrowed, and as they came to a corner, a server holding a tray of hors d'oeuvres approached from the opposite direction. The waiter stopped, raising the tray and pulling his body up against the wall to allow the couple room to pass.

"Where is the wine room?" asked Savanna.

"Just around the corner, miss," replied the server as she slipped past. Then, as Tony squeezed through the narrow passageway, he felt a sharp prick in his beefy backside, enough to cause him to yelp and pull away abruptly.

"Hey, asshole . . . be careful," he said, raising his voice at the waiter.

"I'm sorry, sir. Are you okay? I must have somehow gotten you with the corkscrew in my other hand," said the waiter. He waited for a response, but Tony said nothing, continuing down the hall, the incident now forgotten, his attention focused elsewhere.

Savanna pulled Tony along hurriedly. After they had walked out of earshot of the waiter, she laughed. "Oh my, Senator, that guy could have easily caught us in the act."

When they found the wine room, Tony held the tinted glass door open for Savanna as they moved into another layer of coolness in the softly lit chamber. Once inside, Savanna put her wine glass on a table, turned, and kissed Tony deeply. Then, after taking her time to build anticipation, she began fumbling with his belt, first pulling down his pants and then his underwear. "Well, hello," said Savanna. As she dropped to her knees in front of him, the senator let out a loud groan and began to wheeze.

"Oh my God, I suddenly don't feel very good," said Tony, who began sweating profusely. "Can you find a chair for me? I think I might need a doctor."

"What's wrong?" asked the young woman.

"My chest is tight. I need help, *now*!" said Hecht, his voice trailing off. "Help me, Savanna. Please call an ambulance."

Savanna frantically began searching her purse to find her phone. "Damn, I've got no service down here," she said, jumping to her feet. Kicking off her shoes, she moved quickly, picking her way along the darkened hallway, the unheard cry of "help" echoing off the walls of the old basement. Unable to find a stairwell, Savanna was forced to wait for the elevator as she felt time ticking along relentlessly. Thirty seconds became sixty, which became ninety before the doors opened. When the elevator finally arrived on the main floor, she saw a police officer talking to the man she knew as the host of the event.

"Help!" she yelled, getting the attention of both men. "Please, it's the senator. I think he's having a heart attack."

Chief Marcus Clark immediately yanked the cell phone from his pocket and dialed 9-1-1 before handing it to Brad. "I know CPR," he offered. "Brad, when the EMTs get here, please direct them."

"Where? Where's Tony?" Brad yelled to Savanna.

"Downstairs. The wine cellar. Please hurry." With no other option but to take the elevator, Savanna returned to the basement with Clark in less than a minute. Leading the way, Savanna stopped in the passageway, out of breath. "I can't go on. It's down there, officer," she gasped, managing to point the direction for Clark. Not knowing exactly where he was going, the police chief moved as quickly as he could before he came to the tinted glass door.

When Clark stepped inside, he saw Senator Hecht crumpled on the floor, obviously dead. After the chief checked the senator's neck for a pulse, he saw that the man's eyes were bulging, his large tongue hanging from his mouth, looking like a fish out of water. The fact that Tony was naked below the waist with the young woman reporting his medical issue was inescapable. Clark's first inclination was to find something to cover the senator while waiting for the redhead to arrive with more details. But she never made it to the room.

Then, standing back, Clark noticed something else in the low light. Something like he had seen years before. The number "7" was scrawled in thick, black ink on Tony's forehead.

CHAPTER 2

Detective Chuck Nowitzke was just finishing dinner with his ninety-year-old landlord when his cell phone rang. "Yeah," he answered. "Seriously? No shit. Where to?" His curse drew a look of reproach from Miss Alma. "Have you contacted Anissa? Okay, I'll be there in fifteen," he concluded, clicking off the call. "Gotta run, Miss Alma."

"Chuck, you'll miss dessert. Your favorite . . . apple pie," she said, trying to tempt him.

"Can you put a slice in my fridge? There's a body I need to check out, and I don't know when I'll be back."

"No strip clubs tonight, Detective," she chided.

"No, ma'am. That was Chief Clark on the line. A potential homicide."

"Oh my," said Miss Alma as Nowitzke skipped out the door, unconsciously checking for his gun and badge as he headed toward his new car, a recently purchased faded aquamarine 2008 Ford Escort, seemingly held together by a considerable amount of rust. He'd had the car for only a month and already regretted his choice as he squeezed in behind the steering wheel. In addition to the car being a tight fit for the fleshy detective, Nowitzke had also noticed that the engine continued to run for a full ten seconds every time he turned off the ignition. That, and the air conditioner was on life support just days into the summer heat with several years of payments left to go. *Beautiful.*

The beater car was a reflection of his sins from a prior life. Now in his forties, Nowitzke had split his assets with his ex . . . twice. He was resigned to being a working man for the rest of his days, living from paycheck to paycheck. Following his most recent divorce, he needed a change. He had moved to Appleton, a relatively small city about two hours north of his hometown of Milwaukee, where he had investigated a regular flow of murders. The slower pace at APD suited him. Certainly less stress. He learned long ago that wherever there was a fair number of people, there was crime. A fact of life. However, unlike Milwaukee, the people living in Appleton didn't seem to go out of their way to shoot someone else. After joining APD, he had made his mark early, earning some internal chits. Best of all, he had hit the jackpot, finding a partner he trusted implicitly. Anissa Taylor. Life here was about as good as it got for a single bankrupt detective with a developing drinking problem. But he was free from his past. Another chance to fuck up again. Even he knew that was inevitable.

Standing a shade under six feet tall, the paunchy man with a shock of brown hair, a thick mustache, and a perpetual three-day beard found a piece of gum in the glove compartment to mask the smell of beer on his breath. If not for dinner with Miss Alma, he would likely have been half in the bag by this time on a typical Saturday night. *Thank God for small favors.* Cracking the driver's window to get some air into the stifling vehicle, Nowitzke fumbled with a portable police bubble from the back seat before placing it on the dash and turning on the light. He drove towards the address Clark had given him and realized that he was breaking new ground tonight. Even though the neighborhood was not in a gated community, it was not a part of town where he normally ventured. *Where the other half lives*, he thought as his car rolled up the front drive, parking so it could drip oil on the pavement between a Mercedes and a Porsche.

Several emergency vehicles were already on scene with light bars flashing. Perspiring heavily, Nowitzke peeled his back from the faux leather seat and took a rumpled sport coat from the back of his car.

He didn't know if it matched his jeans and polo shirt, but he didn't really care. Nowitzke nodded toward a uniformed officer, who was also basting in his own gravy and standing watch near the large wooden double front doors of the home. Ducking under the line of yellow police tape, the detective was about to enter the house when he heard the roar of a vehicle approaching from behind. A black Audi TT. Nowitzke barely stifled a laugh as his partner, Anissa, did her best to gracefully emerge from the sports car, a puce bridesmaid gown billowing around her. In her late twenties, the lithe and athletic blonde rarely struggled with much in life, but Nowitzke thought she might have met her match with the unwieldy dress. Looking more like a runway model than a cop, Anissa had more than made her bones as an investigator in their time together. "Nice look, Nis, but the funeral won't take place until after the autopsy," he called.

"Shut up, Chuck. I came here directly from my girlfriend's wedding. Dammit, I can barely breathe in this ridiculous outfit," said Anissa frustratedly, huffing in the sultry air. She approached her partner. "Supposedly women don't sweat, but I'm glowing like a pig."

"But at least you'll be able to use the dress again, right?"

"You're in rare form tonight. By the way, who's dead?" she asked as they moved toward the door.

Before Nowitzke could answer, the officer guarding the entrance to the home greeted them as he held the front door. "Detective Nowitzke. Miss Scarlet . . . welcome back to Tara," he said in his best Southern accent.

Anissa sneered at the smiling uniform as she entered the air-conditioned foyer with Nowitzke. Once inside the cooler air, they collectively exhaled. Marcus was waiting there to brief both detectives and direct them to the body in the sprawling home. Despite his otherwise serious demeanor, the normally reserved Marcus could not resist commenting on Anissa's appearance. "I know it's a formal investigation, Detective Taylor, but you didn't need to dress the part," he offered.

While Nowitzke tittered at Marcus's uncharacteristic remark, Anissa swallowed her tongue, saying nothing in response. "Actually, I appreciate both of you getting here so quickly," the police chief continued. "We've got a situation, and frankly, I don't know if it's a homicide or not. We will need to investigate carefully. Senator Anthony Hecht is dead under at least some suspicious circumstances. You need to see the scene to understand."

They walked toward the elevator. "Nice digs, sir," said Nowitzke, looking around at the heavy wood, high ceilings, and elegant furnishings. "Looks like the owner doesn't spend much time at IKEA."

"No kidding. The home belongs to Brad Hawkins," responded Marcus.

"Seriously? The former DA?" questioned Anissa.

"Well, I think he made most of his money after being a civil servant. Otherwise, we might be investigating him," chuckled Marcus as they stepped into the lift. "Even though he's now in private practice, Brad continues to be incredibly sympathetic to law enforcement. He's a champion for us on many levels, providing his opinion on issues and donating to our cause financially. Beyond that, he's a good guy," he concluded as the elevator came to rest in the basement. "We'll talk with him later, but for now, follow me." Marcus stepped into the lower level, where the temps were noticeably cooler than even the rooms above.

"Damn, I can breathe again," said Anissa as they strode past another officer monitoring entry and exit to the crime scene.

"Hey, I thought you guys were in plain clothes, ma'am," said the cop as they went down the hall.

Anissa shook her head. "Jeez, enough cop humor for a lifetime," she said to no one in particular.

"You know, Nis, this might be a first. No one seems to care about what I'm wearing," added Nowitzke.

When they arrived at the wine cellar, the officers were greeted by Dr. F. Walter Schmidt, the medical examiner. "Glad you could make it," said a snarky Wally. "I've had more than enough time to check out

the impressive collection of wine down here. It took everything I had
to keep from popping a cork." Schmidt, a living caricature of himself,
was a corpulent, bald man, almost as wide as he was tall, with a thick,
greying, bushy beard and large, round black glasses.

"You're looking like a rail, Wally," said Nowitzke. "Have you lost
weight?"

"Fuck you, Chuck," retorted the doctor. "By the way, you look
very elegant this evening, Anissa."

Anissa paused, wondering whether Schmidt was serious or
slamming her like her many counterparts.

In the center of the room lay the body of Senator Hecht. Hecht
had a contorted look of pain frozen on his thick face, his eyes still open
and bulging. He was wearing a jacket and tie but was covered from the
waist down by what looked like a frayed piece of tarp. "Is this the way
the body was found?" asked Nowitzke.

"No," said Marcus. "I was trying to be respectful of the man.
You'll see in a moment."

"What do you make of the number on the senator's forehead?"
asked Anissa, studying the politician's death face. "A seven? Why?"

"I have no idea," Marcus replied. "It's part of the reason you're
here. When I saw Hecht, it triggered the memory of another set of
cases that I need to dig back into."

Both detectives circled the body. "So, what's the story, Chief?"
asked Anissa as she took a camera from her large Shinola bag and
began snapping photos of the scene.

"Brad Hawkins was hosting a fundraiser here this evening for the
senator. I was a guest. At some point, it appears that the senator found his
way down here with a young lady. Quite a looker, by the way. My guess is
that when they started to get it on, Hecht had a heart attack. At least, that
makes sense considering what she told me." When Anissa had finished
her scan of the wine room, she looked at Nowitzke for help in removing
the tarp covering the senator. Before they could, Marcus stopped them.
"Wait! An FYI . . . the senator is naked from the waist down."

Nowitzke and Anissa briefly exchanged a look and then carefully removed the cover like they were unveiling a masterpiece in a museum. Following a pregnant pause, there was a collective gasp in the room. Wally was the first to chime in. "Jesus, looks like the man had an old Foster's oil can in his pants."

It took all of Anissa's energy to quell her urge to laugh at Wally's comment as she began taking photos of the body. "Yes, Wally, the man was packing," she agreed, "but I don't see evidence of trauma. You know, like a gunshot wound, stabbing, or blunt force."

"You said a heart attack, Chief?" questioned Nowitzke, turning to look at Marcus.

"Yeah, but I've got no evidence of that one way or the other. That's what the woman told me after she came upstairs looking for help. Plus, the senator looks like a walking heart attack anyway."

"No shit." Nowitzke considered the comment while unconsciously feeling his paunchy gut. "So, where's the lady?"

"I don't know," replied Clark. "Initially, she went looking for help, which happened to be me. I called 9-1-1 and then followed her down here. Somewhere down the hall, she stopped. She said she was out of breath, but never made it back here. After I found Hecht and confirmed he was dead, I went through the home looking for her. But she was gone."

Anissa cocked her head. "Even though her leaving sounds suspicious, maybe she just panicked. You know, she starts having sex with the senator, who then goes into cardiac arrest. I could see her just trying to get away."

"Anyway, Hawkins must have a security system with CCTV in the house," offered Nowitzke. "We should be able to get a look at her, for starters."

"Chuck, help me turn the senator over so I can get a couple more photos," Anissa said. As they did, Wally stepped forward.

"Whoa, look at the senator's butt cheek. He's got a decent-sized puncture wound of some sort there . . . big enough to draw blood.

But I don't see anything else," concluded the ME. "Let's get the man bagged up. As we've been standing here, I've been racking my brain like Chief Clark. I did an autopsy on a guy who had a number written on his forehead a couple of years ago. I'll need to check my files for specifics, but what I remember of the case was having a problem nailing down a cause of death."

"Wally, I'm tracking with you on the prior cases," said Marcus. "It's what I was referencing before. You handled one, but there was a second case that took place before you were hired as ME."

"We'll give Hecht a full once-over given he was a sitting senator," said Wally.

"Alright, anything you can do to speed up the process might help," said Nowitzke. "Anissa, please get the forensics folks in here to do their work. Then let's try to identify our mystery woman from Mr. Hawkins. Chief, you need to join us since you got a good look at her."

Marcus nodded in the affirmative. "Chuck, one last thing. I've asked Will Porter to come to the scene when you meet with Brad."

"The public relations guy? Jesus," sneered Nowitzke.

"Listen, we're down a senator under dubious circumstances at best. A story with sex, intrigue, and death sells well, even in our little town. Our TMZ moment. The press will eat this up, considering the death involves a politician at the national level. Tongues will be wagging across the country if the whole story comes to light. This needs to be handled with care, and we need Will's expertise. He's on staff and understands homicide investigations from his time in the field. And he needs a break since he was injured in the line of duty."

"He's also a major pain in the ass," muttered Nowitzke quietly to himself.

CHAPTER 3

Twenty minutes later, Nowitzke and Anissa were waiting impatiently in an elegant room, having claimed opposite halves of a brown leather couch. A gentleman dressed in a suit with a tie and vest, presumably a butler, had met them when the elevator arrived back on the main floor and escorted the detectives to a room he referred to as the study, promising that Mr. Hawkins would arrive shortly.

As they sat and drank bottled water, Nowitzke and Anissa quietly studied the space. Clearly, it was Hawkins' office, the centerpiece of the room being a massive antique wooden desk. Surrounded by built-in oak shelves filled with books and memorabilia, the room was softly lit by several well-placed lamps. Nowitzke rose and scrutinized several Indian kachina dolls decorating the fireplace mantel, resisting the urge to pick one up. Then, he moved to the wall behind Hawkins' desk, scanning several of the man's framed diplomas, proclamations, and citations. On the credenza were several personal photos. Some with members of law enforcement, present and past. Others with celebrities and politicians. And finally, a photo of a young, smiling Hawkins taken on a beach somewhere with a cute young blonde girl in a swimming suit who was probably not more than a teenager at the time. While the room had every reason to be pretentious, it somehow managed a cozy feel.

Anissa stood and stretched, looking out the window. "Hawkins has a huge greenhouse lit up out back," she exclaimed. "He must have a team to maintain the grounds here. The whole place smells like money."

Both detectives refocused on the business at hand when they heard a polite knock on the door and a group of four men entered the study, two of which Nowitzke didn't know. The first arrived with a burst of energy as he moved immediately towards Nowitzke. "Detective, I'm Brad Hawkins," he said, shaking the officer's hand warmly before moving toward Anissa. "And you must be Detective Taylor. I've heard so much about you both from Marcus here," he said, gesturing to Chief Clark, who trailed behind the former DA. Brad dropped into his leather desk chair. "Please, take a seat. I've brought along my director of security, Elliott Gordon." Elliott made the rounds, introducing himself to those in the room before plopping into an open chair. The thin man, who was pushing sixty, wore slacks, a button-down shirt, and a sport coat; however, he was most notable for his bookish look, which included jet-black hair fashioned in a pompadour and Clark Kent glasses. "Oh, and I assume you're all acquainted with Will Porter." Porter, who had been described by others on the force as a milquetoast, trailed the group into the study. He was overdressed in a three-piece black suit, and Nowitzke thought he looked more like an accountant than anyone connected with law enforcement. The study door was closed behind Porter by an un-introduced brick of a man who towered over everyone else. Wearing a pressed dark suit and an earpiece, he stood with a far-off, serious glare on his face, his hands folded in front of him.

Hawkins was a sixty-year-old man who had aged well. Still dressed in a double-breasted suit from the fundraiser, the trim six-footer had olive skin and was also blessed with a head full of brown hair that swooped in a broad part, with just enough gray on his temples to give him an aura of instant credibility. Nowitzke liked what he had heard about Hawkins, but for whatever reason wasn't immediately able to size the man up. Hawkins was considered a near legend as an aggressive prosecutor during his time as district attorney. Furthermore, he had a reputation of giving the presumptive benefit of the doubt to any cop in the Appleton PD, whether it was deserved or not. He also held the respect of defense attorneys in the area and had not been prone to cutting deals with accused criminals simply to keep his conviction rate high.

"Detective Nowitzke," said Brad, "can you tell me what happened here tonight? I understand that Tony . . . err, Senator Hecht is dead."

"Yes, sir. Apparently, the senator went down to your wine room with a young lady. Our thinking is that one thing led to another, and well . . . the senator suffered a heart attack while . . . while . . . anyway, we found his pants around his ankles," said Nowitzke, painting the picture for Brad.

The room was quiet for ten seconds before Brad stood and exploded, pounding his fist on the sturdy desk. "That stupid son of a bitch! Tony's been a huge success as a senator, but he's always had a problem keeping his dick in his pants. After his wife died, it only got worse," confided the former DA. "What about the woman?"

"We don't know. She disappeared," said Anissa, entering the conversation.

"We were hoping you could fill in the blanks for us, counselor," Nowitzke responded. "She was the one who came up the elevator to get help. You saw her, well, at least for a second or two."

"The redhead," said Brad, retaking his chair and looking at Chief Clark, who nodded. "I have no idea who she is. I assumed she was a hanger-on with someone invited here. Do you think she had anything to do with Tony's death?"

"The honest answer is we don't know at this point. But I'm guessing not. If she did, why would she run to find help for the senator?" offered the detective.

"Makes sense. I guess it's not unreasonable to conclude that she might have wanted to get the hell out of here if she was having sex with the senator when he died," replied Brad. Nowitzke glanced at Anissa, who was smiling in agreement.

"She remains only a person of interest at this point," said Nowitzke. "We'd certainly like to talk to her, but we'll need to get an actual cause of death. The ME is downstairs working the case as well."

"Aren't you going to mention the puncture mark or the number, Detective?" said Will, who had been listening to the exchange, earning an eye roll from Nowitzke. "That's what Chief Clark told me."

"A puncture mark?" asked Brad.

"Well, we're not sure what it is," said Nowitzke, glaring at Will. "It's something the ME is already working on, but it's an open question in our investigation."

Brad continued to look at Nowitzke. "What's the story about the number?"

"The senator had a number written in black marker on his forehead," said Anissa, answering the question now that the cat was out of the bag. "We have no clue how it got there or what it means. Another reason to talk with the woman. We'd rather not say anything else at this point."

"But it doesn't look like foreplay to me," said Nowitzke dryly, receiving a grimace from Marcus. "Elliott, do you have a CCTV system on the property?"

"Absolutely. We don't have cameras everywhere, but they are on the main floor. Nothing in the lower level or the wine cellar, by the way."

"We'd like to look at any video to see if we can figure out who the woman is," said Nowitzke.

"I'll take you to our monitoring room after the meeting."

"Jesus, what do we tell the press?" asked Brad, now ignoring Nowitzke and looking at Will.

"For starters, Appleton PD will acknowledge that Senator Hecht has died of an apparent heart attack."

"The press already knows the man's dead, by the way," added Marcus. "There's a contingent of reporters camped out in front of your house, Brad."

Will stepped back into the discussion. "We'll tell the press that we are investigating the death simply because it involves the senator and we want to be thorough. Beyond that, we release no other details."

"Like the size of the man's dick," whispered Nowitzke to Anissa, who almost drew blood biting her lip to keep from laughing.

"Detectives, would you please keep me appraised of your investigation? The senator has been a friend for years," Brad said as he rose from his chair, signaling the end of the meeting. He shook both Nowitzke's and Anissa's hands solemnly. "I sincerely appreciate what you do. If you need anything, please contact me," he continued, looking at Marcus while giving each detective his business card. Brad exited the room, followed by his large bodyguard.

Elliott stood. "Let's go see what kind of video we have."

Anissa walked ahead with Elliott and Marcus, followed by Nowitzke and Will. When Anissa's group turned a corner and was out of earshot, Nowitzke slowed Will in the hallway before stopping him altogether and blocking his way. "Listen, dumbass, this isn't your investigation. You're only here for public relations," said Nowitzke angrily.

Will looked surprised by the detective's outburst. "What are you talking about?"

"The puncture wound? The number on Hecht's forehead? Those are details that should not have been released. This is an active investigation. *My* investigation," Nowitzke snarled, his voice measured but rising as he stepped closer, invading Will's personal space. "You weren't planning on releasing those particulars to the press, were you?"

"Of course not," replied Will. "But Brad's one of us, Chuck. A former DA, if you didn't already know. I thought it was professional courtesy."

"The emphasis on 'former.' It's shoddy police work, Porter. In the future, keep your fucking professional courtesy to yourself, especially on one of my cases." Nowitzke shook his head. *It's why you're no longer an investigator.*

CHAPTER 4

Nowitzke, Anissa, Marcus, Will, and Elliott joined a chubby security guard, wedging themselves into a cramped room much too small for six people. Elliott explained the setup to his guests. "We have a guard seated at this console twenty-four seven, watching eight different rotating feeds on these screens from cameras placed around the residence. We cover the main entrance to Ivy House and the main floor, as well as the grounds. But nothing upstairs where Brad lives or in the wine room, as I said. We preserve the recordings for thirty days unless we have an event or suspicious activity. All the external entrances are alarmed when the system is armed in the evening."

"Jesus. Why such an elaborate video system?" asked Nowitzke.

"Well, it's the cost of doing business for Brad. He sent a lot of really nasty people to penitentiaries, and, from time to time, they get out. Some have been rehabilitated, but the security staff and I were hired to guard against those that weren't and may be looking for revenge on the former district attorney. Especially one that has had some obvious financial success in private life," concluded Elliott.

Nowitzke nodded, wondering about the scumbags he had put into prison and patting the Glock on his hip, which was his current security system.

"So, bringing up video of this evening's event is no big deal?" asked Anissa.

"It shouldn't be. The only challenge is that our technology is a bit dated. Black and white, not color, meaning redheads won't stand out," said Elliott. "We're due for an upgrade later this month. Bob, can you bring up tonight's feed from the foyer on screen five?" He looked at Marcus. "Starting when?"

"Well, I made the emergency call at 7:34 p.m. when our girl emerged from the elevator."

"Start there, Bob," said Elliott. The security technician scanned the video tied to the camera on the main floor. The group watched in anticipation as the time marker in the upper right corner of the screen approached 7:34. When it reached 7:33 p.m., the security man slowed the images. The group focused on Brad and Marcus chatting in the hall. Then, a minute later, a striking woman emerged from the elevator, right on cue.

"That's her," said Marcus. "Can you get in closer on her face?"

"Sure," replied Bob, confidently tightening the frame. "I assume you'd like a hard copy photo of the lady?" He pushed a button, making an unseen printer whirr.

"Alright," said Nowitzke. "We've got her image, but we still don't have a name."

"Do you have any facial recognition technology?" asked Anissa.

"No," Elliott responded. "That comes with our upgrade."

Nowitzke scratched his head. "Do you mind if we work with Bob here to look at additional tape to get some clue about who she is?"

"You can have whatever you need from us," replied the security director.

"Anissa and I will keep looking. Will, why don't you and Chief Clark go and meet with the press?" said Nowitzke. "Elliott, you can stay if you want to get really bored."

"No, I'll make my exit now too. The air conditioning can't keep up with all the bodies in this room anyway. Let me know if you need anything else." Elliott opened the door to leave, followed by those who had been excused.

"Where should we start, Bob?" asked Nowitzke after the room cleared.

"We can scan the main entrance to see when the woman arrived, but that won't necessarily tell us anything unless we see her getting out of a vehicle. When the party was raging, it seemed like most people were either in the dining room or the library . . . you know, where the bars were located. Maybe we can spot her talking to someone we can identify and figure it out from there?"

"I like the way you think," said Nowitzke with a smile as he hunched over the cherubic man. "Let's start in the dining room and go from there."

Although the video room was small, Bob found folding chairs for each officer to sit on as they scanned the recording. From time to time, either Anissa, Bob, or Nowitzke recognized the woman walking through the frame. However, she didn't appear to be talking with anyone at length. An hour later, both detectives stood from their chairs and stretched, having not developed any leads.

"Why don't we try looking at video from the library?" said Anissa, as the detectives both sat back down.

Without a word, Bob re-queued the footage and began scanning. "You know, I'd like to be a cop someday," he said off-handedly to Anissa as he worked. Thirty minutes later, they spotted the woman having an extended chat with another couple at a portable bar. The detectives' interest was piqued when the senator entered the frame.

"Look at the time stamp, Nis. 7:25 p.m.," observed Nowitzke.

"This conversation took place just before the senator died," Anissa realized.

The senior detective turned to Bob. "Can you tighten up on the faces of the couple she's talking with?"

"Already working on it, boss. And you won't have to go to Walgreens for your prints," Bob joked. "By the way, I'll print a copy of the video you need and give it to you before you leave."

"Any ideas about who they are?" asked Anissa, pointing at the couple.

"No," said Bob as the printer kicked in again. "I'm pretty new to the company, but I'd bet money that Mr. Gordon will know."

The three of them watched as Hecht and the woman took their drinks and left the library. "Wait," said Anissa. "This might be nothing, but the woman is carrying a wine glass with her. When we saw the later video of her coming out of the elevator looking for help, she didn't have it. Where do you suppose it went?"

"Who knows?" replied Nowitzke. "It could be anywhere. I assume the help here has probably cleaned up the joint by now."

"But the cleaning staff wouldn't have touched the crime scene downstairs," she said, racking her brain. "Maybe there's an empty glass in the wine cellar?"

"Would you call Elliott for us, Bob?" asked Nowitzke.

"I'll get him on his cell."

Nowitzke stood once more with a deep groan and twisted and turned to stretch his back. "Bob, one last question. Who's the monster protecting Brad?"

"You mean the guy who looks like he's been popping steroids like they're Skittles? His name is Leonard Sharp. A human pit bull, with his large, muscled neck and tapered down from there. I guess the shaved head just adds to the effect. He's not very friendly. The good news is that he reports directly to Mr. Gordon and I don't have much interaction with him. Sharp pretty much shadows Mr. Hawkins wherever he goes."

Ten minutes later, the officers met Elliott outside the video room. "Any luck?" asked the security director.

"I think so. Do you recognize this couple?" asked Nowitzke, handing over a photo.

"Oh yeah. Jeff and Laura Reardon. He's an anesthetist. Makes beaucoup bucks and appears to have been a fan of the senator. He's also one of Brad's buddies. You need a phone number and address?"

"That, and another trip back to the wine cellar," replied Nowitzke. After the detectives jumped back onto the elevator and descended to the basement, Anissa led the way with anticipation.

Upon entering the glassed-in room, she smiled. "The holy fucking grail," commented Nowitzke when he saw a stemmed glass sitting on a table. "Maybe we just got some prints." Anissa slipped on a glove and neatly deposited the finding into an evidence bag.

As the detectives exited Hawkins' house, they heard heavy footsteps coming from behind them. It was Bob. "Here are copies of the discs, Detective," he said, handing them to Anissa. "I put my card in one of the jewel cases. By the way, my name is Bob Edwards." He held out his hand as an official introduction. Anissa took the discs, placing them carefully in her handbag next to the wine glass, before shaking his hand. "Any chance I could get one of yours, Mrs. . . . ?"

"Miss Taylor . . . Anissa," she said with a smile. "And of course, Bob. You've been incredibly helpful. Thank you."

****

It was approaching 11:30 p.m. when Anissa's Audi rolled to the curb in front of the Reardons' home. "You think they're still up?" she asked.

"We'll find out in a minute. By the way, any luck finding a guy at the wedding tonight?"

"No," Anissa said in a matter-of-fact tone. "The groomsman I was partnered with tried to make a claim on me. A new college graduate who spent the evening monopolizing my time trying to impress me. I think he thought he was going to get lucky."

Thankfully, they saw that the interior lights of the Reardons' home were still on. "Let's go see what the doc and missus know, if anything," said Nowitzke as they stepped out of the sports car. "So, no action . . . no prospects?" asked the senior detective.

"None, aside from Bob the security guy. By the way, Chuck, it's not like I'd tell you anyway. But let me conclude the latest episode of Anissa's frustrating love life by saying that getting a 10-35 call about someone finding a dead body beat the hell out of doing the chicken dance with Wayne, or whatever the hell his name was," she said as she arrived on the stoop and pressed the doorbell. Although the night had cooled, the air remained thick. Surprisingly, Jeff Reardon answered the door in less than ten seconds, wearing a t-shirt and shorts.

"Doctor Reardon, we're with the Appleton Police," said Nowitzke, holding up his badge. He was flanked by Anissa, who was doing the same. "We're sorry to disturb you at this hour, but we need some help."

"Who's there, Jeff?" they heard from inside the house as his wife Laura, wearing a robe, poked her head into the doorway.

"I'm Detective Nowitzke. This is Detective Taylor."

Both Reardons gave Anissa a queer look, wondering why someone who looked like Cinderella was holding up a police badge on their porch at such a late hour, but they said nothing.

"We're investigating the death of Senator Anthony Hecht," continued the detective.

"Death? What do you mean?" said Jeff.

"We just met him earlier tonight at Brad Hawkins' home," interjected Laura, looking shocked.

"Would you mind if we stepped inside?" Nowitzke asked.

"Of course. I'm sorry," replied Jeff. "You just caught us off guard." He held the door open, allowing the officers into the foyer. "What happened?"

"We think the senator died of a heart attack," replied Anissa. "Considering who Mr. Hecht was, we've been asked to tie up a few loose ends."

"I understand you had a conversation with the senator tonight?" asked Nowitzke, looking at the pair.

"We did. I was so impressed to meet him," said Laura, beaming. "You know, he remembered my name."

Nowitzke held out the photo printed by Bob. "Would either of you be able to identify this woman?" "Of course. That's Savanna," said Jeff. "Quite a stunning woman. We were talking with her when the senator approached us."

"Did you catch her last name?" asked Anissa.

"I believe it was Smythe," Laura chimed in, looking at her husband.

"That's correct," Jeff confirmed. "Is she okay?"

"We think so," replied Nowitzke. "We're just trying to figure out who talked with Mr. Hecht before he passed away. Procedure, and again, I'm sorry," offered Nowitzke as contritely as he could. "How well do you know Miss Smythe?"

"We just met her tonight. We made some small talk. You know, the weather, how hot it's been, politics . . . a reasonably safe topic at a fundraiser, if you're all like-minded," replied Jeff. "Then when the senator approached us, we all focused on him. When we finished our conversation, he and Savanna walked off together."

"My impression is that they knew each other, but I could be wrong," said Laura.

"Turns out, they had a very personal relationship," said Nowitzke.

CHAPTER 5

The following morning, an irritable Nowitzke drove into the lot at Appleton PD just before 9:00 a.m. On a typical Sunday, the detective would have slept in until noon, but with the pending investigation, and a special invite from Chief Clark, Nowitzke finally willed himself from his bed after hitting the snooze button for only the fourth time. He showered, then dressed casually, wearing a wrinkled, navy, plaid, short-sleeved shirt and jeans. On the drive to the office, he added to his unkempt look by managing to dribble McDonald's coffee down his arm and into his lap. Parking his Escort in the department lot, he was completely out of the car before the vehicle finally shut off. Worse, on the short ride in, the air conditioning had made what sounded like a death wail, losing its battle with the humidity. Nowitzke felt the sweat rolling down his back as he passed Anissa's Audi and Clark's pickup truck on the way to the lobby door. After sliding his identification through the card reader, he entered the office area and paused for a moment to suck cool air into his lungs. Then, he lumbered down the industrial blue hallway toward Chief Clark's office. Halfway there, he heard conversation coming from a conference room. Anissa and Marcus, who was still wearing his suit from the night before, were in the middle of a confab when Nowitzke entered.

"Morning, Chuck," offered Marcus, receiving a grunt in reply.

"Chuck," added an enthusiastic Anissa without earning any reaction from her partner. She was wearing a knee-length, green sundress and jumped into a monologue. "I was updating the chief about our findings from last night. The video. Finding the wine glass. Meeting the Reardons. Identifying Smythe. Right now, we're running her name through DMV and checking any wants or warrants," she said. "Oh, and I've already run the glass down to Forensics to see if we can isolate and identify some prints. You can see them all over the bowl and stem of the glass. Maybe we'll get a hit."

"Jesus, Nis, you need to switch to decaf," growled Nowitzke, grabbing a stale, day-old cake donut from an open box on the conference room table before slumping into a chair.

"I know it's Sunday, Chuck, but I've got some important information for you," said Marcus. "Seeing the number seven scrawled on the senator's forehead last night sent my brain into overdrive. It's been years, but I immediately thought of two cases that took place during my time at APD. Technically, they're both closed, but I was never satisfied with the outcome of either. After Will and I did our presser last night, I came to the office to dig through my old files. I ended up pulling an all-nighter searching the archives before I found them early this morning." He pointed to two large cardboard boxes sitting on the table next to the donuts. "I went back through the material so I could give you an overview. But I'd like you to tear into both of these files to see if there is any connection to the senator's death."

Nowitzke sat up in his chair and took a sip of coffee while Anissa pulled out a portfolio to take notes as Marcus continued.

"The first case involves the death of a man in 2008. Kenneth Devine, a white male, age thirty-eight. Devine was employed at a local paper plant. He generally worked the second shift from the middle of the afternoon into the evening around 10:00 p.m. or thereabouts. Typically, after work, Devine would head out to a bar behind the mill and have a few drinks with his buddies. When he didn't come home one night, his wife called the police. I was a detective at the time. My notes say that I met a patrol officer at the tavern, known as Plant Four, that morning at 8:24 a.m. after someone realized Devine's car was still parked in the bar's lot. However, there was no sign of Devine. I talked with the bartender, several coworkers, neighbors, but found nothing. Talking with Devine's wife, Candy, she didn't cop to any problems at home. Based on what I could tell, they were a hardworking blue-collar family with two kids. Kenny was considered a good husband and father. No issues with the law.

"Later that morning, I got a call from dispatch. A couple of kids had discovered a body in a park. It was Devine. Looked like he was sitting under a tree enjoying a sunny day in June. Pretty much like today, only cooler. When I got to the park, we cordoned off the area. There were no signs of foul play or any trauma to the body. But the number four was written in black ink on Devine's forehead."

"A four?" asked Nowitzke, raising his thick eyebrows.

"What was the cause of death?" Anissa probed.

"That's just it. There was nothing obvious. Devine was in good shape. A lean guy without any health issues. The coroner ruled the death by heart attack because he couldn't come up with anything else."

"A coroner?" asked Anissa. "Wait, why not an ME?"

"Chief, you're showing your age," said Nowitzke. "In the olden days, Nis, we didn't have MEs. We had county coroners. Someone who ruled on cause of death. An elected position, meaning the person didn't necessarily have any medical expertise. There are still some counties around the state with coroners."

"That's exactly the way it was. Our local coroner held the position for thirty-plus years . . . Landon Salsbury. Good old Landon. Nice guy," said Marcus, looking off into space, "but as useless as a box of condoms in a nunnery. Landon owned a local grocery store. What he knew about anatomy he learned from butchering cows and pigs. His position gave him the ability to make referrals for help from the state on any case, if he wanted. But that required him to move quickly and make a decision. It always seemed like any serious case we had conflicted with a brisket sale he was running at the store. Landon was more interested in the steady monthly $650 check from the county and the celebrity of being a local politician, if you can believe that. His coroner investigations were largely one-page forms completed with check marks. No photos of the bodies or wounds. No drawings. No notes. No nothing. Just guesses, and some of them not terribly informed. As I understand it, Landon sometimes stored bodies in the store's freezer. His contribution to the county. Picture a stiff or two lying on a stack of frozen turkeys around Thanksgiving. He also billed the county for the freezer space."

"Wow," exclaimed Anissa, shaking her head in disbelief.

"From what I heard, the chief here was able to convince the county managers to get rid of the position and replace it with a medical examiner." Nowitzke chuckled. "Making him responsible for Wally."

"Only the position, Nowitzke, not the man. Hey, even despite all of Wally's eccentricities, he has brought value to the table," concluded Marcus.

"What about the second case?" asked Anissa.

Marcus sighed. "June 2018. Another white male. Kevin Henderson, CEO of a regional financial firm. Age forty-nine. In addition to his professional responsibilities, his resume read like he was shooting for volunteer of the year . . . every year. I mean, the man found time to work with numerous charitable organizations, making meaningful contributions with both his time and money. Married to Mikki, a couple of kids. No criminal record.

"On a rainy Saturday morning, Kevin had just gotten done coaching a youth soccer match. After the game, he went to the restroom in the park, a permanent structure at the complex. Before the kids were done eating their oranges, someone said, 'Where's Kevin?' A couple of dads started looking around for him before finding him in one of the stalls, dead. At least we got some photos of this body. I still remember seeing the man's eyes popping out of their sockets and his hands clutching his chest. He had a number six scrawled on his forehead."

"My God," responded Anissa. "Did Henderson have any health issues?"

"None. He'd passed a corporate physical the week before, according to the file."

"You investigated both cases, Chief?" asked Anissa.

"No. Only the Devine file."

Nowitzke jumped in. "Who was the detective on Henderson?"

"Will Porter."

"Shit, are you kidding me?" retorted Nowitzke. "The guy who couldn't find his own ass in the dark with a flashlight?"

"Will's got some limitations, but he was a competent investigator," said Marcus.

"Which is why he is now in public relations," countered the senior detective, shaking his head.

"What's done is done, Chuck. Frankly, neither Will nor I were able to figure out what had taken place with these two deaths," Marcus said, bringing the matter to rest.

"So, Henderson was ten years after Devine and five years before the senator?" asked Nowitzke. "Four, six, and seven on the bodies. It's hard to say 'victims,' but these cases have to be connected."

"Chief, did you ever run across a white male with a five on their head?" chimed in Anissa.

"You know, I half expected it to happen at some point, but it never did. And why did the numbering start at four? I dug into both cases, looking for any type of link or direction to pursue. Neither of these men ran in the same circles. They were in different lines of work. I don't get it. But, considering the senator's death, I want you to take a fresh look at these cases. In theory, we now have three deaths over fifteen years. You're both better detectives than I ever was. Plus, Wally has documentation on Henderson's case as well as that of the senator. Maybe he can scare up some missing detail. If you need any assistance or resources, let me know." Marcus stood and stretched. "I'm going home to bed. See you tomorrow morning."

"Before you leave, Chief, can you have an officer who monitors traffic look at the tape from last night in the general vicinity of Hawkins' home from an hour before until an hour after the fundraiser?" asked Nowitzke. "It's probably a long shot, but we don't know how Ms. Smythe arrived or left Hawkins' place. It might help us locate her."

"You got it, Chuck. I'll make the call right now, unless either of you have anything else you want me to do," said Marcus. Nowitzke and Anissa exchanged glances and shook their heads.

After Chief Clark left the room, Nowitzke looked at Anissa. "How about if we each take a file and make notes?"

"Then we switch and do the same on the other?" Anissa replied.

"I like the way you think, Nis. We can talk about the cases after we're through. Lady's choice," he concluded, tilting his head toward the boxes.

****

The size of the case boxes belied the actual amount of contents inside. Each file had minimal documentation of the events. Anissa chose the Devine case, and she finished her review in a frustrating forty-five minutes, even taking the time to make painstaking notes. She rose, stretched, and glanced at Nowitzke.

"Sorry, Nis, I'm a slow reader. Give me another fifteen minutes," he said, munching on another hard donut while lounging on his chair with his feet resting on the table. Anissa went looking for coffee. When she returned to the conference room, Nowitzke had already switched gears and was well into the Devine file. While the Henderson record was slightly larger, Anissa found it equally scant on particulars. Thirty minutes later, the two detectives were in a stare-down across the table.

"What do you think?" asked Nowitzke.

"It's exactly what Chief Clark told us," she said. "There are a number of similarities between the subjects, but more than enough differences too. I did make note of a couple of things, though. The biggest is that Devine died on June 16, 2008. Henderson died *exactly* ten years later on June 16, 2018. And we know that Senator Hecht died yesterday, on June 16, 2023. Each died on the exact same calendar date."

"Is there any significance to June 16?"

"I looked it up. National Fudge Day. National Flip Flop Day. Nothing that stood out," said Anissa. "But since each subject had a number on their forehead, this can't be a coincidence."

"Investigators generally don't believe in coincidences," replied Nowitzke.

"God knows what was with this group, but there has to be some connection between them."

"I assume you noticed Wally's autopsy report on Henderson?"

"You mean the puncture wound on Henderson's shoulder?" replied Anissa. "It looked just like the one on Senator Hecht's ass. A similarity. Interesting, but I mean, it's hardly a fatal wound."

"Agreed. Unless there's something more than the actual puncture itself. I wish we had some death photos of Devine," said Nowitzke rhetorically. "I would guess that Wally's gone back through his notes on Henderson. Let's get him on the phone and talk this through."

CHAPTER 6

"Wally, what are you doing on a Sunday afternoon?" asked Nowitzke on the speaker phone from the APD conference room.

"Catching up on work. Plus, it's cool in my examination room. Got the senator chilling on the table over here," replied the ME.

"Anissa and I are on our way over."

"Great. Bring some lunch with you," said Wally. "I'm up to my elbows in Hecht, if you catch my drift."

The detectives decided to take Anissa's vehicle from the office based on its creature comforts, like working air conditioning. After stopping at the drive-up window of a local sandwich shop, they found ample parking in the lot of the Hobart Thompson Memorial Hospital. A rent-a-cop manning the front entranceway waved at the officers as they made their way to the pathology department in the lower level of the building. After a short elevator ride, the doors opened to an antiseptic smell in a darkened hallway lit only by fluorescent ceiling lights that reflected off the industrial tiled floor. Since it was the weekend, they saw no one on their way to the ME's office. As Nowitzke held the door open for Anissa, they both heard Wally in a loud voice. "I hope you didn't bring me fucking egg salad, Nowitzke."

"No, Anissa chose a turkey and cheese wrap for you," said the detective, tossing him the food in a small white bag.

"I knew I could trust Anissa with such an important decision," Wally said politely. The three of them took chairs and huddled around Wally's cluttered desk, clearing space to eat their lunch. The office was austere, bordering on grim, devoid of any personal memorabilia, the lone exception being two large Grateful Dead concert billings posted on one wall.

"Either of you want a beer?" asked Wally. "I keep some in my fridge for night and weekend work . . . along with some sodas."

A skeptical Anissa eyed the old white refrigerator in the corner. "What else do you keep in there? Any body parts or tissue samples that you've taken?"

"Of course not. Well, maybe just the overflow," joked the ME. Anissa deferred, but Nowitzke took a beer.

"Have you had a chance to examine Hecht's body?" asked Nowitzke.

"Yeah, I just got done. Beyond the puncture wound, there wasn't anything else that was unusual. No other trauma. Just as we thought originally. The one thing that is interesting, though, is that the senator received the wound while he was still alive," commented the ME before taking a bite of his wrap.

"How could you determine that?" asked Anissa.

"Well, if you take a close look at the wound, you can see some tearing of the flesh around it. My guess is when someone stuck the senator in the ass, he instinctively jerked away after feeling the pain," Wally replied. "Beyond that, I found nothing else suspicious, at least from a medical perspective. Keep in mind that the man was developing a serious case of cirrhosis of the liver, was significantly overweight, and, in general, was a walking heart attack waiting to happen."

"A heart attack then?" probed Nowitzke before he tore off a bite of his Italian sub.

"I didn't say that."

Anissa considered the ME as she nibbled on her wrap. "Wally, do you have a cause of death?"

"Nothing concrete, yet. I've got more work to do."

"But you haven't ruled out a potential homicide?" clarified Nowitzke.

A frustrated Wally put his wrap on the torn paper bag that was serving as his plate and looked at both detectives. "Listen, all I'm saying at this point is that if you're even assuming someone actually murdered the senator, the easiest person to kill is one you expect to die anyway."

Wally's observation hung in the air for a moment before Anissa moved on. "Have you had a chance to look back in your archives?"

"Yes, I assume you're referring to the Henderson file?"

"We spent the morning going through the documents that Chief Clark mentioned last night," said Nowitzke. "Devine in 2008 and Henderson in 2018." He refocused on his sandwich.

"According to the photos, it looked like Henderson also had a puncture wound on his shoulder," Anissa continued.

"I checked my old notes this morning and went back for a closer look at the photos of Henderson. Damn if I didn't find the exact same kind of tearing as on Hecht."

"Was it something you missed the first time?" asked Anissa carefully between bites.

"No. I remember seeing it when I examined the body way back when. I just could never figure out how it was involved with Henderson's death, if at all," said the medical examiner. "I was convinced that something would turn up on the toxicology report, but it didn't. With the evidence I had, I had no choice but to rule that Henderson died from a heart attack."

"Can you take us through your procedure with toxicology?" asked Nowitzke.

Wally took another bite taking a moment to think through the best way to describe the process. "We work through the state crime lab in Madison. Typically, we ship out biological samples, including blood, urine, and tissue. Sometimes we limit the testing to alcohol or drugs, if that's what the criminal investigators are looking to charge someone with. You know, like when someone is suspected of driving under the influence. There's no sense in incurring the cost of testing for everything. Otherwise, in a typical homicide investigation, we get the full battery of tests because we don't really know what we're looking for," he concluded.

"You said you got a toxicology report back on Henderson?" asked Anissa.

"Yeah. It turned up negative for everything."

The junior detective continued, "What kind of substances does the lab test for?"

"Cocaine, opiates, meth, ketamine, oxy, barbiturates, fentanyl, and carbon monoxide, for starters. LSD was popular for a time," he added with a nod toward the posters on the wall. "But the forensic toxicologists work all the way down the list from heavy metals to acetaminophen."

"Aspirin?" asked Nowitzke.

"Well, technically not Aspirin," Wally corrected, "but an over-the-counter painkiller nonetheless."

"So, the state folks are pretty thorough then?" questioned Anissa.

"Oh yeah," replied Wally.

The room went quiet as they finished their impromptu meal.

"Wally, are there chemicals beyond what might be on the standard list?" asked Nowitzke, launching his wrapper towards the wastebasket.

"Of course. There are any number of substances out there. But again, with the cost involved, it makes no sense to test for them unless you're looking for something specific."

"What do you do when you want to look for something exotic . . . like some kind of off-the-wall poison?" asked Anissa. "You know, something that might bring on what looks to be a heart attack?"

"I've used National Medical Services Labs in Pennsylvania when I've needed to. They do largely what the state crime lab does but have the ability to find unusual things."

"Well, since we have a senator on the slab in there, should we let them take a look?" inquired Nowitzke.

Anissa nodded. "Yes, and what about a sample from Mr. Henderson as another potential victim too?"

"Hecht's sample is easy. But you understand that to get a sample from Henderson, we would need to exhume the body, which requires a court order," countered Wally. "The other thing to understand is that some toxins degrade in the body rather quickly. I mean, they could be gone in a matter of hours or days, let alone after five years."

"Okay, start with Hecht," said Nowitzke. "If you get a hit on something, we can talk to the chief about next steps with Henderson if we think we need to."

"I get the similarity with the puncture wounds and the numbering between the victims, but what else about the deaths makes you think they're connected?" asked Wally.

"Devine, Henderson, and Hecht all died on the same calendar date, June 16, making this even more suspicious," replied Anissa.

Wally considered the detectives with a look of disbelief. "Shit. But what's the connection between the three of them?"

"The million-dollar question, Wally," resolved Nowitzke. "*The million-dollar question.*"

The medical examiner nodded solemnly in agreement. "It will take some time to get back the test results, but I'll keep you both posted."

CHAPTER 7

It was Sunday night, and Nowitzke was thrilled for several reasons. But he was also nervous. First, a cold front had blown through the area in the late afternoon, clearing out the humidity and dropping the temps into the comfortable seventies. The chunky detective did not do well in thick air, so any reprieve in the weather was welcomed. Second, Miss Alma was cooking dinner for him and Anissa. It had become a standing weekly date. As far as Miss Alma was concerned, there was no excuse for missing Sunday dinner, short of a death in the family. Not that Nowitzke ever missed a home-cooked meal or had any family anyway. Yet, he had felt a growing pit in his stomach for a while. Tonight was confession time and he was unsure about the reaction he would get from the elderly woman.

Nowitzke's relationship with his landlord had evolved significantly since they first met. Miss Alma, a long-time widow, was initially pleased at the idea of an Appleton PD detective living in the walk-up flat above her house. In her mind, she envisioned a young, good-looking Dirty Harry–type guy living there. However, after taking his call about the space, the sharp old woman had second thoughts when she first glimpsed the overweight and rumpled man plodding up to her house. It took all of her willpower to resist asking the man to show his badge just to confirm he was an actual officer. Nowitzke, who was hungover at their first meeting, was interested in the place because the rent was well below the going rate in town. But he quickly discovered why when Miss Alma outlined the rules for living under her roof.

Rule one: No smoking.

Rule two: No guns, although she knew she had to make an exception for an officer of the law.

Rule three: No women. This tenet got Nowitzke's attention, even though he was coming off his second divorce and had zero prospects. When Nowitzke questioned her intent, the clarification could not have been clearer. "No fornicating," expounded Miss Alma, the Old Testament phrase still clanging in his head well over a year later. Ironically, as luck would have it, it was one of the first statutes he violated.

Rule four: No alcohol. An idea so far-fetched for Nowitzke that he decided it must be more of a guideline than a rule.

Finally, rule five: No pets. And here was the rub. Typically, such a regulation would not be a problem for the gruff detective. But things changed when he rescued a scrawny tabby cat that he named Sinker. A year earlier, Nowitzke had been walking in a heavy rain in downtown Appleton when he heard an anguished cry coming from a storm drain. Peering into the sewer, he found a soaked kitten losing its fight with the torrent of water. The detective was compelled to kneel, pushing his thick arm into the opening as far as he could. He wasn't a cat person. But he couldn't just stand by and watch a living thing drown either. Pulling the orange tabby from certain death, he resolved to turn the animal over to a shelter the following morning. However, overnight, Nowitzke became smitten with the kitten's purring as it wedged itself against the hardened officer for warmth. In a matter of hours, Sinker had become family.

Nowitzke was a serial miscreant from day one, in line for banishment from Miss Alma's world. However, he scored some early points with the elderly woman, making use of his limited ability to keep her ramshackle home from totally falling apart. On one ambitious weekend, he painted the garage while drinking a concealed twelve-pack of beer. She brought him cookies. He fixed a minor leak under the sink in her kitchen. She baked him a cake. Then he took it upon himself to roll the trash out to the curb each Friday, even though his ulterior motive was to hide the beer and liquor bottles that had piled up in her recycling bin.

While Nowitzke thought he had cleverly disguised most of his transgressions, he found out on a particularly warm day the summer before that the jig was partially up. Miss Alma had asked Nowitzke to come to dinner on the condition of him bringing *his* beer along if she could have a cold one too. In Nowitzke's mind, Prohibition was over. And, while they maintained their distance, they grudgingly got to know each other better.

Then, he and Miss Alma shared a crucible moment. When an attacker threatened Nowitzke and a witness with deadly force on her property, Miss Alma took on the thug with her husband's old shotgun, arguably saving the detective's life. At least that was her version of the story, which had still been hotly debated over many beers since that fateful night. Somehow, they had become family. The old widow who lived alone and the twice-divorced officer who had many acquaintances, but few friends. For Nowitzke, the product of a broken home, Miss Alma became a mother figure, filling a hole in his life that he didn't know existed. Nowitzke wasn't sure Miss Alma would go so far as to say he had taken on the status of a son, but it was clear she enjoyed his company . . . most of the time.

Though they were a grudging family, Nowitzke still held out a healthy level of fear of Miss Alma. Over the course of his law enforcement career, the detective had been involved in numerous gun battles and brawls with hard men who had shot, cut, or busted him open. But in his eyes, Miss Alma channeled an elementary schoolteacher from years before who had wielded a yardstick on Nowitzke's knuckles in the same artful way as a conductor waving a baton in front of an orchestra.

He was a serial abuser of the rules, and she pretty much knew about all his offenses. All except for Sinker. Nowitzke's nerves were unraveling. Potential grounds for termination. So, he had plotted to unveil his solution at dinner, where Anissa would be there to serve as his second if he needed one.

As Nowitzke clomped down the stairs from his apartment, he heard the growl of the Audi as it came to rest in Miss Alma's driveway. Anissa popped out of the vehicle, wearing a light sweater, sandals, and a comfortable pair of jeans. She considered Nowitzke in his open button-down, t-shirt, and cargo shorts, carrying a twelve-pack of beer and a small faux leather bag. "Tonight's the night, huh?" asked Anissa, looking at her boss.

"Listen, I need you for moral support."

"Considering your morals in general, I'm not sure what I can do for you, Chuck," she quipped mockingly.

"How about being nice for once?" he asked in a tone mixed with sarcasm, desperation, and anxiety as he simultaneously knocked and entered Miss Alma's back door.

"Put the beer in the refrigerator, Detective," said the old woman from the other room. As she arrived in the doorway of the kitchen, she saw Anissa. "It's so good to see you again, my dear." Miss Alma reached up for all she was worth to hug the much taller young woman. In the course of her relationship with Nowitzke, Miss Alma had come to befriend Anissa and channeled any excitement from Anissa's life, making her a de facto granddaughter. Once the woman released her death grip hug from Anissa, she looked at Nowitzke without missing a beat. "What's in the bag, Detective?"

"A present," he said sheepishly after taking a gulp of air. Before he could explain, they heard a meow, and on cue, Sinker's head popped out of the bag. Nowitzke placed the sack on the floor, and the orange tabby climbed out, moving toward Miss Alma as if trained to do so. Reaching down, the old woman picked up the scrawny cat, which began to purr.

"What's the cat wearing?" asked Miss Alma.

"A vest that I bought for it. She's a service animal. Good for relieving stress. You can see the writing there on the side. C-E-R-V-E-Z-A. It's Spanish for 'service,'" said Nowitzke with a straight face, almost drawing a laugh from Anissa. "She's yours, Miss Alma. To keep you company."

With the cat now licking her hand, Miss Alma continued to gently stroke the animal's head as she walked to a cupboard. Pulling out a saucer, she then went to the sink, poured some water for the thirsty cat and set both on the floor.

"Thank you," she said earnestly, moving toward the refrigerator to grab each of them a beer. "You know, though, as I recall my Spanish, 'cerveza' doesn't mean 'service.' It means 'beer.'"

"Really?" answered the flustered cop.

"Chuck, why give me the cat now? You've had Sinker for more than a year."

Nowitzke said nothing, but the look of shock and surprise on his face was palpable. Unlike his mother, he had finally realized that he could get nothing by this woman. Breathing a sigh of relief, he reckoned that any question about the "rules" had at least been officially and finally resolved. "Just don't break rule number one, Detective. If you take up smoking, I'll kick you out of here so fast it will make your head spin," concluded Miss Alma, receiving a loud laugh from Anissa.

Following dinner, Miss Alma insisted that her guests relax at the kitchen table while she cleaned up, seemingly ignoring their conversation. With some time before the end of the evening, Nowitzke, nursing beer number three, carefully shifted any conversation with Anissa to work and plans for the coming week. Because the Hecht investigation remained active, the officers spoke in generalities, leaving out details considering Miss Alma's presence. For the next half hour, they quietly rehashed the significance of the four, six, and seven. Was it a code? Did it involve something strange, like a cult? Or was it a clue pointing them to something else? Again, why no five? Anissa and Nowitzke chatted about the consistency between the wounds, the lack of any toxicology results, and the significance of the years 2008, 2018, and 2023. Devine and Henderson had been similar in a couple of respects. Both white males. Family men, yet each with a different background. But what did they have in common with Hecht, of all people? Another white male but living in another stratosphere. Why June 16? And finally, who was the mystery woman? When Miss Alma's kitchen was clean, she joined the officers at the table with a beer. They had come to no conclusions.

"Are you having much luck in resolving the death of Senator Hecht?" asked the old woman.

"It's an open case, Miss Alma. Neither Anissa nor I can really talk about it in detail," offered Nowitzke.

"Are you both thinking he might be the latest in a series of connected deaths in Appleton over the past fifteen years?"

Anissa cocked her head and stared at Nowitzke with a quizzical look given the accuracy of Miss Alma's comment. While the officers thought they had left out specifics, Miss Alma had heard enough to put things together while doing the dishes. "Listen, I'm just an old lady and certainly no detective, and I don't know what you're working on exactly. But if that Will Porter is involved in any part of it, you better find out what he knows. I saw him on television with Chief Clark the other night when the senator died. Porter came off looking like a moron, if I'm still allowed to say that word."

"Why do you say that?" inquired Anissa curiously.

"The man's got no cachet. On such an important case, he spoke without any confidence in his voice. Like he didn't have a clue. Probably why he's not an investigator anymore," she concluded.

Anissa wondered how many of Miss Alma's impressions of Will were her own or were driven by Nowitzke.

"Now I'm not going to tell you how to do your jobs, but if it was me, I'd go back in the archives and look for other strange deaths that happened on June 16 in five-year increments before Devine died. You know, search for numbers one, two, and three to see if there were any. Then maybe number five might fall into place for you," Miss Alma said, dumbfounding the officers, who could only gape back at her. "But what do I know?" She took a sip of her beer.

"Jesus," replied Nowitzke, looking at Anissa with astonishment that Miss Alma had discerned such a clear investigative approach to cases that had stymied local law enforcement for decades.

"Don't blaspheme, Chuck," said Miss Alma.

Anissa drained her beer. "Looks like our plan for the week just added a new wrinkle."

Job's his phone, Chief," said Matt Aften.
Anissa drained her Jacked Lord. "It can plan for one week just
ardeed few wrinkle.

CHAPTER 8

Nowitzke had taken the lead on behalf of his partner in sending a text to Chief Clark requesting an early Monday morning meeting. By the time the three officers convened in Clark's office at 8:00 a.m., several investigative seeds had borne fruit. In addition, the detectives would be asked to take on another assignment.

Nowitzke entered the room carrying a cup of coffee and wearing a black tie that did not match his green-and-blue plaid jacket, yellowing white shirt, or his khaki pants. A trickle of maple syrup decorated his tie. In contrast, Anissa was impeccably dressed in a cranberry business suit with matching heels and a black blouse. "Looks like McDonald's pancakes were on the breakfast menu today," said Marcus, studying Nowitzke's attire.

"Jeez, Chief, maybe you should have remained a detective," replied Nowitzke derisively.

Chief Clark, wearing his uniform, sat back in the chair behind his desk, inviting the detectives to take side chairs. "So, what's up?" he asked.

"We've got a theory on the series of deaths," started Nowitzke. "What if Devine, the guy with the four on his head, was not the first victim? When Anissa and I went through both files yesterday, she noticed that both Devine and Henderson died on June 16."

"The same date as Senator Hecht," added Anissa. "It's a commonality with the three deaths."

"Seriously," replied Marcus.

"Working with Wally, we also learned that Henderson had a puncture

46

mark on his body, similar to Hecht," offered Nowitzke. "We don't know about Devine's body since the coroner left no records or photos."

"Wally's working theory is that both men who received puncture wounds were alive at the time based on the tearing of flesh around the mark," added Anissa.

"Anyway, we want to look at the records for similar deaths that took place prior to Devine," Nowitzke continued. "Obviously, we'd start with the calendar date and look backward five years at a time from the first body discovered to see if there were any others. Is there any reason we can't dig into the APD archives?"

"Actually, yes, there is," replied the chief, drawing questioning looks from both detectives. "Now don't misunderstand, I'm impressed with your theory, and absolutely you need to check it out. But the old APD records are, well . . . incomplete, to say the least." Marcus stood and came around the desk, sat on the edge, and took a deep breath. "When I joined the force here years ago, my predecessor was in the process of destroying our old hard-copy records because they had no more storage space. Whoever did the purge itself didn't know the difference between a closed file and an open one. So, everything went through an industrial shredder."

"No one thought to microfilm the records or have them stored electronically?" asked Anissa.

"Of course not. No one wanted to commit good resources to what leadership thought were a few ancient files." Marcus moved toward his window, deep in thought. "You know, though, we might have an alternative. I think the Appleton Public Library keeps copies of local newspaper stories going back who knows how far. Since you have potential target dates, this shouldn't be a major fishing expedition. Chuck, contact the library and see what they have available. There's a woman there named Maureen Carr, the library director. I met her at several chamber of commerce functions, and she would be a good person to start with."

As Chief Clark was set to move on to another topic, there was a light knock on the door. "Are we ready?" asked Will Porter, sticking his head into the office.

"Yeah, Will. Give us a moment, would you?" Will closed the door as Marcus turned toward Anissa. "We're short-handed on investigative help. I want Chuck to continue to work on the senator's death for now, and Anissa, I need your experience to partner with Will to check out another homicide that was discovered in the last half hour. Apparently, someone found a floater out in the Fox River. It's also an opportunity for you to talk with Will about his investigation of the Henderson death."

"Would it make more sense for me to go to the library?" asked Anissa.

"No, you have fun with Will," said Nowitzke, chiming in. "I recently learned how to read, and I hear the library has books and everything."

"Before you leave, Chuck, you also need to talk with our traffic folks," said Marcus. "They might have developed a lead on the Smythe woman. Did we have any luck with our records check on her?" he asked, looking at Anissa.

"We came up with nothing on Smythe. No fingerprint match. No wants. No warrants. Even the DMV search came up zilch," Anissa replied, rising from her chair.

"Oh," said Will, entering the conversation after poking his head back into the room. He straightened his tie and three-piece suit. "So, we have no information about where to find her?"

"Chuck will handle the follow-up, Will," said Marcus.

Will nodded. "I'll get the car, Anissa, and meet you out front," he offered anxiously.

"One last thing. You two have been invited to lunch by Brad Hawkins at Ivy House," said Marcus, looking at Nowitzke and Anissa. "Give his people a call to set something up for this week. Apparently, the former DA wants to thank you both for your work."

"Wow, lunch guests at Ivy House," said Nowitzke, making his best imitation of Thurston Howell III to Anissa on their way out of the chief's office. "I'm guessing it's not for beer and brats. Hey, by the way, nice try dumping Porter on me."

"Chuck, it just makes sense. Did you even know that Appleton had a public library?"

"Just because I've never been there doesn't mean I don't know about it. Now, what city is it in again?" asked Nowitzke as Anissa shook her head, walking toward the front door of the station.

****

Before leaving for the library, Nowitzke made his way down to the bowels of APD where traffic was monitored. Sitting behind a console of video screens sat a motivated-looking young female officer with "Fischer" on her name tag. "Officer Fischer, Detective Nowitzke," he said, introducing himself with his hand extended. "Chief Clark said you might have developed a potential lead on the Hecht case."

The traffic officer stood and shook his hand in return. "Oh yes," she said anxiously, scrambling to gather her data. "Based on the photo you gave us, I came up with a couple of screenshots of what looks to be the same woman driving through several intersection cameras after the senator's body was discovered." Fischer brought up the images on a screen. "Here . . . " She played a video in slow motion for Nowitzke. "The woman was driving a late-model Lexus convertible with the top down. Here . . . here . . . and here," offered Fischer with three additional still photos.

"That looks like her to me," said Nowitzke.

"I took the liberty to run the plates, Detective. A rental. Hertz said the woman's name is Smythe." Fischer looked down at her notes. "Yes, Savanna Smythe."

"Nice car."

"We got a portion of Smythe's rental agreement. She gave her local contact information, including an address. If it's accurate, she's staying at the Orchard Inn out by the mall. Supposedly, she has the vehicle for another ten days or so. My copy of the agreement didn't include her permanent address or license number though, sir."

"Impressive, Officer Fischer," said Nowitzke. "Can you give me copies of what you've found?"

"Got them right here for you, sir," said Fischer, handing him a manila file, which the detective briefly scanned.

"How long have you been with APD?" asked Nowitzke.

"I'm six months in, sir."

"Lighten up on that 'sir' stuff, Fischer," replied the detective. "For the record, what's your first name?"

"Colby, sir."

"I'd say you're off to a good start, Colby."

CHAPTER 9

Will had signed out a Ford Explorer from the motor pool and parked in front of the building, waiting for Anissa. "Where are we off to?" asked Anissa as she climbed into the passenger seat.

"Alicia Park. We got an anonymous call on the tip line that a body had been found," replied Will, who turned on the emergency lights built into the unmarked vehicle. "It's been a while since I've been in the field. I assume you'll be taking the lead today?"

"Sure. No problem," replied Anissa, who had planned to do so anyway. "Did you get any details about the homicide?"

"No, nothing. Sorry," said Will, negotiating traffic at just over the posted speed limit. The twenty-minute trip ended near the southern edge of Appleton with Will picking his way along the tangled streets of an established neighborhood. The wide and empty avenues were lined with older homes that boasted a pride in ownership, fronted by fully leafed, mature trees. As they neared the park entrance guarded by two large maples, they could hear the white noise of a lawn mower along with the sweet smell of cut grass on an otherwise perfect summer morning. The light bar on a Harley-Davidson Electra Glide and yellow police tape drew them to the site manned only by veteran officer Kenny Hicks, who was smoking a cigarette.

"Morning, Anissa," offered Hicks as both detectives emerged from the SUV.

"Good to see you again, Kenny," replied Anissa, immediately scrutinizing the body of the man lying on the ground at the officer's feet. The victim was dressed in a suit, eyes wide open in horror and surprise, capturing the moment of his death. "What do we know?" she asked with Will shadowing her.

"I got a call to respond at 7:50 a.m. Made it here minutes later. Not sure who spotted the body floating in the river. Subject is a white male. Heavier than he looks. Muscular. Looks like he spent some quality time at the gym. I ended up pulling him to shore, so this is not how he was found. Ironically, he was doing the deadman's float, but got caught up in some tree branches along the shoreline. Don't think he was in the drink too long, though. He's got a nasty knife wound . . . someone slit the guy's throat. Probably bled out in the river," offered Hicks in a staccato speech pattern. "Been waiting on you and the ME before doing anything but marking the territory."

"Nice work, Kenny," offered Will, earning a look of disdain from the older officer. Anissa began her prowl, circling the area surrounding the pale body and making mental notes before pulling a camera from her bag and snapping photos. Will stood a distance back from the corpse. Transfixed on the grisly wound, he was growing greener by the minute, now wishing he hadn't eaten breakfast that morning.

"Dark hair. Brown eyes. You ever run across this guy before, Kenny?" asked Anissa calmly.

"No, he's a new customer from my standpoint. But as I was wrestling him out of the water, I could see his wallet in his jacket pocket. My impression is that he wasn't a robbery victim. Hopefully, our friend here can help us with some answers," concluded Kenny as he glanced up at the approaching white van driven by the ME.

"Morning, Anissa. Another body? We've got to stop meeting like this," called Wally, rolling out of the vehicle. "Officer Hicks . . . Will . . ." He wobbled under the police tape toward the small group. "Where's Nowitzke?" he asked, looking around.

"On another assignment," Anissa replied. "Will's taking his place for the time being."

"Really?" Wally took his first look at the victim. "Oh, wow, that's a horrid-looking laceration. Someone got him good," he added, bending down. "Jesus, I can see the man's spinal column through the front of his neck." His comment drew a shudder from Will. "Any idea who the victim is?"

"No, I was waiting for you to arrive before fishing the man's wallet from his jacket."

"Knock yourself out," replied the ME, who was still kneeling.

Anissa bent down and plucked the man's billfold from his coat. She continued to search the body, looking for pocket litter or items that could provide any additional information or clues. However, even though the river had turned any paper to mush, Anissa found a money clip bearing the initials EP and twenty dollars in ones.

Flipping through the wallet, she found some identification. "Wisconsin driver's license issued to Ernest Preston," said Anissa. "A local, if the address is correct. A couple of credit cards. Visa, Mastercard, both issued to Preston. Interesting that he's got no phone on him."

"It might be at the bottom of the Fox," offered Kenny. "Either way, we can't ping where he came from using the towers."

"Wally, can you fix the time of death?" asked Will, chiming in.

Wally stood and turned towards the young man. "Sonny, you know the official time of death is when the body is discovered. Kenny, when did you pull Aquaman here out of the drink?" he asked, looking at the uniform.

"Probably 7:55 a.m." replied Kenny.

The ME turned back toward Will. "There you have it, Detective. That good enough for you? Now come over here and make yourself useful. I need some help to turn the body over so I can get a look."

Will appeared horrified at the prospect and went very pale, before responding to the medical examiner with a "Who, me?" expression on his face. Wally did not take the bait and certainly didn't care about the nice-looking suit Will was wearing. Realizing that he had no choice but to man up, Will stepped forward, grabbed one side of the dead man's body opposite the ME, and pushed as requested.

Wally scanned the body and quickly put his thoughts together. "Anissa, a couple of early observations for you. My guess is that the victim didn't know the attack was coming. He has no defensive wounds to his hands, and I don't see any skin under his fingernails. Whoever killed him did it from behind quickly, probably grabbing the man's head with one hand and slicing his throat with a very sharp blade. Looks like one clean cut. Given what I'm seeing, I'd bet next month's paycheck that this guy knew his attacker. Finally, rigor mortis has not set in, meaning this is a fresh kill. Maybe in the last hour or two, if that helps."

Anissa made a mental note. "So, the man died early this morning?"

"Yeah, like about the time my baker was pulling his first batch of donuts from the oven. Maybe 6:00 a.m. or so. Now, let's get this guy to my office," said Wally, looking again at Will. The ME retrieved a pair of body bags from the van, keeping one and tossing the second to Will.

"Two bags?" questioned Will with a puzzled look.

"One for the body and another just in case the head falls off when we're moving him," said Wally with a deep belly laugh, joined by Officer Hicks. Anissa turned away to cover a wide grin, doing her best to maintain a level of professional decorum. However, the image was enough for Will, who barely made it to a large evergreen before losing his healthy breakfast.

After Wally bagged and tagged Preston's body, Anissa turned to Hicks. "Kenny, I know this is a long shot and that you're still soaking wet, but would you mind checking the other side of the river for anything unusual that might show where the actual crime took place? You know the drill, blood splatter, flattened brush, anything that stands out from the ordinary."

"You got it, Detective," said Hicks.

"Even though we're still in the city, it's reasonably isolated over there, more industrial than anything else," Anissa added. "According to Google, the Fox flows north. Assuming the body floated for a while, start your search a couple miles south and work back this way. If you find anything, let me know and I'll be there ASAP."

"What about your partner blowing chunks over there?"

"When Will composes himself, we're going to take a stroll down the shoreline on this side and look for the same thing, for what it's worth."

"Those nice heels are going to take a beating," offered Hicks.

"Unfortunately, the price of poker, Kenny."

****

Based on the information provided by Colby, Nowitzke pointed his Escort in the general direction of the airport. Like many other towns with air service, there were a cluster of hotels and restaurants in the immediate vicinity catering to businesspeople and tourists. The officer regarded the Orchard Inn as one of the many decent cookie-cutter places to stay, not that he frequented many hotels. While deep in thought about the details of the developing Hecht case, some chatter on Nowitzke's police radio startled him back to consciousness. "A 10-16 domestic dispute has been reported at 3908 W. Wisconsin Avenue. Unit two, please respond," requested the dispatcher.

The detective realized he was in the general area of the address in question. "Dispatch, this is Nowitzke. Is the reported address a residence or a commercial business?"

"A business, sir," said the monotone female voice. "The Orchard Inn."

"Jesus, I'm pulling into the lot now. I'm on this. But send me some backup." Nowitzke knew the potential danger of this type of call.

"See the manager, Detective. A John Schroeder."

Nowitzke parked near the entrance next to a five-minute "Unloading Only" sign and noticed a slightly built young man with an acute case of male pattern baldness wearing a light-blue shirt, slacks, and a black tie pacing near the front door. As Nowitzke stepped from his car, the man began yelling, "Hey, you can't park that junker there, sir!"

The detective flashed his badge. "You Schroeder?" he asked, towering over the man.

"Yes. You're with Appleton Police?" asked the manager with a look of skepticism.

"Yeah, I get that a lot," said Nowitzke. "What's the deal on your domestic dispute?"

"A member of our cleaning staff heard shouting and several loud crashes coming from a room just a bit ago. One of our end units on the second floor. Room 223. A man and a woman just screaming at each other. Then our employee, Eleanor Foster, said she heard things breaking inside the room. Glass, heavy thumping, furniture being broken . . . you know, like a brawl taking place. Mrs. Foster became very concerned and contacted me. I went upstairs and heard the same and called 9-1-1."

"Who is the room rented to?" asked the detective.

"A single. A young woman named Savanna Smythe," concluded Schroeder.

"No shit," exclaimed Nowitzke, already on his way up the stairs. Stepping onto the second floor, he heard nothing, but placed his hand on his Glock as he proceeded slowly down the long and narrow hallway. If someone emerged from a room with a gun intent on shooting him, he had no place to take cover. "Beautiful. Fucking beautiful," he muttered to himself as he considered his vulnerable situation, now three-quarters of the way to his destination. Aside from the shadows cast by the overhead canister lights, the sun shone brightly through a broken window on the wall next to the end unit. Large shards of blood-stained glass sat on the tattered carpet in front of the broken hotel room door. A cheap framed photo was lying at a forty-five-degree angle between the wall and floor next to a damaged table and pieces of what was previously a cheap ceramic flower vase.

Nowitzke drew his gun as he closed the gap to the room and stood next to the doorjamb. The door was askew. He drew a deep breath before reaching with his left hand and rapping on what was left of the door. "Police," he said in a commanding voice. "Drop any weapons and step outside."

There was no response. Nowitzke knocked a second time, but still heard nothing. Using the barrel of his gun, he slowly pushed the door open. What had formerly been a comfortable room was now uninhabitable with literally everything inside in pieces, akin to what might have taken place during a professional wrestling match. Nowitzke quickly cleared the small space—a single bedroom and bathroom—confirming that whoever had been there was now gone. Based on what he could see, the participants in the melee had exited in a hurry. The floor-length, beige drapes billowed in the breeze coming into the room through the large broken picture window as Nowitzke tried to put together what had taken place. He poked through the closets and the drawers, finding dresses and lingerie. The bathroom held several perfumes and an assortment of makeup and hair products. A suitcase at the foot of the bed remained half-packed. As Nowitzke began rifling through the case, he heard a noise behind him at the door.

"Oh my God, what have they done to the place?" cried Schroeder, coming into the room.

"Whoa, sir. Back up. This is a crime scene. No one is here. I need to look at your records for information about Ms. Smythe. Credit card info, phone numbers, etc."

"We might have some video, well, at least of the lobby area and hallway," offered Schroeder. "What am I supposed to do about the room damage?"

"Call your insurance agent?" deadpanned Nowitzke.

After sifting through the data gathered by the hotel about Smythe, Nowitzke learned that she had paid for the room with cash. He tried the cell phone number she had left at check-in, but it rang continuously, leaving the detective to believe it was a burner phone that may have now been discarded. He would check the email address later but had little confidence that it was going to be much help. There was one positive development, however. The clerk who was working the front desk when Smythe checked in had followed procedure, making a copy of her driver's license. "I'll be damned," said Nowitzke. "Savanna Smythe, Toronto, Ontario, Canada. She's a long way from home." He took a copy for his file.

In the meantime, Schroeder cued up video from the camera in the lobby based on when Smythe first arrived at the hotel. Sitting in the manager's office, the video feed in front of him, Nowitzke had no doubt she was the same woman who had been at Hecht's home and had been seen by APD traffic control. Schroeder then brought up the second-floor hallway tape from the prior hour.

Nowitzke watched as a thirtysomething man wearing jeans and a sport coat entered the screen. When the man got to the end of the hall outside Smythe's door, the detective got a good look at the subject, who briefly glanced up at the camera. He sported a blond buzz cut and a compact build, standing roughly at five foot ten, as judged by the officer. The silent film rolled as the blond knocked on Smythe's door several times. A sliver of light appeared in the hall when the door opened a crack, and the man bull-rushed his way into the room. Then, for the next forty seconds, nothing. Schroeder was poised to advance the film until Nowitzke stopped him. Suddenly, Smythe flew through the door, landing in the hallway with enough force to splinter a wooden table and knock the picture from the wall. When the blond stepped from the room towards the fallen woman, Smythe managed to get to her feet, grabbed the decorative vase, and smashed it into her attacker's face, knocking him down and momentarily disabling him. Then Smythe, who was wearing only a sweatshirt and shorts, built some momentum. Facing away from the camera, she squared up, waiting for the blond to stand. When he did, she delivered a karate kick to the man's groin with enough strength to make both Schroeder and Nowitzke recoil in unison.

"Jesus, an axe kick to the giblets," exclaimed Nowitzke. While the attacker somehow remained standing, but wobbly, Smythe head-butted the blond, further incapacitating him. Now with the advantage, the woman sized up the blond once more before delivering a follow-up kick to the man's chest, sending him through the second-floor window down to the ground. Nowitzke and Schroeder exchanged glances. Although the video showed the images of an intense struggle, it did not capture the screams, shouts, or the sound of breaking glass. Smythe casually stepped toward the window opening and looked down. Then she quickly returned to her hotel room, reappearing thirty seconds later with her purse as she exited down a rear stairway. The action scene, which easily could have been made for a Hollywood blockbuster, was over.

As the video returned to the more mundane look at the hallway, Nowitzke bolted from the manager's office and ran through the lobby and out into the parking lot toward the rear of the building. There was no sign of Smythe's Lexus. The detective, his weapon drawn once more, moved quickly toward the back of the property, expecting to see the blond lying on the ground. But surprisingly, aside from flattened grass, broken glass, and blood stains, Nowitzke found no one unconscious or writhing in pain. Somehow the attacker had gathered himself enough and managed to get away, either by car or on foot.

When Nowitzke returned to Schroeder's office, the manager was still in his chair, muttering. For a person who had spent years in hotel management and had theoretically "seen it all," watching what appeared to be a life-or-death struggle taking place in his building was a new experience.

"Mr. Schroeder, do you have any cameras covering the parking lot or the space in and around the building?" inquired the detective.

"Yes, we have one mounted on each corner of the building and in the entranceway," Schroeder replied.

"Roll back the exterior footage for a half hour and play it at double time," said Nowitzke. "I'd like to see if we can get a look at the guy's car." The hotel manager shook his head at the request and fiddled with his computer, still fretting over the damage to the place. The screen broke into five separate feeds, showing vehicles coming and leaving at an incredible rate. Then, one panel showed Smythe run into the frame before climbing into her car. "Can you slow it down to a normal speed now?" asked Nowitzke, now carefully watching for the buzz cut to do the same. However, the officer saw a flash of the man limping in and out of the picture, away from the premises. "Did I miss something? Is there anything behind the hotel?"

"Nothing. Open space. Green grass. A paved road waiting for someone to develop bars and restaurants around it," replied Schroeder.

There was nothing to follow-up on. No vehicle. No plates. Nothing that might identify the man. However, the devious side of Nowitzke mused that APD could canvass area ice machines if the buzz cut was interested in taking the swelling down on his boys. He also made a mental note of Smythe's physical ability if he was ever called upon to confront her. The detective asked for a copy of the videos and called in a forensics team to gather fingerprints and other physical evidence from the scene. *Man, I've got to meet this lady.*

****

Anissa and Will completed backtracking their side of the shoreline an hour after beginning what proved to be a fruitless search. "Damn, Kenny was right. These shoes are toast," declared Anissa, sitting on a park bench rubbing her feet. As she examined the irreparable damage to her pumps following their nature walk, her phone rang.

"Anissa, it's Kenny. I walked quite a ways back but couldn't find any evidence of a struggle on this side of the river."

"Thanks, Kenny," she replied, clicking off the call. "Shit, that was a waste of time."

Will sat on the other end of the bench. Had it not been for a murder and a second death involving his suit at the hands of the heavy brush, it might have been a beautiful day. "Anissa, can I ask you something?"

"What's up?"

"I get the impression that no one at APD or associated with it likes me all that much. I certainly don't feel like I've got anyone's respect," said Will, contemplating the current of the river. "I mean, everyone else seems to like and respect you. We've been on the force for roughly the same time. I don't understand it."

"You mean because I'm a woman?" she asked with an icy stare from her end of the bench.

"No, that's not it at all. I mean, we've got the same tenure. But this morning, I watched the guys, Kenny . . . Wally . . . they listened to what you said and then did it," said Will. "Even Chuck. Fucking Nowitzke trusts you."

Anissa stopped rubbing her feet, sighed, and pivoted her body towards Will. "I can appreciate what you're saying. Let me tell you that I've worked my ass off to get where I am today. I spent more time listening and watching than talking early on. I studied on my own time. When someone asked for my opinion, I gave it to them, point-blank. Maybe there's some luck involved too. Who knows? Several people did take me under their wings. Chuck stood up for me on more than one occasion. As I understand it, he knocked out an old curmudgeon of a sergeant who was chirping about me getting my detective shield because I was a woman. My impression is you just need to stay with it and pick a direction. Whether it's public relations or being a detective or doing something else, you need to figure it out. Everyone knows you've had a tough go of it lately with your injury. Are you sure you're up to this job?"

"That's a fair question," replied Will. "Physically, I think I'm back from the stabbing, but mentally I'm not a hundred percent yet."

Anissa hesitated for a moment biting her lip but decided she needed to ask the question. "I've heard stories about the incident, but what actually happened?"

"It was a domestic disturbance that I got called to because the suspect was a known drug dealer, an enforcer, and a thug in general. Anyway, for some reason this guy beat the shit out of his wife. I mean really pummeled her. When she answered the door, her face was covered in blood. Several other uniforms arrived about the same time I did and tried to subdue her asshole husband, a big dude who was probably high on something.

Anyway, when the uniforms started reading him his rights, the dealer's old lady figured out it meant her guy was going to jail and she freaked out. I was focused on the suspect and never saw the knife until the woman slashed me." Will pointed toward his abdomen. "Got me good too. My first instinct was to pull my gun, but before I could, I collapsed. Next thing I know, I'm in a hospital with the doctors telling me how lucky I am to be alive. Funny thing was that I didn't feel lucky." He smiled awkwardly. "A lot of stitches and a lot of pain. I'm still working through the counseling process, but I needed to get back to work. Oh, and the best part is that the dealer and his wife both made bail and were back out on the street long before I was released from the hospital."

"So, working the knife attack this morning must have been hard for you," concluded Anissa, shaking her head and pausing. "You know, Will, working law enforcement is a tough gig. But you already know that. Terrible hours. Not enough pay. Always dealing with not-so-nice people who lie awake at night thinking up stuff that most of us can't even conceive. Give yourself a break. Maybe you just haven't found your calling yet."

"Thanks for the pep talk, Anissa." Will continued to look off into space. "Why do you do it?"

"I guess it's the family business. My father is a cop. My hero. I want to be like him." She smiled and put on her battered shoes. "Changing gears, what can you tell me about the Henderson murder?"

"The Henderson case? You mean the guy with the six marked on his forehead?"

Anissa nodded.

Will sat back for a moment as if searching his mind like a computer trying to call up an old file. "It was one of my first assignments as a detective. On the surface, Henderson seemed about as good as they come. Husband. Father. No criminal record. But . . ."

"But what?" asked Anissa.

"There was something about this guy. A big-time area volunteer, involved in his kid's soccer league, all the big fundraisers in town . . . you know the type." Anissa nodded. "Even though no one had a bad thing to say about Henderson, I got this impression that he was working hard to make up for something he'd done in his past. You know, trying to make amends. Of course, it was just a feeling that I couldn't prove. A perplexing case. There was no physical trauma to the body, aside from a small puncture wound that Wally found later. If it wasn't for the six on the man's head, I doubt we'd even be talking about this file anymore."

Anissa sat engrossed in the story and impressed by Will's insights, filing them away in her mind. "You know, you might want to focus on being a detective. I think you've got the makings of a good one."

"Thanks, Anissa," he said with a muted smile, finally earning a win following a tough morning.

CHAPTER 10

Nowitzke stepped into the glassed-in entrance of the Appleton Public Library and immediately felt lost. Anissa had him pegged better than he cared to admit. Considering himself a TV kind of guy, he could not remember the last time he had read a book, let alone been in a library. He guessed he must have checked out a few books sometime during high school but could not recall a single title. Part of him also wondered if he had ever returned any of those books.

Like most of its contents, the building was dog-eared, yet it had the feel that someone was still lovingly caring for it while maintaining a certain order. Nowitzke judged that the current structure was a combination of multiple additions cobbled together over decades. As he stepped into the lobby, he saw a poster on an easel seeking support from benefactors and the taxpayers to build an impressive new chrome-and-glass facility in the coming year. The detective was also struck by the noticeable quiet inside the space despite the number of patrons reading at tables, conducting research on outdated computers, or simply walking the aisles in search of specific titles. The images took him back to elementary school where he and his classmates first learned the universal rule: always whisper in the library. Nowitzke also recalled violating the instruction, having been shushed multiple times, always by a stern, old crone wearing her glasses on a decorative chain around her neck.

Ironically, a helpful-looking teenage girl who was sorting returned books at the front desk spotted the out-of-place man and politely asked, "May I help you, sir?"

"Yeah, miss. I'm looking for Maureen Carr."

"Mrs. Carr is our director. I think she's in the kids section. If you'd like to wait, I can track her down for you," she replied enthusiastically, jumping off her stool before disappearing into the building.

Nowitzke found a comfortable chair and barely got settled before the high-school girl reappeared with a woman wearing a trendy business suit. He judged that the petite woman was likely in her thirties. She was of average height, but was distinguished by thick, dark hair fashioned in a neck-length bob parted down the middle. She confidently strode up to the detective with a helpful smile and an outstretched hand.

"You must be Detective Nowitzke," she said in a calming voice as the officer rose and shook her hand. "Chief Clark said to be on the lookout for you. I'm Maureen Carr."

"Pleasure to meet you, ma'am," replied Nowitzke. "I'm not sure what the chief told you about why I'm here."

"All I know is that you're working on some sort of cold case and that you need to dig into our archives."

"That covers it, except it might be more than one case and it could stretch back for years. Do you have some place we can talk privately?"

"Of course. Let's go to my office," replied Maureen, leading the detective through a labyrinth of bookshelves before approaching a wide set of stairs seemingly carved from a single slab of marbled granite. Upon reaching the second floor, Maureen turned left and entered a space that had an unintended retro feel but was immaculately clean. Nowitzke was drawn to a large window in the office that overlooked the first floor of the library. "Would you like regular or decaf, Detective?" asked Maureen, searching for a cartridge from the chrome tree holding various flavors of coffee, with her finger poised on the Keurig's "ready" button.

"Regular, please," replied Nowitzke, preparing to fill in the blanks of what he needed. However, Maureen, who was working the coffee machine, managed to hold up a single finger in what the officer construed as the equivalent of a twenty-first-century shush. As the coffee brewed, the detective found a seat.

Moments later, Maureen began. "Chief Clark provided broad strokes about what you're looking for. But when he said the word 'archives,' I knew this was beyond my area of expertise. I was a librarian at one point, but now I run the business end. The good news is that we have a local historical librarian on staff that can help you sift through all the chaff. In fact, I've asked her to join us."

On cue, a woman was standing in the doorway. "Natalie, would you like some coffee?" asked Maureen. Nowitzke looked up as the woman silently shook her head and entered the room before lighting on one end of a threadbare couch opposite from where the officer had planted himself. "Natalie Alvera, please meet Detective Nowitzke from Appleton Police," offered Maureen. However, Natalie said nothing and remained in place, requiring the officer to twist and reach across the couch to greet her. The woman accepted his hand but did not make eye contact.

As Nowitzke sipped his coffee, he studied Natalie. He had done a double take when she came into the room, intrigued by an exotic look that she possessed. The Hispanic woman had a thin face with almond skin and large dark-brown eyes. He judged that Natalie was likely in her forties. She was short but maintained a slim frame with more than a hint of curves and wore a sleeveless Bohemian dress along with a hint of perfume that caused Nowitzke to breathe deeply, searing the scent into his brain. However, her most striking feature was a mane of shoulder-length grey hair that had a natural curl. Interestingly for the detective, he noticed a tan line on the third finger of her left hand as she waited quietly on the couch. *No ring.* Natalie apparently had not gotten the memo about the requirement for librarians to wear reading glasses around their neck.

Maureen took a steaming cup of coffee from the Keurig and sat down in a plush chair opposite Natalie and Nowitzke. "Detective, can you tell us about what kind of research you need?"

Nowitzke sat forward toward the edge of the couch and put his coffee down on a side table next to his seat. Then he launched into a monologue about the deaths of Devine and Henderson, the numbering found on their foreheads, the significance of June 16, and the potential of five-year increments, forward and back. He left out any reference to the late senator and details about his ongoing investigation. The officer also explained that old case files at APD had been purged and wondered about accessing the Appleton *Post-Crescent* to look for a pattern of other similar deaths, in keeping with Miss Alma's theory.

"What prompted the timing of this project, if I may ask?" asked Maureen.

"Frankly, the deaths predate me coming to Appleton. Chief Clark wanted a fresh set of eyes to look into this matter," said Nowitzke with a straight face.

"I see," Maureen replied, not necessarily buying what the officer was selling. She turned toward her still-silent employee. "What do you think, Natalie?"

The librarian sat up as tall as she could manage. Then, in a measured tone, her voice deep, she spoke. "This shouldn't be a problem, Maureen. We could go through Newspapers.com. However, sometimes the content at that site is incomplete. If that's what we find, we can search through our own records on microfilm. We have versions of our local paper going back almost to the 1800s, I believe. What year would you care to start with?"

"Well, if the pattern holds, 1993," surmised Nowitzke.

"Do you have any other names or details?" Natalie asked.

"No, none . . . except again that June 16 seems to be the magic date for some reason."

"I gather that any news of a crime or any obituary would likely have been published during the span of the following week?"

"That makes sense to me," conceded Nowitzke. "When could we get going?"

"Let's focus on the microfilm. I could give you a tutorial on how to use the machine tomorrow morning. I can also show you how the records are filed, which will allow you to complete your project. Does 9:00 a.m. work for you?"

"Wait, are you saying that I would be doing this on my own? I thought this was something you would do to help APD," protested Nowitzke, somewhat incredulous at the thought of working alone with the library equipment.

"Of course we will assist you," offered Maureen. "It's just that you'll need to be an active partner. Neither Natalie nor I really know what we're looking for."

"That makes us members of the same club, I guess," Nowitzke replied, standing.

Natalie also rose from her seat. "I'll see you bright and early tomorrow morning, Detective," she said flatly, leaving the office.

Nowitzke's eyes followed Natalie as she left the room, then he looked at Maureen. "Is Mrs. Alvera up for this? I mean, she seemed pretty withdrawn and not terribly excited to work on these cases. Is there anything about her that I should know?"

"Natalie is quiet by nature. She's also a technical genius when it comes to this type of work. I'm sure you will be dazzled."

Nowitzke said nothing, a stony, less-than-confident look on his face.

"For what it's worth, I can tell you that from a personal standpoint, Natalie's plate is full," conceded Maureen, not divulging anything further. "If you two don't click, I'll try to find someone else to help you, but I'm sure she'll warm up as you get to know her," she added. "Trust me."

Nowitzke left Maureen's office and made it to the top of the stairs when his phone rang. Several patrons turned at the sound and shot him disapproving looks. "Nowitzke," he answered full-throated.

"Detective, this is Officer Benson calling from the front desk at APD. Just wanted to give you a heads-up that you have a visitor waiting in your office. A woman named Savanna Smythe. She said you probably want to speak with her."

Nowitzke squinted, his head cocked, wondering for a moment whether he'd heard the officer correctly. "Thanks, Benson. Make sure she doesn't leave the facility," he instructed, then hung up, considering this turn of fortune. He began making his way down the main stairwell when he heard children yelling in excited voices near the entrance of the library.

"Abuelita! Abuelita!" shouted a young boy and girl, drawing head snaps from several patrons followed by a collective *shhh*. As he cleared the bottom rail, Nowitzke saw both kids running eagerly towards Natalie Alvera before she embraced each, then quickly corralled the pair and ushered them out the front door.

Curious about the woman, Nowitzke's eyes followed Natalie until she disappeared into the parking lot. *Damn, maybe I need to get a library card.* As he walked toward the Escort and climbed in, he tried to focus on his meeting with Smythe. *I wonder what "abuelita" means?*

CHAPTER 11

By the time Nowitzke arrived at his office, the redhead had made herself comfortable, reclining in his office chair with her feet on his desk and playing with a snow globe. "You must be Detective Nowitzke," she said cheerfully, popping to her feet and greeting the officer. "I love your snow globe collection. Did you know this zombie one glows in the dark?" She gave the globe one final shake before placing it carefully into the palm of the officer's outstretched hand.

"Yeah, I do," replied Nowitzke, taking the globe and returning it to its place on the credenza next to the fifty other assorted specimens of all shapes, sizes, and styles.

"By the way, I'm Savanna," she said with a perky smile.

"Ms. Smythe, you've had quite a run in your short time in Appleton," offered the detective, shooing her from his chair. He surveyed the eye-catching woman, who was wearing the same top and shorts as in the video at the hotel. She also had a deep cut above her left eye and a developing bruise on her right cheek, along with some faded bloodstains on her sweatshirt that appeared to have been rinsed out. "I saw the tape of your WWE match at the Orchard Inn this morning. That was a helluva finishing move. Can I get you some ice?"

"No, I'll be fine," Savanna replied casually, dropping into one of the side chairs in front of the desk. She fingered the open wound on her eyebrow. "Just some cuts and bruises. No big deal."

"Looks like you could use a couple of stitches," replied Nowitzke. She rolled her eyes. "Are you also a doctor, Detective?"

Nowitzke let the remark and her smug look pass. "Let's back up," said the detective, taking a breath before launching into his questions. "What the hell is going on here? Over the weekend, you meet Senator Hecht, who apparently dies in your company. Days later, you're attacked in your hotel room and then basically kick the shit out of some asshole who forced his way into your room. Now, even though everyone at APD is looking for you, somehow you find your way to me. Who are you?" he demanded.

"I'm a tourist," replied the woman. "Oh, and please, it's Savanna."

"Yeah, I know you're a Canadian. I saw a copy of your driver's license this morning," said Nowitzke. "Let's try again. What are you doing here?"

"As I just said, I'm visiting, eh," she answered in a sarcastic tone. "A first-timer in Wisconsin."

"Who are you visiting?" pressed the detective.

"No one in particular. Is there a rule that I have to be visiting someone? I've just read about Wisconsin and decided to check it out," Savanna replied. "Love the cheese curds and beer, by the way. Thinking about taking the Lambeau Field tour. Maybe buy a Packers t-shirt."

Nowitzke stared down the woman, looking for a tell, but didn't see one. Nonetheless, he wasn't buying what she was selling, given the remarkable past couple of days. "Why are you here at Appleton PD talking with me?"

"Well . . ." she said, eyeing the ceiling. "I figured someone was investigating the death of the senator. I looked up the APD website, and your name came up. I saw that you've been involved in several high-profile cases. And your rank was listed as senior detective. I suspected the police might be trying to track me down, and I thought you were the guy. Am I wrong?"

"No, you're not. Tell me about what happened at the fundraiser with Senator Hecht," said Nowitzke.

"I had read about the fundraiser online. I've always been interested in American politics and thought maybe I'd meet a sitting senator. I bought a dress and some shoes and just showed up," Savanna replied, sitting on the edge of her chair. "They had free drinks."

"How did you get into a private event like that without a ticket?"

"C'mon, Detective. The level of security at the house was no match for my best smile and some cleavage. I fit the profile of the others who were there, except for the big bank account, and just waltzed in. No biggie." Playing with her hair, Savanna sat back and flashed another smile at him.

"Continue . . ." replied a skeptical Nowitzke.

"I drank several glasses of wine. Hobnobbed with some very nice people. Ate some fantastic food. Had a great conversation with a well-to-do doctor and his wife. Towards the end of the day, I finally met the senator. We talked for a while. For an older guy, I found out quickly that he was a bit of a horndog, so we ended up taking the elevator to the lower level of the house, looking for some privacy in the wine cellar. One thing led to another, but before we got too far, the senator started seizing up. You know, grabbing his chest. His eyes began to bulge, and he was sweating profusely," she said with a serious tone, now leaning forward in her chair. "Then, he asked me to call a doctor. I ran to the elevator but had to wait before I made it upstairs. I didn't know if there was a stairway or not. When I got to the main floor, I yelled for help and found someone who knew CPR."

"But I understand that you never made it back to the wine cellar," replied Nowitzke. "Why?"

"I panicked . . . a foreigner involved with an American politician? I didn't want my face on any of the newspaper rags at the grocery store or any headlines like 'Canadian Screws Senator to Death.' I don't know if it was the wine or I just got carried away. Not my proudest moment. Anyway, once I found someone who could help, I pointed the way for him and made for the exits," she concluded.

"Just to confirm, you never saw Hecht's body after you left to get help?"

"No," replied Savanna with a puzzled look. "Why?"

Nowitzke ignored her question. "Did you touch Hecht's body?" he asked.

"What kind of details are you looking for?" She looked askance at him. "Like I said, I might have kissed the senator. I might have even pulled his pants down. But he started having a heart attack almost immediately."

After listening to her story, Nowitzke was still not satisfied. "You don't look like a chubby chaser to me," he said, trying to provoke a response. "Frankly, you are just too good-looking a woman, and I've seen the senator. The math isn't working for me."

"I don't know what else to tell you," replied Savanna.

Nowitzke sat back in his chair, rubbing his temples. "On your trip to the wine room, were you and the senator alone?"

"Several people saw us talking together on the main floor as we got into the elevator," she said, standing to stretch, buying time to think. Ten seconds passed. "Wait, when the senator and I were downstairs, we had to walk through a narrow passageway. We ran into a server. I even asked the guy where the wine room was, and he pointed us in the right direction. Anyhow, there was only enough room for us to go one at a time. I scooted through. Then, when the senator tried, I heard him kind of yelp. The server apologized . . . saying something about sticking Hecht with a corkscrew."

"A corkscrew? How does that happen?" asked Nowitzke.

"Beats me. Something stuck him, but it didn't seem to slow him down. Hecht's mind was on other things."

"Can you describe the server, or could you identify him if you needed to?"

"I think so," replied Savanna. "He was about average height, fairly well-built. Dark hair cut short. There wasn't much light down there, but I did glance at his face when I passed. I think I would recognize him if I saw him again."

"A server, huh?" Nowitzke thought about this piece of information. "Had you seen him during the event or after you met him in the hallway?"

"No, I don't think so."

"What was the deal with the number?" asked Nowitzke.

"Number?" replied Savanna, looking confused. "What number are you talking about?"

Nowitzke studied her face closely, but there was no tell. *Truth.* "Let me ask you this, Savanna. Any chance the server was the same person that you put through the second-floor hotel window this morning?"

"None. Totally different guy. The idiot this morning was blond, kind of wiry strong. Banged on my door saying he was with hotel maintenance, and I made the mistake of opening my door a crack before he barged in. Stupid me, I never checked through the peephole."

"What did he want?" asked Nowitzke.

"I have no idea. At first, I thought he was there to rape me. Then, it took a minute before it finally clicked that he was just trying to kill me," said Savanna, still fingering her cut. "That fucker picked the wrong girl."

"Damn, I'll say," Nowitzke echoed, replaying the video in his mind. "My compliments on the groin kick."

Savanna smiled. "Got him square too. Ten years of martial arts lessons finally paid for themselves today."

"Did this asshole say anything to you?"

"He didn't talk dirty or anything, if that's what you mean," said Savanna, drawing a scowl from Nowitzke. "No, nothing, sir," she followed contritely. "That was the scary part. He showed up and tried to strangle me. Out of the blue. I have no idea why."

The detective let her words sink in. "So, you're saying this was a random attack?"

"I have no other way to explain it."

"You know, Savanna, assaults like this are not typical in Wisconsin," said Nowitzke.

"Tell me about it. The travel brochures never mentioned it as a problem," she said in a snarky tone. "Actually, everyone else here has been very nice."

"You sure you're alright?" asked Nowitzke.

"Yeah, I'll be fine," replied Savanna. Then, after a pause, she said, "I've got to be somewhere. Am I free to go?"

It was an interesting question. While Nowitzke wasn't buying into Smythe's entire story, she supplied enough plausible details to give her credibility. The sex-with-the-senator scenario still didn't make sense to him. But he didn't want a visual. At the same time, Nowitzke knew firsthand that you didn't prosecute someone for making poor choices. If so, he would have been locked up and doing hard time somewhere. Nowitzke didn't believe Savanna was involved in Hecht's death. He was, though, inclined to believe her story about a third party on the way to the wine room that night. It fit with the physical evidence of the puncture wound that Wally was looking into. Nowitzke made a note to follow up with Elliott for information about the staff at the event. The blond subject who lost the brawl at the hotel was another open issue. But as far as Savanna was concerned, he considered her to be acting in pure self-defense. While the hotel's insurance company might be upset that charges were not brought against her, they also would not want to respond to a lawsuit for negligence for the hotel failing to protect a guest. Finally, even though he was worried that she might be a flight risk, he didn't consider her a suspect and had no reason to hold her. "You know, if I can find the server, I'd want you to identify him. How long are you staying in town, Savanna?" asked the detective.

"Another week or so. I still have an agenda."

"Where can I reach you if I need to?"

"At this point, I'm looking for another hotel," said Savanna. "I'll give you my number."

"Give me the real one. Not the bogus one you gave the Orchard Inn," Nowitzke replied.

"Of course, Detective," she said, flashing her brilliant smile once more.

****

Anissa stood opposite Will Porter as he rapped hard on the third-floor apartment door. They could hear rock music playing inside, along with a baby crying. The officers looked up and down the hall of the dull building, waiting another thirty seconds before Will followed up with a heavier knock. "Police," he called. With the dinner hour approaching, both inhaled the smell of cooking food coming from the adjacent apartments.

"Wow, suddenly I'm hungry," commented Anissa.

"Something Italian?" guessed Will, sniffing the air. As he was about to knock a third time, the music disappeared and the baby stopped crying, replaced by the sound of someone jostling with the chain lock.

A short, dark-haired woman in her early twenties opened the door. Anissa judged that she was roughly five feet tall. Her green eyes complemented her delicate face. At any given time, Anissa might have qualified her as cute. However, today she had large bags under her eyes, along with greasy, unkempt hair that suggested she hadn't showered recently. She was barefoot but dressed in an AC/DC t-shirt and plaid pajama bottoms. Her final article of clothing was a powder-blue blanket draped over her right shoulder as she nursed a baby.

"Police, you said?" she asked in a tired voice, seeing both officers holding up their badges. "Can I help you?"

"Is this the residence of Ernest Preston?" asked Anissa.

"Yeah," the young woman warily replied. "Ernie should be coming home soon. Is he in some sort of trouble?"

"Are you married to Ernest?" asked Will.

"No, but we've been together for some time. I'm Angel . . . Angel Stone. This is Ernie's son, Horace." She nodded towards her covered shoulder.

"Miss, would you mind if we stepped into the apartment?" asked Will with a stony face.

Thirty seconds later, and with the door closed, Will continued.

"There is no good way to say this Ms. Stone. Ernest was found dead this morning."

Angel had a bewildered look on her face for a moment before she blinked hard several times and her eyes began to moisten. "How? How did Ernie die?" she asked, her voice trembling.

"His body was found near Alicia Park. We suspect that foul play was involved in his death," replied Will.

"Oh, God." Angel sat down on a ratty cushioned chair as tears streamed down her face. "Why? Was he robbed? Who killed him? I don't understand," she cried.

"We have no suspects at this point," offered Anissa. "And we're still trying to establish a motive. However, Ernie wasn't a robbery victim." The room went quiet, aside from an occasional whimper from Angel and the sound of Horace hungrily nursing. "Can you tell us what Ernie did for a living?"

Angel's green eyes fixed on a point on the bare living room wall, looking past the detectives, and she answered with an automaton-like response. "Security. A private contractor. He did work for many people, but I never knew who it was at any given time," she offered. "Ernie worked odd hours based on whatever the work required. He was just starting to make a go of things after several years in the Army." Then, still in a daze, Angel threw off the blanket, mindlessly pulled up her shirt, gently flipped the infant to her other breast, and recovered herself. "What am I supposed to do now?" she asked.

"Did Ernest have any family in the area?"

"None, besides the two of us," she said with an indistinct twang in her voice.

"We do need you to identify Ernest's body," said Will. While the ID needed to be done, Anissa was struck by the lack of compassion in Will's voice.

"Right now?" Angel asked.

"No rush," said Anissa. "Take care of your little man, and we can go when you're ready. Is there anyone we can call to help you?"

"No, I don't know anybody around here," Angel replied feebly. "Would you take him for a minute while I get cleaned up?" She handed the now sleeping child to Anissa.

Anissa was wide-eyed for a moment. She couldn't remember the last time she had held a baby. But taking the sleeping infant seemed low risk, and Horace could have cared less. Anissa studied the child's peaceful, almost angelic face as she stood, rhythmically bouncing back and forth on her feet. She and Will heard Angel retreat into the bathroom and water beginning to run.

"Not to sound sexist, Anissa, but you look like a natural holding that little guy," offered Will.

"Feels good too." Anissa cuddled the baby. "Hope to have my own someday," she added in a melancholic tone.

Five minutes later, the officers exchanged glances when it dawned on them that while they still heard water running, there was no other sound coming from the bathroom. Then, a loud thump got the attention of both. Instinctively, Anissa handed the baby off to Will and moved quickly to the bathroom door.

Anissa pounded hard with her fist, which woke Horace, who began to cry. "Angel! Angel, are you okay?" The detective rattled the door handle, but found it locked. After no response, she looked at Will and calmly said, "Call 9-1-1." Then, turning, Anissa squared up and rammed the old hollow-core door with her shoulder, but it barely budged. Using her foot, her second try splintered the door enough for her to snake a hand through a small opening to unlock it. As she threw the door open, steam from the running shower mushroomed into the rest of the apartment. Through the fog, Anissa saw Angel lying unconscious on the floor, holding a brown prescription bottle with pills scattered around her. "Fuck . . . Valium!" she shouted as she dragged the woman from the small space into the main room before checking for a pulse and trying to revive her. "Angel, can you hear me?" yelled Anissa. "Will, any ETA on the first responders?"

Before he could answer, they both heard sirens approaching. "She tried to kill herself with these tranquilizers. Get downstairs and point the EMTs up here when they arrive," she ordered.

Will froze in place, wide-eyed, still holding the wailing baby.

"Will . . . goddammit, MOVE!" Anissa roared once more, finally getting his attention. Then, not knowing what else to do, he robotically handed Horace back to Anissa and disappeared down the steps.

Several long minutes later, a fireman appeared at the door of the apartment. Flashing her badge with one hand while comforting the upset infant, Anissa explained. "I think the mother OD'd on these," she said, tossing him the plastic bottle. "Probably not more than ten minutes ago, but I have no idea how full the container was."

The firefighter knelt beside Angel and felt her neck, checking for a pulse. "She's alive, Detective," replied the first responder. "But we need to get her to the hospital now to pump her stomach."

What sounded like a herd of elephants made its way up the narrow stairwell. As reinforcements arrived, Angel spasmed, bolting upright at the waist, and threw up, now semiconscious.

"So much for needing a stomach pump," concluded the EMT. "She should be fine."

The first responders loaded Angel onto a gurney, which several brawny firemen carried down to the ambulance. When the crowd upstairs cleared, Anissa carried the now sleeping baby down to the street, where she found Will sitting on the steps by himself, staring blankly at the ground.

"Sorry. I just checked out," he confessed in a small voice to Anissa's abject silence. "I don't know what else to say."

Anissa sat down next to Will on the brick steps and took out her phone to make a call. In the din of traffic, the three of them sat silently until a vehicle rolled up to the curb.

A middle-aged woman stepped from the car. "Are you Detective Taylor?"

"Yes, ma'am," Anissa replied, standing.

"I'm Carol Vaughn from social services," she said, holding up her

ID. "You called a bit ago. I'm here for the baby." The woman put her arms out to accept the infant. "Wow, he's a cutie." Anissa filled in the sad details of the day, including the death of the baby's father and the suicide attempt by the mother. "Talk about stacking the deck against this little boy," replied Vaughn. "We'll take good care of him." She carefully placed Horace into a car seat and disappeared into traffic.

Anissa sat back down next to Will. "It's been a helluva day. I'm not hungry anymore, but I could use a stiff drink," she concluded. "Care to join me?"

"Only if wherever we go serves doubles."

****

Click – click – click – click – click – click.

As they walked back to the SUV, Anissa and Will were unaware that they were being watched. A wiry, blond man sat across the street from the officers at a bus stop, casually reading a newspaper. At the same time, the autowinder on a 35-millimeter camera positioned down the block began working furiously, taking a series of photos of the area, the man on the bench, and the officers.

CHAPTER 12

Nowitzke returned to the library the following morning, fifteen minutes before its scheduled opening. Armed with a coffee carrier, he brought two large steaming cups, one for Natalie and one for himself. It would be his third that morning, having needed to give his motor some extra priming just to get rolling. He had woken early, hitting the snooze button only twice versus his normal six times. After showering, Nowitzke had used the extra time to shave in anticipation of working with Natalie on the cold case. Wanting to make a good impression, he carefully chose a jacket and tie that were a reasonable match together with his typical khakis and loafers. However, after languishing over his wardrobe choice, he managed to earn a conspicuous grease stain on his best tie when a piece of egg from his breakfast sandwich skittered down the front of him as he ate in the car. Using a napkin to wipe the mess off as best as he could, Nowitzke remained undeterred. At least until the officer reached the door, where he was met by a stony Natalie, who made him wait until the building officially opened at 9:00 a.m.

"Good morning, Natalie," greeted the detective when the door finally opened. "How do you like your coffee?"

"I don't, Detective. I'm a tea drinker," she said brusquely, turning into the library. "Come with me. I have a workstation already set up for you."

Natalie was wearing a stylish multicolored dress and heels, her hair tied back. She said nothing else as she led the detective through the maze of shelves and back up the marble stairs to the second floor, past Maureen Carr's office, to a windowless room at the dead end of an uninspired hallway. Inside was an intimidating piece of equipment sitting on a rickety table, ancient metal desk, and an uncomfortable looking stool. "I've gathered all the microfilm from the week in question in 1993. It's on the desk next to the reader," Natalie said, nodding toward the apparatus.

Nowitzke inspected the stark black machine with the oversized screen, the multiple spools and rollers, and the four buttons. He put down the coffee carrier on the desk as Natalie conducted her lesson.

"Detective, I'll give you this tutorial once. Each roll of film is one hundred feet long, containing roughly six hundred to seven hundred images. Load the film roll carefully so that it clicks into the spool on your left." Natalie's narration continued as she demonstrated how to use the reader. "Thread this around the first roller; the glass panel in the center of the unit will open automatically. Feed the film under the glass panel and onto a catch reel on the right. Insert the end of the film into this slot so that it catches and then tighten it up. If you get confused, the diagram is on the lower panel. Hit the power button twice. When the screen comes on, select the required software." She handed him an envelope. "Here is your pin and password to enter at that point."

Nowitzke's head was still catching up to the diagram, but officially shut down when he heard the word "software."

"If I were you, I'd scan the obituaries to start with," continued Natalie. "From there, you might find stories that connect with any unexplained deaths. Here is where you find the print feature." She pointed to an obscure button on the side of the machine. "Any copies you make can be picked up from the printer at the main desk downstairs." Then, Nowitzke received an admonishment from the librarian about making sure to rewind every wheel of microfilm before proceeding on to another. The demo took less than five minutes before Natalie disappeared with a "call me if you need me" comment that sounded like anything but.

Left alone in the room, Nowitzke took a deep breath and a huge pull of coffee. "Jesus Christ . . ." he mumbled to himself. "Now what did she say?"

In his first attempt to spool the machine, Nowitzke managed to place the film so it displayed an unreadable reverse image. After rewinding the spool, he flipped the film and began the threading process a second time. Halfway through, Nowitzke touched a button on the base unit, sending the entire film through the glass in thirty seconds. Worried that he would tear a film roll in two, he opened the desk drawer where the reader sat, looking for written operating instructions. Not that he was particularly adept at following written directions, or any others for that matter. An hour and a half in, he made one final attempt to correctly spool the film and engage the software, but again failed. In frustration, he drained his coffee and sent the empty cup flying toward the wastebasket in the corner, the dregs splashing the wall. Somehow the cup fell into the receptacle, his only success for the morning. He brooded briefly, thinking about putting two rounds from his Glock into the reader as he debated calling Maureen's bluff about finding someone other than Natalie to guide him through the process. Fuck it. It's not my problem if the library can't find quality help. He resolved to use the restroom and then raise the issue with Maureen.

Nowitzke followed the signs down the hallway, which took him down a second corridor with several small rooms, all but one with their doors open. As he moved down the hall, he heard a soft whimper coming from the room with the closed door. He gently knocked, but the sound immediately stopped. Finally pushing the door open, Nowitzke found Natalie sitting in darkness, dabbing her eyes. "Natalie? Are you alright?" he asked.

"I'm fine," she said curtly. However, a splinter of light entering the room from the hallway shone on her face, betraying her words. Natalie's eyes were puffy and red, and her makeup was smudged.

"Well, you don't look fine to me," offered Nowitzke, noticing a wastebasket full of used tissues. "Can I help you?"

Natalie stood, straightened herself, and smoothed her dress, trying to regain her composure. She picked up the half-filled box of tissues from the small table in the room and tried to get past the detective.

"Listen, I'm sorry for disturbing you. But I need your help on my project," he said with a pleading look in his eyes. "This is an important assignment, and I'm struggling."

"With what part?" she asked.

"Pretty much all of it. I'm not good with technology."

She hemmed and hawed briefly, taking a deep breath before replying, "Alright, let me go to the ladies' room, and I'll be right back."

Five minutes later, Natalie poked her head into the small room holding the microfilm reader. She had put herself back together, even offering a hint of a smile as she assessed Nowitzke's progress. "Gee, you really didn't get very far, did you?" she said, shaking her head in amazement.

"No shit," he replied in agreement, followed by an apology. "Sorry for swearing."

The two exchanged glances, followed by a shared laugh. "I've heard worse, Detective," she said.

Then, in the abject silence of the room, Nowitzke's stomach growled loudly. "Natalie, after screwing around with this machine all morning, I'm starving. Would you mind if we got some lunch and a fresh start?" he asked.

Natalie briefly studied the detective before taking pity on him. "Okay, but I need to be back in an hour. There's a diner around the corner."

They had beaten the lunch rush, having the place largely to themselves. The restaurant, Ellie's, was a single-room café with large windows. Shabby, brown industrial carpeting covered the floor, while several old-fashioned metal-legged kitchen tables were spread about the room. Small caddies holding ketchup, mustard, and napkins sat on the small Formica tabletops that were heavily scarred from years of hard use. The chairs were roughly the same style yet were multiple colors of vinyl with silver backs and legs. Natalie chose a table in the corner. Once she and Nowitzke were seated, a stooped elderly woman, presumably Ellie, dropped two one-page laminated menus on the table and disappeared. Nowitzke surmised from the prices on the menus that they had not changed in years.

After ordering, Natalie a salad and Nowitzke a cheeseburger with fries, they each sipped iced tea until she broke the silence. "Detective, I apologize for my unprofessional behavior today. I don't want to make any excuses for myself, I've just had some things on my mind . . ." She trailed off, then stammered, "I'm generally a happy person, but . . ."

Nowitzke studied the woman's face as she talked. "A divorce, huh?" he asked matter-of-factly.

Natalie looked stunned. "Does it show that much?"

"Lucky guess. I'm a detective, remember. Since you showed up for work this morning, I assumed there were no deaths in the family. Also, when we met yesterday, I noticed that you weren't wearing a wedding ring, but you had a tan line, like you'd taken it off recently." Natalie unconsciously moved her telltale left hand under the table in response as Nowitzke continued. "For the record, I'm a charter member of the club. Repeat offender, no less. I'm sorry," he offered as Ellie delivered their food.

The silence returned as Natalie poked at her salad. "It's weird," she replied. "We've been married for twenty-two years. We love each other . . . well, at least I love him. There's been no drama, no third parties, or fourth parties for that matter. No financial issues. I was happy with my family life and my job. Then one day about ten months ago, with no explanation, my husband announces that he can't be married to me anymore. He says he can't even explain why. We've been separated since. I can't figure out what triggered this, and I sure don't understand it." She took a sip from her tea as her eyes glistened for a moment. "It just feels like I've always been married to him. And the change has me a little scared. We're now in the process of finalizing the divorce, which ripped all the old emotional scabs off me," she concluded.

The detective listened intently to Natalie's story as he munched on his cheeseburger. "Your husband just came up with this out of the blue?"

"Yes."

"No other woman involved, huh? I mean, I'm not trying to get into your personal business, but it makes no sense to me either," he replied. "As a cop, I've heard a lot of bullshit stories over the years, but your husband's moves right near the top. Let me just say that a guy leaving a woman like you without a damn good reason must be an idiot."

Natalie grinned at the officer's conclusion.

"Wow, after this morning, who would have believed you have such an amazing smile," added Nowitzke sincerely as he cocked his head.

Natalie took a deep breath. "So, you've been divorced twice?" she asked with an almost imperceptible cringe that Nowitzke picked up on.

"Yeah. I'm not good at relationships . . . at least that's what I've been told. The original Mrs. Nowitzke was a barmaid with whom 'until death do you part' lasted about eighteen months. I picked up number two on the rebound. A dancer, no less."

"Really, a dancer?" she questioned.

"A polite word for stripper. Mercedes," he replied, nodding his head. "In her case, wedded bliss went down in flames in about a month. A personal best for me. I served thirty days but feel like I'm still doing time."

Natalie said nothing at Nowitzke's revelation, continuing to chase a tomato around her salad bowl. "Can I ask . . . did it hurt? You know, emotionally?"

The detective chewed on some fries as he contemplated a question he'd never considered before. "I guess it should have, when I think about it. But for me, no. Maybe that means I was never really in love to start with. Either time."

Both Natalie and Nowitzke remained silent for the rest of the meal, each deep in thought. When they finished, the detective stood. "Would you give me a hand with the microfilm, Natalie?"

"Of course," she replied.

At four that afternoon, Maureen Carr poked her head into the microfilm reading room. Nowitzke and Natalie were sitting side by side. "Any luck?"

"I think so," said Nowitzke, looking at the notes he'd scratched onto a yellow legal pad. "Since we really didn't know what we were looking for, it was harder than I thought. But Natalie found an obit for a guy named Frankie Brock, age twenty-three. There were no details about the death, so we searched further. Nothing specific came up until we saw a small article in the June 20, 1993, edition of the *Post-Crescent* about a junkie found dead in an alley downtown off Franklin Street. Nothing else seems to fit the time frame with deaths that year. At this point, I've got enough to go back to work."

"Was Natalie everything I said she would be?" asked Maureen.

"That and more," he replied with a smile at Natalie, who beamed. "I would like to come back and do a follow-up search for other potential individuals. For now, though, I'll get started learning more about what happened with Brock."

"Then I'll leave it to you two to figure out any next steps," said Maureen proudly. "Glad we could help." She left the room.

Nowitzke packed his notes into a manila folder provided by Natalie. "Detective, I'm curious about what other years you're interested in," Natalie commented.

"Well, I guess if the pattern holds, 1998, 2003, and 2013."

"Only those years?"

"Yeah, only those years." He laughed, realizing that this was going to be a much bigger undertaking than Natalie probably thought. "I'll be in touch soon. Here's my business card . . . uh . . . my personal cell number is on the back," he said ham-handedly.

"Thank you, Detective. And here's my card," she said, placing it in his beefy palm.

Nowitzke stood and breathed deeply, just to take in a final whiff of Natalie's perfume before he left. "By the way, some people call me Chuck."

****

From the library parking lot, Nowitzke called Clark. "Chief, I might have a lead on the death from 1993. A guy named Frankie Brock was found dead in an alley. Any ideas about who might have investigated this for APD?"

"Chuck, this is well before my time. From what I understand, APD didn't have multiple detectives back then. My guess would be a guy named Mack Bordon, probably."

"How do I find him?"

"How the hell would I know? Not to sound rude, but you're the detective." Chief Clark laughed as he signed off. "By the way, nice work."

Nowitzke stood in the lot, thinking this through. Thirty years had passed. And who knew if this Mack Bordon was still alive. The detective pivoted from his car and walked back into the library directly to the main desk staffed by the teenage girl from the day before. "Hello, sir," she said, recognizing the officer. "Welcome back. Are you looking for Mrs. Carr?"

"No, actually just a local phone book, if you even have one . . . " said Nowitzke, squinting at her name tag.

"Rachel," she replied, filling in the blank. "No problem." She reached under her desk and handed him a yellowed copy. "Do they still print these things anymore?"

Nowitzke could only shake his head at the question. He took the book to a table and paged through the B's. There was no Mack Bordon listed. However, he found three other Bordons. Resisting the urge to tear the page from the phonebook, he flipped open his manila folder and jotted down the names and numbers. "Thanks, Rachel," he said as he returned the book to her, getting a smile full of braces from the bubbly girl.

From his car, Nowitzke began calling the Bordons listed in search of a relative named Mack, taking the time to explain who he was and what he wanted. It took until the third number before the detective spoke with John Bordon, a son of Mack's. John explained that his father and mother were in a local senior home, largely because of her dementia. However, Mack, who was now in his eighties, remained sharp. John provided Nowitzke with his dad's mobile number. Even with this information, Nowitzke decided it was best to visit the man personally.

As Nowitzke neared the senior living center, he had a feeling that someone was following him. Checking his rearview mirror several times, he changed lanes randomly as he made the trip, but never noticed any suspicious vehicles. Just that feeling. Ultimately, he concluded it made no sense that someone should be tailing him on a trip to talk to a retired cop about a death that had taken place thirty years earlier.

The Oakdale Village facility was a series of well-maintained one-story brick buildings connected to a large main structure with a vaulted entranceway. As Nowitzke parked the Escort near the front door, he felt his blood pressure rising. Aside from Miss Alma, one of the few things he feared in life was entering a nursing home. He hadn't visited many over the course of his life and couldn't pinpoint where the dread came from. Maybe it was knowing the residents were in various stages of contemplating their own mortality. Or worse, knowing that many of them were unable to do so. Or perhaps it was just the smell he associated with such places. Nowitzke took a deep breath, pried his sweaty hands off the steering wheel, and told himself to grow a pair and do his job.

Much to his surprise, the place looked more like a hotel than any nursing home he had ever been to. Nowitzke went to the front desk, flashing his badge out of habit. "Would you happen to have a Mack Bordon here?" he asked the young man, who was wearing light-green scrubs and a ponytail.

The man behind the counter eyed Nowitzke. "Is there a problem, Officer?" he asked with some trepidation in his voice.

"No. I was told that Mr. Bordon is a resident here. He's a retired cop, and I need to speak with him about a case he might have worked back in the day."

"Interesting. Yeah, I know Mack . . . cool dude, by the way. Can I tell him who's calling?" asked the man.

"Detective Chuck Nowitzke."

While he waited on Bordon, the detective curiously studied the large lobby. Painted in a light beige, it was well-lit and cheerful. The walls held professionally mounted photos of local landmarks, including the Hearthstone Historic House Museum, Lawrence University, and, ironically, the Appleton Police Department. The green carpet covering the expanse looked new and clean, based on what Nowitzke could see. Surrounding the main desk were clusters of stuffed chairs near reading lamps. He also noted several wooden tables and chairs interspersed about the space. For whatever reason, the comfortable area sat empty. Poking his head into an adjacent room, he found a dining hall that looked more like a restaurant. Nowitzke watched as the staff made their final preparations for dinner that evening, putting menus at each place setting. While he could not identify the aroma, the smell of whatever was cooking set his large stomach rumbling.

An elderly man ambled toward the lobby. Trim, but slightly stooped, he had the appearance of having shrunk from his former self based on the way his clothes hung on his body. The man's grey hair was receding, and he wore heavy glasses. *Thick enough to burn ants on a summer day*, thought Nowitzke. Combined with the shape of his head, he had the look of an owl with a sharpness that belied his years.

"Detective?" he croaked, his voice gravelly. "I'm Mack Bordon."

"Chuck Nowitzke, sir. Good to meet you," said the officer as he thrust out his hand. "I was wondering if you had a few minutes."

"Well, only a couple. Dinner will be served shortly . . . the highlight of my day. Pork chops tonight. Damn tasty. Don't know what the cook does with them, but they're better than any my Vivian could make," he said with a mischievous smile. "Just don't tell her that."

They found an open table in the lobby away from the main desk.

"Mr. Bordon . . ." Nowitzke began.

"Call me Mack. Everybody has since I was a kid."

"Alright, Mack. Were you a detective at APD?"

"I was, but I've been retired for quite a while."

"I'm working a case that you might have been involved with about thirty years ago," Nowitzke explained, pausing. "Do you recall the death of a man named Frankie Brock?"

Mack scratched his head, thinking for a minute. "Yeah, I do. If memory serves, Brock was found in an alley downtown. Don't recall too many specifics, but it was warm outside, you know, like summer. Probably June. I got called when the city garbagemen almost tripped over the body. Sad case, Brock. He was a young guy. Did some background work on him. He was a decent student and a top-notch athlete in high school. Not sure what happened. Anyway, he had no family, and no one ever claimed the body. He was cremated and buried in a potter's field somewhere around town."

"Do you recall the cause of death?"

"Drugs," he said bluntly. "Turned out Brock was a junkie. Several homeless people we questioned filled in the blanks. The thinking at the time was that Brock OD'd. Probably heroin."

"Was there any medical inquiry or an autopsy?"

"The coroner came out and ruled it an overdose. No one thought to do anything else," replied Mack.

The easiest person to kill is one you expect to die anyway. Wally's words rang in Nowitzke's head as Bordon spoke. "Was there anything else about this case that stood out to you?" asked the detective.

Mack got up and walked to a picture window fronting the street, deep in thought. "Yeah, there was," he said with a large blink behind his heavy lenses. "It was the darndest thing. Brock had the number one drawn on his forehead in a black marker. Never saw anything like it before or after. Never figured out why it was there either."

"You just answered my next question about finding any other bodies with numbers on them," replied Nowitzke.

"Do you know what the number means?" asked Mack.

"No. I've just been asked to look into this case by the current chief, for what it's worth."

"That sounds like bullshit," retorted Mack, momentarily becoming a cop again. "Considering the timing of our conversation after all these years, my guess is there must be others just like Frankie."

Nowitzke chuckled. "You're pretty quick, Mack."

"You know, I kept waiting for another body to show up at some point, but thankfully none ever did . . . at least none on my watch," he concluded, his head cocked, staring into Nowitzke's eyes.

"You looking for a job back at APD by any chance?"

"I wish. My best days are behind me, Detective. Need to take care of my Vivian. We've been married for fifty-four years, and I'm not sure we'll see fifty-five together," rasped Mack, trailing off into a prolonged stare.

Nowitzke rose from his chair. "Mack, I can't thank you enough for your help," he said, bringing the former officer back into the moment. "You take care." The detective, becoming anxious at the conversation, made a quick exit to the door.

CHAPTER 13

Elliott Gordon was a man unaccustomed to clandestine meetings. He was also used to having information from a variety of sources on any subject relevant to his business. Given the circumstances, and with background information recently obtained on his new prospective contact, he grudgingly agreed to meet. A proponent of hiding things in open spaces, Elliott took a stool at the elegant bar of the CopperLeaf Hotel on College Avenue in downtown Appleton. He wore a comfortable pair of jeans, loafers, and an open-collared white shirt under a blue sport coat, looking like any number of businessmen after hours. Not being familiar with the bar, he arrived ten minutes early to get the lay of the land and see how crowded the place was. He was pleased to see that, aside from the bartender, there was only one couple having a quiet conversation on a couch on the far end of the room. Elliott ordered a Drambuie straight up and stared mindlessly at a baseball game on the television perched above the bar, waiting for 8:00 p.m.

His counterpart arrived precisely on time and took a seat at the bar, leaving a stool in between himself and Elliott. The man ordered a beer. After unbuttoning his jacket, he took his drink and moved to a highboy table. Elliott followed moments later.

Click – click – click – click – click – click.

"Good evening," said Elliott. "What's going on in my world?"

"Quite a bit actually," launched the man. "The police are stymied on Ernie Preston's death. The medical examiner and the investigators have developed quite a bit of information, though. They have a promising theory that Ernie likely knew the perp, which we both know was the case. The cops also went to the man's address and interviewed his girlfriend. By the way, when she heard about Ernie, she took a handful of pills."

"Did she die?"

"No, she's still around. Before her little incident, she told the detectives that her boyfriend worked as a contractor doing security work. Nothing tied back to you . . . yet," he cautioned, taking a swig of his beer.

"Listen, you're not giving me much of anything I don't already know," protested Elliott.

"Bullshit. I told you that Smythe was staying at the Orchard Inn. Your boy should have been able to take care of business. Frankly, with the information he had, courtesy of me, he screwed the pooch before he took a header out the window," he said with a chuckle. "The hotel recorded some of the big fight, and the police have the video. It's only a matter of time before they identify your associate."

Click – click – click – click – click – click.

"Then Smythe met with Nowitzke in his office. I'm not sure what she told him, but afterwards, Nowitzke didn't take her into custody, which seems to mean he believed what she said."

"Who the hell is she?" demanded Elliott quietly, his face animated. "What was she doing in the house the night the senator died? It's hard to believe she just happened to show up at Hawkins' house without some agenda."

The contact rolled his eyes.

"Can you get more information about her?" Elliott asked.

"Maybe. Smythe's supposedly still in the area but keeping a low profile. One more thing. I tracked Nowitzke to Oakdale Village. Does the name Mack Bordon ring a bell? You know, the investigator on the Frankie Brock case?" asked the contact. "Elliott, you've got a developing shitstorm on your hands." He shook his head.

Elliott paused, then swallowed the rest of his drink. "Okay, you seem to have some interesting tidbits I might be able to use. But before we start a working relationship, we have a couple of things to clarify. First, you report to me and no one else. We operate in Brad Hawkins' house, but he is outside the loop without any clue about how we operate or what we do. Do not talk with anyone you *think* are my associates either."

"Got it."

"You and I should only meet when you have something of value. If it's an item that requires immediate attention, text me at this number," he said, sliding an otherwise blank sheet of paper across the table. "*Never* call my personal cell number. Understand?" The man nodded. Elliott then pushed a thick manila envelope across the table. "I hope two thousand a week still works for you?"

"It does."

"Don't be unreliable. If you fuck up, or I get even a hint that you might, you'll get to meet our blond friend in person and end up like our pal Ernie."

"Unless I decide to toss him through a window first," the contact said with some bravado, putting the envelope in his breast pocket.

Click – click – click – click – click – click.

Elliott snickered at the comment, rose from the stool, shook the man's hand, and disappeared out onto the avenue. Once Elliott was gone, the contact downed the rest of his beer and left by another exit.

A photographer with a telephoto lens positioned across the street captured the meeting, unbeknownst to either man, before sending a text:

Hey asshole. Next time smile. I know your secret!

When Elliott heard his phone ping, he took it from his pocket and read the incoming message. His head snapped around to look over his shoulder, but no one was on the street. "Shit," he murmured angrily to himself before replacing the phone and continuing on his way.

CHAPTER 14

I t had been a long week. Nowitzke woke with a start and an immediate "oh, shit" moment. As his brain kicked in, he remembered that he and Anissa were to meet Brad Hawkins for lunch at Ivy House. While he knew of Hawkins' reputation as a former prosecutor and staunch defender of law enforcement, "lunching" was not a verb in Nowitzke's vocabulary. However, Chief Clark had made it clear that attendance was mandatory.

Nowitzke sauntered into the office around eight thirty after picking up coffee and a half-dozen donuts. He hadn't seen Anissa in several days and looked forward to exchanging information with her on their respective cases. His partner was in her office concentrating on her laptop, wearing a black business suit with matching shoes and a white blouse. He rapped on the glass window and entered, taking a seat in front of her desk. "Donut?"

"Already had my yogurt and fruit this morning," she replied, eyeing her boss. Nowitzke was wearing a grey pinstripe suit with a blue shirt and a wide bright-yellow tie. "You know we're having lunch with Brad Hawkins today, right?"

"Is that a slam against my donuts or what I'm wearing?" he asked.

"Both . . . I guess. As your partner, I'd advise you to lose the tie, Chuck."

"Aren't power ties yellow?"

"Not when they're large enough to be a lobster bib," she commented. "But at least it's not stained. Changing gears, let me bring you up to speed on the body we found." Anissa launched into a recap of the sad story of Ernie Preston, the overdose by Angel, and the fate of young Horace, who was picked up by social services. "The mom survived, but she'll have a bitch of a time getting her baby back," concluded the junior detective.

"How did your boy Will do?" Nowitzke asked.

Anissa looked down at her desk briefly.

"That good, huh?"

"Chuck, why do you always see the worst in him?" asked Anissa.

"Why are you always defending him?" he retorted.

"Will's got some strengths. We chatted about his future. He's got his issues, but I think he's a good person down deep," she concluded to a silent and smug Nowitzke.

"Don't misunderstand. I'm sure Will's got his talents. It's just that I haven't seen any of them in his current line of work."

Anissa remained silent, leaning back in her chair. "What have you been up to?"

"Well, our traffic people were able to identify where Savanna Smythe was staying. Went out to the Orchard Inn. But some asshole beat me there, intent on killing her."

"Are you kidding me?" questioned Anissa.

"Best part is that I saw her beat the shit out of her attacker on the hotel's video system. Kicked him in the sack and then put him through a window. A second-floor window, no less. Then she disappeared. The bad guy too. Waiting on some fingerprint results from Forensics," he added.

"Sounds like my kind of girl," Anissa smirked. "I'd like to meet her."

"Well, you should have been in my office near the end of the day, cause guess who showed up?"

"Smythe?"

"Bingo. Still had some battle scars from her scuffle, but even then, she's a doll. Found her relaxing in my desk chair playing with a snow globe."

"Uh-oh."

Nowitzke shook his head then ran his fingers through his hair, still thinking about his first impression of Savanna. "Anyway, we had quite the conversation. She copped to being in the lower level of Hawkins' home with the senator, but said Hecht started grabbing his chest before they got busy. Told me that she went upstairs to get help and then just kept on going."

"Meaning she wasn't the one who put the number on the senator's head."

"Correct. But the most interesting thing she said was that on the way to the wine room, they ran into a server. A guy who supposedly bumped into Hecht with a corkscrew . . . even apologized to the senator."

"That's where the puncture wound must have come from."

"Yeah, my assumption too. Anyway, Savanna said the guy had short, dark hair and was well-built. She thinks she could identify him if she ever saw him again. Based on the time frame between when Savanna left for help and when the chief showed up, the server also has to be the one who put the number on Hecht's melon."

"Sounds like a topic for lunch today with Hawkins when things get boring," replied Anissa. "So, I take it that you believe her?"

"About not having anything to do with the death of the senator, yeah. She's a badass of some sort, and my instincts say that she's telling the truth . . . at least on that account. But she's also peddling a load of shit about just being a Canadian tourist who happens to be in the area."

"Where is she now?" asked Anissa.

"Beats me. I had nothing to hold her on. Couldn't charge her with anything. I asked her about her plans, and she said she had some more business to attend to, but she's a flight risk for sure. She gave me her number."

Anissa sucked in her lower lip as she processed this new information. "The timing of Savanna seeing the server and the attack on her is curious to say the least."

"Agreed. We're following up on both incidents. Right now, I don't know if or how they might be related. Am I missing something?" As

Anissa was about to answer, Nowitzke's cell rang. "Hello, Natalie," he said with an uncharacteristically chipper voice. Anissa listened to his half of the call. Minutes later, she heard "We'll be there shortly" before the senior detective clicked off. "Grab your stuff. We gotta go," said Nowitzke.

"Where to?"

"The Appleton Public Library. My new librarian friend says she has something to show me."

Anissa closed her laptop as both detectives stood to leave. "Chuck, the answer to your question before is no. I don't think you've missed anything about the connection between the server and the attack on Savanna."

Nowitzke shrugged. "I hope you're right."

As they made the trip in Anissa's Audi, Nowitzke filled in the gaps about the microfilm search the day before, Frankie Brock, the number one, and Mack Bordon's investigation. Before stepping into the library, Nowitzke ditched his tie, tossing it into the back seat.

Following introductions, Anissa and Nowitzke hovered over Natalie, who was sitting behind the microfilm desk in the second-floor room. "Chuck, after you left yesterday, I decided to look for any victims that fit your criteria for 1998," said Natalie. "I couldn't find a one. Then, I expanded my search outside of Appleton to include all of northeastern Wisconsin. But I came up empty again. Nada. Then I decided to jump ahead to 2003 and did another search. I came across an obit in the *Green Bay Press-Gazette* for a guy who died on June 16 named Myles Tucker. Tucker lived in Fish Creek, a small town in Door County, north of here. He was a doctor. Seemed like he died out of the blue, but there were no other details. I hope this helps you," she concluded with a smile.

"Thanks, Natalie," said Nowitzke, dumbfounded.

"Also, I couldn't find any possible matches for 2013 anywhere around here."

"When did you do all this work?" he questioned.

"Last night. I was up until three this morning. I had nothing to go home to and was intrigued by the circumstances."

"I . . . we need to check this out. I also need to find some way to repay you for your time."

"No, you don't. It's part of my job." Natalie handed him a printout of the findings with some background on Tucker.

"Natalie, I'm sorry we can't talk more, but we've got to run. We have a meeting to get to," stammered the detective. Before he left, he took a moment to discreetly drink in her scent once more.

Walking back to the car, Nowitzke noticed that Anissa had said nothing yet, a smirk painted on her face. Stopping in his tracks, he put his hands on his hips. "What?"

"Nothing. Natalie is a beautiful woman with a brain."

"It took all of your detective powers to figure that out?" he said tersely.

"She's also got the hots for you, Chuck," teased Anissa. "Looks like it might be a two-way street too."

"Shut up and drive."

****

The Audi purred to a stop in front of Ivy House. The entrance to Hawkins' home looked conspicuously different than on their first trip to the place, now sans first responders and law enforcement personnel. On the drive across town, Nowitzke had quickly read through the documents provided by Natalie. As Anissa turned off the engine, Nowitzke looked at his partner. "Nis, you up for a trip to Fish Creek? Looks like Tucker had a wife, Anne, according to the material that Natalie gathered."

"Of course. Door County is wonderful at this time of year," she concluded as she rang the doorbell next to the imposing set of front doors.

The same butler who had guided them to the study on the night of Hecht's death recognized them. "Detectives Nowitzke and Taylor. Welcome back," he said in a monotone voice, holding the door open for them. "Mr. Hawkins is in the garden, and lunch will be served shortly." He then led the officers through the home to their destination.

"Detectives . . . welcome," called Brad enthusiastically as they entered the garden. Dressed in slacks and a polo shirt, he popped out of his chair and extended his hand. "It's good to see you both again. Can I get you something to drink before lunch?"

Anissa and Nowitzke exchanged glances, wondering if this was a test of some sort, before settling on iced tea. "Thomas," said Brad to his butler, "two iced teas and a glass of white wine for me, please." Brad studied his guests, waiting for one or both to change their minds. "Officers, as far as I'm concerned, this is a friendly get-together and you're both off-duty."

"Alright, I'll have a white wine too," said Anissa.

"I'll take a beer if you've got one," Nowitzke added.

As they waited for Thomas to return, Nowitzke looked around the area.

"Something wrong, Chuck?" asked Brad.

"Just wondering if the Incredible Hulk is hiding in the bushes."

Brad looked at Nowitzke quizzically for a moment until he made the connection. "Oh, you mean Leonard. It's his day off. I assumed I would be reasonably safe in the company of two of Appleton's finest." He laughed. Shortly thereafter, the drinks and lunch arrived, and the three enjoyed a relaxed conversation over grilled salmon and salad. Despite not being a fish eater, even Nowitzke was impressed.

"Brad, I understand you were a helluva prosecutor in your day," offered Nowitzke. He glanced around at the expansive property. "What do you do now?"

"Good question. I consider myself a recovering attorney," replied Brad. "My work now is pretty much just serving on corporate boards, both locally and around the country. I paid the bills for this place primarily through corporate law. Technical stuff, boring as hell, but the compensation was incredible. I also did some personal injury stuff, but only took on select cases. However, none of it is as exciting as prosecuting criminals.

"As I look back, I've had several careers that were pretty diverse.

Believe it or not, I graduated from the University of Wisconsin with a degree in biology. My passion, frankly. I did well enough in my undergrad studies to earn a fellowship to study in Columbia. When I returned from South America, I remember being so fired up, ready to pursue an advanced degree. First a master's. Then a doctorate. Wanted to change the field in some way," he said, then drained his wine glass.

"How did you get from biology to law?" asked Anissa.

Brad stood and straightened himself for a moment, then poured another glass of wine and topped off Anissa's. "Fate," he said, sitting back down. "I have . . . had, a younger sister. Ten years younger. Sandra. Our parents had both passed away, and I became responsible for her. My career was really taking off about the time she graduated high school. Sandy had it all, the potential to do whatever she wanted in life. She told me she wanted to be a doctor someday. Graduated at the top of her high school class, had big ACT scores, and earned an academic scholarship to Wisconsin. Before she graduated, my gift to her was a choice. Sun and fun in Maui or skiing in the Rockies."

"Nice," said Nowitzke. "She must be the girl with you in the photo in your office."

"You're a quick study, Chuck. Yes, as you could tell, Sandy picked Hawaii. Man, we had the time of our lives. Surfing, sun, biking, great dinners. Then . . ." He paused, staring off into space, a blank look on his face.

"What?" asked Anissa.

"We came back to Appleton all tanned," Brad continued, his voice taking on a more ominous tone. "Sandy was fired up for college and a new chapter of her life. She walked at the ceremony, as the valedictorian, of course. I was so proud of her. Later, there was a post-graduation party at a local park sponsored by the parents. A safe party. No drinking. She told me not to wait up. And I didn't. But by noon the following day, I still hadn't heard from her and got worried. Later, Sandy called me and told me she was staying with a friend and not to worry. Then I got the same type of call the next day too. I thought something was up, especially for Sandy, who was definitely not a party girl. Several days later, she came home, but was sullen. Something was wrong. I tried talking with her, but she said everything was fine and blew me off. A day or so later, Sandy disappeared."

Sitting on the edges of their seats, Nowitzke and Anissa both paid rapt attention to Brad.

"The police were all over Sandy's disappearance. I told them about her state of mind and wondered whether something had happened at the party. The investigating officer talked with Sandy's friends and people at the event but came up with nothing. Then, several detectives came to our house and looked around, asking me a ton of questions. Did she have any boyfriends? Did she have any enemies? Was anything missing from the house? Was she involved with drugs? All no. When the police and I searched Sandy's room, nothing appeared to be missing aside from her purse, which I assumed she had with her. A couple days later, they dragged the Fox River, looking for a body. Part of me wanted them to find her, just for some closure, you know. But another part of me hoped they wouldn't. As the year went by, I was told that bodies sometimes turn up during hunting season. But that didn't happen either. She was never found. The police never had any suspects. It remains a cold case." Brad stood, but didn't move, trying to gather himself after reliving the moment.

Eventually, he downed the rest of his wine and put his glass on the table. "Anyway, I said 'screw it' to my career. I was so incensed by the situation that I decided to go back to law school with the idea of prosecuting criminals. If nothing else, to get some level of justice for Sandy or people like her. I was accepted at the UW law school. When I graduated, I came back to Appleton, where I took a job as an assistant district attorney. The caseloads were huge, and the pay was lousy, but I didn't care. I was doing good work. While I met some great people around town, I was equally amazed at the level of trailer trash living here too. You know, some people who do really bad things. Later, when the time came, I was elected as district attorney, determined to make life miserable for people who broke the law."

Anissa piped in. "I read your bio, Brad. I understand you were an early advocate for women's rights and an early adopter of using rape kits in the state."

Brad dropped back into his chair. "I was. I heard about this police officer down in Chicago named Louis Vitullo. He worked as a microanalyst in the city's crime lab. He had quite the resume and was involved in several high-profile cases, like the one involving Richard Speck, who killed eight nurses in the 1960s. However, his biggest claim to fame was in developing the nation's first rape kit. The early model was a cardboard box with some instructions, swabs, slides, a comb, that type of thing. Anyway, with my biology background, I was intrigued and wanted to learn more. So, I called him before he retired to pick his brain on the subject. Interesting guy, to say the least. Even though most people know about rape kits today, Louis was largely forgotten. Anyway, he challenged me to become a thought leader on the subject in Wisconsin. I tried to make the effort, looking to give something back."

"Why did you leave the DA's office?" asked Nowitzke.

"I became fed up. The system sucked. After years of prosecuting murderers, rapists, thugs, and the scum of the earth, I was just burned out. Over the years, though, I had made enough contacts in the business world that made it easy for me to move into private practice. Ivy House is a legacy of that work. The good news is I made a fortune so that I could hire the people to protect me if and when the unrepentant came calling. They do from time to time, as I'm sure they must for people in law enforcement that have been around the block," he concluded, looking directly at Nowitzke.

"How did you meet Elliott?" asked Nowitzke.

"We go back a long ways. Elliott worked for APD, and we teamed up on many cases. When I left the DA's office, I needed an investigator . . . you know, someone who could keep up with the ambulances," he joked. "His job morphed over the years into full-time security for me, along with other one-off things, like handling the details surrounding the fundraiser for Tony."

"Did he arrange the catering?" asked Nowitzke.

"Yes. Why?" asked Brad, shifting in his chair, cocking his head at the detective. "Is there an issue?"

"Well . . ." Nowitzke chose his words carefully. "I was able to interview the mysterious redhead from the wine room."

Brad sat forward in his chair at the disclosure. "Seriously? Who is she, and what did she tell you about Tony's death?"

"Her name is Savanna Smythe, and not a whole lot. She took me through what happened that day, writing things off to using bad judgment with the senator."

"Was she the one who put the number on Tony's forehead?"

Nowitzke grimaced, thinking of Will Porter's slipup, and glanced at Anissa. "No, I don't believe so. Your next question will probably be about the puncture wound that was brought up the other night too."

"Yes," replied Brad, nodding.

"Smythe said that when she and Hecht were making their way to the wine room, they passed a server who inadvertently stuck the senator with a corkscrew." The detective let that thought sink in for a moment. "She says she can identify the man."

"Jesus," replied Brad. "What's your take, Detective?"

"Well, Smythe looked confused when I asked her about the number out of the blue. I don't think she was faking. Anissa and I are working closely with the ME as he develops his findings on the cause of death. Frankly, I'd like to talk with Elliott about the identity of the server and find out what he knows. Remember, at present, the working assumption is that Hecht had a heart attack."

Brad took his cell from his pocket. "Elliott, can you come to the garden?" He clicked off the call. "He'll be right over." There was a prolonged silence as the group waited for Elliott to arrive.

After several minutes, they heard "What can I do for you, Brad?" coming from Elliott, who approached them at a quick pace. "Detectives, good to see you again. What's up?"

"Elliott, Anissa and Chuck were here for lunch today, and our discussion rolled back around to Tony's death. They identified the woman who was with him, and the long and short of it is that she had an odd encounter with a server on the lower level of the home. The officers here wondered if you could fill in the blanks about the identity of the man."

"The quick answer is that I don't know," said Elliott. "I hired the catering firm, and they brought their own staff. My team did a brief security screen on each of their employees, just to be safe, but there were no red flags. I've kept a file with the contract and the background check we ran, complete with photos. You're welcome to the data . . . I can make copies for you."

"That would be great," Anissa replied.

"Stop by the security room when you're done here. I'll leave the details with Bob," said Elliott.

"Thanks, Elliott," replied Nowitzke. "We appreciate the ongoing cooperation."

As Elliott left the garden, Brad looked at Anissa and Nowitzke. "Thank you for coming today. Anything else I can do for you?"

Anissa looked sheepish. "Would it be an imposition to get a tour of your greenhouse? I'm a flower fan but live in a condo with no real space for gardening, and my job leaves me with little time. I'd love to see what you've done. Maybe it will give me some ideas."

"Absolutely." Brad grinned. "Biology is still my first love, and I rarely get to show off the hothouse. Grab your wine glass or a beer, and I'll give you both the nickel tour."

Although it was a comfortable day in the garden, it didn't take long for the group to notice the increased heat and humidity after stepping into the hothouse. Five minutes into the tour, beads of perspiration were forming on Anissa's forehead. Nowitzke started breathing heavily and took off his jacket, revealing large sweat rings under his arms. "Damn, it is *hot* in your hothouse, Brad," commented the senior detective. Nowitzke considered the size of the greenhouse, which he judged to be roughly seventy-five feet long, twenty-five feet wide, and fifteen feet tall at the apex of the gabled glass roof. Inside was a series of lighted pathways constructed of patio block that wended through the thick greenery rising from black dirt.

"Basically, I try to keep the temp like a jungle," said Brad. "I've spent a fortune getting the right plants and trees in here. If you look closely, you might see some indigenous, exotic little critters running around to add some realism," he added proudly.

On cue, a beautiful, small two-toned blue frog hopped onto the path in front of the group. "Just like my little friend here," continued Brad. "If you stay long enough, you might see some other species too. Maybe a snake or two, some beetles, that type of thing. Nothing illegal, mind you." He chuckled.

"Do you keep this open all year?" asked Anissa.

"Yes, I do. In the dead of winter, I trudge out here and take an afternoon minivacation once in a while. Nothing like going from minus thirty to ninety degrees in seconds. This is really my only hobby. I never married or had kids. This is my baby, I guess," Brad concluded, wiping his brow with the back of his hand. "I've got everything in here from cactuses to small palms to fruit trees. Seeing lemons growing in January always adjusts my attitude. The staff is also free to enjoy my little jungle as well."

"Thank you, Brad . . . for everything," said Anissa as the three stepped out of the conservatory and into the relatively cool air.

"We really appreciate your time today," Nowitzke added, shaking Brad's hand before hesitating for a moment. "Brad, can I ask you one last question about Sandy? What year did she disappear?"

"1988," he said matter-of-factly.

"Thanks," replied Nowitzke, who made a mental note.

"Anything for my friends in blue. Let me know if I can ever be of help."

The officers found their way back to the security office. Nowitzke rapped lightly on the door, and within moments, Bob opened. "Hey, Anissa. So glad to see you again," said the portly security guard. "You too, Detective Nowitzke. Mr. Gordon asked me to give you this packet." He handed Anissa a manila envelope. "How was lunch?"

"Great," said Anissa. "Quite the place."

"Well, as you might guess, I saw you both on camera in the garden," said Bob. After a short pause, he continued, "Anissa, do you have a minute?" The tone of his voice signaled that it was a personal question.

"Sure," replied Anissa as Nowitzke bit his lip, gave her a sideways glance, and excused himself, plodding toward the front door.

"I've been meaning to call you," said Bob timidly. "Any chance we could get together for coffee or a drink sometime?"

Anissa paused at the unexpected question but smiled as she thought of a polite response. "The truth, Bob, is that right now I'm buried in the Hecht investigation. It has taken on new life, along with a couple of other assignments. But can I call you when things calm down?"

Bob grinned from ear to ear. "Of course. You've got my cell, right?"

"I do," she replied, exiting the small room. When Anissa returned to her car, Nowitzke was already waiting in the passenger seat. "He's got the hots for you, Nis," he chortled.

"Shut up. As someone once said, you used all your detective powers to figure that out?"

CHAPTER 14

The following morning, Anissa pointed her Audi north, turning onto Highway 41 just before 7:30 a.m. Nowitzke wanted to get an early start on the two-hour trip to Fish Creek but regretted it immediately upon waking. They made it past all of one exit before pulling off to get coffee from a McDonald's drive thru. Given her boss's history as a walking grease stain, Anissa requested additional napkins, just in case.

Once Nowitzke felt the caffeine surging through his system, he brought his partner up to date on the agenda. "I talked with the officer last night who investigated Tucker's death in 2003. Scott Aldrich, a deputy sheriff with Door County. He said he's got time for a late-morning breakfast at a place in Ephraim called the Old Post Office. He's got a hard stop, needing to be in Fish Creek at noon for a presentation at the local high school. Our second stop is at the Tucker residence in Egg Harbor. Stay on 41, follow the signs, and eventually we pick up Highway 42 north."

"Got it," replied Anissa. For the moment, traffic was light on an otherwise beautiful summer day. "Chuck, what's our approach with Mrs. Tucker? I mean, her husband died in 2003. Sounds like there was an investigation and some sort of conclusion. If after our meeting with the deputy we think Tucker's death is related to the others, we might be ripping a bandage off a scar that's already healed."

"I know. That's why we'll start with Aldrich. If it turns out that Tucker is number three, according to Miss Alma's theory, maybe Anne

Tucker can give us some background about her husband that might be useful. I figure it's going to be a tricky conversation depending on what she was told about her husband's death."

Anissa's car phone chirped, interrupting their conversation. She hit the touch screen on the dash.

"Anissa, it's Teddy Shaw from Forensics," the voice said through the speaker system.

"Morning," replied the detectives in sync.

"Morning Chuck. Just wanted to give you a heads-up that we drew a blank on both prints and DNA on the attacker at the Orchard Inn. Suffice it to say, the cleaning staff doesn't necessarily wipe down every surface in each room after a stay. Probably not possible, when you think about it. Anyway, while we got prints galore, there were so many that we ended up with a lot of clutter, not knowing who any of them belonged to."

Anissa shuddered at the thought of the room's cleanliness.

"Thanks, Teddy," replied Nowitzke as he studied the screen, trying to end the call. Once he did, the phone chirped again. "Nowitzke," he said by force of habit.

"Chuck. Will Porter here. Thanks for the opportunity to check into the catering firm and their employees. For the record, the company is Elite Events. Pretty reputable based on what I saw on the web. Anyway, I told them that despite the previous background checks of their people, I needed to do some additional follow-up given the senator's death. So, I . . ."

"What's your conclusion, Will?" replied Nowitzke impatiently, cutting off Porter.

"Well, the company accounted for all their people. They have no employees who match the description of the person you referenced. Without a photo of the guy in question, we don't have much to go on."

Nowitzke focused on the clouds on the horizon, thinking while the car hurtled along. "I suppose the man could have just posed as a server. I mean, for as much as Hawkins' people talked about security, it was pretty much a shit show that day. Anything else?"

"No, that's everything. Are you with Anissa?"

"Morning, Will," she said, jumping in.

"I can hear you're in the car. Where are you off to today?"

"Doing some follow-up work on Hecht's death," said Nowitzke, being intentionally vague. "Have a good one, Will." He signed off, now having figured out that much of the Bluetooth phone system.

"Nice to see that you're giving Will another chance," commented Anissa.

"Against my better judgment, mind you. I still think he's a walking fuckup. But, after our conversation, I decided to give him the benefit of the doubt." Nowitzke took a sip of his coffee. "Hey, can I make a call from your car?"

"No, I only bought the incoming service," she said with a smirk.

"Okay," said Nowitzke, relaxing back in his seat as Anissa laughed. "Of course you can call from the car, Chuck."

Nowitzke shook his head, realizing he'd been duped. "Smart-ass. You know I know nothing about technology. My old Escort doesn't have this option."

"Did they even have cell phones when they built your car?" she replied.

"Very funny. Would you call Natalie at the library for me?" he asked, giving her the number. The phone rang twice before Natalie picked up. "Morning, it's Nowitzke."

"Hello, Chuck," came the throaty reply.

"Can I ask you to use your microfilm skills for another favor?"

"Sure," she said, smiling through the phone receiver.

"In 1988, a young woman named Sandra Hawkins disappeared. Local law enforcement investigated. For that matter, the FBI may have even been involved. As described to me, it must have been a big deal . . . you know, a high school girl going missing. Stuff that doesn't happen much in this part of Wisconsin. Would you see what kind of local newspaper coverage this got? Based on what I heard yesterday, probably May or June time frame."

There was a brief pause from Natalie's end. "Just making notes,

Chuck. I should have it for you later today if you want to call my personal number tonight," she said.

"Talk to you then," he replied, hitting the "end" button on the touch panel yet again before settling back into his seat. "Hey, Nis, do you know what the word 'abuelita' means?"

"It's been a couple of years since my high school Spanish classes. Give me a few minutes to think," replied Anissa as she negotiated Green Bay traffic. Even though the road remained a four-lane highway, both officers noted an increase in the number of recreational vehicles and cars hauling boats or travel trailers as they all moved north towards Sturgeon Bay.

"Looks like we caught up with the vacation crowd," observed Anissa as she sped past most of the traffic. Once they were north of Sturgeon Bay, the road went from four lanes down to two. While they were making good progress, Anissa's attention was drawn to the rearview mirror. "Chuck, I've got this strange feeling that we've got a tail."

Nowitzke turned around discreetly but had difficulty seeing much over the high-backed seat or through the small rear window of the TT. He then tried to use the side-view mirror on the passenger side but couldn't identify any suspicious vehicles. "You know what, I had the same feeling the other day when I went to meet Mack Bordon. I never spotted anything unusual, even after taking a couple of soft moves to throw the potential tail off." Looking ahead, he saw a sign for a roadside farm market. "Pull in there," he said, pointing to the large red barn on the right. "Let's see if anyone comes with us."

Anissa cruised into the parking lot, followed closely behind by a line of RVs and cars. She took an open space, and the detectives decided to walk through the store, watching the flow of people. Fifteen minutes later, after sampling baked goods and fresh-cut apples, they climbed back into the car and continued their journey.

"What do you think?" asked Anissa.

"You tell me, Nis. You had the feeling," Nowitzke replied as he turned to take a final glance over his shoulder.

"I'm not getting that vibe anymore. It's certainly tougher to follow someone on a two-lane road and be stealthy. Probably a good exercise, but why would anyone be shadowing us for a death case from 2003?"

"I agree. Pretty much wondered the same thing the other night."

The road eventually curved down a long grade into Ephraim, where it hugged the edge of the bay. The tourist season was in full gear with people jogging or walking up and down the sidewalks between shops or on their way to the beach. Anissa spotted the restaurant and found a parking space five minutes before their scheduled meeting. Nowitzke emerged from the sports car, stretching like a bear coming out of hibernation. "Man, something smells really good," he growled as they stepped onto the porch towards the front door.

"This is just gorgeous," said Anissa, admiring the thick forest in the distance over the chalky white bluffs and the gentle waves of Eagle Harbor lapping against the shoreline. Several people were on the porch of the historic white building watching a woman on a cement dock toss a dog toy for her chocolate Lab, who jumped enthusiastically into the chilly water, entertaining the crowd. "I need to spend some time up here," she concluded, before stepping into the eatery.

The restaurant boasted large windows showcasing the water view. The interior was bright and airy, filled with white tables and chairs and decorated in cherry-themed wallpaper. Light classical music played in the background. Even though it was midmorning, the place was almost full. However, it was easy to spot Deputy Aldrich, who was dressed in uniform sipping coffee while seated at a corner table. He rose upon seeing Anissa and Nowitzke navigating through the tables of patrons.

"Welcome to Door County," he said, extending his hand.

"How did you know who we were?" asked Anissa.

"Well, you're in vacation territory. Not too many people wearing business clothing here," he replied, nodding towards her grey suit. "The heels gave you away . . . you must be Anissa?"

"Yes, that's me."

"The shoes were the first clue, but you being paired with a guy in a sport coat in Ephraim was a dead giveaway. Chuck?"

"Good to meet you," replied Nowitzke, shaking the deputy's hand before taking a seat.

"Call me Scotty. Even though I graduated, my high school nickname has stuck with me for some reason."

The gregarious officer looked like a perfect fit for the area. Nowitzke judged that he was a laidback sort who worked well with the locals and the out-of-towners with money. "What's good here?" asked Nowitzke, picking up a menu.

"Everything," replied Scotty. "If you want to be done eating for the day, get the Belgian waffle." He drained his coffee and signaled the waitress. After she refilled his mug and took their orders, Scotty got down to business. "So, why the interest in the Tucker death after all these years?"

"Good question," said Nowitzke. "Anissa and I investigated a recent death that had an unusual element to it. Based on what happened, our chief asked us to look into some older death cases with fresh eyes. Right now, we're testing a theory that there may be others that are in some way connected. The original cases took place years ago, long before either of us joined APD. But they all seem to have the same interesting twist to them, including a thirty-year-old death we just learned about in the last couple of days. We're wondering if Myles Tucker's case might fit with the others."

"I noticed that you never used the word homicide in your description. Was that intentional?" asked Aldrich.

"Good catch." Nowitzke smiled. "It was. In theory, none of the deaths in any of these cases were ruled as murders. What can you tell us about Tucker?"

Scotty emptied his coffee again as a tray of food arrived. Once the waitress delivered breakfast and left, he took a deep breath. "You play your cards pretty close to the vest, Detective," the deputy said. "There were some interesting elements to Dr. Tucker's death. For example, the coroner at the time ruled that the doc died from a heart attack. However, based on what I saw, that was bullshit. Tucker didn't look like a heart attack kind of guy to me. He was fit, a thirty-three-year-old triathlete, no less. You know the type, like you could strike a match on him."

"Who found the body?" asked Nowitzke before diving into his eggs and bacon.

"A couple from Illinois who were walking through the park. Over there," he said, pointing through the front window at the land jutting out across the bay. "Peninsula State Park. Supposedly, Tucker was stricken while riding his bike. It looked like the doc pitched over the handlebars and landed on the asphalt, leaving a trail of blood before ending up in the ditch. There was very little trauma, aside from some broken bones he sustained in the fall."

"Was he alone at the time?" asked Anissa.

"Hard to say conclusively," replied Scotty. "There aren't any cameras in the woods. According to his wife, Myles liked to train by himself. I studied the scene at the time, looking for any evidence of a collision with a car or another biker, but couldn't find any. I did notice the front tire of the bike was flat, though."

"Any witnesses?" Anissa questioned. "By the way, you were right on about the waffles." She carved off another piece.

"To Tucker's death?" he asked, getting a nod back from Anissa. "None. While it's a huge park, it's also used heavily during the summer. Surprisingly, no one ever came forward with any information."

"You sound a little unconvinced even this many years later," said Nowitzke. "Tell me about the body."

Scotty reached under his chair, pulling out a folder. "Here's a copy of the file for you. The doc must have been traveling pretty fast when he had his 'heart attack,'" he said, using air quotes, "because when he hit the asphalt, his left shoulder and arm were pretty torn up. There was something else unusual, though." He took a dramatic pause. "Someone wrote the number three on the doc's forehead."

Neither Anissa nor Nowitzke reacted to Scotty's revelation. "Here's one of the photos that was taken," Scotty said, discreetly sliding it across the table to Nowitzke. The detective scrutinized it briefly before pushing it over to Anissa. The photo captured the image of a taut-looking man with gaping eyes and a three clearly drawn on his forehead below his bike helmet.

"Who knows about the number?" asked Nowitzke.

"No one," said Scotty, "not even his widow. The others involved in investigating the death held that detail back, not sure what to make of it. The whole incident had the feel of a murder, but we couldn't come up with a motive, let alone a suspect. Tucker was on his way to becoming a huge success. Frankly, the area was happy to get him. An orthopedic surgeon in a county with a built-in clientele of old people?" He paused, rubbing his chin. "There was no evidence of weapons . . . no marks on the body."

"None?" asked Nowitzke quizzically.

"Nothing I could see."

"Any puncture wounds?" Anissa added to clarify.

Scotty let her question sink in for a moment, his eyes narrowing before he responded. "I didn't see one, but I wasn't looking for one either. If it was on his left side, the road rash might have scraped it off," he concluded.

"Any autopsy?" questioned Nowitzke.

"No. The sheriff lined up with the coroner. An accidental death. The body was cremated with Tucker's ashes scattered over the park. I take it you've found other bodies with numbers on them?"

Nowitzke and Anissa nodded together but offered no details. The three officers finished their breakfast, with Nowitzke picking up the tab.

"Scotty, aside from all the death talk, the meal and setting were amazing," concluded Anissa as they stepped out onto the front porch, looking across the water at the park.

"Come back sometime and we can do dinner. They have a mean fish boil here. The tourists line up for it every night." Scotty took a deep breath of the fresh air. "Are you planning on meeting Mrs. Tucker?"

"Yeah, why?" asked Nowitzke.

"No reason. A nice lady. Never remarried, even though she was so young when her husband checked out. Oh, and she's loaded," added the officer. "Let me know if you ever figure out more than what I told you," he said as he walked toward his SUV.

Anissa's car waited to turn left from the parking lot as a stream of out-of-state vehicles went by before she got a break in traffic. Heading south, they backtracked toward Fish Creek, proceeding through the quaint village filled with even more tourists before turning right onto a side road moving west. The faded and patched blacktop meandered around and through several farm fields filled with corn doing its best to be knee-high by the Fourth of July. Then the scenery gradually morphed into a heavily wooded area full of maples and oaks, and the elevation of the road dropped considerably, snaking through several switchbacks. After a mile, the road flattened as the shoreline of Green Bay appeared. When the Audi's navigation system announced that they were at their destination, Nowitzke looked to his left, spotting a carved, weather-beaten wooden sign that simply said "Tucker." Anissa turned down the short, steep grade onto a broad paved courtyard in front of a massive home.

As they exited the car, a trim and deeply tanned woman wearing a light-blue golf shirt, matching sweater, and shorts stepped out the front door. "Hello, I'm Anne Tucker," she said with a confident stride. Anne's friendly face was framed by brown hair just long enough to touch the collar of her shirt. "You're right on time."

Nowitzke took the lead, introducing himself and Anissa before their host led them into and through the house to a stone patio overlooking the bay. "Please have a seat," Anne said. "I've brewed some coffee and bought some fresh Door County cherry turnovers from the bakery in town. They are to die for." She nodded toward the pastries.

"Mrs. Tucker, I love your place," said Anissa. "Is that the mainland of Wisconsin across Green Bay?"

"Yes, it is. Michigan starts over there somewhere to the north. The view here is what sealed the deal for Myles and me when we bought the place years ago," she volunteered. "I could watch the white boat sails bobbing in the deep, blue water all day long during the summer. And the fall colors here are just amazing. Spectacular, in fact. I'm also told that you can watch winter storms blow in from across the water too, although I've never seen it."

Nowitzke looked puzzled at her final comment.

Anne leaned in toward the detective. "I get out of Dodge when the temperature dips below the freezing mark. I've become a confirmed snowbird," she confided. "My other home is in Phoenix. I have no interest in spending another Wisconsin winter here."

After pouring coffee, Anne sat down and crossed her legs. "Now, what can I help you with, Officers?" she asked, looking back and forth at Nowitzke and Anissa across the table.

"Well, the long and the short of it is that we've been assigned to look into some old files," said Nowitzke, choosing his words carefully. "The original case goes back to 1993."

"Okay," Anne replied with some apprehension. "What does this have to do with Myles' death?"

"Frankly, we're not sure it does," said Anissa. "We've talked with Deputy Aldrich about the details of what took place. We'd like to get some background about your husband."

"Myles died while biking twenty years ago on June 16. That date haunts me even now. I kissed him goodbye just before he took off that morning, and he never came home. No one in law enforcement or at the coroner's office has ever said this was anything but a heart attack. But the way you two are poking around, you're almost hinting that it could have been something more?" she asked brusquely, her voice rising.

"Mrs. Tucker, the facts of Myles' death are clear," said Nowitzke. He tried to change gears. "I know this is awkward, but can you give us some background information about your husband? I understand he was an orthopedic surgeon?"

Anne sat thinking about the question and why these two detectives were on her patio, the only sound being the wind moving through the birch trees. "Yes, he was a marvelous surgeon. He was just hitting his stride when he died."

"How did you two meet?" asked Anissa in a soft voice.

"At college . . . Wisconsin in Madison. He was a senior pre-med student, and I was an undecided sophomore. For whatever reason, a mutual friend of ours, Dan Warren, set us up. We agreed to meet for a beer, but that turned into dinner. I don't remember where we were or what we ate, just that we talked all night. After that first date, I knew we were meant to be together forever, even though we had totally different backgrounds. I'm originally from Milwaukee, a terrible student, and from old money. Myles was from a small town and was incredibly smart . . . the salutatorian of his class," she added. "He came from a blue-collar family, which meant that he was always working hard to pay for tuition and living expenses. My God, I never knew how he was able to do everything so well. School, work, time for me. I eventually concluded that he must have slept only a couple of hours a night," she said with a giggle.

Both detectives sat quietly in their chairs, listening intently. "What led you to Door County?" asked Nowitzke, gently prodding Anne to continue with her story.

"I've always been a Door County person. Daddy had a home near Ellison Bay up north, and I grew up spending summers here. Anyway, after I graduated from college, Myles was in his last year of medical school before interning in Green Bay. Then, out of the blue, he insisted on spending a year in Ukraine working for Doctors Without Borders. He told me it was payback for past sins," she added as an aside. "When he returned from Kyiv, we got married and honeymooned here. We both fell in love with Door County. A couple of years later, he was offered an opportunity at a clinic in Fish Creek. We took the leap and moved here. My life's dream . . . at the time." Anne paused, looking out onto the lake. "But I guess dreams change," she continued. "After Myles died, I was alone, left with a life insurance settlement. Daddy helped me learn about finance and investing, so I've been self-sufficient ever since. Everything I have is because of Myles, and I am so grateful for the time we had together."

Anissa and Nowitzke sat in silence, exchanging glances. "Sounds like a wonderful man," said Anissa.

"Can I ask . . . what do these cases you were talking about have to do with Myles?" she asked pleadingly.

"You know, I'm not sure that any of it does, Mrs. Tucker," said Nowitzke contritely. "I think we had some bad information. We're sorry to have bothered you or upset you in any way." He handed her his business card as he stood.

Anne waved at the Audi as it turned out of the driveway and back up the short hill to the main road. "Damn, that was rough," said Nowitzke. "Other than upset her, I'm not sure what we accomplished with Mrs. Tucker."

"Agreed," replied Anissa. "However, someone must have been near Myles before he died. While we'll never be able to prove it, the number on his forehead links him to the other deaths. A killer who looks to be an opportunist with a hard-on for June 16 for some reason."

"Thinking this through, Myles might have actually had an accident. Scotty said that the front bike tire was flat. Maybe someone set it up, like dropping a branch in the road to cause the flat tire. If Tucker went down as hard as Scotty said and was injured, he would have been easy pickings for the puncture and getting the number."

"Okay. So, in theory, we have a junkie, an orthopedic surgeon, a CEO, a working man, and a senator all connected by a numbering system. One with holes in it or other victims we haven't found yet. Chuck, despite what all the official documents say otherwise, we must be looking for a serial killer."

"I agree. But where are victims two and five? And where the hell is Wally in his investigation of Hecht?" wondered Nowitzke.

CHAPTER 15

Anissa dropped Nowitzke off at APD to pick up his car. As he pulled out his phone to call Natalie, Anissa powered the driver's window down. "Hey, Chuck, I forgot to tell you. 'Abuelita' is a term of endearment for 'grandmother.'"

"You sure?" asked Nowitzke, his eyes squinting at the news.

"Absolutely. I just looked it up. You plan on dating a grandma, Chuck?" she said with a laugh as she drove off.

Nowitzke flipped Anissa the bird as she left, wondering if her translation was accurate. He paused on making his call and considered how he should approach his conversation with Natalie. He was obviously attracted to her. According to Anissa, the feeling seemed to be mutual. Yet, in the detective's mind, the term "grandma" meant someone who was *old*. By the pure logic of it, if who he was dating was *old*, what did that make him? Nowitzke had never known his own grandparents and had little personal experience with anyone who was, aside from Anissa's grandmother, whom he had met previously. Virginia Taylor was the epitome of the term. A petite, kind white-haired woman who probably made excellent cookies. Nowitzke, now in his mid-forties, had never had solid relationships in his life, particularly of the romantic type. Neither of his exes had any maternal instincts whatsoever. Then he recalled the fact that he had never really met a librarian before working on this case. *Let alone a sexy librarian.*

He shook his head and punched in her number, getting her on the first ring. "Natalie. Nowitzke here."

"Chuck, I've been waiting for your call. I was able to find a ton of stuff on the Hawkins girl. Such a sad story. I've got a folder here with copies of everything for you."

"Can I meet you somewhere?"

"How about at my house? Have you had dinner yet? I can take you through what I was able to gather."

Nowitzke paused, thinking about the invitation before relenting. "Sure," he replied, taking down the address. "I'll see you in a half hour." He knew the area where she lived, on the south side of town. An older neighborhood with smaller family homes, a throwback to the sixties when most of them were built. On the way, he stopped at a local liquor store after deciding that he should bring something with him. He stood in the wine aisle, overwhelmed with trying to pick something out before remembering that he knew nothing about wine anyway. Ultimately, he bought a cold twelve-pack of Corona.

Nowitzke arrived at the house just as the sky turned to dusk. Natalie had left the outside light on for him. The small white home was well-maintained, with two large flower boxes on the porch flanking each side of the front door. As he walked up the concrete front walk, he wondered if he was making a mistake. However, his fears melted away when Natalie greeted him with a smile through the screen door as if she had been waiting for him. No longer looking like the librarian he knew, she seemed relaxed, with her hair down and wearing a tank top, jeans, and sandals. As he approached, he caught a whiff of her familiar scent.

"Thank you for bringing some beer. After I asked you over, I checked the fridge. You would have had your choice between Kool-Aid and a juice box," she volunteered. "Weird as it sounds, though, I do have limes for the Coronas."

They each took a beer before she led him out the back door to a patio surrounded by more flowers and an expanse of grass in a fenced-in yard. A small wood fire was snapping in a rusty fire ring near a set of padded lawn chairs.

"Nice place, Natalie," offered the detective as he dropped into one of the seats. "Own or rent?"

"My soon-to-be ex-husband and I bought the place fifteen years ago. It was a dump at the time. But we threw ourselves into making it better. A change every year, some bigger, some smaller, depending on our finances. Once the divorce is final, the house is mine . . . *my* home," she said proudly, yet sadly. There was a pregnant pause as she took a sip of her beer. "Did you and Anissa make any progress on your investigation today?"

"Yes and no, but thank you." Nowitzke smiled, raising his bottle toward her as if making a toast. "You were right about Tucker. We would not have made that connection based on my microfilm skills. Still, a sad story involving a woman who is still grieving years later," he said, staring into the fire. "I didn't help matters today by stirring the pot looking for information."

"You were just doing your job, Chuck," she replied.

"Well, like Cool Hand Luke once said, 'Calling it your job don't make it right.'" He drained his beer, then asked politely, "Do you mind if I get another?"

"It's your beer. You might as well bring me another before I fire up the grill," Natalie said, watching him as he went toward the house.

"The grill? What's for dinner?"

"I planned ahead. Burgers and beer." She smiled. "Since you brought beer."

"A Nowitzke favorite," he replied with a new bounce in his step. When he returned to the fire pit, two new beers in hand, he asked, "Did you find anything interesting about Sandy Hawkins?"

"Not too much. It was pretty much like you said. She was a young woman who seemed to have everything going for her, the valedictorian of her high school class, an active member of several service clubs, a scholarship to Wisconsin, a real cutie too, based on the photos. Then she turns up missing, reported by her brother, Bradley. According to the papers, the cops dug in, looking at several homeless men in the area as likely suspects. That didn't make any sense to me, but I guess they felt the need to blame someone. One reporter did an article with Sandy's best friend, a girl named Kelsie Cantrell. She talked about losing Sandy and not knowing what happened to her. Just heartbreaking stuff to read. Anyway, the police never found the girl's body," Natalie concluded, taking a pull on her beer. "No one was ever arrested."

Nowitzke nodded. The story largely jived with what he had heard from the former DA.

"There was one attention-getting wrinkle though, Chuck. Maybe it's not a big deal, but her brother, Brad, had Sandy declared dead after five years. I guess that's Wisconsin law, the minimum time on a missing persons case. It must have been hard for him to do that."

That fact caught Nowitzke's attention, and he made a mental note of it. "I appreciate you digging into that case for me."

"No problem. I've got a file with all the articles printed out for you on the kitchen table. Hope you don't mind that my grandkids decorated the file cover with some pictures in crayon."

"Of course not," said Nowitzke, the open personal question no longer in doubt. "Do the kids live with you?" he asked, fishing for more details.

"Only for a couple of hours a day. My daughter is a nurse at one of the hospitals, and she works the afternoon shift until ten during the week. Her husband works third shift at one of the paper plants. I also get Nino and Chloe for a couple of weekends every month. Noisy and high energy, but they are the loves of my life," said Natalie, laying her cards on the table.

"Your daughter and son-in-law are lucky to have you so close."

"Well, it's the way families work." It was news to Nowitzke. "On that note, let me throw some meat on the grill."

An hour later, Nowitzke had polished off his second burger. "Damn, Natalie, you can make dinner for me anytime," he said, relaxing by the fire pit with another beer. "Can I return the favor for you this weekend?"

"You cook?"

"No, but I can make a reservation. My best thing. It's the least I can do for you for all the help."

Natalie said nothing, but she closed her eyes as her body noticeably stiffened for a moment. "Chuck . . ." she finally stammered. "I'm not sure what to say. Are you asking me on a date?"

"I guess . . . well, yeah."

"It's just that I'm not divorced yet, and I'm struggling with the idea of being single again, even though I've been on my own for almost a year. And now the idea of dating?" Natalie hesitated, shaking her head.

"Alright, not a problem," Nowitzke said, standing with a resigned look on his face before he drained his beer. "Thank you for the information and dinner." He left her by the fire as he moved toward the back door of the house.

"Chuck," called Natalie, catching up with him as he reached the door. "Yes. Yes, I'd really like to have dinner with you. I'm sorry for being so indecisive. Maybe change is good? Let me get the Hawkins file for you."

They moved through the house back to the front porch after she grabbed the file from the kitchen table. "Good night, Natalie," said the detective, giving her an awkward hug before walking back to his car. "Call you tomorrow?"

She waved as he got in the car and then watched him disappear into the night.

CHAPTER 16

E lliott was perturbed by the text: *Need to see you with an important update. 7:00 a.m. coffee at Bobo's downtown?*

"Goddammit," he cursed to himself as he scanned his phone, his legs over the edge of the bed before responding with a terse "yes." Even though he constantly needed updated information, he was already feeling buyer's remorse with his newest contact. Foremost, Elliott hated early-morning meetings. Not his best time of the day, and they threw off his entire routine. Something he was a slave to. Today, the meeting meant no workout. No leisurely breakfast. And, after this unplanned get-together, he knew he would have no time to do anything else constructive short of going to the office and getting an early start to an already long day. "This better be worth it," he mumbled to himself.

Thirty minutes later, Elliott stepped into Bobo's, a tacky hole-in-the-wall coffee shop manned by a single barista, an extremely large bald man with "BOBO" tattooed across his forehead. As he waited to place his order, Elliott's attention was divided between studying the chalkboard menu and watching Bobo flip through his vinyl record collection that was stashed in an old milk crate. Finding his next selection, Bobo dropped the needle on Canned Heat's "Going Up the Country" before ambling toward a growing line of paying customers. Already upset at the idea of this meeting, Elliott felt his blood pressure rising by the minute before receiving his pour-over and turning to look for his contact. With no place to sit indoors, Elliott found his man relaxing at a patio table outside, off to the side away from any other customers.

Click – click – click – click – click – click.

Elliott sat across from the man, took a sip of coffee, and tried to calm himself. "Listen," he said in a stilted tone, speaking through his teeth. "No early-morning meetings. No shitholes like this anymore. You just let me know when you have something, and I'll set the timing." He took another sip of his coffee. "So, what's so important?" he asked the smiling man.

After being chided, the man shifted in his chair and looked askance at Elliott. "Nowitzke and Taylor were in Door County yesterday chasing down details on the death of a Myles Tucker from 2003."

Elliott's eyes grew large and he began to fidget, visibly agitated at the news. "Jesus, how did they figure that out?" he asked.

"Beats me. Both detectives are clever. And they seem to be working on a larger plan of some sort."

"What did they learn?"

Click – click – click – click – click – click.

"I'm not sure. But they spoke to the deputy who investigated the Tucker case before spending some time with the missus. I've got no details beyond that."

Elliott sat back in his chair and cocked his head, processing this information. *Shit!* "Well, get some. What have you learned about Savanna Smythe?"

"Nothing more . . . yet."

"What am I paying you for?" he asked gruffly. "You like the money, right? It's enough to cover your habit?"

"What are you talking about?" replied the man, now nervously drumming his fingers on the metal table.

"You're a fucking addict is what," said Elliott matter-of-factly. "I know you got hurt on the job. I suspect you developed a taste for painkillers when you were off on work comp. Now my guess is you're running short of prescription meds and have to find a replacement on the street or wherever."

"How do you know that?"

"It came up on my background check on you," Elliott replied. "From my standpoint, addicts are unreliable." He paused, then leaned forward. "If you want to keep the flow of cash coming, do your damn job and get me the information I need." He stood, picked up his cup, and left.

After Elliott departed, Will Porter sat back in his chair, closed his eyes, and exhaled loudly. *How the hell did I get here?* Several minutes later, he shook his head, stood, put his empty cup into a trash bin, and walked to work.

As he did, a photographer positioned half a block down the street repacked their camera into a bag and took off in the opposite direction.

****

Nowitzke approached his morning with excitement, dread, and a throbbing headache. After returning home from Natalie's place, he had one too many celebratory beers, finishing off a six-pack before passing out in his living room chair. He woke hours later to an incessant beeping that started small, gradually creeping into his consciousness before he realized it was the alarm clock in his bedroom. From where he sat, he was incapable of stopping it short of physically moving. He finally surrendered to the idea ten minutes later, summoning the will to rise, his back and knees popping and clicking as he straightened from the chair. Lumbering into his bedroom, he put a fist into the snooze button to quiet the clock before clicking it off. Even so, the beeping continued in his head as he eyed his mattress, which called to him like a siren's song. But he fought the urge, taking off yesterday's clothes before stepping into the shower, where lukewarm water pelted his body.

Remembering his pending date with Natalie, Nowitzke found a renewed spring in his step as he moved down the stairs before squeezing into his Escort. He stopped at Dunkin' Donuts, ordered two large coffees, both for himself, and a box of powdered donut holes. Still in the drive-thru lane, he washed down a pair of Aleve, mentally declaring himself ready to take on his day. By the time he made it to the office, his dark-brown jacket and khakis were covered with a fine layer of powdered sugar.

Even though he tried to keep a reasonable attitude, he felt a growing sense of dread as he moved down the hall toward his office, waiting to see the condition of his desk. Nowitzke was an excellent investigator, but his workspace was yet another reflection of his approach to life that extended to his living quarters and the bulk of his relationships. As he rounded the corner, he saw a mountain of paper and files centered on his desk, a phenomenon that always happened after being out of the office for even a day. Furthermore, his desk phone was blinking, ironically keeping time with the now dissipating beeping in his head. Nowitzke pushed aside the files, creating space for both coffee cups just as Anissa walked by with a cheery morning greeting.

"Morning, Chuck. How are you and the abuelita getting along?" she chortled as she passed by, unable to make out Nowitzke's garbled snarl in response.

As he was trying to decide how to attack the mess on his desk, his phone rang.

"Detective Nowitzke, it's Brad Hawkins. Do you have some time to meet this morning?" he asked, with an urgent tone in his voice. "Something has come up along the lines of our recent discussion."

"What time works for you, Brad?" asked Nowitzke in a gravelly voice, his eyes still mindlessly scanning the desk.

"Any chance you could come right now?" replied the former DA.

"Yeah, sure," said the detective as he hung up the receiver, freed from the paperwork for the time being. "Nis, you got a minute?" he yelled toward her office.

A moment later, Anissa poked her head into his open doorway. "What's up?"

"Brad Hawkins wants to see us. Says it has something to do with our conversation from the other day. He was speaking at about twice his normal speed, like he was shook up for some reason."

"I'll get my keys, and let's see what's on his mind."

Anissa's Audi parked in the same spot on Hawkins' driveway as on their previous lunch date. Thomas opened the front door as the detectives emerged from the car. "Good morning, Detectives," he said. "He's waiting for you in the study."

Ivy House was quiet aside from the clicking of Anissa's heels as she moved down the tiled hallway. Thomas gave a warning knock on the study door, simultaneously opening it to invite the visitors into the room. Brad, who was wearing a button-down striped shirt with pleated trousers, rose from behind his large wooden desk with a nervous smile, greeting both detectives. "Thank you both for coming so quickly. Please have a seat. Coffee for anyone?" he asked.

Anissa begged off while Nowitzke accepted. "With cream, please," he added.

"Me as well," said Brad to Thomas as the butler left the room. "While we're waiting, let me get right down to business. This package arrived here by UPS this morning," he began, standing over a cardboard box that rested on his desk. The flaps were open with the only visible contents being crumpled newspaper. Before he could continue, Thomas disrupted the heightening mystery, served the coffee, and left the room. After the door closed, Brad put his hand into the container and gently removed a small, tattered blue bunny, placing it gently on the desk. "This was my sister Sandy's favorite lovey when she grew up," he said. "She called him Bobilly. Turns out that Sandy was trying to say 'blue baby,' but the original name stuck. Anyway, as a young girl, she carried it everywhere with her." His face grew pale. "When she got to be a little older, I told her to stop bringing Bobilly to school."

"When was the last time you saw this doll?" asked Nowitzke.

"That's just it," replied Brad. "I'd forgotten all about Bobilly until I opened the package this morning. I haven't seen him in years . . . decades?"

"When we chatted about Sandy's disappearance the other day, you said her room was undisturbed when it was searched, aside from her purse being missing," Anissa observed.

"I know," said Brad. "I must have missed Bobilly when we went through Sandy's belongings back then. This baby was always in her life, even though it was not the same fixture when she was eighteen," he concluded. "I do remember the day, though, when she packed him in a box that was going with her to college."

Anissa glanced at her boss. "Who do you think sent you this package, Brad?"

Brad slumped into his desk chair, pondering both the question and the shabby-looking kid's toy. "There's only one person it could be," he finally concluded. "Sandy! She must be alive, somewhere. She has to be. I mean, who else would have the doll, let alone know of its significance, besides her?"

The detectives traded puzzled looks. "If Sandy is alive, why would she send you this package? I mean, why not just pick up the phone and call?" asked Anissa.

"Beats me," the former DA conceded. "I don't know."

"Brad, are you sure that this is Sandy's rabbit?" asked Nowitzke skeptically. "I mean, is there any chance someone is playing a cruel joke on you?"

"No, this *is* Sandy's doll." He handed the rabbit to Nowitzke. "No doubt, in fact. Check inside the ears. It's the first thing I did when I saw Bobilly in the package. When Sandy was younger, I put her initials with a permanent marker in the one on the left, just to make sure no other kid ever claimed the doll as their own."

Nowitzke twisted the rabbit in his hands to take a closer look before spotting a faded "SH." He passed the doll to Anissa so she could see it as well. "Can I look at the package?" Nowitzke asked, putting on a pair of rubber gloves taken from his jacket pocket. He examined the box. "No return address, as you might guess. But someone taped up the seams. We'll take the package and check for prints, if you don't mind."

"Take it, by all means. Do you want the bunny too?"

"No," said Anissa. "We can't get prints off of a soft surface."

Silence filled the room as brains began working on what should happen next. Nowitzke finally spoke. "Brad, I understand you had Sandy declared dead in 1993."

"Yes, I did," Brad replied, sitting forward in his chair. "Two reasons. One, to make sure her estate could be fully settled, not that she owned any property. She had a small life insurance policy. Something like ten thousand dollars. Nothing in the grand scheme of things. The other reason was that I needed closure." He stared Nowitzke in the eye.

"We'll check the package," said the senior detective. "Frankly, I need some time to think. We're breaking new ground for me with investigating a missing person who has been declared dead. Rest assured, though, that we will dig into this for you."

"Thank you both," said Brad before bending forward in his chair with his head in his hands. Nowitzke took the cardboard box as they exited.

Once they were alone in the hall, Nowitzke looked at his partner. "What do you make of this, Nis?"

"I have no clue. Do you think Sandy is alive after all these years? I mean, to send such a personal item as if trying to make sure her brother knows it's her."

"Again, why not just show up?" questioned Nowitzke.

"Maybe she's thinking that it would be too jarring for her brother after all this time," Anissa speculated. "Who knows what goes on in people's heads?"

"Okay, let me play Mr. Sensitivity for a moment. How about a call from Sandy before showing up?" he asked rhetorically. "I mean, why the games?" They passed the entrance to the small room where Bob and his people were typically keeping electronic tabs on the place. The door was cracked, but no one was in the room.

Thomas stood near the front door, waiting for them. "Hey, Thomas, where's Bob and the security crew?" asked Anissa. "Just wanted to say hi."

"I'm sorry, Ms. Taylor. We have a vendor here today making a system upgrade. Bob and the staff are off-site at a week-long training course, learning the capabilities of the new system."

"Okay. Thanks anyway," replied Anissa as the officers exited the home.

"When we get back to the shop, I'll walk this box down to Teddy Shaw in Forensics," said Nowitzke. "I'm curious to see if we can pull any prints from the tape."

"I agree, but for some reason, I think you're going to draw a blank," Anissa concluded.

"Me too," replied Nowitzke. "I'll also talk with UPS about where the package originated."

Nowitzke spent the balance of his day in his office on the phone and working to move most of the mountain of paper from one side of his desk to the other. He also learned from the local UPS office that the shipment to Brad originated at a drop box located in downtown Green Bay, one of the busiest in the metro area. In the meantime, Shaw confirmed Anissa's best guess that there were no viable fingerprints anywhere on the package.

As he was set to leave work for dinner with Natalie, Nowitzke finally dug down to the metal top of his desk, where he found a slim package in a black plastic wrapper hiding under a file. While the contents inside felt like paper, he wasn't one hundred percent sure. The packaging reminded him of how his monthly edition of *Playboy* arrived at his door back when he was a subscriber. The mailing address on the exterior of the package named him specifically. Relying on his instincts, he opened his desk drawer and found a pair of evidence latex gloves to wear before using the pocketknife on his money clip to carefully slit open one end of the parcel. Inside, he found a red folder. Nowitzke flipped the cover open to find a dated newspaper article from the *Stillwater Gazette. Minnesota?*

The packet included several pages of the newspaper, yellowed with age, and other official-looking documents. Nowitzke studied the external packing material closely. "Of course, no return address," he mumbled to himself, shaking his head. Then, he checked the envelope to find the postmark that would tell him where it was mailed from. He found it, but it was of little help. "Banff, Alberta, Canada?" he said out loud as he read. "What the fuck? Never been there." *Who sent me an old Minnesota paper via Canada? And why?* He scratched his head, remembering a case he once investigated in Minnesota. But he had no real connections there. Looking at the clock on his credenza, he realized that time was growing short. He was supposed to meet Natalie in ten minutes and being late was not an option. Nowitzke carefully replaced the material back into the folder. *It will have to wait until tomorrow*, he thought to himself as he flipped off the lights in his office.

They had agreed to meet for Italian at a popular place downtown called Victoria's, which boasted outstanding food served in generous portions, generally more than enough for another meal the following day. The restaurant was literally a stone's throw from APD, so Nowitzke walked from his office, following the smell of garlic that wafted in the air for blocks.

When he arrived, the place was packed. But he spotted Natalie immediately, sitting at the end of the bar with a glass of red wine, chatting with the bartender as he worked. She looked beautiful in her bright pastel summer dress and sandals. He stopped by the door, taking a moment just to watch her. Then, when she turned around and realized Nowitzke was there, she smiled, gracefully sliding off the barstool. She approached him and gave him an unexpected hug. Even though the smell of her perfume was lost to the garlic, her touch more than made up the difference. Nowitzke ordered a beer and stood off from the crowded bar behind Natalie as she swiveled the seat of the chair around to face him.

"Well, Detective, any more assignments for me?" she asked.

"Nothing at the moment, but you just never know," replied Nowitzke, thinking about other potential unknown victims, if Miss Alma's theory was correct. "Should we ask about getting a table?"

"I've already got my name on the waitlist. Still quite the popular place," Natalie replied, marveling at the crowd of patrons. "I haven't been here in several years. Last time was for my anniversary a couple of years ago . . ." Her voice trailed off, her face becoming flush. She took a moment to gather herself. "I'm sorry, Chuck. I had a little flashback of another time."

"No apologies necessary," he replied as the hostess approached, indicating that their table was ready.

They moved into a rear dining room decorated with cheap wallpaper, large wall mirrors, faux greenery, and large hand-painted frescos of popular tourist sites in Italy. Thankfully, the din of the bar faded into background noise, allowing them to chat comfortably. They placed their orders with their waiter, a clean-cut young man. Twenty minutes later, he returned with a platter holding a large order of chicken parmesan, a pasta dish with mixed vegetables, and another round of drinks. After more polite small talk, Nowitzke looked at Natalie. "Can I ask why you became a librarian?"

Natalie put down her fork, wiped her mouth with her napkin, and took a sip of her wine. "Since I was a little girl, I have always loved books. They took me to places that I never thought I would go, kind of like going on a vacation," she said. "When I was young, my grandmother and I often went to the library together. It was our special time since I had her all to myself. I've tried to carry on mi abuela's tradition with my daughter and my grandchildren."

"Do you like to read anything in particular?" asked Nowitzke.

"I read pretty much everything, but I guess I'm drawn to mysteries. You know . . . trying to figure things out before the end. What do you like to read?"

Nowitzke thought back to the black plastic envelope, but nixed the idea of saying, "*Playboy*, but just for the articles." He took a draw of beer. "To be honest with you, I'm not much of a reader. I spend most of my time looking over police reports and autopsy records. I've got enough mysteries in my life without the books."

"But, Chuck, you are kind of like me . . . you know, you like figuring things out too."

"I guess you're right," he replied.

"Why did you become a police officer?"

Nowitzke smiled. "Well, when I was a kid, I was not a very nice person. My parents didn't really care about me. I was a delinquent, a thief, and just a punk. I dropped out of high school, destined to meet with a judge who would give me a choice between the military and spending time in jail, or worse, prison. Then, for some reason, a local cop took me aside one day after arresting me. He knew I was on a bad path. I've seen it in other soon-to-be felons since I became a cop. Anyway, he said I had the potential to do more than go to jail if I wanted to. He told me to get my ass back to school and work at it. He took an interest in me. Anyway, when I finished high school, he came to my graduation, the only person there for me. I decided to make some money and took a job in a foundry. Decent wages, but a hot, dirty place to work. It motivated me to go back to school, and I ended up going through the police academy. I didn't know it at the time, but that old cop was my mentor, and I ended up just like him."

Natalie smiled. "Where is your friend now?"

"Dead." Nowitzke took a healthy swallow of beer. "A couple of years back, some scumbag murdered him during an arrest gone bad. He died in the line of duty."

Natalie reached across the table and put her hand on his for a moment. "I'm sorry," she said somberly.

Nowitzke shrugged, remaining silent, and took another heavy pull of his beer before turning his attention back to Natalie. "My turn to ask a personal question?"

His tone caught her off guard. "I suppose."

"How is it possible that such a beautiful woman can be a grandma? You're way too young. I just don't get it," he said.

"Ah, the detective in you comes out with a direct question. For the record, you're right, I am way too young to be a grandmother. I got married young. Despite being a good Catholic girl, I turned up pregnant when I was eighteen. Where I was from, I had no options other than getting married. Funny, though, after my husband scored a goal with our first, we never had another child. My daughter, Blanca, at least got the order right, but she also started early, having her first when she was twenty-two."

Nowitzke did the relative math on Natalie before concluding that they were roughly the same age. Abuelita or not, he felt relieved.

"Chuck, since we've moved into personal territory, do you have any children?"

He laughed. "No. I told you about both of my mistakes. Neither of my wives had any maternal instincts. Not that I'd have been much of a father. Thank God that was not in the cards for me," he said, taking a moment to reflect. "I think the closest I've come to feeling what it must be like to be a parent is how I feel about Anissa. The daughter I never had. I can't tell you how proud I am of her and the progress she's made." He beamed. "She's a helluva cop."

Hearing Nowitzke talk about his relationship with Anissa was a relief for Natalie. "No other family?"

"Just Nis," he said. "Turns out I also have an adopted mother, Miss Alma. Technically, she's my landlord, but that's a story for another night."

They finished their drinks, each picked up a Styrofoam container of leftovers, and they stepped into the cool evening air. "Let me walk you back to your car," Nowitzke said, taking Natalie's hand. They slowly strolled a block before she stopped.

"This is me," she said, nodding toward a Prius parked on the street. "Chuck, I really enjoyed spending time with you." She reached up and kissed him on the cheek. His sinuses now clear of garlic, Nowitzke immediately refocused on Natalie's perfume, watching as she left.

****

Anissa maneuvered into her parking stall at her condo. On the way home from work, she had promised herself that she would enjoy a glass of red wine and some soothing music while soaking in her tub infused with a lavender bath bomb. Interestingly, the bath bomb had been a

Christmas gift from Nowitzke. She wagered that, prior to someone coaching him up, Chuck likely thought a bath bomb was something that needed defusing underwater. Laughing at the thought, she set the hand brake of her car when her phone rang.

"Taylor," she answered.

"Anissa," said the man's voice through the car's speaker.

"Yes?"

"It's Bob Edwards. You know, Bob from Brad Hawkins' security team." His voice quavered.

Anissa sighed for a moment before continuing. "Yes, good to hear from you, Bob. What's up?" she said with a cheery tone nonetheless.

"I need to see you. Sooner rather than later," he replied with a sense of urgency coming through the phone.

"Can we schedule a time for tomorrow? We could meet for lunch at . . ."

"No, Anissa. This can't wait. I found something today that you and Chuck need to see. Evidence."

"Of what?" she asked warily.

"Please? Can you meet me in a half hour, seven o'clock, downtown at Tiana's Café . . . the little coffee shop off College Avenue?"

Anissa drummed her fingers on the steering wheel before relenting. "Sure, I know the place. See you in a bit." Still sitting in her car, she did the math. With travel time to Tiana's, she would have all of ten minutes to herself to do nothing if she went up to her condo. Anissa shook her head and gritted her teeth, thinking about missing her date with the warm water. "Screw it," she said to herself, slamming the Audi into reverse before pulling out of the garage. *Maybe Bob will get there early too.*

Twenty minutes later, Anissa stood in line, waiting to order her drink. Tiana's was a reasonably new bohemian place downtown, fighting for dollars with other local sole proprietorships and corporate coffee. A tall, pale girl with a nose ring, purple hair, and a sleeve of tattoos took Anissa's order. The shop was largely empty, as most of its clientele likely had moved on to alcohol at a local watering hole by this time of the day. Anissa took her latte and found a seat in the back of Tiana's that let her watch both the front door and the local news on a muted television perched in the corner. Seven o'clock became seven fifteen, which became seven thirty. She called Bob, but his phone went straight to voicemail. Anissa resolved to give him another thirty minutes, ordering a second latte. When eight o'clock approached, the staff began stacking chairs and cleaning the floors in anticipation of closing time. Anissa looked at her watch before making one final attempt to call Bob. The phone rang twice, then stopped as if someone had picked up. Anissa cocked her head, concentrating on the phone receiver, unsure if anyone was listening on the other end. She heard nothing but breathing. "Bob? Is that you?" she asked as the call dropped.

CHAPTER 17

For the second straight day, Nowitzke's morning began with a call from Brad Hawkins. "Chuck, I really hate to bother you, and I know I'm not following proper channels, but we've got a situation over here. Do you remember Bob Edwards, one of the security guards at Ivy House?"

"Bob, yeah, sure," responded Nowitzke. "What's up?"

"Well, he's missing. Bob was at a training session for our tech upgrade yesterday but disappeared sometime after lunch. Elliott tried to call him to see if he was ill, but he never picked up his phone. Anyway, one of the security guys volunteered to check on him at his apartment on the way home from work last night, but no one ever came to the door. But Bob's car was parked out on the street. Then, this morning, Bob never made it into work. Elliott again made several calls to him that went unanswered. It's just not like the guy. Bob hasn't been with the company long, but he's incredibly sharp. Normally, he's here at least fifteen minutes before his shift, kibitzing with the team coming off duty about anything that he needs to know before starting his day. Frankly, I'm worried about him. I know Bob hasn't been missing for at least twenty-four hours and that it's not your job to do wellness checks, Chuck, but . . ."

"No problem, Brad. What's his address?" Nowitzke asked, biting his lip almost through just as Anissa passed within earshot on her way to her office. "Can you text me a photo of Bob, too?" The junior detective stopped, waiting for Nowitzke to complete his call. "I'll get right on it," he said, signing off.

"What's up, Chuck?" Anissa asked.

"Do you remember our buddy Bob at Brad Hawkins' place?"

"Yeah," she replied, her eyes growing wide.

"Brad thinks he's gone missing."

"Jesus," Anissa said, looking down. "Bob called me last night. Said he had something for us. Evidence ... of something. He didn't say what, but he sounded nervous. Anyway, we agreed to meet last night, but he stood me up. I tried to call him several times, but we never connected."

"Let's go," said Nowitzke, moving quickly out to the parking lot.

Anissa guided the Audi east towards an older portion of town. "Brad called you about Bob's disappearance?"

"Yeah. I think I'm now his official police bitch," replied Nowitzke.

Rolling up the street in front of Bob's apartment, they parked behind a Chevrolet Impala. A license plate check confirmed that the 2011 vehicle was registered to Robert Edwards. From the car, both detectives turned their attention to the building. Bob lived in a shabby duplex. It appeared that no one had mowed the lawn in several weeks, now overgrown with large, noxious weeds. The large front window of Bob's apartment was covered with a blanket to keep the light out. As the officers made their way to the front door, they passed a scrawny young man with dirty-blond dreadlocks flopping from under a faded ball cap and a Bob Marley t-shirt who had come out of the adjacent apartment. When he saw the detectives approaching, he immediately froze, looking guilty and uncertain of whether they were coming for him. Both Nowitzke and Anissa stopped, flashing their badges.

"Good morning," said Anissa politely. "We're here on a wellness check for Robert Edwards ..."

Marley stopped, not sure of what to do or say.

"... *your neighbor*," she concluded.

"Ah, oh man, you mean Pudge? At least, that's what I call him ... if we're talking about the same guy."

Nowitzke pulled out his phone. "Is this the guy?" he asked, bringing up the photo.

Marley examined it closely, having difficulty focusing his bloodshot eyes as the officers exchanged glances. "Yeah, man, that's Pudge."

"When did you see him last?" asked Anissa.

"Man, like I don't know. I mean, like, I'm not my brother's keeper," said Marley sarcastically. "A week ago? I'm not sure. Why are you grillin' me, man?"

Nowitzke took a step forward. "Listen, asshole. Right now, you smell like probable cause to me. If you want me to come back with a warrant after talking with Edwards, keep it up. We're just looking for a little cooperation, that's all."

Marley took off his hat, holding it with both hands in front of himself, looking contrite for a moment. "Oh, man, I'm sorry. I haven't seen Pudge in a while."

"Thanks for your help, Mister . . ."

Marley stood up a little straighter. "Sadowski . . . err, Johnny Sadowski."

"Marvelous," replied Nowitzke derisively. "One of my Polish goombahs. Have a nice day, Mr. Sadowski," he said, dismissing the man.

"Class act," Anissa concurred as the officers stepped onto the front porch. She knocked on the door. Nothing. Thirty seconds later, she tried again. "Bob, it's Anissa and Chuck. Please open up." But neither of them heard any activity from inside the apartment. Nowitzke peered into the apartment through the door window but saw no one. The front door was locked, as was the back door they found after circling the house.

"What do you think?" said Nowitzke. "Should we get a warrant?"

Anissa shrugged, giving him a look like he needed to do something quickly. Nowitzke sighed in response, reaching into his pants pocket and pulling out a pick before unlocking the back door in thirty seconds. When the door swung open into the kitchen, both officers knew they had a problem.

The apartment had been ransacked. Anissa called for backup as they drew their guns and stepped inside, Nowitzke taking the lead.

Following their training, they worked as a pair, moving methodically back and forth from room to room, clearing the small house, stepping carefully to avoid the mess on the floor. As they finished, they heard the yowl of sirens approaching. Bob was nowhere to be found.

Nowitzke stood in the living room and surveyed the scene. "Bob was no housekeeper, but the entire place has been tossed, Nis. I mean, it doesn't look like he had much in the way of value here, so whatever happened wasn't a burglary."

"Agreed," she replied. "The only good news is that I don't see any blood smears anywhere."

Retrieving the SLR camera from her car, Anissa began to photograph each room of the house. Nowitzke donned gloves before sifting through the carnage. Based on what he could tell, there was no evidence of a break-in, meaning that someone had a key, Bob had intentionally let someone into the place, or the lock had been picked à la Nowitzke. Kitchen drawers were left half-open with cooking implements strewn about the scuffed linoleum floor. The few contents from the refrigerator lay on the floor amidst broken jars. A bookshelf had been pushed over with paperbacks and old DVDs falling onto the ragged living room carpet. The flatscreen television was smashed. As they entered Bob's bedroom, Nowitzke saw that someone had used a knife to shred the mattress, sending foam and padding material everywhere. Dresser drawers were askew, with underwear and socks strewn about the place, along with Bob's shirts and pants from the closet. Interestingly, the only things that seemed untouched in the apartment were a set of keys sitting on the kitchen counter and a cheap-looking wall clock in the main living area.

"We've seen all that we need to. Nis, get an evidence team in here to begin dusting for prints and any unseen blood spatter, starting from the exterior and working through the house," concluded Nowitzke.

Several frustrating hours later, Nowitzke stepped onto the porch for a breath of fresh air and to think. Spying a weather-beaten spring patio chair, he wondered if it would hold him. After giving it a test push with his full weight, he took the risk, gently lowering his body onto the chair, which responded in kind with a gentle bounce back. Bob's house was now surrounded with yellow police tape as numerous officers continued their work moving in and about the area. Two uniforms were assigned to canvas the neighborhood in the hopes that someone saw something. However, the preliminary reports from the officers were all negative. As Nowitzke relaxed, bouncing in the chair, his eyes came to rest upon Bob's Impala sitting on the street.

"Oh shit," he said as a thought entered his brain. Bolting to his feet, Nowitzke went to the kitchen counter to retrieve the car keys. Putting on another set of protective gloves, he inserted the key into the trunk lock, carefully opening the lid. As light entered the compartment, the detective found Bob staring back at him, wide-eyed, with two holes in his forehead and his mouth gagged. Nowitzke studied the face, puzzled by a number of strange-looking welts on Bob's body. The entire upper torso was covered in blood, now coagulating with grey matter in a thick stew on the trunk floor. With the growing warmth of the day, a stench was beginning to build.

Nowitzke called Wally Schmidt, asking that he come to the scene. Then, the detective partially lowered the trunk lid and clomped back into the house to find Anissa. Unfortunately, only a portion of the mystery was over.

****

"Based on the wounds and the imprint of the gun barrel, you don't need to be an ME to see that the victim took two to the back of the head. You can see some stippling on the skin around the wound caused by the gunpowder," Wally explained to Nowitzke and Anissa. "A large-caliber handgun would be my guess. Execution-style, the victim's hands zip-tied behind his back. Since I couldn't find any evidence of blood spray or brains anywhere in the car except the trunk floor, my impression is that the actual homicide took place somewhere else."

"What's the story on the welts?" asked Nowitzke.

"I was just getting to that, Chuck. They aren't welts. They're burn marks. It took me a while to figure it out . . . the cigarette lighter."

"Dear Jesus," exclaimed Anissa.

"These are the ones you can see on his face. However, the vic's abdomen and back are covered with them too. Somebody tortured this poor bastard for hours. Didn't need any exotic tools, just standard equipment on an old Chevy Impala," the ME replied, shaking his head in disgust.

"So, every time Bob came up with a bad answer, the bad guy punched in the lighter to heat it up," said Nowitzke. "Bob must have screamed his head off."

"Another reason why I think this happened elsewhere. You know, somewhere incredibly private. Definitely not in a small residential area, even a questionable one like this. If someone was shrieking in the house, a neighbor would likely have called the police," concluded Wally.

"Except for maybe the asshole that lives next door," Nowitzke offered. "Nis, get our forensic folks back out here and focused on the car. After that, we'll need to have it taken to impound."

"Got it," she said, moving toward the house before stopping halfway up the walk and turning around. "You know, Chuck, everything fits with what we saw inside the apartment. I don't think that whoever did this was necessarily after Bob. They tore the place apart like they were looking for something."

"But what did Bob have that was enough to get him killed?" asked Nowitzke.

CHAPTER 18

What did Bob have that was enough to get him killed? The question haunted Nowitzke for the balance of the day. Needing to mentally switch gears, he returned to his office to get back into other work waiting for him. Although new mail had arrived on his desk, his attention was immediately drawn back to the red folder that had been mailed from Canada. He took a deep breath, trying to purge his mind of Bob's death face before digging into the details.

The *Stillwater Gazette*, dated June 18, 1998, provided a glimpse into a slow news day in Minnesota long ago. There were no major stories aside from some articles about flooding in the area. However, below the fold was a story about the death of a local prison guard, Jacob McClary. McClary had been found dead in his home earlier that week, the victim of an apparent suicide. The man's name rang no bells for the detective, but the date of the death immediately got his attention: June 16. Paging through the balance of the paper, Nowitzke noted an editorial about the mental strain experienced by prison guards and a correlation to higher suicide rates in the profession. A separate section of the paper contained McClary's obituary, including a photo of a buff-looking man dressed in uniform. Scanning the obit, Nowitzke saw that McClary had worked in the Minnesota prison system for five years after earning a degree from a technical college in nearby Eau Claire following graduation from high school in Neenah, Wisconsin. The single man was twenty-nine. Nowitzke sat back in his chair. *Neenah? A local kid?*

In the folder, he also found a copy of a police report from Stillwater PD about McClary's death stamped "confidential." The document looked like the genuine article to Nowitzke, detailing much of what he had already read in the obit. It also confirmed that the death took place on June 16. However, when he saw the cause of death, he raised his eyebrows. At one point, the blank had held the word "pending." Then, "pending" had been crossed out by someone who then scribbled in "heart attack." Nowitzke noted that the report had been completed by a detective, Sam Boylan. Even with Nowitzke's limited computer skills, he found a phone number for Stillwater PD, intent on tracking down the investigating officer. His call was answered at the main switchboard at SPD, and when he requested to speak with Boylan, he was immediately transferred, taking it as a good sign that the man still worked there. But Nowitzke was wrong. When the call was picked up, a woman's voice answered. "Boylan."

Nowitzke paused for a moment. "Sam Boylan, please."

"You got her," she said in a soothing radio voice. "How can I help you?"

"Ms. Boylan, I'm Detective Chuck Nowitzke, Appleton PD, over in Wisconsin. I'm investigating some old open death files in my local area. We haven't concluded that they're necessarily homicides at this point, but each case has some interesting consistencies. Anyway, I just received a packet in the mail about the death of a guy named Jacob McClary that got my attention. Do you happen to recall that name by any chance?"

"McClary . . . yes, I do," replied Sam. "He's been dead for quite a while. When did you say you received this material?"

"Yesterday. Regular mail, postmarked in Canada."

"Seriously?" exclaimed Boylan. "Let me pull up a copy of my electronic file." Through the phone, Nowitzke recognized the clicking sound of keys on a computer. After a short pause, she continued. "Now, what can I help you with?"

"Detective, can you confirm the official date of McClary's death?"

"June 16, 1998."

"What can you tell me about the guy?" asked Nowitzke. "Anything curious about his background?"

"McClary was a regular working man. White guy. A prison guard here in Stillwater. No issues with the law. He was unattached, aside from an on-again, off-again relationship with a local gal. He worked, paid his taxes on time. From what I remember, people said he enjoyed Friday night fish and beer at his local tavern. You know, if anything, he might have died of boredom," Sam concluded.

"What do you show as *the* cause of death?" asked Nowitzke. "The folder I received had a copy of your local paper that reported it as a suicide. However, I'm also looking at a copy of a police report that appears to have finally settled on a heart attack."

There was silence on the other end of the phone. "How did you get a copy of our report?"

"Open records? Beats me. Some anonymous Canuck shipped it to me."

"Okay," Sam replied in a more hushed tone. "The cause of death was a bone of contention on this end. The early thinking was suicide. It's just that the evidence wasn't clear. Talking with his girlfriend, we found out that McClary hated his job, his life, where he lived, pretty much everything . . . you know . . . depression. Everyone thought he likely OD'd on something, at least until his toxicology report came back clean. After a lot of hand-wringing, the ME eventually concluded that the man died of a heart attack because he needed to fill in the blank with something."

"But you didn't buy that?" questioned Nowitzke.

Sam hemmed and hawed for a moment. "No," she said. "Frankly, I didn't know what to make of the cause, but heart attack didn't work for me."

"Sam, officer to officer, can you tell me if the man's body had any unexplained or unusual wounds?"

More silence from Minnesota before Sam finally answered as if doing so on the sly. "Yeah, I remember this clearly. The ME found a puncture wound on McClary's back. Nothing major, mind you, meaning not enough to kill him. It was suspicious, but the ME was pretty quick to dismiss it. I didn't know what the mark meant, if anything, but the examiner's conclusion didn't necessarily fit the heart attack narrative. McClary was a well-built guy. According to the notes I made after talking with his girl, she said he was in the weight room constantly. You know, a prison guard who wanted to make sure he could take care of himself if he needed to when handling prisoners."

"But no drugs in his system," repeated Nowitzke to himself, waiting for an objection from Boylan that never came. "Sam, this will sound weird, but did your guy have a number written on his forehead?"

"Fucking A!" she exclaimed, almost exploding through the phone. "How the hell could you know that? We held that back from everyone here, including the press."

"Like I said, I'm finding similar fact patterns with other deaths. McClary's death seems to fit for a lot of reasons. The date . . . the puncture . . . the number." *Another body. But someone needed to lead me to this one,* he thought, shaking his head.

"When we found McClary's body in his home, someone had written the number two on his head in black ink. It's why I fought the ME's conclusion," said Boylan. "I mean, the situation made no sense to me, especially after finding evidence in McClary's home that he had visitors before he died. And no, not the girlfriend. But we don't know who. Unfortunately, this incident took place long before the invention of doorbell cams. Anyway, the issue for the ME was that there was no real trauma to the body. At the end of the day, we had nothing further to investigate. It is technically a closed file."

Nowitzke scratched his chin as he pondered this information. "One last dumb question, Sam. Did you ever determine whether McClary had any connection to Banff, Alberta?"

"Canada? No."

"Told you it was a dumb question. Would you mind sending me

a copy of what you developed, along with any photos of the body?" asked Nowitzke.

"Only if you keep me apprised of any developments on similar cases," Boylan replied.

"Thanks. Hey, if you ever get to my area, the first beer is on me," said Nowitzke as he provided Boylan with his contact information, then signed off the call.

An email from Boylan arrived just as Nowitzke put his phone in his pocket. Clicking through the attachments, he saw another copy of the official report, the ME's material, and the photos of McClary. The same young man from the obit was laid out on the floor wearing a "2." Nowitzke had now developed information on victims one through four, six, and seven, fitting the edges on a puzzle that was years in the making. However, there were still so many open issues, not the least of which was any connection between the victims.

While Boylan had been helpful in detailing elements of the McClary death, she had only addressed the contents within the package received by Nowitzke. The other serious question, which she couldn't help with, was who had sent him the parcel. His first reaction was that the Canada connection seemed too obvious. First Savanna, now this. Still, it was worth a call. Picking up his phone, he punched in the number she had provided, wondering if it would connect. Surprisingly, Savanna answered on the first ring.

"Hey, Chuck! What's up?"

"I need some help, Savanna. I just got a package from Canada. Banff, in particular."

"Alright . . ."

"What do you know about Banff?"

"It's a small town out west in Alberta. Lots of mountains. Great skiing. Cool bars. About a couple thousand miles away from where I live. You know, like the distance between Appleton and Los Angeles."

Nowitzke paused. The logistics involving Savanna made no sense, especially since she had been in the States for some time.

"Anything else?" she asked. "Vancouver is nice too. Also, check out the Maritimes. Planning a trip to Canada, or am I your 'phone a friend' on *Who Wants to Be a Millionaire?*"

"Thanks for the information," replied Nowitzke, shaking his head. "Are you enjoying your vacation in Wisconsin?"

"Of course," retorted Savanna before clicking off the call.

He sat for a moment thinking before he rose and went to an old four-high metal filing cabinet in the corner of his office. Rummaging through the contents of the top two drawers, he found what he was looking for. An outdated world atlas. Flipping to the index of the oversized, well-thumbed paper book, Nowitzke found the page number and coordinates for Banff. Studying the map of Alberta, he located the small town. The closest major city was Calgary, a little more than an hour away. *Who would have sent me information about an old Minnesota death from Banff?* Mindlessly, he grabbed a snow globe from the credenza and snapped his wrist. Black flakes from an old coal-fired power plant erupted in the liquid-filled keepsake as he put his feet on his desk to think. Several minutes later, having come to no conclusions, Nowitzke sat up towards his laptop and typed "Banff" into a Google search. The chamber of commerce website appeared, introducing the town as being in a national park in the Canadian Rocky Mountains. According to the site, Banff had roughly eight thousand residents and was a place that largely catered to tourists. Nowitzke was impressed by the photos of the thick forests, mountains, wildlife, deep blue lakes, and winter snow. But any connection between Banff and McClary or any of the other victims for that matter continued to elude him. Then, he heard Anissa frantically call for him from her office.

"Chuck, you there?"

"Yeah," he yelled back. "What's up?"

"Get in here. You've got to see this," she replied. Considering the urgency in her voice, Nowitzke quickly jumped out of his chair and went around the corner into Anissa's office. She was sitting at her desk, transfixed by the screen of her laptop. "You're not going to believe this.

Step around back here," she said. "These emails just started arriving minutes ago."

Nowitzke watched the screen from behind Anissa as she began clicking her mouse. The first image showed a man with a blond buzzcut and a white bandage over his nose standing in the home of Bob Edwards. "Jesus, Nis, that's the guy who went after Savanna at the Orchard Inn," exclaimed Nowitzke. Each succeeding photograph showed the unknown man in various stages of trashing Bob's living room, apparently looking for something. "Where did you get these?"

"The first email said it was 'care of Bob Edwards,'" she said, flipping through a total of ten pictures. "Bob was a tech geek. He must have set up a motion-activated stationary camera in his house as some sort of security."

"You mean he might have been worried that someone would break into his place . . . like maybe his Polish Rastafarian neighbor, Sadowski? From the angle of the photos and considering they're all in the same room, the camera must have been in that cheap clock on the wall."

"I agree. But Bob must have taken the time to reprogram his camera to send the photos to me, thinking he was in some sort of trouble. You know . . . maybe part of the reason he wanted to see me the other night. Look at the time stamp in the corner. Exactly twelve hours ago. He must have also put a delay on the transmission time for the photos to be sent, for some reason," she concluded.

"Yeah, but you said Bob had some sort of evidence for you," said Nowitzke. "This isn't the evidence, just photos of someone searching for something, like maybe whatever you were promised."

"Bob must have thought this guy would come looking for whatever, with the logical starting point being his house," Anissa offered.

Nowitzke scrutinized the photos once more. "If nothing else, Bob left us a record from the grave of the sadistic asshole who likely killed him."

"We can check the house again for prints, but based on the photos, you can see the man's wearing gloves."

"Skip it. Forensics has been there twice. How do we get copies of these photos?"

"We print them, Chuck," Anissa replied, trying not to laugh. "I'll even save them to a flash drive, just in case." She took a new device from her desk drawer.

Ignoring his partner, Nowitzke asked, "What did Bob get himself into?"

"Well," said Anissa, taking a breath, "I'm not sure I can even guess. I can't believe Bob was personally involved in anything illegal, like the drug trade. I mean, this is a guy who wanted to be a cop."

"Unfortunately, I've met a lot of law enforcement types over the years whose side hustles involved narcotics," replied Nowitzke. "But I agree with you about Bob."

"What was he hiding, and where is it now? Also, what's the connection with the guy who presumably killed Bob and assaulted Savanna?"

"No idea on the first question. The only common thread between Bob and Savanna is being at the fundraiser at Brad's house."

"Maybe we should go ask Brad about this guy," Anissa suggested.

"We don't have much to lose," agreed the senior detective.

CHAPTER 19

Nowitzke turned the tables on Brad Hawkins, calling him to ask for some time to meet to provide him with an update on Bob Edwards. With an already tight schedule, Brad offered fifteen minutes at the end of the day. On the drive over, Nowitzke provided Anissa with his findings about victim number two, the details of his conversation with Sam Boylan, and the mystery around the postmark.

Because Nowitzke and Anissa were now regulars at Ivy House, Thomas greeted them and merely pointed the way to the study, saying, "He's waiting for you." As they moved down the hallway, both detectives noticed that the security team was back in its room before happening upon Leonard's large shadow outside the study's open doorway. He gave each of the officers a dour nod as they passed. *Wow, he's in a good mood today*, thought Nowitzke, giving a slight courtesy knock before they entered the study.

Brad was not his usual ebullient self, and he stiffened visibly upon seeing the looks on the detectives' faces. Dressed in a black tuxedo, he peered up from his desk and motioned the officers to the side chairs across from him. "I'm guessing you have bad news based on your demeanors," he said to start the meeting.

"Yes, sir," replied Nowitzke. "We found Bob's body this morning in the trunk of his car outside his house."

"Jesus." Brad grimaced, his head briefly swooning as his eyes closed, processing the news. "I know I'm no longer a member of local law enforcement, but can you give me any details?"

Nowitzke sat back in his chair. "Bob was shot in the back of the head, execution-style. But before that, someone tortured him, like he was being interrogated."

"About what?"

"Frankly, we're not sure," said Anissa. "However, we have photos of a suspect who was rifling through Bob's house, apparently looking for something." She slid an eight-by-ten photo of the blond across the wooden desk to Brad. "We believe this is the man responsible. Have you seen him before?"

Brad picked up the photo, sat back in his chair, and studied it. As he did, Nowitzke carefully examined the former DA's face and eyes. While he wasn't a human lie detector, Nowitzke had become quite accomplished over the years in recognizing tells in people who were trying to deceive him. "It's been a long time since I was involved in prosecuting anyone like this, but no, I don't know him," said Brad, pushing the photo back to Anissa. "Any idea who is he?"

"No," Nowitzke replied, shaking his head. "But there is something interesting about the suspect. Not only is he wanted for murdering Bob, but he also tried to kill the woman who was in your home with Senator Hecht when he died."

"No shit," replied Brad, seemingly out of character. "That's quite a coincidence, Detective."

"To say the least, sir."

"Let me see the photo again. I was thinking in terms of someone I helped convict years ago, but . . ." Brad's brow furrowed as he inspected the picture once more before finally shaking his head, putting the photo back on his desk. "No, I'm sorry. I've never seen this guy before. Absolutely positive."

Nowitzke was convinced. *Truth.* "Brad, you said that Bob was in a training class when he disappeared?"

"Yes. We're upgrading our security system."

"Bob seemed like a pretty straitlaced kind of guy," offered Anissa. "Were you aware of any problems he was having with coworkers or any enemies he may have had?"

"No," Brad replied emphatically. He glanced at his watch. "Like I told Detective Nowitzke earlier, he was a fairly new employee who seemed to be doing well here."

"Well, we wanted you to hear about Bob from us," said Anissa, standing from her chair. "By the way, you're looking sharp in your tux. What's the occasion?"

"Thanks. I have a dinner tonight. I'm being honored with a lifetime achievement award for my time as district attorney by the local bar association." His face colored with embarrassment. "I'm sorry if I rushed you. Again, if I can be of any help, please call me," he said as he stood. "You know, if you have some time, stop over at the Hilton and check out the event. It was put together by a friend of yours."

Nowitzke and Anissa replied silently with questioning looks on their faces.

"Yes," continued Brad. "Will Porter put together all the details for this little soiree."

"Really?" asked the detectives simultaneously.

"Hope to see you there. I'll be buying drinks."

Once they were back in the Audi, Anissa looked at Nowitzke, trying to refocus on their case. "What do we do now? It feels like we're making progress on the individual files, but we just don't have much to show for it overall."

"Agreed," said Nowitzke. "The coincidence between Bob and Savanna with the blond bothers me, but I have no reason to question Brad any further. I guess we need to keep working. All it takes is one piece of evidence for everything to fall into place."

****

Anissa dropped Nowitzke off at APD to pick up his car. While it was already late afternoon, he felt compelled to go back to his office to take care of several items. His first order of business was a call to Wally, looking for an update on Hecht's toxicology report.

"Medical Examiner's Office, Schmidt here."

"Hey, Wally, any word back from your experts on Hecht yet?"

"Chuck, if I'd heard, you would have been my first call. Remember, time and money. Oh, and these are busy people too. Not like they wait around for me to send them samples to keep the lab in business. But I'll keep after them," he said, signing off.

Nowitzke shook his head. He was not a patient person, at least when it came to his work. Moving on to the next item on his mental list, he scanned the material generated by Natalie regarding the disappearance of Sandy Hawkins. He was interested in talking with her former best friend, Kelsie Cantrell, but had none of her personal information. Since multiple decades had passed since Sandy's disappearance, who was to say that Cantrell would even be in the area anymore. Although Nowitzke had difficulty with technology, he had mastered a few programs that allowed him to find people. He began with a review of CCAP, Wisconsin's automated program regarding court activity. If Cantrell had picked up a misdemeanor or felony over the years, she would be listed. But he drew a blank on his search. Then he checked the county website devoted to property ownership. After plugging in her name, he got a hit. Fortunately, Kelsie Cantrell had kept her maiden name, hyphenating it with her husband's, Michael Holland. Together, they owned a home somewhere on the north side of Appleton. However, the records did not include a phone number. Nowitzke dialed the Outagamie County Clerk's office, hoping that at least one city employee would still be working until 5:00 p.m. He was in luck.

"County Clerk's Office," said the tired voice of a woman on the other end of the phone.

"Ma'am, this is Detective Nowitzke at the Appleton Police Department. I need some information about a resident, please. A phone number for a Kelsie Cantrell-Holland, based on the property tax records."

"Sir, we're officially closed. You'll have to call back tomorrow," came the monotone response.

"Who am I speaking to?" asked Nowitzke.

"Monica."

"Listen, Monica, I'm investigating a missing persons case, and the phone number is critical." With no response, Nowitzke continued, "Jeez, I said please."

He got nothing but dead air before he heard a deep sigh. "Alright . . . what was the person's name again?" asked Monica in a slow voice that showed she was accustomed to working at the speed of a veteran civil servant. Nowitzke repeated the name. Then, more dead air.

The detective picked up a snow globe featuring a shrunken head off the credenza and sat back in his chair, expecting that he would be waiting for some time. However, Monica must have had a date because she was back to him in moments with a number. After thanking her, Nowitzke was pleased with himself as he made his next call.

A man answered on the second ring. "Hello."

"Is this Michael Holland?"

"Who wants to know?" came the suspicious reply.

"This is Detective Nowitzke from the Appleton Police. I'm working on an old case and would like to speak to Kelsie if I could."

"Well, she's out of town. What's this about?"

"Years ago, she had a friend named Sandra Hawkins. A young woman who disappeared from the area."

"Oh yeah, I recognize the name. Kelsie's talked about her over the years. In fact, I think the whole idea still bothers her. Why are you calling now? I mean, didn't this happen back in the eighties?"

"Yes, it did. It remains an open case, and I'm trying to track down a couple of leads. When do you expect Kelsie to return home?" asked Nowitzke.

"She's on a wilderness camping trip. You know, no phones, no showers, no bathrooms . . . no fun, as far as I'm concerned," said Michael. "I've reached the age where my idea of camping is when the hotel door opens directly to the outside."

"I'm with you there," replied the officer.

"She's been gone for a while, and I never know when she'll be back. But I'll let her know you called," Michael offered.

Nowitzke was out of luck. He gave Michael his cell number, clicking off his phone to hear an unusual silence in the office. It was the end of a frustrating week, checking off boxes, finding pieces, but, as Anissa said, feeling like they were slogging uphill on an escalator buried in mud. As far as he could tell, he was the last person in the office. He retrieved his sport coat that was hanging on the back of his door. Shaking his head, he decided to take Brad up on his offer and check out the Hilton. He resolved to stay for one drink and then find something to eat before heading home.

****

The young man's face belied a brief moment of horror as the Escort rolled up to his valet stand. Gathering himself quickly, he stepped around the vehicle and opened the door for the burly driver. Nowitzke stepped out of the car, handing the keys to the kid. "Be careful. It's a collector."

"Yeah, it looks like it," said the valet, his eyes doing a once-over of the rust bucket.

Nowitzke flashed his badge. "Keep it close. I won't be long."

"No problem. I'll put it between the Ferrari and the Jag," the young man replied in a derisive tone.

Entering the main lobby of the Hilton, the detective followed the signs and growing clamor of people and music as he trailed through the halls toward the ballroom. From what he could gather, the dinner and festivities surrounding Brad's award had concluded, replaced by after-dinner drinks and dancing. Nowitzke knew he was seriously underdressed in his red-and-black plaid sport coat, beige trousers, and loafers, and even though he felt eyes boring into him, he was undeterred as he walked through the heart of the crowd toward one of the bars.

Once the bartender finished an order for an elegant couple at the other end of the movable bar, he turned his attention to the heavy-set man in the tattered clothing. "This is a private party, sir," said the man in the black bow tie, ruffled white shirt, and vest.

"Yeah, I know, Shane," replied Nowitzke wryly after stealing a glimpse at the man's nametag. "Here's my invitation." He took his badge from his jacket pocket. "I'm a friend of Brad, the reason for this shindig. What do you have on tap?"

"Nothing, sir. Bottles only and spirits," replied the barkeep, backing down.

"Alright, I'm flexible. Jack Daniels, straight up." Nowitzke pried a five-dollar bill from his wallet and put it in the tip jar. Upon receiving his drink, he asked, "How much?"

"Drinks are complimentary from your host," said Shane.

The detective smiled and nodded toward the bartender in appreciation. "Catch you later." Taking his drink, Nowitzke walked the entire room, watching shiny people dancing to classic big band music put out by a fourteen-piece ensemble. Finding a previously used but now-empty table in a corner, he pulled up a chair, studying the decorations and details associated with the bash. *Will Porter was responsible for arranging all of this?* he thought, shaking his head. Then, from behind him, he heard someone call his name over the music. "Chuck?"

As if on cue, there stood Will. "I thought that was you. Didn't realize you were a guest tonight," Will said, trying to reconcile the man's shabby plaid jacket.

"I'm not, since my tux is at the cleaners. I had a meeting with Brad late this afternoon, and he said to stop by if I had a chance. He also told me you put this event together for him."

"From scratch. Came up with the idea, the signage, the invitations, the seating chart, the band, the menu . . . you name it," replied Will proudly.

"How many people were here tonight?"

"Three hundred. It was quite a tribute to Brad."

"I've got to tell you, Will, this is pretty impressive," said Nowitzke, raising his glass to salute the man. "And you look happier than I think I've ever seen you."

Will could scarcely contain his glee upon receiving such long sought-after praise from the senior detective. "Can I get you another one of those, Chuck?"

"Only if you'll join me," offered the detective. He watched Will walk to the bar, where several hotel staff members approached the man, seemingly asking for direction. From what Nowitzke could tell, Will answered their questions and sent the people on their way.

Will returned with the drinks and put them on the table before pulling out a few chairs and sitting next to Nowitzke.

"Cheers," said the detective as the pair touched glasses. After downing a long swallow of whiskey, Nowitzke cocked his head, considering Will. "How did you learn to organize stuff like this?"

"In college, I had a part-time job in the hospitality business to pay for my tuition. After working this type of event a couple of times, it just became second nature for me."

"What was your degree in?"

"Police Science," replied Will flatly, taking a sip of his drink.

The two sat silently as the band broke into a set of Glenn Miller music before Will felt compelled to fill the void. "Chuck, is there a reason you don't like me?"

Nowitzke exhaled deeply, pushing his chair back on the floor, making a loud scraping sound. "Will, I don't dislike you, if that's what you think. We just don't have much in common." Nowitzke studied the brown liquid in his glass for a moment before he looked up at Will. "Can you tell me why you wanted to become a police officer?"

Will blinked hard, silent for a moment. "I've just always wanted to be a cop, from the time I was in grade school. 'Get good grades,' they said, and 'You can be anything you want to be.' So, I worked hard all the way through school, was on the track and debate teams, earning multiple participation awards before college. Finished my degree with a GPA just under four. Did some ride-alongs. Learned to shoot and got a qualifying score on my second try. Went to the police academy and graduated in the top half of my class."

Nowitzke took a long sip of Jack. "You know, when I was a kid, I used to watch every rocket launch I could find on television. I thought it would be so cool to become an astronaut. Loved the space suits. The helmet. Even the danger didn't make me think twice. I thought it was for me. But my dream lasted until the eighth grade when I started algebra. Turns out that as hard as I tried, I couldn't do math. It never dawned on me that astronauts needed to do higher mathematics than pretty much everyone else on the planet. Then I found out astronauts worked with computers. Something I knew and cared little about. I was bummed. But later on, I realized that even if I was able to figure out all that math and learn computer skills, there was no way I could ever wedge my fat ass into a space capsule. I just thought astronauts sat on top of the rocket, took a ride, maybe did a spacewalk, became heroes, and answered questions in interviews on day-time TV. All along, I heard the same crapola that you did. 'You can be anything you want to be.' Maybe that's the case for a lot of people, but there are limits."

"Your point?" asked Will.

"My point is that I was trying to become what I thought something was, not realizing what was actually involved with the job. You know, the skills and the ability. Even if I had done all the work, turns out there's a ton of competition to get a handful of spots. My odds of achieving my dream were doomed before I even knew it. Certificates of participation weren't going to cut it. But I was lucky and became a cop. Something I was reasonably good at, that was legal, and I could make a living at. Also, something I like."

Will looked confused for a moment before dropping his head and looking dejectedly at the floor. "What are you telling me, Chuck?"

Nowitzke closed his eyes and pinched the bridge of his nose. "That maybe police work isn't your thing, Will," said the detective, pausing for a moment to let the words sink in. "I don't see that you have any passion for the work. And you never look happy. Not like here, in this room. Watching you, there's no doubt who's in charge in this place. Plus, you've obviously got some skills in the hospitality line of work." He looked around the ballroom. "Short of a bridezilla, your odds of getting shot or injured seem much smaller."

"But . . . but, I love my job."

"All I'm saying is that you seem happier doing this type of work, and my impression is you do it better than most. At some point, you should think about making a choice. Would you like to be an excellent event organizer or an average police officer?" *At best.*

Will looked up, his face flushed red with anger. Standing, he kicked the chair back from under him. "Dammit, I *am* a good cop. I'm improving every day. Maybe I don't quite make the Nowitzke grade, but someday I'll prove it to you, Chuck. I will. I'll do something you never could," he said, turning on his heels and getting lost in the crowd.

Nowitzke shook his head and drained the last of his drink. "I hope so, kid. For your sake."

****

Halfway home, Nowitzke's phone rang. His disposition lightened immediately upon seeing Natalie's name on his caller ID. "Hey, stranger, what's up?" he said in as friendly a tone as he could muster.

"Just thinking of you, Chuck. I had a full day at work, and then my grandkids were here for dinner. I love them to death, but they sucked the last of whatever energy I had left right out of me before their mother took them home. It's quiet here now, and I'm looking for some adult conversation."

"Everyone else on your list was busy before you got to my name?"

"I made a pitcher of margaritas, got most of a cold pizza left over, and you can hang out with me by the fire if you're interested."

"That's a pretty tempting offer. What kind of pizza is it?"

"Listen, are you coming, or should I call the pizza guy back? He looked like he might be interesting," she said.

"That's how your classic porno starts," quipped Nowitzke. "My car's already on the way," he said, signing off.

An hour later, they were each on their second margarita, huddled near the fire ring under a wool blanket as the night air cooled. Natalie took a sip of her drink. "You seem like your mind is a million miles away from me tonight," she said.

"Sorry," Nowitzke replied. "It's been a long day that began with a homicide investigation. Maybe one of the most brutal killings I've seen in a while. I'll spare you the details."

"Thanks," said Natalie, shuddering at the thought. "I would guess you've handled a lot of murders over your career?"

"Yeah, too many. This one bugs me because I knew the victim. A nice young guy who deserved better. I can't get his face out of my head for some reason," he said, taking a breath. "The weird thing is we haven't figured out the motive." He looked up contemplating the stars as if they would give him an answer.

Natalie said nothing but nodded. "Can I buy you another drink?"

"Sure," Nowitzke replied with a smile. Natalie stood, bent at the waist, kissing him on the top of his head, and turned toward the back door of the house.

"I need to make another batch," she said. "Sit tight."

Nowitzke lay back in his chair, trying to take stock of what was going on in his life. It felt like he had been taking one step forward and two back lately, aside from finding Natalie. He remained puzzled by what she saw in him, but he resolved to enjoy her company while it lasted, even though he knew a black cloud always seemed to hang over his relationships. Inside the house, the grinding of the blender carried from the kitchen to the outdoors. The little man in his head told him to relax. He was having drinks with a beautiful woman on a near-perfect starlit night in front of a fire. *Enjoy it while you can, dumbass.*

"Chuck, would you come here for a moment?" Natalie called to him through the window.

When Nowitzke stepped into the kitchen, she wasn't there. The hairs on the back of his neck went up. Poking his head around the corners into the adjacent rooms, the detective found them dark and empty. "Natalie?" he called, feeling to make sure his Glock was in place.

"Upstairs," she called back to him.

Breathing a sigh of relief, he traipsed up the stairs, got to the landing, and looked around.

"In here," she called again.

Stepping into what looked like the main bedroom, Nowitzke found her, although it took him a moment to process what was going on. Natalie was smiling, sitting against the headboard of her bed, buried under strategically placed blankets, holding a full pitcher of margaritas in front of her. "I thought we could enjoy the second batch indoors," she offered, managing to also throw back the blanket. Nowitzke couldn't help but stare at her naked body but said nothing. "Are you disappointed?" she asked.

"Are you kidding? You're gorgeous, Natalie. I told you that the day we met," he replied, adding awkwardness to the moment. "I guess I'm just surprised is all. Are you sure about this?"

"Maybe it's the tequila talking, but I'm as sure as can be," said Natalie timidly. "It's been almost a year since Georg left me, and I'm incredibly nervous since I've only ever been with my ex. Is it okay that I made the first move?"

Nowitzke leaned over and kissed her deeply on the lips. "Wow, kind of like getting an unexpected present on Christmas morning!"

"So . . ."

"Feliz Navidad!" replied Nowitzke. "Let's put the margaritas on the nightstand and enjoy them later, when we're thirsty."

CHAPTER 20

Nowitzke woke to a gentle nudge, tangled in a pile of sheets and blankets on a brilliant sunny morning. He raised his head, looking around at the unfamiliar space in the light of day, trying to figure out where he was. Then he heard a woman's voice whisper, "Chuck . . . Chuck," followed by another prod as he put everything together.

"Morning," he croaked upon seeing a smiling Natalie sitting on the bed with a cup of coffee and reaching toward him with a second one. Based on what he could tell, she had already showered. Wearing a comfortable-looking bathrobe, she also had a towel wrapped around her head. "Thanks," he said, sitting up to take the cup from her.

She leaned toward him and kissed him. "Chuck, I had such a nice evening with you. It feels like the weight of the world has been lifted off my shoulders. I want to know when we can spend some more time together, but I have a favor to ask." She scrunched up her face. "My daughter, Blanca, and her kids are coming to the house in about an hour. She has been struggling with the whole divorce thing, as have I. Right now, I'd prefer to avoid a lot of extra questions," she apologized in advance. "I'd like for you to meet my family soon. It's just a timing thing."

"So, use me for sex and kick me out?" Nowitzke said with a grin. "I get it. You don't need to explain. Do I have time to drink my coffee?"

"Of course," she replied.

"Time for anything else?" he asked with his eyes raised.

"Not this morning," she said, stealing a glance at the alarm clock. "But keep me on your short list."

"How about coming to dinner tomorrow night at Miss Alma's house? A Sunday tradition for me and Anissa . . . you know, my family."

Natalie's face registered a look of surprise and apprehension. "Are you sure?"

"Absolutely. Also, I won't send you packing afterwards," he joked, giving her a kiss before he padded off to the shower.

They said their goodbyes before Nowitzke's Escort pulled away from the curb just as Blanca approached from the opposite direction. The detective drew nothing more than a thoughtless glance from the young woman as she and her kids passed by. It was a beautiful Saturday morning, and Nowitzke had absolutely no plans. A day to give his head a break from the developments of the past week. As he mused about taking an afternoon nap, his body was begging for more coffee and something to eat. His car found its way to a Dunkin' Donuts, and the senior detective sat in the drive-thru lane, having barely popped his first donut hole into his mouth when his cell phone rang. Trying to wipe away the powdered sugar from his hands, he triggered the speaker button with his clean pinky and snarled "Nowitzke" to whoever was on the other end.

"May I speak to Detective Nowitzke, please?" asked a woman.

"Speaking."

"Detective, you recently left a message for me. My name is Kelsie Cantrell-Holland."

"Yeah, Mrs. Holland, thanks for returning my call. I wasn't sure when I'd talk to you," he said in a surprised tone. "What can I do for you?"

"My partner and I have been taking a fresh look into the disappearance of Sandy Hawkins."

"Michael, my husband, said something along those lines."

"My understanding is that you were a friend of Sandy's. I'd like to come out to your house and ask you a few questions."

"Sure," she replied. "But after all these years, I'm not sure that I'm going to be much help. Would today work? Say, an hour from now?"

"See you then," said Nowitzke, signing off before punching in Anissa's number. She picked up on the first ring. "Just got a call from a woman who was supposedly Sandy's best friend, at least according to an old newspaper article I read. Interested in tagging along?"

"Stop out in front of my building, and we'll take my car. By the way, I'm dressed pretty casually today."

"No problem," replied the detective, realizing he was still wearing his clothes from the prior day.

Kelsie's address took the officers to the outskirts of Appleton, where the scenery turned from suburbs into farmland. Anissa's Audi sent up a plume of dust as she drove down the gravel drive, approaching a classic-looking farmhouse with a wide wraparound porch. Several outbuildings on the property were in various stages of disrepair. When they emerged from the vehicle, neither had any doubt they were visiting a working farm based on the smell. Both stepped carefully across a small patch of green grass, shooing chickens away before walking up a short flight of steps to the well-rusted screen door. Nowitzke knocked, making the door shudder on its frame and sending red particles into the air.

"Coming," they heard from within the house before a buxom, well-tanned woman wearing patched jeans, a tank top, and working boots appeared through the mesh. "I'm Kelsie," she welcomed, opening the door. As Anissa and Nowitzke entered the kitchen, Kelsie made a vain attempt to tidy up. "You gotta excuse the mess. Never been much for housekeeping." Most of the flat spaces in the room were covered with used pots and pans, dirty dishes, and open food containers. Nowitzke thought the room smelled like lard. "Pull up a chair," offered Kelsie as Anissa discreetly looked for the cleanest one before plunking down in her newest pair of jeans. Even Nowitzke was skeptical of finding a suitable place and risking his pants and worn jacket. Both detectives offered Kelsie a look at their badges as they sat down at the sticky table.

"How was the campout?" asked Nowitzke.

"I loved it. I get out a couple of times a year, just for the solitude. Hiking. Fishing. Catching up on old novels. Living in the real wilderness." Then, she closed her eyes for a moment before changing topics. "Now, you wanted to talk about Sandy?" asked a sincere Kelsie.

"Yeah," Nowitzke began. "Sandy's disappearance came up in connection with another case we're investigating."

"Did someone find her body?" she asked nervously, taking a deep breath. Kelsie's hands were folded so tightly in front of her that her knuckles were beginning to turn white.

"No," replied Nowitzke.

Kelsie loudly exhaled. "Thank God. You know, even after all these years, I'd like to think she's still alive. So, what can I help you with?" she asked with a puzzled look on her face.

"We saw your name in an article in the *Post-Crescent* from back in the day," said Anissa. "It said you and Sandy were friends. Would you tell us about her?"

"Sure. I guess you could say we were what the kids now call 'besties' despite ourselves. I came off the farm . . . third generation. Liked hunting, wrangling animals, shoveling hay. I could fix a tractor engine by the time I was fourteen," Kelsie boasted.

"Sandy wasn't into those things?" asked Anissa.

"No. Not even close," the woman hooted. "She was city through and through. A girly girl. Liked getting her nails done." Kelsie held up her own discolored and unkempt nails by way of comparison. "I don't think she was ever on a farm. Sandy preferred going to the mall. Sports. Pretty much everything I hated. She was smart. I wasn't."

"How did you come to be such good friends then?" asked Nowitzke.

"I guess it goes back to the first day of seventh grade. Our assigned seats were next to each other. Luck of the draw. Two scared girls at a new school, without any friends, each worried about what everyone else thought about us . . . even if for different reasons. We had lunch together that day at a table all by ourselves. But we didn't care. We just started talking and talking. I liked her from the start, even though we had nothing in common. Through the years, it stayed that way. We always shared secrets. You know, guys we were crushing on, the latest gossip. We hung out together every day just like that all the way through high school, until . . ." Kelsie's voice trailed off.

"What did you think happened when Sandy disappeared?" Nowitzke asked.

"The worst. You know, finding her body in a ditch or something like that. Even though I was only eighteen at the time, I pretty much knew that nothing good was going to come from this. It wasn't like Sandy would magically reappear with a smile on her face, like nothing happened."

"Did Sandy have any boyfriends?" asked Anissa.

"Friends who were boys, but no real boyfriends. That's not to say several didn't give it a try. Sandy had serious brains, a tight little body that got some attention, and a fun personality. But she was focused on the future. Bigger things. Getting out of here. She knew what she wanted to be when she grew up and didn't have time for any distractions," concluded Kelsie.

"Anything else you might be able to tell us?" Nowitzke probed.

Kelsie looked at the ceiling for an answer. "I'm sure I told this to the cops when this all happened, but I assume you know her brother offered her a graduation gift?" she asked, drawing nods from the officers. "A choice between two pretty cool places. She ended up going to Hawaii." Nowitzke remembered the beach photo from Brad Hawkins' office. "She was so excited," continued Kelsie. "I was excited for her. My God. Hawaii. Haven't been there yet, but it's still on my list," she added as an aside. "Anyway, when she got home, I couldn't wait to hear every detail. But she blew me off. It was like she wasn't the same person. At first, I wrote it off to time zones. You know, getting your body clock straight. But even after a week, I could tell something was different. I pressed her to find out what was wrong, but she kept brushing me off. For so many years, there were no secrets between us, but it felt like she was holding something back. Can't prove it, just a feeling. After that, we only saw each other a couple times, but her head was always somewhere else." Kelsie's eyes started to glisten. "Then she was gone . . ."

Anissa made a note, as did Nowitzke.

"Even now, after all these years, I still miss my friend," said Kelsie. "It's weird how your life is changed by something as simple as a seating chart in junior high."

Nowitzke and Anissa both fidgeted, each surreptitiously trying to find a position where they didn't think they were sitting in something. However, Kelsie waxed on. "I often wonder how people's lives are affected by seemingly meaningless things. Like, if Sandy had made a different choice."

"About what?" asked Anissa.

"You know, about her graduation gift. Maybe she would still be here if she had gone to Canada instead," offered Kelsie. "Who knows?"

"Canada?" said Nowitzke.

"Sandy told me it was the other option," Kelsie replied. "I'd never heard of the place before, but I guess it's supposed to be amazing."

"Do you remember where?" Anissa asked.

"Some dinky little town in Alberta, I think. Banff?"

****

By the time the officers made it back to the Audi, Nowitzke's brain was racing. A week before, he had never heard of the Canadian village. Now, within the span of a few days, this speck on the map had surfaced in connection with two different cases he was working. *WTF.*

The vehicle had yet to leave the Holland farm before Anissa started the conversation. "Chuck, this can't be a coincidence. Someone sends you a package of documents about the death of Jacob McClary postmarked from Banff, a decades-old case we would never have found without someone pointing the way."

"Yeah, then the best friend of a young woman who disappeared from the area thirty-some years ago mentions the place out of the blue. That, on top of Brad Hawkins receiving a package containing a prized possession of Sandy's," added Nowitzke.

"Enough so to convince Brad that Sandy must still be alive," Anissa followed. "In a weird way, there's a certain symmetry about this. I mean, Sandy was offered a choice. Then she visits Hawaii, her first option. Do you think when Sandy disappeared, she may have left the States and relocated to her second choice in Canada?"

"But why? It still doesn't make any sense. A talented girl with her whole life in front of her drops everything she's worked for and then leaves without telling anyone. I'm just not clicking with this scenario," Nowitzke replied.

"We need to dig into this, Chuck. Sandy's missing persons case remains open. Maybe she's still alive and living in Canada. It's a plausible scenario that we need to investigate further."

"Agreed. Do you have a passport?"

Anissa raised her eyebrows and tilted her head as she gave her boss a suspicious look. "Of course I do."

"Good. Let's give the chief a call. He's going to need to write a check to cover your expenses for your trip to Canada," said Nowitzke.

"Me? Why me?"

"I don't think this requires both of us, Nis. You're a great investigator, and I need to keep churning on the other cold cases."

An hour later, they met Chief Clark on the steps of his home. In less than fifteen minutes, he agreed with his detectives' assessment, authorizing the trip for Anissa. After driving back to the office, Anissa did a quick internet search to find the phone number to establish contact with the local detachment of the Royal Canadian Mounted Police in Banff.

"Inspector Ian Floyd speaking," said the voice over the conference room phone. Nowitzke took the lead, introducing himself and Anissa before explaining to the RCMP officer the circumstances of Hawkins' disappearance and the recent lead.

"Inspector, let me ask the most obvious question first," said Nowitzke. "Do you have any record of a Sandra Hawkins living in or around Banff?"

"Give me a minute while I run the name," said Ian. The officers in Appleton could hear the clicking of a keyboard in the background. "Can you give me some additional details about the woman? When did she disappear?"

"1988," Anissa chimed in. "Assuming she was eighteen when she vanished, that would put her in her fifties now, if she's still alive."

"Do you have any photos of the girl?"

"Yes. Nothing handy now, but we'll email all the information that we have about Hawkins," added Anissa.

"That would be handy, eh," Ian replied. "Guys, I'm not coming up with anything, either in Banff proper or anywhere in our system, which covers the balance of the country. If she is or was here, Miss Hawkins lives a clean life. Without much information to go on, I'm not sure how much help we can offer."

Sitting back in his chair, Nowitzke rubbed his eyes, thinking through the situation and wondering if they would be spending good money after bad. "Ian, I'd like to send Anissa to your area so we can say we went the extra mile on this case. While it shouldn't be a factor, the missing girl is a sister of a former district attorney. Frankly, I'd like to help get some closure on this for our friend and our local department, if that's possible."

"We will extend every courtesy to our brothers and sisters in blue from the States," echoed Ian through the conference speaker. "Send me the docs you have so I can get a head start. Anissa, if you need help with lodging recommendations or whatever, please call my mobile number. When do you plan on arriving in Banff?"

"Monday afternoon, if the flights work," she replied.

"Safe travels," Ian responded before the phone clicked off.

CHAPTER 21

Nowitzke woke in a panic. For the past several hours, he had been playing catch-up on sleep lost from the prior week. While he lay on his couch, cool air gently filtered through his apartment accompanied by the soothing sounds of baseball from the television, making for ideal napping conditions. At least until he realized he was a half hour late for dinner. After splashing some water on his face to wake up, he quickly lumbered down the wooden steps outside his apartment, beating a path for Miss Alma's kitchen.

When Nowitzke was in earshot of her back door, he heard laughter coming from inside the home. He opened the screen, and the three women in the room—Miss Alma, Anissa, and Natalie—slowly turned their heads toward him in unison, immediately becoming silent. For a torturous ten seconds, they held their gaze as Nowitzke froze in place like a deer in the headlights. Then, almost on cue, they burst into raucous laughter as if he were the butt of some private joke.

"Glad you could make it, Detective. I was about to send for the paramedics. You've never been late for dinner," Miss Alma said, keying more female glee at his expense. "Help yourself to a beer. Natalie was very thoughtful, bringing two bottles of wine. I don't remember wine ever tasting so good . . . even at the Lord's Table," she whispered, which sent the women into more hysterics. Based on what Nowitzke could tell, Miss Alma was in rare form and half in the bag.

Dinner led to polite and meaningless light talk before Miss Alma looked at Nowitzke and Anissa. "How are you two coming on my theory? You know, about other victims. Are you making any progress?" she asked between bites.

Natalie drew back for a moment. "Are you the one who came up with that idea? I did some follow-up work here with Chuck trying to find deaths that fit the scenario. Wow, Miss Alma, you're like a modern-day Miss Marple," she offered. "You know, she is still one of my favorite characters. A big reason why I love mysteries so much." She glanced at Nowitzke.

"What's your favorite Agatha Christie novel, dear?" asked Miss Alma.

"I'd have to say *The Murder at the Vicarage*. The first one I read, when I was just a girl. I think the story probably inspired me to become a librarian."

"You know what, that's my favorite Christie book too," concurred Miss Alma. "I also read it when I was a girl, even though it was considered a new release in the 1930s," she conceded.

"My grandmother put me on to Miss Marple," chimed in Anissa. "That character is one of the reasons I wanted to become a detective."

"Chuck, do you know about Miss Marple?" asked Miss Alma as all eyes at the table now focused on him.

"Sure, wasn't she once married to Donald Trump?" he said. Nowitzke received confused looks in return.

"I think you're talking about Marla Maples," replied Miss Alma, sending the women into stitches.

When the evening ended, Natalie walked out into the cool night, thanking Miss Alma for dinner. "You know, we're in the process of building a new library downtown. When it's finished, I think I can arrange a private tour for you. Oh, and I'll keep an eye out for any new mysteries coming out too."

"Thank you, Natalie," replied the older woman, giving her a hug. "Please come back anytime." As Natalie moved on to Anissa to say her goodbyes, Miss Alma took Nowitzke aside. "Detective, Natalie is delightful. What are your intentions regarding this young woman?"

Intentions? Jesus! It sounded like a question the father of a teenage girl might ask a young man coming to his house. Nowitzke had intentions, but nothing he wished to share with his landlord. "Natalie and I are just getting to know each other, Miss Alma. She's almost done with a tough divorce from an idiot who couldn't explain why he left her and didn't know what he had," he replied, dancing around her question.

"Well, she is smart, and I like her a lot. My impression is that she would be good for you. So, don't be the next idiot in her life and lose her over something stupid," she chided, turning to go back into the house. "Oh, and Chuck, make sure you've got a rubber," added Miss Alma in almost a whisper. "At least, I think that's what the sailors called them back in the day, anyway." She stifled a laugh.

Surprised at Miss Alma's comment, the stunned look on Nowitzke's face was his only response, even unable to come up with a snappy reply. *At least rule three doesn't seem to be an issue anymore.* Anissa approached Nowitzke, offering him a hug. "Keep me posted about your trip to Canada," he said.

"Will do," the junior detective replied.

Natalie and Nowitzke watched the Audi pull out of the yard. "How did it go with Miss Alma?" asked the officer.

"She's a lovely lady," Natalie replied. "By the way, she's pretty sharp for her age. She also seems to be reasonably fluent in Spanish."

"I didn't know that," said Nowitzke. "How did that come up?"

"Well, after we talked for a while, I must have passed a personal test of some sort. She asked me point-blank what an attractive woman like me was doing hanging out with a guy like you."

"What did you tell her?" he asked curiously, wondering the same thing.

"For the sex, of course," she said, laughing. "Then Miss Alma looked at me very seriously and said, 'Sin gorrito no hay cumpleaños!'"

"Which means?"

"'Without a little hat, there's no birthday.' You know, about wearing a condom. Not much gets by her." Natalie took Nowitzke's hand and tugged him toward his apartment. "I hope I'm that with it when I'm her age," she concluded as they got to the top of the stairwell.

CHAPTER 22

After Anissa's plane touched down in Calgary, she skated through customs and immigration before picking up a rental car to begin the ninety-minute scenic journey west on the Trans-Canada Highway. Her path took her through the expansive rolling plains of Alberta, then up a sneaky incline before she realized she was passing through the still snow-covered mountains that had formerly been on the horizon. After securing her pass to enter the national park, Anissa continued taking in the scenery before pulling off onto an interchange into the quaint village of Banff.

Using a GPS, Anissa quickly located the small offices of RCMP on Lynx Street, pulling into an adjacent parking lot shortly after 2:00 p.m. local time. As she prepared to pull out her identification for the young female receptionist in the small anteroom, the woman quickly sized her up. "You must be Officer Taylor from the States," she said with a smile. "We've been waiting for you. Let me buzz Ian. Can I get you anything?"

"Bottled water, if you've got it. Is it particularly dry here?" asked Anissa.

"Oh yes, ma'am. We're at roughly 1,400 meters in elevation," replied the woman, excusing herself to get the water. Like every other ugly American, Anissa had no clue what 1,400 meters meant. Her only real experience with the metric system was knowing what a two-liter bottle of Coke looked like.

With a minute to herself, she smoothed her fashionable grey

flannel suit, feeling a bit naked without her Beretta, which was locked in a safe at her condo.

Moments later, a tall, thin, impeccably dressed sixty-something-year-old man with brown hair, matching eyes, and a pencil-thin mustache appeared with a bottle of water, along with the receptionist. "Here you go," he said. "Let me know if you need another. Hydrating is important, especially for a flatlander from Wisconsin." He gave her a toothy grin, then offered his hand in greeting. "I'm Inspector Floyd, but call me Ian. By the way, 4,500 feet is the answer to the question in your head. Canada adopted the metric system in 1970, but what's actually used is a hodgepodge of measurements, leftovers of the English system and, of course, the influence of the States. In the winter, when our local television weatherman says that we received ten centimeters of snow overnight, I'm still not sure whether I need to put on boots until I look outside," he volunteered with a laugh.

Ian's easy way made Anissa relax after her trip. But very quickly, the inspector became all business. "We received the packet of material from you yesterday and began digging into the facts around your missing person. In fact, I've got something interesting for you to see. Follow me."

The two of them stepped through a doorway into a larger room, which was still fairly small, especially after squeezing in four office cubes. The space was drab, with dated mustard-colored furniture that Anissa doubted had ever been in style. However, the feature element of the room was a large window with a spectacular view of the mountaintops around the village.

"I can't imagine ever getting tired of the view out your window, Ian," said Anissa.

"I know what you mean, Detective. Unfortunately, I generally get so wrapped up in work that I don't appreciate it."

"By the way, please call me Anissa. We're pretty informal in our office too. I'm curious about what you've found."

Ian led Anissa to his workspace and rolled his chair around his desk next to the lone side chair he had for her. Then he flipped his laptop around so they could both see the screen. Within minutes, it became readily apparent that whatever the RCMP might have lacked in spending on furnishings had been invested in technology.

"When we got the newspaper photo of the Hawkins girl, we started with a process just to sharpen the image. Once that was done, we fed the result through another program. To give you some background, the RCMP has worked with the Ontario Science Centre in Toronto and in partnership with a private contractor on a piece of software that studies the effect of time on subjects. The output gives us a potential glimpse into the future by aging the subject. The primary application of this program is to show kids what they'll look like over time if they smoke or do meth. Scare tactics that may or may not work for invincible young people, but it makes for some fun. Several television special effects people have used the program as well. However, this tool is perfectly suited for law enforcement in situations just like this.

"Based on my notes from our conversation yesterday and the date of the newspaper articles, we projected that Hawkins would now be roughly fifty-three years of age," continued Ian. "We ran the girl's photo through the software, adding and deleting for things like smoking, but also sun exposure and weight gain shifts in body mass index. The outcomes offer several potential views of the aging Ms. Hawkins." He brought up the data.

Anissa sat forward in her chair as Ian flashed through the images of Sandy, watching her morph from a beautiful young woman in her twenties, through her thirties and forties, before lighting on the target age. After previewing the first group of pictures, Ian then introduced some of the other factors into the mix, altering the output. The outcome was stunning as Anissa considered the various possibilities of what Sandy might look like today if she bumped into her on the street.

Ian sat up in his chair. "I'm assuming we have no additional information about Sandy's medical background or other habits?"

"Correct," Anissa answered. "So, what is the next step with these photos?"

"Well, in America, they might end up on a milk carton or featured on one of those late-night docudramas on some obscure television network. But, since you asked about Banff in particular, I took the liberty to circulate a couple of these photos to a few people in town," said Ian. "Remember, this is Banff, population 8,300. Not Chicago or New York. Anyway, I got a call back almost immediately."

"Seriously, Ian, you're doing all my work for me," replied Anissa. "Who was it? When can I meet this person?"

"Dr. Rebecca Underwood, the president of the local hospital. We're set to meet her tonight for dinner. Looks like you've got a couple of hours to yourself to see some of our fair little town and accomplish your work, and I can expense the meal. I'll pick you up at 6:30, and we can have a drink. I'd love to pick your brain about what's going on in the States these days and why. Where are you staying?"

"The Fairmont," replied Anissa.

"Very nice," Ian said, nodding. "American police travel per diems must be substantially larger than those of their Canadian counterparts."

"Hardly," Anissa said with a laugh. "I've read about the Castle of the Rockies for years, and when I learned I was coming to Banff, I absolutely had to stay there . . . even if it meant giving up my wine allowance for a couple of months."

"Or maybe years," countered Ian. "Dress casually, and I'll meet you at the main entrance later. Also, bring a sweater because it cools off quickly here in the evening."

At the hotel, after a cat nap and a quick shower, Anissa changed into a white sweater, black dress slacks, and matching heels. Feeling her second wind, she wandered about the luxury resort on a self-guided tour. As she stood on the front steps, the stone structure gave her a sense that she had been transported to a château in Europe. The sprawling hotel's architecture incorporated castle-like designs with a series of steep copper roofs, dormers, and gables on the eleven-story main building. The interior was equally impressive, featuring oaken beams and paneling, stone archways, iron chandeliers, Terrazzo floors, and stained glass. Strolling through the halls, she found multiple restaurants and bars, along with windows throughout that offered unreal views of the mountain scenery. She completed her walk, finding her way to the lower level to explore the spa and pool area.

Anissa had timed things perfectly, stepping into the chilled evening air outside the lobby entrance just as Ian arrived in a Grand Cherokee. "You look refreshed," he said as she climbed into the vehicle.

"Ian, the travel brochures don't do justice to this place."

"And you haven't seen much of the town itself, aside from the RCMP office. Tell you what . . . let me play the role of docent on the way to dinner." Ian turned onto Spray Avenue, paralleling the Bow River, on the way towards town. "Unfortunately, being on the main road won't give you all the views of the river," he said, pointing towards the water through the wooded area. "If you have time tomorrow morning, step out of the hotel on the back side. There's a path that will give you a better look. It's a nice, quiet walk through the pines that will take you along the river and the roar of the water as you get to Bow Falls. Well worth the trip, in my view."

"Do you have to worry about the wildlife here?" Anissa asked.

"Worry is such a strong word," said Ian. "We live in a national park, so you might catch a glimpse of caribou, raccoons, porcupines . . . . animals typically found in forests. Just be cautious. Occasionally, we have a sighting of a brown bear in the area."

"A brown . . . you mean a grizzly?"

"Well, yes." Ian turned right across a bridge, followed by another right down a paved road on the other side of the river. "Remember, bears are incredibly fast. If possible, take someone along that you can outrun," he joked. For some reason, Anissa's mind went directly to Nowitzke. Ian pulled over and nodded towards a wooden platform off to the side of the road, then asked Anissa if she would like to see some more scenery.

Stepping onto the deck, they were rewarded with a view of the castle rising out of the pines in the shadow of the Rocky Mountains. Anissa felt compelled to use her phone camera to capture the moment.

"I've never been to the mountains before. The scenery here is awe-inspiring," she marveled.

Five minutes later, Ian parked in front of The Maple Leaf Grille. "Hope you like it. It's one of my favorites," he offered. Upon entering the bustling lounge, they were greeted by a hostess. She found his name on the reservation list, then told Ian that the wait time would be a few minutes, just as he spotted Dr. Underwood sitting at the curved wooden bar. Ian led the way as the officers navigated their way through the crowd. "Anissa, please meet my friend, Dr. Rebecca Underwood," he said, holding up a hand to hail a bartender.

Underwood was a sprite of a woman, trim, with a precise aura about her, extending from the beige jacket and skirt she wore to the understated gold chain hanging about her neck right to her brown hair fashioned in a tight bun. As she sat on the barstool, Underwood's feet dangled just short of the floor, making Anissa guess that she was only about five feet tall. However, she also had a friendly smile and greeted Anissa warmly after sliding off her seat. "Welcome to Banff. First time?"

"Yes, but definitely not the last," replied Anissa while taking in the interior of the restaurant.

"It's quite the place, isn't it?" Underwood observed as she watched Anissa. "Whoever designed The Maple Leaf did a great job of making it feel like a log cabin with all the pine and the local rock on the walls. Casual with a touch of mountain elegance. By the way, please call me Rebecca," she added. "Ian, make sure you put the drinks on my tab."

Just as they received their drinks, the hostess approached and led them to a quiet table on the second floor of the restaurant. "Cheers," said Ian as the three clinked glasses after they were seated.

A college-aged young man approached with menus and the evening specials. While she briefly pondered ordering the bison steak, Anissa settled on the salmon, as did both of her tablemates. "Ian, you're a detective," she said. "Why is it that if I'm near the west coast, the salmon is imported from the Atlantic Ocean, but if I'm on the east coast, it comes from the Pacific?"

"I would guess it must be a corollary to the use of expert consultants. You know, the further they come from, the smarter . . . and more expensive they are," he responded with a smile.

"You've noticed that too," chimed in Rebecca, taking a sip of her chardonnay before leaning toward the American detective, signaling that it was time to get down to business. "Ian gave me an overview of the details on your missing persons case. I get chills anytime I read about that type of situation. Anyway, he sent me several variations of the Hawkins girl after the photos went through the aging software."

"My understanding is that you think you recognized the person in the photo?" asked Anissa.

"Yes," Rebecca said as their salads arrived. "I have no doubt the woman pictured was Dr. Amanda Hartsell. When I saw the first photo, I knew it immediately. Amanda was an incredibly talented physician that I personally hired to come to work at the Banff Mineral Springs Hospital sometime around 2012."

"You're talking about Hartsell in the past tense," Anissa noted.

"Yes, unfortunately," Rebecca replied, wiping her mouth with her napkin. "Amanda and her husband, Alex, were killed in a terrible house fire about five years ago. It was a loss felt by the entire community." She looked at Ian, who nodded in agreement.

"What do you know about her background?"

"Amanda graduated from the University of Waterloo before attending Michael G. DeGroote School of Medicine in Hamilton, Ontario. Good school . . . very difficult to get into, by the way. I looked at her personnel file today just to make sure I had my facts straight for tonight," said Rebecca. "Interestingly, though, something jumped off the page today that I'd never considered. Amanda never listed her high school or a hometown, not that I cared at the time. I was primarily interested in her college and medical credentials. Anyway, I do know that Amanda spent a couple of years working with the underprivileged in greater Toronto. We added her to our pediatric team, but she came as part of a package deal with her husband, Alex, a plastic surgeon."

"How would you describe Amanda?" asked Anissa, sipping her wine.

"Friendly, smart, but also quiet, guarded . . . a bit withdrawn, I guess. You know, I was never sure I fully got to know her as a person. At the same time, she took exceptional care of her patients, having an outstanding bedside manner with the kids and parents. She was someone that just exuded a sense of compassion and empathy. Qualities that even some of the smartest physicians would give their eyeteeth for."

Anissa nodded. "Can you give me a physical description of Amanda, for what it's worth?" she asked. These were potential details to check on when she returned home.

Rebecca shrugged. "I'm no police officer." She smiled, looking at Ian. As Rebecca thought about the question, the waiter returned with a small team of servers, swapping out the salad plates with their entrees. Ian ordered another round of drinks. "Amanda was attractive, tall, slender build with a nice figure . . . blonde hair, at least when I knew her."

"Did Amanda have any family?"

"Yes, she did. She spoke about a daughter and a son, both of whom lived back east. For some reason, one of the suburbs around Toronto comes to mind. They were older and out of the house when Amanda and Alex moved here. I met them at the funeral. Chatted briefly with the young lady. Both nice-looking kids."

"No relatives living in Banff or the surrounding area?" asked Anissa.

"No, not that I know of." Rebecca took a bite of her salmon. "Would you like to see a photo of Amanda?" she asked.

"Of course."

Rebecca dug into her purse, pulling out her phone. "This is one from our website and also displayed in the lobby of our building, the Hartsell Wing, named for both Amanda and Alex after they passed." She handed the smartphone across the table.

Anissa studied the picture of the woman. While Amanda was not smiling like the girl in Hawkins' graduation photo, the detective had no doubt that Sandy was staring back at her. The poses in the photos were almost identical, right down to the angle of her head and the profile of her nose. "Ian, I don't suppose that Amanda's remains are anywhere in the area so we could do a DNA test?"

"No. Both Amanda and Alex were cremated, with their remains scattered on the mountain. That same thought crossed my mind too, assuming this lead had potential. But I guess we'll never know."

"What about the fire?" asked Anissa. "What was the cause?"

"Nothing suspicious, if that's what you're asking. Again, great minds think alike," said Ian. "According to the investigation, the wood stove was the actual cause, compounded by the fact that there were no working smoke detectors in the home."

Anissa leaned back in her chair and closed her eyes for a second to consider any other questions she had possibly missed. "Do either of you have any idea how I might get in touch with Amanda's kids?"

Both Ian and Rebecca shook their heads. "Another dead end that I've already looked into," said Ian.

Before coming to Canada, Anissa would have bet money that she would find Sandy Hawkins alive. The ember had been stoked by Brad with the delivery of the favored kids toy that had disappeared years before. Even though Nowitzke learned that the tattered rabbit had been sent from Green Bay, Brad took it as a sure sign that his sister was living. But now, Anissa was convinced that the girl who disappeared from Wisconsin so many years before had died tragically in Banff as Amanda Hartsell. Thinking through Brad Hawkins' description of his sister, everything seemed to fit. An attractive woman with brains who wanted to be a doctor someday. Anissa guessed it wasn't the path Sandy had envisioned for herself when she graduated from high school, but it appeared she had accomplished her professional goals. But another unanswered question nagged at Anissa. Who had sent the McClary packet of materials from Banff to

Nowitzke? Based on everything she had learned, Banff was looking like a dead end.

With the primary purpose of her trip accomplished, Anissa tried to enjoy the rest of her meal with her Canadian hosts but was now focused on the trip home

****

"We've got to stop meeting like this." Elliott glared at Will, who was sitting in the bar at the CopperLeaf Hotel. They were the last customers in the place, sauntering in separately around 9:30 p.m., a half hour before closing, clearly aggravating the bartender who had largely cleaned up for the night. Nonetheless, the server painted on a smile and delivered a scotch and a beer to the two men, who promptly stole away to a quiet corner of the bar. "Do you understand that you haven't been adding much in the way of value lately?" said Elliott with a stern demeanor.

"What are you talking about?"

Click – click – click – click – click – click.

"Information. Like providing me with *nothing*," Elliott added for emphasis. "I have it on good authority that one of my former employees, Bob Edwards, likely shipped a disc to a person at APD."

"Wait, Bob Edwards," questioned Will. "I know that name. Nowitzke just investigated his death. My understanding is Edwards was tortured before taking two bullets to the head."

"Very talented guy but could have stood to lose a hundred pounds or so. Also, he was a little short on the concept of loyalty. Such a tough quality to find in employees these days," lamented Elliott. He took a sip of his scotch. "According to my source, Bob had a hard-on for a local detective. A friend of yours . . . Anissa Taylor." Will's eyes opened wide at the mention of her name. "Our guy was too smart for his own good. He found out we had recording devices in the lower level of Ivy House, mind you after I specifically told the detectives who investigated the death of the senator that we didn't," Elliott continued in a methodical, but even voice. "Supposedly, there's a disc out there somewhere with enough information to make trouble for me, to say the least. I also have it on good authority that Bob's dying words were that he sent a copy to Taylor."

"What do you want me to do?" asked Will.

"Well, jeez, Will, at a minimum, you need to check her desk to see if she's received any packages. If you can, get into her work account and scan her emails. Do I need to draw you a picture? I need that disc back!"

As he finished his sentence, a wiry blond man with a crew cut entered the room, briefly made eye contact with Elliott, and sat down alone at the bar.

Click – click – click – click – click – click.

"Listen, checking a desk is one thing, but getting into the system requires her password. You know that." Will looked at the floor but continued his conversation. "The good news is that Anissa's out of the office on a business trip and flying home tomorrow night," he volunteered. "I have a window to check her mail before she gets back. If the disc is in her office, I'll find it and email you immediately."

"No, this time you call me, either way," Elliott said with a growing menace in his voice. "If you can't make this work, I go to plan B, which escalates things significantly. Now, get to it and earn your goddamned keep." He slid a manila envelope across the table.

"You're not going to hurt Anissa, are you?" asked Will nervously, wondering if his slip about his friend traveling had already provided too much information about her.

"Not if you do your fucking job," said Elliott.

Will slipped off his chair and quickly departed out the front door. As he walked dejectedly to his car, he replayed the entire conversation in his mind. The situation had quickly gone from bad to worse. His depression was spiraling out of control. But worse, he feared that he had put a friend in jeopardy. *What should I do?*

After Will left, the blond picked up his drink, walked over to

Elliott, and sat down. "Looks like that dumb fuck did half your work for you," Elliott said, downing his drink. "Taylor is arriving at the airport tomorrow night. You need to check incoming flights into Appleton and figure it out. Then, once we clear up this mess with the disc, I've got another assignment or two for you to tie up some loose ends, including taking care of my junkie friend. Consider your dance card full."

Click – click – click – click – click – click.

Elliott said nothing more, rose from his seat, and stepped out onto the avenue, followed by the blond five minutes later.

Will had walked a block toward his car, still wrestling with the unsaid by Elliott as he fingered the envelope full of money inside his jacket. Suddenly, he stopped and turned around, resolved to clear his conscience by confronting Elliott, returning the money, and getting himself clean. But when he got back to the bar, he saw through the window that Elliott was now talking to a blond man. Will watched the conversation momentarily, making the connection before slipping back into the night unseen, except for a photographer positioned across the street who continued to snap photos of the bar until the server turned off the lights. The photographer concluded the evening by sending a text.

Elliott heard his phone ping as he stepped into his Jaguar. He read the message but didn't recognize the number of the sender.

Hey Elliott, how's your friend doing after flying through a window? I know your secrets.

He responded,

I don't know who you are or what you want, but if you're smart, you'll steer clear of me.

Thirty seconds later, Elliott got his reply.

I'll be coming for you soon!

CHAPTER 23

"Get out of my goddamned chair!" Nowitzke howled at Savanna Smythe, who was lounging comfortably in a t-shirt and jeans, her bare feet resting on his desk. She had been amusing herself with a California snow globe taken from the credenza where a stovepipe hat was floating above lumps of coal and a carrot that rested on the bottom. "We used to have security in this place to keep people from waltzing in here. But here you are *again* . . . in my space, sitting at my desk, playing with one of my snow globes. Who the hell let you in here anyway?" roared the detective, setting his morning coffee down on the desk.

"The female officer out front. She remembered me from the last time. We hit it off. Told her I wanted to surprise you this morning." Savanna gave him a Cheshire smile. "SURPRISE!" she mock-shouted with a shocked look on her face while holding her hands up. "Did you bring me a coffee?"

"Move," said Nowitzke impatiently, scooting the woman around to one of the side chairs in front of the desk. "And no, I didn't."

"Bummer. I figured I'd check in on you after getting your question about Canadian geography," she continued. "Anything on your mind, Detective?"

"You probably don't know the name Bob Edwards, but he was on the security team at Ivy House working for a guy named Elliott Gordon," replied Nowitzke while searching his desk for a file. "In particular, Anissa and I worked with Bob on their closed-circuit video system to identify a nice-looking redhead who had crashed

189

the party and was in the presence of the senator."

"Whoops," said Savanna, sitting back in her chair smugly, twirling her hair. "So what's going on with Bob?"

"Bob was murdered. Actually, tortured, then killed," Nowitzke replied, finding the file he had been looking for. After pulling several police photos of Bob's body, he slid them across the desk to Savanna.

Savanna calmly paged through the graphic pictures, never once wincing. "What are these rings on the man's face and back?" she asked matter-of-factly. "They look like burn marks."

"Turns out that Bob drove an older vehicle that had a cigarette lighter. Best we can tell, some sadistic asshole made him suffer, trying to get information from him before he was shot."

"What does any of this have to do with me?" Savanna questioned, pushing the photos back to Nowitzke.

"A day later, Anissa's laptop lit up with a series of emails that had been sent from a hidden camera in Bob's house. Guess who we saw inside the house, apparently looking for something," he said, sending another series of photos across the desk to Savanna.

The woman studied the photos and shook her head when she saw the blond man featured. "Could you tell if he was limping?" she asked with a laugh. "So, the jerk who attacked me presumably also killed Bob?"

"Certainly looks that way," replied Nowitzke. "Also, the only connection between you and Bob that anyone can come up with is that you were both at Hecht's fundraiser that afternoon. Do you have any explanation for that?"

"How would I? I never met Bob. In fact, I didn't know who he was until you just told me." Savanna shifted in her chair. "Do you have a theory on this?"

"No. That's just it. I don't."

Savanna reached into a portfolio that she had placed on Nowitzke's desk and removed a large mailing envelope. "As long as we're playing show-and-tell, I brought something for you. Recognize our friend?" she asked, handing him a blown-up photograph of the man who had attacked her at the Orchard Inn. Nowitzke picked up his coffee and studied the close-up.

"Where was this taken?"

"Downtown on the street . . . while I was doing some sightseeing in Appleton," said Savanna casually. "Didn't have a chance to reintroduce myself to him . . . yet. But I will. Anyway, take a close look at where he's sitting and who's near him." She passed another picture to Nowitzke from a longer view.

"Jesus! Was this asshole following Anissa and Will?" exclaimed the detective upon seeing his colleagues sitting on some steps roughly one hundred feet from the man in question.

"Well, I don't think he was waiting for the number twelve bus to go see the Houdini exhibit," Savanna replied. "As I understand it, your detectives were just wrapping up their investigation of the death of that man who was found in the river. I saw that on TV. I took this photo later in the day when a social worker showed up to take custody of the guy's baby after his girlfriend tried to kill herself. I would guess blondie had something to do with that murder too," she offered.

"You know that?" asked the detective.

"No, I don't. But why else would he be trailing your people?"

"Good question."

Savanna slid to the edge of her chair toward Nowitzke. "Detective, you don't look like a man who believes in flukes. I mean, what are the odds that this guy, who may be involved in several murders, just happens to be sitting at this bus stop close to the officers investigating a crime he's potentially responsible for?"

Nowitzke took a long draw on his coffee and reclined in his chair far enough to make it squeak from stress. "Savanna, how did you come to take these pictures? I need a straight answer."

"I was following Anissa and Will. Will in particular," she said plainly.

"Why?" asked Nowitzke, giving her a quizzical look as he leaned forward towards the woman.

"Got time for a story?" Savanna asked rhetorically, playing with her hair before jumping in. "On the night of the fundraiser, I got back to my hotel room and turned on the news. It was no shock that the senator's death was the lead story on the local channels. I just wanted to see what was going on. Anyway, sometime during the broadcast, they flashed to Will Porter, your PR guy, giving a statement to the press about Hecht. I had no clue who he was.

"The next morning, as I'm on my way down to the hotel breakfast, I see Porter sitting in the lobby. In fact, I did a double take, wondering if it was really the cop I had seen on television the night before. I didn't think too much of it at the time. But when I started to head back to my room a half hour later, he was still sitting there, drinking coffee, doing a whole lot of nothing. I went to the elevator just around the corner, stepped in, but then jumped out as the doors closed and hid where he couldn't see me. Then I watched Porter pick up his phone and make a call. He went to the front desk, flashed his badge at the clerk, and started asking a lot of questions.

"Later in the day, I saw Porter several more times. First, talking to a different desk clerk. After that, he sat in his car in the hotel's parking lot, watching who was coming and going from the main entrance. It was then that I realized he was stalking me for some reason. Not that he was very good at it. I think I saw him more times than he saw me, frankly. I was pretty sure that the Appleton police were looking for me, but he never approached me. The following morning, the blond guy just happened to show up at my hotel door, and you know the rest.

"Are you saying that Will told the blond where you were staying?" asked Nowitzke.

"I can't prove it, if that's what you're asking. But for me, the timing between seeing Porter lounging around in my hotel and the fight of the century is curious to say the least," Savanna answered. "So, I decided that I would do some research on APD at large to see if your unit was on the up and up, which gets me to these photos. When I came to your office to meet you the first time, I was satisfied you were old-school. Based on your bio, everything I'd read about you, and my first impression, I thought you were solid."

"Don't blow any smoke up my ass, Savanna," Nowitzke replied.

Savanna rolled her eyes, ignoring the comment. "And even though I haven't met her yet, I got the same impression about Anissa. Serious skills, from what I'm told. By the way, where is she?"

"Out of town on business. She'll be back in the office tomorrow."

"Okay," Savanna continued. "But something's up with Will. I understand that he was seriously injured not long ago. Studying him, he seems like a weak link. Anyhow, I decided to change the rules of the game and began following him and taking photos. Chuck, Will goes to some interesting places, not the least of which is the Orchard Inn. After thinking more about it, I'm pretty damned sure he was making a drug deal with the desk clerk."

Savanna's observation jarred Nowitzke noticeably. "Seriously? Why do you think that?"

"It was just the way Will handled himself. For a cop, he seemed nervous as hell…you know, looking around like he was doing something he shouldn't be," she concluded. "I've seen that look on people before. In my opinion, the guy's better suited for public relations or being a realtor or washing cars. Anything but detective work."

Nowitzke tried to stifle a smile but unconsciously nodded in agreement. "You're pretty astute for a tourist. Who do you think the buzzcut was watching? Anissa or Will?"

"No clue. But something's up. My impression is that all the good guys need to be watching their asses." Savanna took a breath and glanced down, digging back into her portfolio. "I've got one last photo for you," she said, pulling out an eight-by-ten and handing it to Nowitzke. "Will's having a drink with Elliott. I didn't know those two were buddies."

"Neither did I," said Nowitzke, scratching his head.

"It's just interesting," Savanna offered. "No conclusions. No judgments."

Nowitzke sat back, put his elbow on his chair, and stroked his chin while considering Savanna. Her smile belied much more than a pretty face. This woman had confidence and instincts and the ability to put things together. On top of that, she could take care of herself when the shit hit the fan. The detective shook his head and leaned forward again, squinting at Savanna. "Tell me who you are and what you're doing here. No more bullshit."

"Detective, I've already told you. I'm on holiday enjoying the best of what Wisconsin has to offer. Heading to a beer tasting for lunch. Want to join me?" She stood and left his office, sending a smile to him over her shoulder. "See you soon, Chuck," she said as she disappeared down the hall toward the front door.

Nowitzke pivoted in his chair, turning toward the credenza before picking up the snow globe that Savanna had been playing with. After trying to process their conversation, he shook his head. It was another unsatisfying encounter with this woman. They were playing mental football, where she gave him a leg but then yanked it away, leaving the detective grabbing at air. Based on what he knew of her, she was a helluva lot more than some tourist. In his gut, he was convinced that Savanna was somehow involved with law enforcement. Yet while some things fit with that idea, other parts of her story just didn't jibe. Why was she alone with the senator in the wine room? When the blond asshole attacked her with every advantage, how was she able to kick his ass? And, while he had little use for Will Porter as a detective, this woman was now pretty much saying that the man was buying drugs on the street. Even more amazingly, he tended to believe Savanna's story about Will identifying where she was staying for the buzzcut.

Nowitzke rose from his chair, finished his coffee to the dregs, and pitched the disposable cup into the trash before taking a walk downstairs to the traffic unit. Officer Fischer was on duty and in the middle of a conversation on her headset when she spotted Nowitzke. She smiled and waved him over to the console before telling whoever was on the other end of the line, "Gotta go." Then, she unconsciously straightened her uniform, stood, and mechanically put out her hand in greeting. "Detective Nowitzke. What can I do for you?" she asked.

Nowitzke shook her hand. "Colby, the other day when I was down here, you gave me a heads-up on the woman involved with Senator Hecht. It was impressive work, and we're still working the leads you developed."

Colby listened intently to every word from the senior officer. "Thank you. Is there something else I can help you with?"

"Question for you. Did anyone else from APD ask you for information about the woman? You know, what you gave me?"

The officer paused to think, her eyes focused upward as if consulting the files in her brain. "Yes, sir. I gave Chief Clark some advance notice that morning since he had asked our unit to do a search of our local traffic cameras. It was high-level, without much detail. For the most part just that we had completed the exercise. He told me that you would be coming down to talk with me. But, as I think about it, there was another detective who came down here asking questions . . . right before you showed up. Detective Porter. Don't know him well. He wanted to know what we had learned, so I gave him an overview. At the time, I thought it was kind of weird, but I wrote it off to him assisting you and the two of you not having talked between yourselves."

"He had access to everything you gave me?" asked Nowitzke. "The photos? The details about the rental car? The hotel where the woman was staying?"

"Yes, sir. He was a superior officer who said he was working the case," said the serious young woman. "Is there anything wrong?"

"No," Nowitzke replied blankly as he turned to leave, then stopped. "Colby, you did your job very well."

As he slogged back to his office, Nowitzke took out his phone and spoke to an officer in the records unit. "Can you bring me the working file of when Detective Porter was injured? . . . Great . . . Thanks." While he had a poor opinion of Will's abilities as a police officer, the veiled allegations coming from Savanna were another matter that needed looking into.

****

After receiving the threatening text from the unknown person, Elliott Gordon decided to begin practicing another level of personal security, particularly when he either arrived or left his office at Ivy House. He knew he had accumulated his share of enemies, whether as a cop years before or in his work with Brad Hawkins. Threats came with the territory, but few ever materialized. Still, it cost him nothing to keep his head on a swivel and pay closer attention to his surroundings. Elliott also decided to develop some new patterns, as painful as that was for him. That morning, he left his comfortable lakeside condo and steered his Jaguar on an indirect route through town on his way to work, keeping an eye out for any cars tailing him. But there were none. Adding five minutes to and from work was no big deal in the grand scheme. The aggravation came from the idea that someone felt they could tweak him and get away with it. Worst case, if a threat materialized, he was confident in his backup plan involving the nickel-plated Beretta 92FS 9mm handgun he wore under his jacket.

Carefully scanning the area before emerging from his car at work, he saw little activity in the area aside from a fit-looking woman in a sweat suit, sunglasses, and a hat jogging through the neighborhood like she did every day around 9:00 a.m. Grabbing his briefcase, he shook his head at himself, wondering if someone had gotten into his mind and he was now overreacting to the texts.

CHAPTER 24

A nissa's trip home from Banff had been one from hell. She had woken early, made the long drive back to Calgary, negotiated the morning rush traffic, dropped off the rental car, and still managed to get to the airport well in advance of her departure time. However, the line through immigration and customs looked like she was at Disney working her way to the entrance of Space Mountain. The monkey maze in the great hall snaked back in forth in pattern, which made it difficult to determine how quickly she was moving to the front. Anissa marked her progress by watching the same people ahead and behind her countless times as they all worked towards the same goal. By the time all her documents were stamped, she then followed her new friends in another line through security before missing her flight by five minutes. Anissa had an animated conversation with the gate agent, even stooping to flashing her American police badge. But nothing she could do was enough to convince the airline employee to open the door to the plane, even though she knew her seat was still available.

After rebooking her flight, she passed the time drinking coffee and reading, but mostly focused on mentally playing back the conversation she had with Ian and Rebecca about Sandy. Frustratingly, she came to no new conclusions. She waited several hours at the gate before getting a middle seat for the trip to Minneapolis. Upon arriving, a slender airline employee gave her more news, both good and bad. The bad was that she had missed her connection. The good was that the agent had booked her on the final flight of the day, getting her to Appleton around 10:30 p.m.

Anissa's plane touched down as scheduled, but she still had to wait to collect her bags with a planeload of other groggy-looking passengers all intent on completing their journey. She finally claimed her suitcase and trekked out of the airport into the evening air. After locating her car, she exited the lot, already reconciled to the idea that it would be a short night before going to work in the morning. Anissa breezed down the largely deserted streets and was within sight of her building, pulling up to the final traffic signal separating her from her bed. While she waited, she pushed the button on her visor and got the desired response as the door to the underground garage of her condo began to open. But before she could make the turn, an SUV behind her slammed into the rear end of her Audi.

"Shit," Anissa said to herself. *Probably a drunk on his way home.* As she stepped out of her car to examine the damage, she saw the other driver also exit his vehicle and began to move toward him. She looked at the blond man with the short haircut, who smiled strangely, holding one of his arms out toward her. By the time Anissa realized that the other driver was the man in the photos from Bob's house, her reaction was a half second too late. In an instant, the prick of two barbs dug into her chest, along with the sound of crackling as electricity flowed through her body, sending her into nothingness.

****

When Anissa regained consciousness, she was disoriented but recognized her underground garage as the man wrestled her out of the trunk of her vehicle, her hands zip-tied behind her.

"Let's go up to your condo and have a chat," he said with no emotion in his voice.

"Hey, asshole, you're in deep shit," she said. "You just carjacked a police officer."

"Yeah, I know. You're Detective Anissa Taylor," he replied. "Carjacking would only be an additional charge on top of something much worse. How much worse depends on you. Now, we have some urgent business to take care of." They got onto the elevator in the garage. "Looks like a nice place," the man said calmly. "What floor?"

"Three," she replied, leaning heavily against the wall of the lift.

"Anissa, you can make this easy on yourself. Just tell me. Where is the disc?" he demanded with an evil smile.

Confused by the question, she looked askance at her kidnapper and shook her head. "Disc? What disc? I don't know what you're talking about."

"Well, I guess we'll just have to see. By the way, are you doing okay? I mean with the Taser. It didn't burn you, did it?" he asked incongruously.

"No, I'm fine," she brusquely replied. "I just don't know anything about a disc."

"A friend of yours sent it to you. Bob. Bob Edwards."

Anissa's body noticeably stiffened at the mention of his name. "Why did you kill Bob?" she hissed angrily.

"I just told you. To find the goddamned disc." The man shook his head back and forth with each syllable, like a kid's gesture, as the elevator reached the third floor.

"Well . . . what's your name again?"

"You can call me Black," he replied. "Mr. Asa Black." *Not that it will matter much longer.*

"I assume you trailed me from the airport, so you know I've been gone for a couple of days. Have you checked my mail slot, genius?"

"Good point," he said. "What floor?"

"Back to the main level," Anissa responded, now having fully regathered her wits and trying to buy time for herself. She strained at the zip ties in hopes of pulling a hand free, but Black had cinched them tight. When she resigned herself to the idea that she couldn't make them budge, her brain searched for another means of escape. Anissa felt both her blood pressure and stress level rising as time seemed to be running out for her. She knew that a trip upstairs to the privacy of her condo would likely have been one way for her. The thought of what this animal had done to Bob sent a shiver up her spine, but also increased her resolve.

When the elevator doors opened, they found a maintenance person wearing a baseball cap and a grey jumpsuit just finishing up mopping the tile in the lobby. Black looked at Anissa and whispered in her ear, "Any shout from you and the cleaning guy buys it right here." Anissa and Black stepped out of the elevator, watching as the staff member slowly limped away down the hall. "Which way?" he asked.

With a tilt of her head to the left, Anissa quietly said, "There," gesturing toward a bank of brass mailboxes against the wall. "333. The key is on my ring. The small one. Take your disc and leave."

Black turned his attention to the slots, taking seconds to find her mailbox. Shuffling through the keys on her ring, he found the correct one and gave it a turn. However, before he could open the small metal door, Black's face and body slammed heavily into the wall before he slumped to the floor. Anissa had summoned every ounce of strength and got a short running start before launching her body shoulder first, strategically targeting Black's head and neck, delivering the blow with all the intensity she could muster. However, even though the man was briefly stunned, Anissa had landed on her side on the tile, unable to get up with her hands still bound. From where she lay, she began kicking frantically at the still-stunned Black while screaming for help. Black sat up, shook his head, spit some blood onto the floor, and quickly gathered himself. Now standing, he turned and delivered a series of heavy kicks to Anissa's side. "Shut up, bitch," he snarled. "You just found trouble."

With Anissa temporarily incapacitated, Black again turned toward the mailbox. Suddenly, the blade of a knife tore deep enough into his upper back to make him drop to his knees. Screaming, Black turned at the waist to see the maintenance person cut Anissa free using the still-bloody blade.

"Hey, fuckhead, you need to quit picking on defenseless women," said Savanna, pulling off her cap while brandishing her knife and dropping into a combat stance. Seeing the blade, Black slowly rose to his feet and instinctively reached around his back, drawing a handgun from a holster hidden under his jacket. But when he leveled his gun at the redhead, his groin caught fire as Anissa's foot got him flush from behind. The power behind the blow was enough to send Black's weapon skittering down the hall. Anissa slumped back to the floor, gasping for breath.

Battling to stay conscious, Black spit out a "Goddammit" as he tried to remain standing. Despite the surge of pain, he remained focused on Savanna. He pulled a switchblade from his back pocket and faced off with the woman, hand-to-hand, as the two circled each other, each looking for an advantage.

"Wow, another clean shot to your nuts," Savanna taunted. "You'll probably never be able to have kids now."

Enraged, Black charged Savanna, but she managed to sidestep him and slash deeply into his upper arm. Black turned, storming back at the woman with an overpowering series of wild swipes. Although she managed to counter and dodge several of the slashes, the final one cut through her jumpsuit and across her abdomen, deep enough to elicit a loud yelp, sending both her body and her knife to the floor. With Savanna disabled, Black turned his attention back to Anissa on the tile still writhing in pain. "I need that goddamned disc!" he yelled as he closed the distance to her with each step.

"Fuck you," said Anissa from her prone position, summoning her last ounce of energy to defend herself in what might be her final stand. But before Black could close the gap, Savanna ferociously reengaged in the fight, throwing herself on his back with a blood-curdling scream. She pummeled Black's wounded arm relentlessly with a series of blows, almost dropping him to the tile. Then, somehow, he managed to fling Savanna so that she bounced off the wall and onto the floor. With the tile covered in blood and the sound of sirens growing, Black cursed and staggered to the front entrance, holding his arm before making his escape.

Fully spent, Savanna watched the man's retreat before slowly pulling herself across the floor towards Anissa. "Are you alright?" she asked the detective.

"I think so, but my entire side is screaming," said Anissa, gritting her teeth.

"By the way, nice to meet you. I'm Savanna Smythe," she said as her eyes rolled into the back of her head and she passed out.

CHAPTER 25

Nowitzke arrived at the Hobart Thompson Memorial Hospital after Chief Clark had woken him from a dead sleep, telling the detective that Anissa and a second unidentified female had been attacked and were en route to the hospital. The chief explained to a relieved Nowitzke that none of Anissa's wounds were considered life-threatening. However, it was the final detail that caught the detective's attention. Both women had clearly identified their attacker as the blond buzzcut.

After processing the information from Chief Clark, the normally slow to wake detective bolted from his bed, startling Natalie, who had been sleeping beside him. Feeling a sudden burst of adrenaline, he jumped into an icy cold shower to hasten the waking process before pulling on a wrinkled collared shirt, jeans, and loafers and heading to the hospital.

A middle-aged nurse with short pearl grey hair wearing cranberry scrubs watched from behind her desk as the bull in the china shop that was Nowitzke entered the emergency room. After flashing his badge at the nurse, he began peppering the woman with questions. When he stopped to take a breath, the nurse took control, looking at him with both a level of confidence and calm that seemed to transfer to the police officer. "Please relax and take a seat, Detective. I was told to expect you. Both women arrived here safely and are currently being treated by the doctor on call."

"Can you tell me how they're doing?"

"Yes," said the nurse with a smile. "While I can't go into too much detail, one of the women suffered multiple broken bones, a concussion, numerous contusions, cuts, and abrasions. The other had similar injuries that also required multiple stitches. Nothing life-threatening for either. Both are doing fine, and you should be able to see them shortly. In the meantime, we have freshly brewed coffee and some cookies at the station in the corner." She pointed the direction. "Help yourself. Maybe you can talk with the other police officer who's already waiting in there."

Nowitzke breathed a tentative sigh of relief at the news but remained anxious to confirm for himself that his partner would be alright. He went to the coffee stand and picked up one of the paper cups, shaking his head at the size, which he judged to be close to a large shot glass. Filling his cup, he also snatched two chocolate chip cookies, immediately popping one into his mouth. When he turned the corner into the waiting room, he found Will Porter sitting by himself, staring blankly at a television featuring a late-night infomercial.

"Will?" said the detective in greeting but got no response. "Will?" Nowitzke repeated a little louder, rousing the other officer from his trance.

"Jesus, Chuck," replied Will. "I'm sorry. Isn't it terrible? Anissa was attacked on her way home from the airport tonight."

"What do you mean? Where?"

"From what I heard from the officer on scene, Anissa was outside her condo when someone rear-ended her. But the guy who hit her car zapped her with a stun gun, tried to kidnap her, and brought her into her building. Then there was a big fight between the attacker, Anissa, and another woman who just happened to be there."

Nowitzke shook his head. *A Good Samaritan? A woman who just happened to be there? In the middle of the night? Bullshit! There's more to the story.* "Any idea as to why Nis was attacked?"

"I don't know, but I don't think it was random," he replied. "Chuck, I just feel so . . . I don't know." Will put his face into his hands.

"I know you're friends with Anissa. The nurse on duty just told me that Anissa and whoever this other woman is are both hurting but are going to be fine," said Nowitzke. The detective sat down opposite Will and drank his coffee with one large slurp. "You know, Will, I think I owe you an apology."

Nowitzke's unexpected statement caused Will to look at him, eyes wide in surprise.

"I took another look at that domestic disturbance file when you were injured. You had a helluva wound. It was a bad situation, like a lot of those kinds of calls. I never gave you your due." Will could not hide the look of shock on his face as the detective continued, "I heard you had a serious knife wound. Very painful, from what I've been told. Have you recovered from your injuries?" he asked, sitting back in his chair.

"I'm not going to lie. I've still got issues with the whole situation, not the least of which is the ongoing pain from the injury," Will replied. "I also still have some nightmares, but I'm doing my best to put this behind me. It's given me pause, and I've spent a lot of time thinking about our little conversation from the other night. But thanks for asking." His face brightened.

Nowitzke nodded. "Will, can I ask you something about the Hecht case?"

"Of course."

"How well do you know Elliott Gordon? I mean, I'm trying to get a read on the guy. He seems cooperative and all, but . . ." Nowitzke trailed off, leaving Will to fill in the blank.

"I'm not sure I can help you. I only met the guy once at Ivy House on the night Senator Hecht was killed," replied Will, looking at his feet. "Sorry."

Nowitzke listened closely to Will's answer but was more intent on studying the man's face and demeanor as he talked. He recognized Will's tell but, more importantly, heard the lie. The stone-faced detective rose to refill his mini cup just as a young woman wearing a white coat over dark-blue scrubs entered the waiting area, a stethoscope around her neck.

"Detectives?" she called. "I'm Dr. Stacy Frazier." She reached over to shake the hands of both officers. Frazier had deep brown eyes, stylish shoulder-length hair, and a smile much too bright for the time of day as far as Nowitzke was concerned. "You've got some tough ladies in there," she concluded. "They each sustained significant injuries that we're treating, but they'll both fully recover with some time to heal. You can see both women shortly, but only for a limited time. I will be admitting each of them overnight for observation. Barring something unusual, they should be home by lunch tomorrow . . . I mean later today," she corrected as she looked down at her watch.

"Thanks, Doc," said the senior detective, exhaling loudly with relief. "I'm Detective Nowitzke. This is Detective Porter. Just to confirm, one of your patients is Anissa Taylor, correct?"

"Yes," said Frazier.

"Who's the other?"

"A feisty young woman named Savanna Smythe," offered the doctor. Nowitzke shook his head. *I should have known.*

"By the way, Ms. Smythe probably has the more significant of the injuries," said Frazier. A nurse approached the doctor from behind and whispered something into her ear. "Gentlemen, my associate tells me you can see both patients now. Through that door and turn right down the hall. Fifteen minutes tops," she warned before leaving the room.

Will glanced at Nowitzke and then down at his shoes. "I've got to go. I just needed to know that Anissa was okay. When Chief Clark called to tell me about the attack, well . . . I'm just happy she's fine," he stammered. "Got an early shift coming up." He stood and turned to leave.

"Are you alright?" Nowitzke asked. "Fifteen minutes. You heard the doc. Enough time to say 'hi' and 'bye' and we're out."

"Tell her that I'll catch her later," said Will, looking relieved yet downtrodden. When he reached the doorway, he turned back towards Nowitzke. "Hey, Chuck, watch your ass out there. Chief Clark told me the guy who attacked Anissa was the same one who went after the woman at the hotel. He's still out there."

Nowitzke was puzzled at Will's comment. "You too," he finally responded blankly.

"Thanks again for asking about how I've been doing. It means a lot," Will said, then disappeared out the automatic doors.

Nowitzke turned down the hall, trying to remember Frazier's directions to the treatment room before hearing the sound of women cackling. He found both Anissa and Savanna relaxing on matching beds, waiting to be transported to private rooms for the rest of the evening. As far as he could tell, they had been joking, doing their best to make light of the situation by trying to make the other laugh, which coincided with more than a wince of pain. Upon seeing them, it was immediately clear to Nowitzke that each woman was heavily medicated.

However, the laughter quickly devolved into tears when Anissa saw Nowitzke enter the room. "How are ya, Nis?" he asked, reaching to hug his partner, who was sitting up on her bed.

"I've been better." Anissa wiped her eyes, any emotion quickly passing. "The bastard broke five of my ribs, which makes breathing painful. Got some scrapes and bruises. Probably some other minor injuries I won't feel until morning." Then, taking a deep breath, she continued, "It was him, Chuck . . . the guy who killed Bob and attacked Savanna here."

"Yeah, I heard." Nowitzke turned to see the auburn-haired woman smiling at him, fighting through whatever pain she was feeling. From what he could see, Savanna's body had added new bruises to those earned from her first go-around. And even though she was confined to a bed, any movement was done gingerly, protecting wounds that weren't exposed. Beyond that, she looked spent.

"What? No hug, Detective? Bring it in here, big guy," said Savanna.

"How are you?" he asked, leaning into the woman, who gave him as big a bear hug as she could muster.

"I'll live. My second big fight with this dickhead in a week, and I'm 2–0. He slashed me across the midsection. Thank God he didn't drive a blade into me, but I've got more stitches than I can count. Of course, this had to happen during the height of bikini season," she said, sending Anissa into a mix of laughter and pain. "We need to talk tomorrow, the three of us. Supposedly, I'll be out by late morning," she concluded as an orderly entered the room.

"Ms. Smythe," called the young man wearing green scrubs.

"Yeah, that's me," Savanna replied, holding up a heavily taped arm with tubes running from the back of her hand to a stainless-steel IV stand behind her. "Oh, and based on the second attack, you can guess what kind of Yelp review I'll be giving the greater Appleton area." She looked at Nowitzke as she was wheeled from the room. "You can tell the chamber of commerce people that it won't be five stars, Chuckles!" yelled Savanna loudly from down the hall, sending Anissa into stitches once more.

"Sorry, Chuck. I'm sure it's the morphine talking," said Anissa, embarrassed for her new friend. "Maybe it's just the painkillers, but everything seems funnier." She stifled her own laugh.

They were alone briefly, but only had moments to talk before Dr. Frazier would return and shoo Nowitzke away. "You sure you're okay?" he asked Anissa, taking her hand.

"Yeah," she meekly answered, her eyes half-closed as if she were on low battery.

"What happened?"

Realizing she might only have seconds before losing consciousness, either from her injuries or from whatever drugs the hospital staff had given her, Anissa had a brain dump. "I was asleep at the switch on this," she said, shaking her head. "I mean, I never felt this attack coming. It happened at the traffic light right outside my place. I thought a drunk had nailed my car from behind until I saw his face. Before I could react, he hit me with the Taser. I keep wondering how he found me. All I can figure is that he must have tracked me from the airport. Told me his name . . . Asa Black. And he kept asking me about a disc of some sort. Something from Bob Edwards? It must have been what Black was looking for when he tore up Bob's place. Anyway, I steered Black to my mailbox. I'm not sure he ever got the chance to look before

WrestleMania got started. Look in my purse and find my keys, Chuck. You need to check out my mailbox." The pace of Anissa's speech was slowing to half its normal speed. "Hey, would you mind calling my dad?" she asked from her haze. "Just not until morning. You know the old saying about nothing good happening after midnight."

The same orderly who had taken Savanna to her room returned for Anissa. "We need to talk about Canada tomorrow too," Nowitzke said.

"Are you ready to get to your room, ma'am?" asked the orderly, drawing a brief sneer from the fading Anissa, who detested the term when applied to her.

"One last thing, Chuck. I don't know what you think about her, but Savanna saved my life. No doubt about it. She took a beating but she was so damn ferocious." Anissa closed her eyes as sleep overtook her.

"We'll take good care of her, sir," the orderly said to Nowitzke. The detective leaned over and gently kissed Anissa on the forehead.

Nowitzke was now alone and wide awake. It would not be dawn for several hours. A part of him mused that he had been up at this hour many times before, but he was generally on his way home rather than starting his day. He resolved to find someplace that sold coffee. A *full-size* coffee, or three, fuel for the next several hours, which would include a visit to Anissa's condominium complex. Plodding back through the deserted hospital, he had a thought upon seeing the admitting nurse in the cranberry scrubs. "Ma'am, I'm looking for a male . . . muscular . . . blond crewcut."

"Aren't we all?" The nurse smiled.

"The guy I'm looking for may have come here looking for treatment for wounds from a fight. Knife wounds, bruises . . ."

"You mean the jerk who beat up your friends?" asked the nurse. "Unfortunately, no. I've been here for several hours, and aside from the ladies, it's been a quiet night. But if he comes in here, how do I get in touch with you?"

"First, call 9-1-1," said Nowitzke. "But here's my card."

The Escort balked briefly before Nowitzke hit the streets on a coffee mission. Finding an open Dunkin' Donuts, he turned into the drive-thru, emerging on the other side with two large coffees and a pair of cream-filled long johns. By the time the detective arrived at Anissa's condo, he had managed several dribbles of coffee down his shirt. He stepped out of his vehicle in front of the building, his breath visible in the cool early-morning air, and held Anissa's electronic key up to the reader near the oversized main entrance doors. Hearing a buzz and the click of the lock, the detective entered the eerily quiet lobby.

For whatever reason, yellow police tape was still up, cordoning off an area where the detective presumed the brawl had taken place. Ducking under the tape, he quickly located a bank of mailboxes adjacent to the scene. Nowitzke clumsily swapped his coffee and keys between hands, moving the latter to his right. After inserting the smallest key on the ring into the lock, he opened the gold-plated door. Inside was a handful of pieces of mail: a health magazine, what looked like a couple of bills, and some junk mail in the form of clothing catalogs. But there was no disc or any packaging that looked like it held a disc. Nowitzke jammed his fleshy hand into the empty box as far as he could, but still felt nothing. Using the flashlight app on his phone, he peered into the opening, confirming the mail slot was now empty.

Sitting on a designer metal bench, Nowitzke needed a moment to think. He sipped his coffee, contemplating the steam rising through the opening in the plastic cover. *Where's this supposed disc? What am I missing?* Drawing a blank, he replaced Anissa's mail in the box for her to find later.

As he closed and locked the door, he was startled by a voice behind him.

"You know that it's illegal to tamper with the U.S. mail, Detective Nowitzke."

Turning, the detective came face-to-face with the blond crewcut, who was crouching with a handgun leveled at him. "How do you know me, Mr. Black?"

"Your reputation precedes you," Black said, nodding. "Kudos on learning my name. It was my mistake to tell Ms. Taylor."

"Unfortunately, your reputation is known too, dickhead. You've had your hands full trying to beat up a pair of women, but got your ass kicked instead." Nowitzke chuckled. "By the way, you're bleeding through your shirt," he added, searching for any potential edge. "My advice is not to fuck with me."

"I don't plan on it. I see you didn't find my disc in Taylor's box. That was my first order of business. Looks like I'll just have to move on to plan B of my agenda," replied Black, briefly lowering his gun.

"What's on this disc that's so important?" asked Nowitzke, subtly moving closer to Black while buying time for himself.

"You're never going to know." Black raised his pistol, taking aim at the detective's center mass.

"Murdering a police officer gets you life in prison in Wisconsin," Nowitzke retorted, still inching imperceptibly toward the armed man. "But you look like a guy who might enjoy years of anal sex in the slammer. By the way, even a rookie prosecutor in the DA's office should have no problem convicting you with all the cameras here in the lobby." He pointed to the upper corners of the room to his left and right. When he saw Black momentarily break concentration with a glance upward, the detective went with an all-or-nothing move. On a good day, Nowitzke's typical speed was considered a slow lumber. However, Black was surprised and dismayed at the quickness and agility of the big man, who was suddenly upon him. Nowitzke threw what was left of his hot coffee into Black's face, the move yielding a loud scream that echoed in the entryway. The sound of Black's yell was rivaled only by the discharge of his gun. Nonetheless, Nowitzke got close enough to throw a haymaker with his right hand, catching the blond's jaw hard enough to make him drop his weapon and knock him flat on his back. Having disarmed the man, Nowitzke kicked the gun, sending it across the lobby floor before jumping on top of Black with his full weight and hammering the man's injured arm mercilessly, evoking even more shrieks and cries. Now in control, Nowitzke reached behind his back to grab his handcuffs, but then everything faded to black.

CHAPTER 26

When he regained consciousness, Nowitzke was staring into the soft eyes of Dr. Stacy Frazier. "Where am I?" he asked gruffly. "What time is it?"

"At Hobart Thompson Hospital. 9:05 a.m. You're yet another casualty brought in by ambulance from Ms. Taylor's condo. Must be a rough place," she offered sarcastically. "You were lucky, Detective."

"Yeah, I feel like I just won the lottery," he said groggily.

"You sustained a pass-through gunshot wound to your left shoulder. If the bullet had moved a millimeter this way or that, it would have been considerably worse, especially since you were on the floor bleeding for God knows how long before a security guard found you. You lost a lot of blood, but you also have some friends who were willing to lend a hand," concluded Frazier.

As he became more aware, Nowitzke realized he was surrounded. In a good way. Standing at the foot of the bed were Anissa, Savanna, Natalie, and Miss Alma. "We each gave a pint, Chuck," offered Miss Alma, stepping forward and taking his hand.

"Thanks," he rasped in a tired voice.

"How *are* you feeling?" asked Anissa on behalf of the group.

"Beat." Nowitzke looked at Savanna. "I won't be giving the chamber of commerce five stars on my review either."

"Jeez, did I actually say that?" asked the redhead with an embarrassed look. "I thought I dreamed it."

"What about Black? Where is he?" Nowitzke questioned.

"He got away," said Anissa. "I went back and watched the video from the lobby. Looks like you finished some of the work that Savanna started. Black was hurting pretty bad. His arm was hanging weirdly when he hit the push bar on the front door."

"Any idea how he got into your building in the first place?"

"There are a lot of gaps in security at the complex. I'll be taking it up with the management."

Nowitzke turned to Frazier. "When can I get out of here?" he asked as he tried to slide his feet over the side of the bed, attempting to stand but feeling a wave of pain run through his body instead. Natalie stepped forward and put her hand on his chest to deter him.

"What's the rush?" said the doctor, getting a scowl from her patient in return. "Tomorrow, maybe. A couple of days most likely. That's assuming you're a good boy and don't do anything stupid that might tear out the stitches I put in you." Then, looking around the room, Frazier declared, "The show is over! My patient needs his rest."

Natalie walked around the edge of the hospital bed and squeezed Nowitzke's hand. "Please get some sleep. You know, when they told me you were shot, I was afraid I was going to lose you," she said, her eyes welling up. "I can guess you don't like to follow directions, but you must listen to your doctor. I'll see you tomorrow." She leaned over and kissed him on the lips. "I have to get Miss Alma home. Please take good care of him," she said to Frazier.

"Looks like we'll have to postpone our meeting," said Nowitzke, looking at Anissa and Savanna. "By the way, there was no disc in your mailbox, Nis."

"Don't worry about it. We'll figure it out," replied Anissa reassuringly as she and Savanna moved toward the door.

Finally, Miss Alma sidled up to Nowitzke. "See this controller attached to the bed?" she asked in a whisper. "If you push this button, a nurse will come running. I found out when I was a patient here. They'll bring you food or whatever you want. Chicken parmesan if you're still around for lunch. I checked. Also, if you ask nicely, a handsome young man will come and give you a sponge bath," she concluded, her eyes wide open, giving him a knowing nod.

"Just what I need, Miss Alma," he replied before drifting off.

****

When Nowitzke woke for the second time that day, the sun was fading. After he got his bearings, he remembered he was at the hospital. The lights were subdued, and it was quiet, the only sound being the unintelligible dialogue from a television in the background. Scanning his room, the detective found Anissa sitting next to his bed, her head buried in the same magazine that he had found in her mailbox earlier. He assumed she had been discharged since she was now wearing a red sweater and jeans. Savanna was lounging in a chair on his other side, watching the cop drama on TV, wearing a well-worn Rush t-shirt and shorts.

"What time is it?" croaked Nowitzke. He grabbed the oversized water jug sitting on the tray over his bed and took a healthy drink. Both women jumped to their feet upon hearing his voice.

"Around 10:00 p.m.," Anissa offered. "You've been out for hours, Chuck. Are you up for a conversation?"

"Yeah," said the senior officer, pushing a button on the bed controller to raise his upper body. "Looks like you're both back up to snuff," he observed. "Bring me up to date."

"Well, first of all, the two of us went back to my condo and looked in my mailbox," said Anissa, nodding toward Savanna. "It held my normal mail, but no disc, which you had already told us. Then we went into my place on the off chance that a package was somehow slipped under my door. But, once again . . . nothing. We even made a run to the office to check my desk but came up empty there too. If there is a package coming to me, I have no idea where it is," she concluded.

Nowitzke's eyes blinked heavily. "You said that you thought Black must have picked you up on your way home from the airport. How could he have known you were flying into Appleton?"

"I have no idea. I've been racking my brain all day, but haven't come up with a good answer," Anissa replied.

Both officers turned to look at Savanna, who shrugged. "You were in Anissa's building and saved the day," said Nowitzke. "How did you happen to be there?"

"Chuck, I told you the other day that I was concerned for Anissa's safety after showing you the photos of Black watching her and Will."

"Wait a second . . ." Anissa sat upright, jumping back into the conversation. "The asshole was tailing us?" she asked Savanna.

"Yeah. You had just wrapped up your investigation of the dead guy who was in the river, after his girlfriend OD'd. Black was scary close. It certainly wasn't by chance," she said. She looked directly at Nowitzke. "Anyway, I decided I would quietly follow Anissa when she returned home from her trip."

"How did you figure out Anissa's travel plans?" asked the senior detective.

"You pretty much told me. At our meeting, you casually mentioned that she was out of town on business. I assumed that meant she was flying. I kind of staked out the airport and waited," she replied contritely. "But, when I got there, guess who was the first person I saw? Mr. Asa Fucking Black," Savanna added. "I didn't know which airline you were flying or even where you were coming from. The good news is that the Appleton airport is small and there isn't a high volume of traffic. I stayed in the shadows watching Black as he waited for Anissa.

"When it got down to the last couple of flights for the day, I went out to the parking lot so I could follow you from there. Just as I thought, Black was behind you when you stepped out of the doors," she told Anissa. "When you left the parking lot, he followed you, and I trailed. I knew your address, so I sped through town, trying to get to your building before you and Black did. When I got there, I parked behind the condo, jimmied a lock, and waited for you in the lobby disguised as a maintenance person. Sorry that I missed all the drama out in front of your building."

Both detectives cocked their heads, looking at Savanna. "Who are you?" they asked simultaneously.

Savanna rose from her chair. "Chuck, I told you I'm a tourist."

"Enough with the bullshit," spouted Nowitzke loudly, shaking his head. "I need a better answer."

Savanna took a deep breath. "Okay, I'm a tourist who also happens to be a Canadian police officer," she said, pulling a badge from her back pocket. "Royal Canadian Mounted Police. RCMP for short. I'm a staff sergeant with O Division in the London, Ontario office." She produced a business card for each detective.

"You know, I had a feeling that you had a law enforcement background of some sort," Nowitzke replied.

"What gave it away?"

"Couple things. Just the way you handle yourself screams cop. One of the biggest things for me, though, was that you didn't flinch when I showed you the death photos of Bob Edwards," said Nowitzke. "I didn't realize the RCMP trained people to be so rough and tough."

"Yeah, well, everyone thinks Canadians are 'nice,'" she explained, using her fingers to make air quotes. "We have our share of criminals, so our team needs to be prepared to handle themselves."

"No shit!" marveled Anissa. "Though you seemed to crank it up a level or two with your knife against Black in the lobby."

"I guess my background is a little amped up too. Before I joined RCMP, I was with Canadian Armed Forces . . . Infantry."

"Infantry? You mean out in the field, slogging it out with the enemy . . . living in a hole for days or weeks at a time?" asked Nowitzke.

"Yeah," Savanna responded casually. "I'm one of a handful of women who made the grade in Infantry. Did two tours in Afghanistan. And I always carry my jump knife, standard issue to the CAF for decades." She took the eight-inch stainless-steel knife from her purse, passing it to Anissa, who handed it to Nowitzke for a look. "We trained extensively on hand-to-hand combat," she concluded.

Nowitzke passed the knife back to Savanna. "How are you involved with this investigation?" he asked.

"I told you I'm not," answered the redhead. "I made the mistake of going to Hecht's fundraiser, which got me into someone's crosshairs. Whose, I've got no idea." She shook her head. "I told you about the server on the lower level of Hawkins' house. The real question is who's this Black guy? He attacked me. He went after Anissa. He even had the balls to throw down with you, Chuck. Who's next, and why?"

"He's also the prime suspect in the Edwards homicide," added Anissa.

"Listen, guys, I'd love to help you get this bastard . . . if you'll let me. Part of the RCMP's role is to preserve the peace and uphold the law. For me, the motto isn't restricted by geography. My impression is we need to have a serious discussion with Will Porter too. My gut tells me that something's up with the guy."

"Why?" asked Anissa.

"How many people knew you were out of town on business, Anissa? Chuck here, me by accident, the airline, and who else? Could Will have found out and passed the word along to Black?"

"Whoa!" Anissa yelled, shaking her head violently. "Are you saying Will is working with Black?"

"Not necessarily, but what are the odds of Black showing up at the airport looking for you? I told Chuck that I spotted Will at the Orchard Inn just before I was attacked. How could Black have found me without some help?"

"Nis, I did some follow-up," added Nowitzke, chiming in. "Will talked with our traffic people. He was trying to find Savanna the day after Hecht died. He was downstairs just before I showed up and asked the same questions I did. You know Officer Fischer?"

"Colby?"

"Yeah. She confirmed it for me."

"Maybe Will was just trying to show some initiative," said Anissa.

"Maybe," Nowitzke conceded. "But it wasn't his case, and he never passed the info on to me. And there's more." He looked at Savanna to fill in the gap.

Savanna turned to Anissa. "I think the man's got a drug problem. I know he was seriously injured. I pretty much watched as he scored something from some low-life dealer when he was at my hotel. My guess is he's still struggling with pain."

"Will told me he was," added Nowitzke. "Even to the point of looking into a career change. Nis, I know he's your friend, but I'm leaning towards believing Savanna. You know, Will was in the waiting room at the hospital this morning when you were being treated."

"He was? Why didn't he stop by?" she asked.

"I have no idea. I thought it was strange. He left after the doc said you could have visitors. I could see that he was relieved when they said you would be okay, but he also looked guilty as hell of something. Then, he out-and-out lied to me. Savanna had shown me a photo of Will having a drink with Elliott Gordon, so I asked Will how well he knew the man. He said he'd only met him once, on the night of the senator's death."

"What does Elliott Gordon have to do with anything?" asked Anissa.

"Don't know. We need to do some checking. Maybe have a conversation with Brad Hawkins," Nowitzke offered.

"One last item," said Savanna. "On the night I took the photos of Will with Elliott, something else happened. Elliott passed Will an envelope. I don't know what was in it, but I can only assume it was cash. Will took the envelope and put it in his pocket. While they were talking, Black came into the place and took a seat well away from them. Then, when Will left, Black picked up his drink and moved to sit with Elliott for a short conversation."

"When did that take place?" asked Nowitzke incredulously.

Savanna looked at Anissa. "The night before you got home from your trip. Maybe Will told Elliott, who then gave your travel info to Black?" she surmised.

Anissa said nothing, but stood and walked to the window, gazing out at the lights in the adjacent buildings, thinking. After several minutes, her head dropped. "I guess we need to talk with Will too."

"We can figure that part out tomorrow when I get out of here." Nowitzke groaned in his bed as he shifted to face Savanna. "Would you mind stepping out of the room? I need to talk with Anissa about another case."

"Sure. Call me when you want to talk. You both need to watch your asses. Black might be wounded, but he's still out there," she said as she left the room, closing the door behind her.

"Sandy Hawkins is dead," Anissa blurted out as plainly as she could. "Apparently, Sandy moved to Canada, went to college and medical school, got married to another doctor, had a couple of kids, and somewhere along the way became Dr. Amanda Hartsell. She and her husband, Alex, were pillars of the Banff community until they both died in a house fire. The cause was not suspicious," she added, looking at her partner, defeating his next question.

"Are you absolutely sure?" asked the senior detective.

"The local police took the photo of Sandy we sent and ran it through some sort of software that ages people. Its primary purpose is to deter young smokers," she offered as an aside, "but it's an incredible tool for a long-term missing persons case. Anyway, my contact at RCMP shared the aged photos of Sandy, sending them to several people in the area. He got a hit almost immediately at the local hospital. Hartsell's boss, the administrator there, swore on a stack of Bibles that it was Sandy. No doubt. No hesitation."

"Can we check Sandy's DNA?"

"No, she was cremated with her husband."

Nowitzke stroked his beard for a moment, thinking. "Did Hartsell have any relatives living in the Banff area?"

"None. As I said, she had two kids . . ." She removed a portfolio from her bag to check her notes. "Yes, a girl and a boy. The locals I spoke with told me that no one there ever really knew the kids. Apparently, they were older when the accident happened and living east, somewhere in Toronto."

"Then who sent us the file on McClary postmarked in Banff?" asked Nowitzke.

Anissa shrugged. "I've got no idea."

"Shit," Nowitzke replied, now feeling fully spent. "At least we have a pretext to talk with Brad. I'd also like to give the chief a heads-up about Sandy Hawkins beforehand." Nowitzke studied Anissa's body language during a long, awkward pause between them. "You okay? I mean, with the whole Will thing?"

"No, of course not. I'm trying to keep an open mind, hoping there's a logical explanation. Maybe I'll come up with one by tomorrow. Sleep well," she said dejectedly as she left for the door.

CHAPTER 27

Nowitzke was discharged from the hospital late the following morning. Anissa judged that her boss, a slow mover at best, had somehow managed to find an even lower gear as she watched him cautiously slog down the short walk to her waiting vehicle in the patient pickup zone. "Thanks, Nis. How's your morning going?" he groaned, gently entering the Audi.

"Will's disappeared," she replied point-blank even before she left the curb. "He didn't show up for work and never called in. I was up all night grinding away to come up with a reason for his behavior, following our discussion with Savanna. You know, waiting to confront him and then deciding how I could gauge whether he was telling the truth." She sighed, her eyes fixed on the road. "Without any explanation from him, I'm coming to the same conclusion as you that Will might be playing for the other team, whoever that is."

Nowitzke shifted in his seat, hoping to find a more comfortable position. "Let's swing by his apartment and see if he's there."

"Great minds, Chuck. I checked his address before I left the office to pick you up, and that's where we're headed. You don't think Black might have turned on him like Bob, do you?"

"Who knows? Put your bubble on the dashboard to clear the way," said Nowitzke as Anissa picked up speed.

The address was a modest, well-kept brick four-plex in the downtown area. From the street, nothing looked amiss. A couple of kids were playing basketball in the parking lot, taking advantage of the weather. A garbage truck was working its route. A young woman with her hair in a ponytail and wearing a tank top and cut-off jean shorts was watering a window box of colorful impatiens.

"Miss!" called out Nowitzke after delicately righting himself from the car. "Does a Will Porter live here?"

The woman turned her head toward the detective but continued to water her flowers. "Yes. Apartment A on the first floor. We're neighbors. Who are you?"

"Detectives Taylor and Nowitzke," announced Anissa, holding up her badge. "And you are?"

"Heather Nystrom," she replied, turning off the spigot on the hose and pivoting towards the officers. "Isn't Will a cop too?"

Nowitzke moved across the lawn towards her. "Yeah, he is. When did you see him last?"

"A day or so ago. He was finishing his laundry downstairs just as I was starting mine."

"Did you talk with him?" asked Anissa.

"I guess. It was only a couple of minutes, maybe. Chitchat, mostly stupid stuff, you know . . . like the weather. That kind of thing," she replied with a growing look of concern on her face. "Is Will okay?"

"How well do you know Will?" Nowitzke probed, dodging the woman's question.

"We're just friends, I guess, maybe more like acquaintances. We see each other in passing," offered Heather. "He's a good-looking guy. I've been kind of hoping that he would ask me out, but he hasn't. I read online that he was hurt a couple of months ago while making an arrest. He's kept to himself quite a bit since then. Have you checked his apartment?"

"That's our next step," replied Anissa. "If you see Will, please let us know." Each officer handed Heather a business card. With that, she turned mindlessly back to watering her flowers as the detectives stepped into the small lobby of the building.

The interior of the place matched what they had seen outside.

There was new paint on the walls, which held artwork that was a step up from the typical institutional pieces found in some apartment buildings. From the looks of it, the deep-brown carpeting had been recently replaced as well. Anissa knocked on the heavy door of Apartment A and waited a few moments. As she was about to try again, Heather entered the building.

"Oh, by the way, Will's car is gone," she said, opening her door down the hall. "I just checked his space out back, and it was empty."

"Do you have a manager on premises?" asked Anissa.

"No, but the owner is pretty responsive when there's a problem. I have his number in my apartment if you'd like me to get it for you."

"Thanks, but we've got a couple other places to check out in the meantime," Anissa replied.

Heather smiled and stepped into her unit, closing the door behind her.

"What do you want to do?" asked Nowitzke as Anissa glanced at his pocket, her intention registering with him. He sighed. "Then stand over here to block Heather in case she comes back into the hall." Using his partner as a screen, he took a lockpick from his pocket and opened the door.

Upon entering Will's apartment, nothing jumped out at either officer. Will's place was just as Nowitzke had imagined: immaculate. Spotless, in fact. The exact opposite of his own apartment. As the officers moved from room to room, they saw no dirty dishes, a clean bathroom, and meticulously ironed shirts still hanging in the closet next to pressed suits. A place for everything, and everything in its place. Nothing looked missing in the form of clothes or suitcases that would suggest the man had left hastily. "Maybe something just came up?" offered the senior detective.

"Wow, I thought I was particular, but this guy puts me to shame," Anissa concluded, still glancing around. "I guess we'll wait for him to call us. He hasn't been gone even a day. But the timing on this and recent history makes me nervous," she explained. "If we don't hear from him by tomorrow, we can file a report."

****

An hour later, Anissa briefed Chief Clark regarding her trip to Canada, with Nowitzke observing. "Has anyone told Brad Hawkins yet?" asked Marcus after Anissa finished.

"No," Nowitzke replied. "We thought we should talk with you first. Closing a missing persons case after so long, particularly one involving his sister, might get you a call from him. We wanted to give you some advance notice on this is all. By the way, Anissa did some outstanding investigative work on her trip."

"Actually, RCMP did most of the heavy lifting," conceded Anissa.

"Is there any doubt in your mind that Sandy Hawkins died as Amanda Hartsell?" asked Marcus.

She shook her head without any emotion. "None."

"Then talk with Brad and close the file. Nice work."

As they walked back to their respective offices, Nowitzke offered to contact Brad. "Haven't talked to my buddy in a couple of days," he said derisively. "Just give me a minute to clear out my voicemail first."

Next to the stack of new mail, the message alert on Nowitzke's phone blinked at him even before he flipped on the lights. Although he expected more than just two messages, each intrigued him for different reasons.

The first was from Brad.

"Chuck, this is Brad Hawkins. I just received a package in the mail. It's disturbing to say the least. Call me as soon as possible. I've got a problem."

Nowitzke returned Hawkins' call but got an answering machine and left a message in kind.

The second voicemail was from Kelsie Cantrell-Holland. She was not specific about the reason for her call, asking only that Nowitzke contact her. He dialed her number but got a bad connection to her cell.

"Hello . . . would you . . . farm today . . . in an hour or so? . . . remembered something . . ." was all Nowitzke heard before the call dropped altogether. He tried to call her back but was unable to reconnect. Even though he was already worn-out, he gave a shout-out to Anissa.

"Nis, I just had half of a garbled conversation with Kelsie Cantrell. The gist of it was that she remembered something and wondered if we could go back to the farm. Like now. From there, I need a ride back to your place. Unless it's been stolen or the management of your building had it towed, my car's still sitting there?"

Anissa appeared at his door. "Who would steal your old Escort, Chuck?" she said with a smirk. "Any luck in connecting with Hawkins?"

"No. Had to leave him a message. He left me a voicemail earlier saying he just received a package and was 'disturbed' by it but left no details."

****

Pulling onto the gravel road leading to Kelsie's farmhouse, Anissa shook her head. "You know, I just got my car washed this morning. Whatever she has better be something worthwhile."

The Audi came to rest in a cloud of dust under the large oak in the yard. Nowitzke creaked slowly and carefully from the low-slung car as the rusty screen door opened and Kelsie poked her head out. Wearing a grubbier version of her original uniform, she yelled to the detectives, "Wasn't sure whether you got my message or not! I've had a problem with my cell lately. Come on in. Got some coffee brewing and some fresh blueberry muffins just coming out of the oven."

They sat at the same gummy kitchen table after Anissa and Nowitzke each fruitlessly searched to find a clean chair. Kelsie fretted as she poured coffee and served the muffins. "I hope I didn't get you both out here for nothing. I haven't been able to sleep much lately since your first visit. I keep thinking about Sandy." Sitting across from Anissa, Kelsie saw the officer's expression change at the mention of her friend's name. "What? Something's happened?"

Anissa and Nowitzke exchanged glances before he nodded, giving her the go-ahead. "Sandy's dead, Kelsie," said Anissa impassively.

Kelsie froze, tears instantly forming as she went ashen. "Oh God," she cried. "When? How?"

Nowitzke saw a box of tissues on the counter and passed them to Kelsie as Anissa outlined what she had learned in Canada. Kelsie paid close attention and asked questions during her interchange with the detective. "A house fire? How weird is that?" she asked ironically as they sat in a house that looked like a tinderbox. When Anissa finished her story, Kelsie stood solemnly and excused herself to go to the bathroom while Nowitzke buttered a second muffin.

Five minutes later, Kelsie returned and sat back down, recomposed. "Well, by the sounds of it, at least Sandy had a good life. A doctor . . . wow. Helping other people. Kids, no less," she said impassively, reflecting on her friend while staring at the wall right through Anissa. She poured herself another cup of coffee and added, "Thank you. At least now I know."

Nowitzke felt the pull of his pants sticking to the chair as he shifted his body. "You left me a message?" he asked awkwardly, trying to change subjects.

"Oh, yeah. You know, thirty years is a long time, and I think most people only remember the good about others. Especially when you find out they're gone. Detective Taylor, you asked me before if Sandy had any boyfriends. I think I told you she didn't have any. But after tossing and turning for the last several nights, I remembered someone who had the serious hots for her. A decent-looking guy. They started off as friends, then quickly became an item. Then they were on-again, off-again several times," she added, sipping her coffee. "When they were together, they were a cute couple. But when things were not so good, the guy was a total jerk and started spreading vicious rumors about Sandy. I mean just terrible things. Stuff like Sandy had been raped . . . and that she loved it. That she was a slut." Kelsie's jaw tightened as she uttered the words. "Thank God it was near the end of our senior year and their relationship didn't last long. Sandy deserved better. Years later, I heard the bozo died, and I couldn't help but think good riddance."

"What was the guy's name?" asked Nowitzke.

"Yeah, see, that's been the tough part. You know, trying to remember a name I thought I'd erased from my brain. Then last night it came to me. Dan Warren."

Anissa and Nowitzke swapped looks, recognizing the name from their conversation with Anne Tucker. "You said you think he's dead?" Anissa probed.

"I think so. I could have sworn I read it in the newspaper years ago. He had moved away from the area. My brain says Oregon, but it was somewhere out west. I think Dan still has some family living in Neenah, just down the road. You might be able to track someone down there, if you're interested in finding out more about him," she offered.

"Kelsie, you were Sandy's best friend. What was your opinion of the rumors?" asked Nowitzke.

"They were a bunch of crap!" Kelsie said defensively, her voice rising. "Sandy had no dark side, and she wasn't a slut. Like I said, she had this one boyfriend during the entire time I knew her. I thought the rumors were just that. In fact, if anyone asked me about it back then, I'd have slapped them for all I was worth," she added, ending the discussion.

****

Kelsie waved from the front porch of her home as the detectives left the yard. "Nis, can you get Natalie on the phone?" asked Nowitzke.

Anissa scanned the numbers on the touch screen of the car and pressed the dial button. "Public library, Natalie Alvera," she answered in a husky tone.

"Hi, Natalie, it's me, and I'm in the car with Anissa. Hey, can you go into your archives again and look up the name Dan Warren for me? We just talked to someone who told us the guy had a relationship with Sandy Hawkins."

"The woman Anissa went to Banff to find?"

"Yeah. The weird thing is that the man's name came up when we were interviewing the wife of Myles Tucker, number three in your program, if you're keeping score."

"That's not very nice, Chuck," replied Natalie, earning a silent smile from Anissa.

Nowitzke ignored the comment. "Anyway, this Warren guy was supposedly from the area, and some of his family might still be here. He died a while back, but I've got no other details. You know how sometimes a family posts an obituary in a local paper to announce what happened even if the person doesn't live there anymore? Well, I'm wondering if that was the case here."

"It's going to cost you big-time."

"Add it to my tab."

"I'll see what I can do," she said, signing off.

Anissa let a minute pass before speaking. "Looks like your relationship with Natalie is heating up," she said, shooting a comment across Nowitzke's bow.

"Yeah," he replied, surprising Anissa with any kind of response. "Gorgeous, smart, sexy . . . I'm still confused about what she sees in me. Sometimes I think things with her are going almost too good. You know I don't have much of a track record with relationships. Things always seems to get in the way. Mostly me, I guess, doing something to mess things up, but I could see myself settling down with her. Natalie is so different from my first two felonies. Maybe the third time *is* the charm?" Nowitzke mused. "At least once her divorce is final. Who knows?"

CHAPTER 28

Anissa could see the Escort still positioned in front of the building where Nowitzke had left it. After parking in one of the many open guest spots, she tried to help her boss out of the sports car. However, the maneuver was more complicated than she had bargained for, for a couple of reasons. First, she was also nursing an injury, so any strain on her body was still painful. Nowitzke's body had tightened up as the end of the day approached, his pain level pushing the envelope. The more practical issue was that there were only so many places she could or would grab the large man to help him stand, making any help awkward at best.

In a delicate dance, Anissa finally wrangled the man from the car. The senior detective was standing, but stiff. "Listen, Chuck, you shouldn't be driving considering how you're feeling," she said, assuming she would be picking a fight. However, Nowitzke didn't object. "Let me call Natalie back. She can Uber over here so we can get your car home."

Anissa made the call, but Natalie wouldn't get off work for at least another hour. "Let's go up to my place so you can relax in the meantime," she offered. "I'm pretty sure I've got a scotch upstairs that will help take the edge off."

Nowitzke grunted a "Yeah," and they moved in slow motion towards the front door, with Anissa holding his arm. "Nis, don't hurt yourself. You're still smarting too."

After making it through the front door, Anissa guided Nowitzke to the same bench where he had sat on the night when he and Black had gone toe to toe. As she checked her mailbox, a smallish, fussy-looking man with slick, black hair and a Hitler-like mustache snuck up on her from behind. One Salvatore Montgomery, building manager.

"Ms. Taylor, Ms. Taylor," he said in a puckish manner, trying to get her attention.

Anissa recognized the voice immediately without needing to turn around. *Shit, he's going to yell at me about my car parked out front.* But she was shocked when he didn't.

"Ms. Taylor, I need to apologize to you. We've had some personnel issues in our front office as of late. Several episodes of malfeasance, shenanigans, and sloth on the part of a member of my administrative team. I had to let the man go, with the blessing and support of our condominium leadership team and, of course, our attorney," Montgomery said with some zest in his voice. "Were you by chance expecting a package? We received something too large for your box, and our employee didn't follow proper procedure by providing you with a notice that we were holding it."

"How long has it been here?"

"A couple of days. When I discovered it, I believe you were away from home. But I personally held it for safekeeping in my office under lock and key," he assured her.

"Would you mind getting it for me?" Anissa asked.

"Of course. Immediately. When I saw you across the lobby, I was just in the process of calling a tow truck to have that disgrace of a vehicle removed from our front drive. That Escort has been leaking oil in our parking lot for several days."

"Wait," she said, taking Montgomery aside. "You see the man sitting on the bench over there?" The building manager peeked around Anissa for a better look. Nowitzke was sitting with his hands wrapped around the edge of the bench, his eyes clenched shut, seemingly trying to manage his pain. "He's an Appleton police detective who parked his car here to investigate the incident where a man beat me up and knifed another member of law enforcement."

"Seriously? Him?"

Anissa continued, "Then that same suspect, who is wanted in several murders, attacked Detective Nowitzke there, shooting him in the process . . . here in *your* lobby." She waved her arms about the area. "The detective will recover but spent time in the hospital. Do you really want to have his car towed?" she asked, combined with a grimace.

"Ms. Taylor, right is right. Our manual expressly states that . . ."

"Salvatore, Sal . . . listen to me. My counsel here is to use some good judgment. If you're going to stick with your plan, then go over and tell the detective what you're going to do. But just a note of caution, Detective Nowitzke's in a bad mood since his pain meds are giving out," she warned. "Go ahead and explain the rules to him."

Montgomery took a slight step back, his eyes moving back and forth, thinking through the advice while trying to size up the brawny man. When he finally took a step towards Nowitzke, Anissa gently grabbed his arm.

"Take your chances. My guess is that when the condo board finds out what you've done to one of APD's finest, especially one who's been injured in our building, you'll probably be out on the street looking for another job."

Montgomery blinked several times, thinking through Anissa's message before swallowing hard. "Ms. Taylor, we fully support our friends in blue. I think I'll use my executive power to cut some slack for the detective. Now, let me get your package," he said, quickly excusing himself.

Moments later, the persnickety man returned with a box covered in brown paper. "I'm sorry for any misunderstanding, Ms. Taylor. Please forgive me."

Putting the package under her arm, Anissa left Montgomery in her wake and collected her boss, leading him to the elevator. "Chuck, this has to be it. The disc must have been here all along," she explained. "Luckily, it was delayed by some internal mail snafu here. Let's go up to my condo and have a look."

Once in the condo, Nowitzke scanned the great room to find what looked like the most comfortable chair before plunking down heavily. Anissa poured scotch into two large tumblers, then sliced open the parcel with a kitchen knife. Inside, she found a one-page note scrawled on a sheet of yellow lined paper torn from a notebook. She assumed the handwriting was Bob's.

Anissa, hope this helps in your investigation of the senator's death. Please be careful.

BE

Anissa turned the box on its side as if pouring cereal, and a red jewel case slid into her hand. After booting up her laptop, she connected the computer to her large-screen TV and inserted the disc. The machine *whirred* as the internal disc drive began churning. Nowitzke reclined in the deeply padded chair with his drink like it was movie night. Moments later, the screen filled with blackness aside from one blurry point of light in the background and a time counter in the upper left corner that registered 7:28 p.m. Anissa backed into the couch and sat, her eyes never leaving the screen as they heard a man and a woman laughing and some otherwise unintelligible conversation. Savanna and Hecht entered the frame and approached the camera as the screen split, offering output from a second camera. As the picture lightened, it was clear that the pair was in a narrow passageway. More giddy laughter came from Savanna until a microphone picked up a distinct sentence. "Which way to the wine room?" she asked a server, who entered the other half of the display. The man was dressed in a white shirt and a black vest, his face partially obscured.

"Just around the corner, miss," came the reply. As the detectives watched the stout senator negotiate the turn, they heard the dialogue quickly shift back to Hecht.

"Hey, asshole . . . be careful," he snarled.

"I'm sorry, sir. Are you okay? I must have somehow got you with the corkscrew in my other hand," came the explanation.

When the waiter eventually turned back down the passageway, the television revealed a full-screen shot of the man.

"Holy . . ." said Anissa, standing near speechless, reaching for the controls on the laptop as the video continued. "That's Ernie Preston. The floater Kenny Hicks lugged out of the river the day after Hecht died."

"Are you sure?"

Anissa pushed the rewind button to get a second look at the man before pausing at the precise moment when Ernie's face filled the screen. "No doubt. I couldn't see when Ernie stuck the senator, but the conversation couldn't be clearer about what took place."

"Hit 'play'," Nowitzke directed as the image switched to another camera in the wine room. The film followed the script offered by Savanna, showing her kissing Hecht and then pulling down his pants, dropping to her knees just as the senator began clutching his chest. By the time they saw Savanna leave the room screaming for help, the detectives were both convinced her story was exactly as she had told it. The video rolled on as the microphone caught the *whoosh* of the door opening. Preston entered the wine room. Walking up to Hecht, he felt the senator's neck, searching for a pulse. Satisfied the man was dead, Preston nervously glanced over each shoulder before pulling a thick marker from his pants pocket and drawing a "7" on the senator's forehead.

"Pause the video Nis," interrupted Nowitzke. When the screen froze, the detective looked over at his partner. "Even though we couldn't see it, your boy Ernie must have injected something into the senator when they passed each other."

"Agreed. It had to have been some fast-acting poison, because Ernie looked reasonably confident that he'd find a body when he returned to the wine room to decorate Hecht's forehead."

"Finally, some progress," replied Nowitzke, making a mental note to contact Wally for an update. "Let's see what's left on the tape." Anissa hit play and the video picked up as Preston left the scene, fading into the darkness of the lower level. Several minutes later, Chief Clark appeared, found Hecht's body, and checked for a pulse. The chief shook his head and rummaged around the room before finding an old painter's tarp in a cabinet. He covered the senator's corpse, then left. The video then automatically fast-forwarded to the conversation between Nowitzke, Anissa, Marcus, and Wally. Anissa clicked off the player when the disc stopped.

Both Anissa and Nowitzke sat silently, each taking long pulls of their scotch. "What did we just see?" Anissa finally asked.

"An old senator and a beautiful redhead getting ready to give him a BJ before the man goes into cardiac arrest in the worst sex tape ever made," said the senior detective derisively. He shook his head. "Aside from that, it was something we were told did not exist. That son of a bitch Elliott lied to us."

"In fact, he made a specific point in telling us there were no cameras in the lower level of Ivy House," Anissa observed. "And it just dawned on me that whoever recorded this heard our entire discussion right from the beginning of the investigation."

"On its face, that seems pretty incriminating. Why would he lie about something like that?" Nowitzke asked. "Can you think of any legitimate reasons why Elliott would tell law enforcement there were no cameras downstairs?"

"Well, maybe he didn't know about them."

"Okay. So, he's not a liar, just incompetent," replied Nowitzke. "Try again."

"Maybe an attempt to protect his boss from any embarrassment if the story about Hecht ever leaked out?" Anissa surmised.

"Thin at best, Nis. I can't think of *any* good reason. The lie makes me think Elliott is dirty somehow."

"Dirty how? Lying to us about having a camera system in the lower level? Big deal. Even though we saw Hecht die on the tape, we can't even prove there was a murder, let alone tie it to Elliott. Remember, everyone thinks the senator died of a heart attack. Short of some conclusive answers from Wally, it's impossible to prove otherwise at this point."

"Damn, it's the same dilemma that Scotty Aldrich, Mack Bordon, and Chief Clark had with their cases," concluded Nowitzke before draining the last of his scotch. He paused. "Let me ask you this. If you're Elliott and you know there are cameras downstairs, what's your first impulse after this little episode?"

Anissa never hesitated. "It's a no-brainer. I'd want to see what's on the tape."

"If you were on the up-and-up and just lied about the fact that the cameras were in place downstairs, what would you do?"

"Suck it up, admit the oversight, and turn any evidence over to the person responsible for investigating the death."

"Exactly. And if you had any involvement in the senator's death, you would . . ."

"Keep the disc secret and take care of any smoking guns," she replied, finishing Nowitzke's sentence.

"Which is pretty much what happened. In our little scenario, Elliott reviews the tape, finds he's got a major problem, and sics Mr. Black on the two loose ends. A day later, Ernie turns up doing the dead man's float in the Fox River, his throat cut. Later, Savanna, the only person who could identify Ernie, was attacked by the guy in her hotel room," said Nowitzke. "Everyone on that video, short of Savanna, is now dead."

"Poor Bob was another casualty too," added Anissa. "He must have figured out that there were cameras in the lower level. Maybe when the security team had their upgrade training? Remember when Brad explained that Bob just left the session and disappeared?"

Nowitzke exhaled heavily. "So, Bob found the video and knew that Elliott lied about the cameras. Then, when he saw what was on the tape, he made copies, shipping one to his wannabe girlfriend. Black must have gotten to Bob when he stood you up for coffee."

"Jesus, Chuck. All I can think about is that I sat on my ass waiting for Bob while Black tortured him," she said, thinking through the timeline.

"When Bob wouldn't give up the disc, Black killed him, tossed his apartment looking for the copy, and then came looking for you and the disc here," concluded Nowitzke.

Anissa took a sip of her drink, considering the details. "The whole thing sounds plausible." She hesitated before continuing. "By the way, when we were processing the crime scene near the river, Wally surmised that Ernie must have known his killer. No defensive wounds. He never saw it coming. Savanna thought it was Black's handiwork. Maybe Ernie and Black somehow knew each other?"

Nowitzke held up his glass for a refill. "Do you know what Ernie did for a living?"

"His live-in said he was a private security contractor," replied Anissa as she stood, retrieved the bottle, and poured her boss a couple more fingers of scotch. "I think you need to call your new buddy Brad so we can get a look at the various security contractors used by Elliott to see if our theory holds water."

"Will do. In the meantime, I need to make another call." Nowitzke pulled out his phone and dialed Savanna, getting her on the first ring. "Hey, we've got some video we need you to see. We're at Anissa's condo. Bring all your photos along, including the ones with Elliott and Black." He clicked off. "She's on her way," he said to Anissa.

"Chuck, she's still at risk," she reminded him. Topping off her glass, Anissa had another thought as the room went silent. "If Elliott was involved in murdering Hecht, one fitting a pattern where the victim has a number on their forehead, does this implicate the man in all the deaths?"

The loaded question sucked the air from the room as the detectives continued to think. Nowitzke finally spoke. "If we could figure out a single motive for all the deaths, then yeah, Elliott has to be."

"But even though the connection between the individual deaths is easy to establish, we have no evidence he's involved," offered Anissa. "It's a big leap from heart attacks to murder." More silence. The condo's buzzer startled both officers, who were deep in thought.

"Hello, it's Natalie," they heard through the tinny speaker. Anissa walked to the intercom.

"C'mon up, third floor, 333," said the detective, pushing the buzzer to unlock the front lobby door.

"One final question for you before Natalie gets here," said

Nowitzke. "Do you buy the theory that Will was feeding info to Elliott?"

Anissa contemplated the question with her back to her boss. "Will lied to you. Savanna's got photos of him and Elliott together. Now Will's AWOL," she said before turning and nodding. "Yes, Will must have told Elliott."

There was a quiet knock on the door before Anissa let Natalie in.

Natalie gave the young detective a hug and wandered over to Nowitzke, who was still slouched in a chair. After kissing Nowitzke on the forehead, she said, "You owe me dinner, Chuck," then dropped an oversized envelope on his lap. "According to these records, Dan Warren was from the area. He died on June 16, 2013, in Newport, Oregon." She paused, cringing as she recognized the significance of the calendar date. "The obit said he died of a heart attack. He had been a principal at a middle school for a couple of years. Divorced. No kids. At the time of his death, the article mentioned he had family living in Neenah. A father, Gaylord, and a mother, Gloria. I've got copies of everything I could find for you. After checking some other records, I even got a local phone number and an address for the mom," she said, handing him a separate note with the particulars.

"You're the best," Nowitzke exclaimed.

"Instead of working at the library, maybe you should be an investigator for APD," commented Anissa as the lobby buzzer went off again.

"Anissa, it's Savanna."

The detective touched the buzzer once more, replying, "333."

Moments later, there were several loud knocks that continued until Anissa opened the door. "Greetings," said Savanna, entering the condo. "Looks like the gang's all here. And you must be Natalie," she added with a smile, approaching the librarian with her hand extended.

"Anissa and I were just working through a timeline of what's taken place since Senator Hecht died. Can you show us the photos you took of Elliott, Black, and Will?" asked Nowitzke.

"Sure," she said, taking a chair at the expansive granite island in the kitchen and digging into the portfolio she had brought. "Here you go." She removed a set of enlargements and sent them around the group that had now gathered around her. "One of Elliott, alone. Mr. Black shadowing Will and Anissa. Another of Elliott with Black. That one was taken right after this picture with Elliott and Will in a downtown bar. One of Elliott passing a suspicious envelope across the table. And the pièce de résistance, the final one of Will pocketing the suspect envelope, which likely contained cash for reasons I've already given."

Nowitzke shook his head. "Considering the timing of the conversation, my take is that it'll be difficult for Will to explain this away, even not knowing exactly what was in the envelope."

Anissa studied the last picture and quietly nodded in agreement.

"It was never my intent to smear the man, especially if there was something going on that I wasn't aware of. But, by the looks of it, that's not the case here," Savanna concluded. "What's the plan for Elliott?"

"For what?" Nowitzke slowly rose from his chair. "Even though he might be pulling the strings, we can't prove anything aside from the fact that he lied to Anissa and me. On the face of it, that's not a crime. We have several deaths, but no motive. We don't have any evidence suggesting the deaths are even murders, including Hecht's. I'd love to corner Will, but he's missing in action. And as much as we need to confront Elliott, we should focus on Black. We've got him cold on several serious charges, with the likelihood of adding more. Maybe he leads us to Elliott?"

"The disc finally arrived," said Anissa, turning to Savanna.

"Marvelous," she replied, shaking her head. "I suppose the video shows everything . . . like me and Hecht?"

"Yes, just like you said. It also confirms the identity of the server, Ernie Preston, the guy who was dumped in the river. Would you like to take a look?"

"Well, I don't need to see any of that," said Natalie. She looked at an exhausted Nowitzke. "Still up for dinner, Chuck?"

He managed a smile. "Dinner it is. You get to drive my car, which is currently in primo parking downstairs," he replied. "Nis, I'll try to run down Warren's mother for an interview tomorrow. And plan on a stop at Ivy House to find out what's on Brad's mind. We can give him an update on Sandy," he added as an afterthought as Natalie took him by the arm and led him out the door toward the elevator.

CHAPTER 29

Dusk had arrived with the promise of comfortable sleeping weather. Nowitzke took in a deep breath of the clean air before sliding into the front passenger seat of the Escort. He felt what amounted to a dull ache where his wound was. Even though he was tired, as if he had been awake for days straight, he was now getting his second wind. And he was hungry. Natalie carefully drew the seat belt around his injured shoulder, then climbed into the driver's side. Amazingly, it fired up immediately. She took off as darkness quickly fell, and they drove together in silence for several minutes before Natalie started a conversation.

"Chuck, I know this is a bad time with your injury and all, but we need to talk."

Shit! "That doesn't sound good," replied Nowitzke. "What's up?"

Natalie was quiet for a moment, presumably choosing her words carefully as she negotiated downtown traffic on College Avenue, a wide four-lane thoroughfare. Moving into the curbside lane, she was on watch for an empty parking spot while negotiating from stoplight to stoplight, keeping pace with the other cars around her. "I got a call from a lawyer today. The one who represents my soon-to-be ex."

"Don't tell me the asshole changed his mind and now wants your house."

"No. It's worse than that," she replied as the car came to rest at a red light. "He wants . . ."

What sounded like an explosion interrupted Natalie mid-sentence, followed by a shower of broken glass and the sensation of bullets cutting through the car. Any pain or fatigue Nowitzke had been feeling suddenly disappeared, replaced by a burst of adrenaline as he simultaneously reached for his Glock. His first instinct was concern for Natalie. She was slumped over the steering wheel, unconscious and covered in blood. Nowitzke checked her neck and found a pulse. Then, looking past Natalie, he made eye contact with Black, who had an assault rifle in his hands as he emerged from a car stopped in the center lane alongside the Escort. Black had a surprised look on his face upon seeing Nowitzke sitting in the passenger side of his vehicle. All traffic in the immediate area around the developing firefight froze in place as the occupants scrambled from their cars to find safety wherever they could.

Black flashed a wicked smile and walked with purpose, rounding the front of his vehicle. He leveled his weapon and sprayed more rounds into the windshield of the Escort leading to where Nowitzke had been sitting. But the detective had managed to slip out of the car, finding temporary refuge on the pavement against the rear bumper of his auto, his weapon at the ready. He quickly scanned the area, looking for better cover while also trying to keep one eye on his assailant. Cold sweat covered much of Nowitzke's body as his heart pounded furiously inside his chest. *Fuck.* Trying to calm himself enough to think, he banged his back against the car several times in frustration. *Fuck.* Finally, he spotted his next hide, some twenty feet away. Fighting the urge to make a mad dash, the detective told himself to wait until Black needed to replace the clip in his weapon. When that pause took place, Nowitzke bolted across the broad sidewalk, diving behind a large dumpster that sat on the corner near a building under construction.

The shooting resumed, and multiple pings ricocheted off the heavy steel. Rising from a kneeling position, Nowitzke took a quick look over the top of his hiding space. Black was no more than fifteen feet away and narrowing any means of escape for the trapped detective. Nowitzke emptied his handgun in the direction of Black, earning yet another volley from his attacker. With Black now only a few feet away just on the other side of the dumpster, Nowitzke quickly reloaded his final clip into the Glock. Crouching, he played cat and mouse, doing his best to keep some space between them. In his mind, the detective knew that any standoff would buy him time, allowing other members of APD to respond. But he also knew that any further delay in getting medical attention to Natalie might be the difference between life and death.

With his back facing traffic, Black bent down to slam more ammo into his rifle before making his final assault on the detective. "I'm coming for you, Chuck!" he yelled as he stood looking over the top of the dumpster. However, even though he was intently focused on the detective, Black suddenly recognized the reflection of headlights approaching from behind just before hearing the roar of the SUV. Turning at the last second, the blond managed to hose down the oncoming vehicle as it moved towards him at a high speed along the sidewalk. An instant later, the heavy vehicle caught Black at the hips, crushing him back into the dumpster and sending it flying along with Nowitzke, who was on the other side. Black's body was almost torn in two by the impact. Whether it was by intent or his nerves reacting to the devastating injury, Black's finger continued to squeeze the trigger until he was out of ammo.

When the sound of bullets stopped, Nowitzke carefully rose with a heavy groan from where he had landed. Peering over the top of the container, he took in the chaos, doing a hasty onceover of his body to check for any new injuries. Warm fluid ran into his eyes, down his face, and into his mouth. Recognizing the taste of blood, he wiped his eyes with his jacket sleeve and carefully approached the bullet-shredded SUV before seeing Black's mangled body lying on the sidewalk. Convinced the threat was over, Nowitzke holstered his weapon and went back to Natalie. She was alive but still unconscious as he dialed 9-1-1 for help. Hearing the scream of the approaching sirens, Nowitzke made his way toward the SUV to check on the driver who had saved his life.

The man's face rested against the steering wheel, obscured by blood and powder from the airbags that had deployed with the heavy front-end collision. Black's final effort had sent bullets through the windshield into the cab of the vehicle. Sticking his arm through the broken side window, Nowitzke searched the driver for signs of life amidst a sea of red. Then, the man came to, surprising the officer by asking, "Are you alright?"

"Yeah, you saved my life. Thanks."

The driver raised his head before rasping, "I got that fucker, Chuck?"

Nowitzke recognized the voice. Will Porter sat behind the wheel, choking up blood. Looking further into the SUV, the detective saw blood gushing from several holes in Will's chest and immediately knew that the wounds were fatal, but never changed his facial expression. "Jesus, Will. Where did you come from?"

"I'm sorry for everything," Will gasped. "I knew that Black would come after you again to finish things. I tracked him . . . waiting for him to make his move. I wanted to be there for you . . . to do my job. To do it so you could be proud of me. They took advantage of me . . . used me to provide information about the redhead, the security tech . . . Anissa. Some friend I was," he added, wheezing. "I told you I could be a good cop . . ." Will's voice faded away.

Nowitzke felt Will's neck but couldn't find a pulse. Taking a moment, the hardened detective exhaled loudly and wiped away a tear with his fingers. *Goddammit, Will. Why didn't you go into the event organizing business?*

Circling back towards Natalie, Nowitzke saw that the first responders had taken her from the wreckage and placed her on the ground, working hard to stop the bleeding. "How's she doing?" asked the detective, holding up his badge.

"She took a bullet to the abdomen and has several other wounds. We have her stabilized, but she'll need surgery," replied the lead EMT, hovering over her patient. "We'll be ready to transfer her to Hobert Thompson shortly." She looked up at Nowitzke while her partner continued to work. The medic suddenly stood, exclaiming,

"Detective, you've got a head wound! Come to the back of the ambulance so I can have a look."

Reluctantly, Nowitzke sat on the tailgate of the rescue vehicle as the EMT gave him a large sterile pad. "Hold this on your head," she said. "Keep pressure on the wound and hop in back. We need to go!"

After climbing into the ambulance, the detective sat next to the gurney holding Natalie as another medical technician monitored her vitals. Looking down at her, Nowitzke took her hand. She briefly regained consciousness and smiled at him before drifting off again. "You're going to be fine, Natalie. Just hang in there."

CHAPTER 30

"Y"ou looking to earn frequent visitor points, Detective?" asked Dr. Stacy Frazier as she cleaned the gash on Nowitzke's head. "Or do you have a thing for me? You know, some psychological issue where you look to get hurt and then seek attention?"

"Been through a bunch of psych tests, Doc, but I'm not sure if anyone ever went looking for that problem."

"You are one lucky SOB. Shot twice in one week. A pass-through wound and now a bullet grazing your head," she said, continuing to work on the officer. "Of course, I'm sure you know that head wounds bleed like crazy. I'm going to put some glue on it. You won't need stitches, and any scarring will be minimal. In a week or two, your girlfriend won't even notice."

He cocked his head, looking at the doctor expectantly, hoping he had correctly interpreted what she said. "Does that mean Natalie's going to be fine?"

"They're prepping her for surgery, giving her fluids and blood. With all the privacy laws, I can't tell you much except that she has several bullet wounds, which you already know. Amazingly, none of her major organs appear to have been damaged, based on my preliminary look, but she'll have some pain for a while. Beyond the normal risks, though, I'm not anticipating any problems with the surgery. She also took a round to the heavy bone in her upper arm that looks to have stopped the bullet. I'll patch up the flesh wound after dealing with the cracked humerus. Based on the story I heard about the number of shots fired, things could have been much worse for her and you. Maybe the two of you should go halfsies on a lottery ticket!" Dr. Frazier said, placing a large bandage on Nowitzke's forehead. She took a step back to admire her work. "There. Now, if you can find a flag along with a fifer and a drummer, you can be a Revolutionary War reenactor."

"Thanks, Doc," said Nowitzke, sliding off the exam table. "Any idea when Natalie will be out of surgery?"

"Give me a couple of hours."

Nowitzke wandered back to his spot in the waiting room. Aside from a smartly dressed Hispanic man in the room watching television, Anissa and Savanna were the only other people there. They had been talking quietly, drinking coffee, until they saw the detective emerge from the treatment rooms wearing a bandage on his head. Both women stood and gave him hugs.

"Chuck, we brought you a large," said Anissa, handing him a Styrofoam cup with steam coming through the hole in the lid. "What's the story on your head wound?"

"It's no big deal," he replied, sitting down as they followed in kind. "Of all the bullets that Black sent my way, he only managed to bounce one off my head, giving me a cut that didn't even need stitches. The headache's the worst part," he confided.

"And Natalie?"

"Took at least one to the gut along with several other wounds. She'll be in for surgery for a while. Lucky woman."

"What happened?" asked Savanna.

"We were on our way to dinner. Turns out Black was trailing us. As we sat at an intersection, he pulled up alongside and emptied an automatic weapon of some sort into my car. I think he was expecting that I was driving because he looked shocked when I got out of the passenger side. I knew that Natalie had been hit, so I moved away from the car and behind a dumpster to draw fire. But my Glock was no match for his weapon, and I was cornered. Then, out of the blue, a car crashed into Black, killing him." He paused. "It was Will. Crushed

Black like a bug with an SUV but took several rounds in the process. He died at the scene."

Anissa closed her eyes, and her head dropped at the news.

"Said he was sorry that he gave up info on you, Nis," said Nowitzke, then looking at Savanna, he added, "And you too. Then he goes and saves my ass." He shook his head before taking a sip of coffee.

"Chuck, you're on fumes," offered Anissa. "Let me take you home so you can sleep."

"I can't leave," he protested.

"There's nothing you can do for Natalie here anyway. We've got it all worked out. Savanna will keep a vigil and call you when she gets out of surgery. I'll bring you back in the morning so you can see her."

Anissa anticipated that Nowitzke would resist but was surprised when he agreed with her plan. Shortly afterward, she dropped her boss off in the driveway of Miss Alma's yard.

Nowitzke emerged from the Audi and thought for a moment about talking with his landlord, but the lights in her home were off. He stuck his head back into the vehicle. "I'll catch Miss Alma in the morning to let her know about Natalie," he said to Anissa. "We need to corner Brad Hawkins tomorrow and circle back on Gloria Warren." He gave his partner a wave as she took off, then he plodded up the stairs to his apartment. "Oh, and I get to go car shopping again. Fucking A," he muttered to himself as he opened the door, grabbed a beer from the refrigerator, and collapsed into his favorite chair, the can unopened.

CHAPTER 31

The Audi entered the yard just as Nowitzke was leaving Miss Alma's house by the back door. He trudged toward the car and slowly climbed into the passenger seat. As the car pulled away, the old woman smiled and waved through a window to Anissa, who responded in kind.

"Morning, Chuck. How did it go?"

"About as well as you would expect. Miss Alma saw the footage of the shoot-out on the local news and knows Will Porter died in the process. She's concerned about my gunshot wound and whether I'm okay to be working. She also knows you've taken a beating and is worried about you too. When I told her that Natalie had been shot and was in the hospital, she said nothing, but her eyes started welling up as she stared at the bandage on my head. She said it felt like her whole world was coming apart," concluded Nowitzke as they continued their journey to speak with Brad Hawkins.

****

Thomas greeted both detectives at the door of Ivy House as the morning grew overcast with clouds that the local weatherman said were a precursor to rain. "Mr. Hawkins is in the study. May I bring you anything? Water? Coffee? Tea?" he asked politely.

"Coffee with cream, if you've got it," said Anissa.

"Make it two," chimed in Nowitzke.

As they moved down the hall, the man mountain stationed outside the study opened the door for them as they approached. "Did I catch you smiling by accident today, Leonard?" asked Anissa cheerfully to the expressionless security guard as they stepped into the room.

Brad had been absorbed with his laptop. When he heard the door open, he looked up, popped to his feet, and stepped around his desk to greet the detectives warmly. "Please have a seat," he said, nodding at Leonard to pull the door shut. Brad did a double take upon seeing the bandage on Nowitzke's head. "I heard a rumor that you were involved in the shoot-out downtown last night. And the news about Will Porter," he added somberly. "Are you alright, Detective?"

"Been a long week," Nowitzke conceded tiredly without offering any details. "You left a message that said you got a package and had a problem?" he questioned, dispensing with any pleasantries and moving right to business.

Brad dropped into his chair and opened the center drawer of his desk, pulling out a silver disk and holding it up for the officers to see. "Do you know what this is?"

"Lemme guess." Nowitzke took a chair opposite Brad and sat back. "Video of your friend Hecht and the redhead in *your* wine cellar just before he checked out."

"How did you know that?" asked Brad with a shocked look on his face.

"Because I got the same disc," said Anissa, who sat down next to Nowitzke. "I'm assuming you've seen it?"

"Yes," he replied, his hands starting to shake.

"The server in the video was Ernest Preston. It's hard to tell from the tape, but we surmise he injected Hecht with a poison before writing the number on the senator's head," said Nowitzke.

"Wait, I'm confused. I thought Tony died of a heart attack?" asked Brad, his voice trailing off.

"We're still waiting on an official ruling," Anissa added. "However, during the autopsy of Hecht's body, the ME found a puncture wound that seems to match the conversation on the disk."

"Okay, but you're saying the puncture wasn't the cause of death, but there was some sort of poison. Did the toxicology tests identify what type of poison?"

"We've got nothing official back as yet," conceded Nowitzke.

"So Hecht's death was a homicide?" Brad stood, his voice rising. "I've seen the tape, and I'm not so sure, even with the number on the man's head. Have you arrested this Preston fellow and charged him with anything?"

"We would have," replied Anissa. "However, by the time we got to him, someone had already slit his throat and dumped his body in the Fox River."

The blood drained from Brad's face at the revelation. "Preston was murdered? Do you have any suspects?"

"Remember the photo we showed you of the blond guy who's connected to the attack on Savanna, the redhead?" asked Nowitzke.

"Of course."

"We've identified him as Asa Black. We're pretty sure he was responsible for killing Preston. And Bob Edwards too."

"Why would Black have killed both men?"

Nowitzke and Anissa traded looks. "It's part of a cover-up that starts with the video," replied the senior detective.

"That's the problem I mentioned in my message," replied Brad, his voice adding decibels. "This video shouldn't exist."

"Agreed. On the night of Hecht's death, we were told there were no cameras on the lower floors." Nowitzke's statement hung in the air until they heard a gentle knock on the door. Thomas entered, holding a silver tray with a small urn, two cups, and a cream pitcher. After setting the tray down on Hawkins' desk, he made a hasty retreat, feeling the tension in the room.

"When the surveillance system was installed, I gave specific instructions that it was only for the main floor, entrances and exits, and the compound," countered Brad.

"Who was responsible for the installation of the cameras?" Nowitzke asked.

"I don't know the name of the company. That was Elliott Gordon's call."

"Exactly my point. For some reason, Elliott lied to you and us about the cameras," Nowitzke replied. "Why would he do that?"

"I have no idea. Elliott's out of the office for the moment, but you can bet I'll be having a chat with him," said Brad. "Are you implying that Elliott is somehow working with Black?"

"Our theory is that Preston was tasked to kill the senator, probably for payment of some type. But he made a mistake by showing up on a video he didn't know existed. None of the staff knew either, at least until your man Bob Edwards discovered the evidence and was promptly killed by Black. The thinking is that since Elliott was the only one who knew of the CCTV in that part of the house, he directed Black to kill off everyone associated with the disc."

"For the record, Black also kidnapped and threatened me, searching for a copy of the video he knew was sent to me," Anissa added. "And last night, he went after Chuck and his lady friend with an automatic weapon, killing Detective Porter in the process. If there is any justice in the world, Will managed to take out Black with his vehicle."

"My God!" exclaimed Brad, slumping back in his chair, astonishment showing on his face as the detectives outlined their case.

"Good summation, counselor," Nowitzke offered.

"You're saying that everything ties back to Elliott?" asked the former DA, leaning across the desk towards Nowitzke.

Nowitzke reached into his portfolio. "Take a look at these and you tell me," he said, sliding several enlarged photos across the desk to Brad. "Looks like Elliott and Black hanging out together. By the way, we got separate photos of Elliott with Will Porter, which makes me wonder about that relationship too."

Brad rose from his desk and began to pace about the study. "This is all speculation. Circumstantial evidence at best. There's nothing illegal about meeting with sketchy people. Sometimes security professionals move in the shadows to gather information. Frankly, that's why I hired Elliott. I don't want to know if someone is coming for me. His job is to protect me. I've known the guy forever, and I'm disturbed by the photos and what you're insinuating." His eyes searched the room, buying time to think. The former DA then put on his lawyer hat. "Detective, break this down for me. What kind of motive would Elliott have to kill a sitting senator?" he asked, moving back to his chair to sit down.

"Frankly, we haven't found one yet," replied Nowitzke. "Any thoughts on the subject?"

"None," said Brad forcefully, his fist hitting the desk.

"What would motivate Black to kill all these people?"

"I have no clue. I'm assuming you never had a chance to question him?" Brad asked.

"Correct," replied Anissa. She tried to defuse the moment. "Brad, can you look into your records to see if you have anyone on your payroll named Preston or Black? Or payments to independent contractors?"

Brad turned toward his laptop and began to type. When the appropriate screen appeared, his head bobbed as he searched the entries. "I can assure you we have no employees by either name. For simplicity's sake, we have only a handful of people on staff, and I know them all. However, with regard to independent . . ." He stopped, his eyes scanning the screen. "Damn, it looks like multiple payments have been made to an Ernest Preston over the last several months . . . upwards of twenty-five thousand dollars! But I don't see anything issued to anyone named Black," he concluded, turning the laptop for the officers to view.

Brad closed his eyes as his fingers tapped the desk nervously, his brain engaged, deep in thought. "However, you both know that there are other ways to funnel money to someone without making a direct payment. Cash. Checks to seemingly unrelated entities. Payments to pseudonyms," he offered as he stood, came around toward the detectives, and sat on the front edge of his desk. "Let me play district attorney one last time regarding your theory about Elliott. To get a conviction for murder, an attorney needs to establish means, motive, and opportunity. If anything, the video implicates Preston, not Elliott. Dismiss the idea that Elliott lied about the placement of cameras and met with some rough people, even though they are things that don't necessarily make me feel good. He won't be our employee of the month, but on the face of it, he did nothing illegal. Here's the upshot. At this point, the ME hasn't ruled on Hecht's cause of death, so we don't have a homicide. And *you* don't have a motive. Based on what you told me, Chuck, even the means remains unclear. There's no weapon . . . no smoking gun. A puncture wound. Death by corkscrew? I think not. And I'm not sure exactly what the opportunity was. You've got some major holes in your case before you can prove that Elliott Gordon is some sort of mastermind behind it all. Based on my experience, there's no way I could get a conviction based on what you have here."

Nowitzke's face reddened with anger and frustration.

"Looks like you've got more work to do," concluded Brad. "Maybe you're both onto something that's taking place here under my nose. However, if Elliott is involved in this situation, my reputation is on the line. When you can establish a case with direct evidence, I want to be one of the first to know about it." He stood, signaling the end of the meeting. "I also apologize if I lost my cool today."

Nowitzke breathed in heavily and stroked his chin, thinking about what he had said relative to Elliott and what was now coming. "Brad, we need a bit more of your time, and I think you should be sitting down."

The former DA looked askance at Nowitzke but acquiesced, dropping back into his office chair with a questioning look on his face as the detective nodded toward Anissa.

"It's about Sandy. She's dead," she said matter-of-factly before launching into an overview of her trip to Banff. The graduation photo of Sandy and the software that RCMP used to enhance the aging process. A thumbnail of Sandy's life in review. Her education. Her work as a physician. Her role as a wife and mother of two children. Then her untimely passing, capped by the confirmation from those who knew her best that Sandy had died as Amanda Hartsell. Fifteen minutes later, Anissa slid a file containing a copy of her report across the desk to Brad.

Brad sat stoically, remaining impassive throughout Anissa's monologue. Nowitzke observed that he never even reached for the file, as if Sandy might still be alive somewhere if he didn't look inside. Several minutes later, Brad sat forward in his chair and looked at the officers, sucking in his bottom lip, fighting back his emotions. "I don't know what to say. After all these years . . . ." He stood again and picked up the photo of Sandy smiling on the beach in Hawaii that had been taken decades before. "Banff?" he asked, running his fingers through his hair. "Never been there. How ironic, though. It was one of the places I offered to take Sandy for her graduation. Looks like she made it there before me." He carefully replaced the photo on his desk. "Thank you, Anissa, for your fine work. Chuck, I'm in your debt as well. At least I've got some closure. I don't know what else to say."

Nowitzke and Anissa took his last comment as an opportunity to leave. As Nowitzke opened the door, Brad had one final question. "Anissa, you said Sandy died in 2018?"

"Yes."

"Any ideas who sent Bobilly to me? You know, her rabbit?" he asked.

Anissa exhaled heavily. "None," she replied.

CHAPTER 32

"F uck! Fuck! Fuck!" yelled Nowitzke as they emerged from Ivy House. "I totally screwed the pooch, Nis. Brad shredded me, my theory, and my credibility."

"Relax," Anissa replied. "The man was giving us the perspective of a prosecuting attorney. He didn't call you out or try to embarrass you, so don't take it personally. Basically, he told us what we already knew. We've got more work to do."

"I know. I just feel like I made a goddamned rookie mistake."

"Well, at least you didn't have to tell Brad that his long-lost sister was dead."

"True. What did you think of his reaction?"

"He keeps his emotions in check better than Mr. Spock. I think when reality hit him, he regrouped quickly. Never really lost his composure. Maybe it's one of the reasons he was considered such a great trial lawyer?" she offered.

Nowitzke nodded his head in agreement, calming down as he got in the car. "Hey, would you mind if we took a quick trip to the hospital? Savanna left a message last night that Natalie was out of surgery and things went well. But I was totally unconscious and didn't see it until this morning."

"Sure. Then off to meet Mrs. Warren?"

"You got it."

Anissa stayed in the car to make some calls as Nowitzke went to the front desk of the hospital to get Natalie's room number. However, as he stepped into her room, he did a quick double take, thinking he was in the wrong place. The moment for pause was due to the well-dressed fifty-something Hispanic man sitting in the corner reading a book next to Natalie, who was sleeping. It was the same man Nowitzke had seen in the waiting room the night before.

"Hello? I'm Detective Nowitzke," he announced with a confused look on his face. "And you are?"

"Georg . . ." the man replied. "Georg Alvera. I'm Natalie's husband." He stood and moved towards Nowitzke, offering his hand in greeting. "Are you investigating the shooting?"

"No, someone else is working the case. I was in the car with Natalie when the man opened fire last night," the detective said awkwardly. "Just so you know, the shooter died at the scene, so there's wasn't too much to wrap up."

Georg cocked his head, looking at Nowitzke. "How do you know each other?"

Nowitzke held the man's gaze while he scratched his chin. "I met Natalie through the library. She's been researching several cold cases for me. We were on our way to dinner when the shooting started," he concluded.

"You two are friends then?" asked Georg.

"Yeah. We've become very close, in fact," Nowitzke replied in a distracted tone. "Listen, I gotta ask, Georg. Natalie told me she was going through a divorce?"

"Yeah, she's right. We are. Or we were, anyway. I left her. Never gave her a reason. Didn't really have one. I'm fifty-two and started wondering what I had accomplished with my life. You know . . . the grass must be greener on the other side. Well, turns out it isn't. I concluded that I had acted stupidly by leaving what I had with her. Anyway, our daughter, Blanca, works here at the hospital and called me last night, telling me that her mother had been admitted with a gunshot wound. I felt this need to come by, if nothing else just to tell her I was sorry for any pain I had caused her about the whole divorce thing. Frankly, over the last couple of weeks, I've been having second thoughts, and this put it over the top. Now I'd like to stop the whole process and have us get back together. I screwed up, Detective," Georg declared as he sat back down. "I've been praying all night that she'll take me back."

This must have been the reason for the call from the lawyer that Natalie mentioned. "Well, good luck to you. My contacts here at the hospital tell me Natalie will pull through. Any idea on when she'll be released?"

"Probably not for the better part of a week," Georg offered meekly.

"Would you tell her I stopped by when she wakes up?" Nowitzke turned towards the door, then stopped. He reversed course and went to Natalie's bedside before leaning down and kissing her on the forehead. "Take care," he whispered before he left. Just in time for Georg to put things together.

****

"How's Natalie doing?" asked Anissa as Nowitzke climbed into the car.

"Great. She was sleeping, but her husband was there visiting her."

"Her husband?" exclaimed his partner. "What the fuck? I thought Natalie was getting a divorce."

"Join the club. The guy who walked out on her is now having second thoughts. What a dumbass! Fucking around with people's lives," he said, shaking his head.

"What are you going to do, Chuck?"

"Well, wait for Natalie to heal, and then we need to talk. Right now, I don't think she knows that old Georg is keeping a vigil. Or whether she has any feelings left for the guy. For the time being, I'm in limbo." Refocusing on the next order of business, he asked, "You got your bearings on Warren?"

"Yes."

Nowitzke mindlessly sat back in his seat, his mind elsewhere. "How much worse can the day get?"

****

After the short drive to Neenah, Anissa stopped in front of a one-and-a-half-story home in an older neighborhood located between a major thoroughfare and the interstate. Stepping out of the car, Nowitzke immediately heard the drone of traffic coming off the highway. The neighborhood was in a state of transition, with some of the modest homes staying well-maintained while others had fallen into disrepair. Nonetheless, it appeared to be an old-school area where kids could still play safely in their front yards while old men living next door yelled at them to stay off their lawns.

The Warrens lived in a ramshackle house that had seen better days. Large sheets of fake brown-and-red brick siding had torn away from the walls, exposing a black underlayment, and several shingles from the roof were lying in the overgrowth of what was once the yard. Nowitzke assumed it was garbage day by the presence of two large containers sitting on the curb. As he stepped past them, he opened the lid of the recycling bin, spying an impressive collection of empty vodka bottles.

Anissa came around the car to join Nowitzke, taking a moment to smooth her pin-striped business suit, before they moved down the short, uneven flagstone walkway towards the front door of the home. The senior officer knocked on the wood frame surrounding the metal screen door. A heavier interior wood door was wedged open while an oscillating fan moved back and forth, sending air through the living room. Getting no response, the detective pushed his face up to the screen and cupped his hands around his eyes to peer into the house. Since he could see and hear a television tuned to *The Price is Right*, he assumed someone was nearby. Just as Nowitzke moved to knock a second time, both he and Anissa heard a grinding noise coming from inside the house. Snoring? Someone was sleeping in the room, prompting Anissa to gently call "Hello?" through the door. Her second try worked as the snoring stopped abruptly, followed by a snort and a loud fart.

"Coming! Yeah, I'm coming," yelled a woman gruffly. A minute later, she appeared in the doorway, a cigarette dangling from the corner of her mouth. The short, thin woman had shoulder-length, frizzy, grey hair and wore a ragged, loose-fitting floral bathrobe that she held tightly at the neck with one hand. A pair of fuzzy, pink open-toed slippers covered her feet. In the woman's other hand was a white coffee cup. "What're ya sellin'?" she asked curtly, blowing cigarette smoke through the screen.

"Nothing," replied Nowitzke as he and Anissa held up their badges. "Are you Gloria Warren?"

"Yeah." She squinted warily before taking a sip from her cup. "Thought you might be Jesus people at first. But neither of you look like it . . . you, in particular," she offered, staring at Nowitzke. "And you, Princess . . . I'm still figuring out what you're up to, but you're too goddamned pretty to be a cop."

"Do you have a minute to answer some questions about your son?" asked Anissa softly.

"Danny? He's dead!" the woman loudly exclaimed. "Been gone for ten years, for Chrissakes. Back in 2013. There ain't much to talk about."

"It won't take long," said Anissa. "Would you mind if we came inside?"

Gloria hemmed and hawed for a moment, then exhaled disgustedly before unlocking the metal door and pushing it open. "Better get your asses in here before it starts raining. But make it snappy, Princess, 'cause my soaps come on TV soon," she admonished.

Once inside, both officers smelled alcohol on Gloria's breath, strong enough to cut through the odor of nicotine. The interior of the house was a mess, filled with clutter, looking like it hadn't been cleaned in a while. The formerly beige walls were stained yellow from cigarette smoke, the carpeting was in shreds, and the place smelled like a small animal had recently died within its walls. "Now what do you want to know about my Danny?" Gloria asked, dropping into an old wooden rocking chair held together by duct tape. Next to the chair sat a table holding a bottle of cheap vodka and an ash tray that was overflowing with butts. She pointed the officers to a pair of folding chairs near her line of sight. "Have a seat, but not in front of the TV," she cautioned, refilling her coffee cup with vodka. "That Drew Carey still gets me dewy."

Anissa sat, forced a smile, and softly said, "Tell us about Dan."

"Well, he was a good boy," said Gloria, her tone softening. "He went to college down in Madison. Made his way in the world. Became a school principal." Her slight smile revealed crooked yellow teeth. "Rose above all this to become a successful educator just to drop dead from a fucking heart attack. Only the good die young," she lamented, her voice cracking. "God, I miss him."

"Did you have any other children?" Nowitzke asked.

"No. Only my Danny."

"And Mr. Warren?"

"Gaylord? Died of cancer a year ago. Fucking disease ate up all his innards."

Anissa continued, "Where did Danny live?"

"In Oregon. Some pissant town out there. Never saw it. Supposed to be on the coast," replied Gloria.

"Was he married?"

"No. Never found his princess, Princess."

"He just dropped dead?" asked Nowitzke.

"Are you a little slow, Detective? Like I said, he just keeled over. Got the death certificate upstairs. If you can read English, you can look for yourself," she said. "Stress, I'd guess . . . chasing around all those little bastards at the school. If you wanna see the paper, c'mon with me." She added another slug of vodka to her cup for the trip then stood unsteadily, lurching briefly. Nowitzke reached out to grab her arm. "Get your paws off me," she growled. "You fucking perve, trying to get a feel!"

The three slowly moved up the steep stairway with Gloria in the lead, laboring one step at a time while clinging to the wooden railing. Although the first floor of the home was a mess, the second floor looked like it could be a candidate for *Hoarders*. All the rooms were strewn with clothing, odds and ends, old newspapers, and empty liquor bottles, and many corners showcased piles of rat droppings. Anissa stopped at the top of the stairs, unwilling to proceed and risk her outfit. Nowitzke took a whiff of the area, content to wait as Gloria slowly angled through the debris and moved directly to the correct stack of paper. "Here it is," she said, holding up an official-looking document before pivoting and working her way back to the detectives. "See . . . a myocardial infarction. Doctor words for a fucking heart attack," she yapped at Nowitzke, pointing to the cause of death on the form. She shook the document at him. "Told you."

Nowitzke gently took the paper from Gloria, nodding in agreement after scanning the document. "Danny died on June 16, 2013, in Newport," he said, flashing five fingers at Anissa while raising his eyebrows. "Did Danny have any friends in Oregon that we might be able to speak to?"

"Probably. But I couldn't tell you who they were," she muttered. "Never went there for a visit."

"Ma'am, this might sound strange, but did Danny know a girl named Sandy Hawkins?" asked Anissa.

Immediately, Gloria's face tightened, her eyes flashing with anger. "That fucking slut!" she snarled. "She was Danny's girlfriend for a time. Nothing but trouble as far as I was concerned. She broke my Danny's heart, dumping him for some older guy. Then I heard she up and disappeared. The little bitch." she added, her voice trailing off.

"So, Danny did know Sandy?" repeated Nowitzke.

"That's what I just said. Do you have some sort of learning disability, Detective?" she said disgustedly.

"When were they together?" asked Anissa.

Gloria thought for a moment. "A long time ago. Probably sometime near the end of their senior year in high school."

"And was there anything unusual about why they split?"

"I don't remember exactly. Mothers never really know what's

going on with their sons and their relationships. Danny later told me that Sandy was a tramp and he wanted nothing more to do with her. Supposedly, they got into a pissing contest, and Sandy told my boy she could cause big trouble for him if he wasn't careful," said Gloria, now working her way back towards the top of the stairs. "*The Bold and the Beautiful* is coming on in a minute, and I need to get back to my chair."

As Nowitzke and Anissa followed the woman, they passed an unopened door, the only one of several upstairs rooms that was closed. "What's in here?" asked Nowitzke.

Gloria glanced back at the detective. "Oh, that's my Danny's room. Still like to keep it the way it was when he went off to college. I think he might have made it home for a couple of weekends before he went to the left coast for his job. Been a long time since he was here. Help yourself and go on in. Take your time. I can hear my soap starting downstairs," she said, proceeding deliberately step-by-step back down to the first floor.

Once Gloria was downstairs, Nowitzke and Anissa stood outside the door and swapped looks. "Ladies first," he offered with a smile, trying to envision the chaos on the other side.

Anissa shook her head. "You're senior, Chuck."

"Just wondering if my tetanus shot is up to speed," Nowitzke replied as he turned the antique crystal doorknob and gave the dark-stained door a shove.

Much to their surprise, Danny's room was in pristine condition. "Wow, this place is like a museum from decades ago," observed Anissa as she stepped into the room. Although the air was musty and stale, there was no doubt that the bedroom belonged to a teenage boy from another era. The single bed was made, ready for the evening in case Danny showed up unexpectedly and decided to spend the night. At the foot of the frame stood a large boxy television that looked like it weighed some fifty pounds. A poster of a blonde "Playmate of the Month" hung on the wall above several cheap fiberboard bookshelves holding a combination of comic books, a couple of paperback Hemingway novels, and a series of high school yearbooks. An oversized desktop computer with a small green screen monitor sat on Danny's desk next to his high school graduation photo, along with several bowling trophies that were draped with assorted sports medals. The closet held several now-faded but crisply ironed shirts hanging next to a cluster of empty wire hangers.

"I wonder if Gloria tossed out Danny's baseball cards?" asked Nowitzke, lamenting that his own mother had trashed his collection years before.

Anissa sat on the bed, trying to make any sense of it all. "Gloria might actually dust in here," she said. "Do you really think Danny is victim five?"

"Not sure. If nothing else, the dates line up. Another fairly young guy having a heart attack? I'd like to get an officer on the line out in Oregon to fill in any gaps," Nowitzke said, pulling out his phone to search for a number. He continued talking as he did his Google search. "You know, there are just enough threads here to think this is somehow all connected. First, Anne Tucker, the wife of victim three, mentions Dan Warren's name. Then we hear it from Kelsie Cantrell, Sandy's friend, who tells us that Sandy happened to be Danny's girlfriend. Too small a world for me, Nis."

As Nowitzke dialed, Anissa examined Danny's room more closely. Initially, she was fascinated with the monstrous piece of hardware on the desk, wondering if the computer still worked. In the background, she heard Nowitzke connect with someone only to hear her boss growl after being placed on hold. Continuing to look through Danny's things, Anissa was drawn to the bookcase. She was a fan of Hemingway and managed to wrench a copy of *The Sun Also Rises* from the shelf where it was wedged. During high school, she had become enamored with the story about the running of the bulls in Spain. However, after paging through the novel, she was unable to replace it back into the tight shelf. She made several tries before concluding that she might be able to create space by pulling out another book and replacing them together. However, as Anissa attempted to solve the

puzzle, she inadvertently caused one of the yearbooks to fall and hit
the floor on its spine. She replaced the two novels and looked down
to see the annual. The 1988 edition of *The Rocket* from Neenah High
School had opened to a series of photographs of clubs. As Nowitzke
continued to wait on hold for someone halfway across the country,
Anissa picked up and perused the book.

Thinking back to her own high school years, she smiled as she
looked at the young faces. The DECA group. The French Club.
The Math Team. Young Democrats. Young Republicans. Then,
as she flipped to another page, something caught her eye. A picture
of a group labeled the "Achievers Club," featuring eight students:
one young lady, seven males, and an advisor. Anissa immediately
recognized a smiling Sandy Hawkins. Then she read the names of
the other Achievers listed under the photo. McClary. Brock. Tucker.
Hecht. Devine. Henderson. Warren. The smiling faces of each of the
victims were staring back at her, captured in time. Anissa's eyes grew
wide as her heart began to race, especially when she saw the name of
the group's mentor. Elliott Gordon.

"Chuck!" she called excitedly. "Put the phone down! We just made
our connection."

CHAPTER 33

It had been several days since Elliott received a threatening text. He wrote the experience off to tough guys getting out of prison, getting drunk, and looking to cause him problems, even if they had no intent of following through. It had happened before, and it would happen again. Part of the territory in his line of work. And, like other previous occasions, Elliott maintained a sense of high alert before lapsing back into complacency.

It was just after noon as he turned into his normal parking space at Ivy House following several outside morning meetings. After he shut off the engine, he took a cursory glance around, looking for anything unusual. Seeing no threats, he popped out of the Jaguar before making his way to the front door. The rain clouds above him were growing, and off to the side, he caught a glimpse of a female jogger working her way towards him. Glancing at the approaching woman, he waved, getting a smile in return, his subconscious continuing to process the image of the woman as he turned toward the front door. As he scanned his card in the electronic lock, he concluded that it was the same woman he typically saw when he arrived at work . . . at his normal time. Then, his brain finally registered something more unusual. The woman was carrying something in her hand. A dark object. Jesus, it was a pistol.

Before Elliott could react, a blunt object tore into the skin on the back of his head, sending him slumping to his knees in pain. The woman ripped off her baseball cap, unfurled a mane of red hair, and looked directly into the camera positioned above her while pointing at the front door with her weapon.

****

While Anissa continued to pore over the old high school annual, Nowitzke took the wheel of the Audi as they quickly made their way to Ivy House to speak to Elliott. "Chuck, guess the date of the high school graduation in 1988 at Neenah High."

"June 16?"

"Yes," Anissa confirmed. "Something must have happened on or after graduation since every victim died on the five-year anniversary of that date."

"Yeah, a helluva way to celebrate reunions. What's the story on Elliott? You said he was listed in the photo as an adviser for this club?"

"He must be older than the students. Based on the photo, it doesn't look like much. He's definitely not part of the graduating class, if the yearbook is accurate."

"Looks like a good place to start our questioning with Elliott. We're still looking for a method and a motive," Nowitzke concluded as Anissa's phone rang in the car. She answered using the touch screen, and the voice of Wally Schmidt echoed through the vehicle.

"Batrachotoxin!" exclaimed the ME. "Anissa, I couldn't find Chuck. Is he with you by any chance?"

"Yeah, Wally, I'm here. We're in the car, and you're on speaker. Now, batracho-what?" asked Nowitzke.

"Toxin. Batrachotoxin. It was something new, even for my lab colleagues in Pennsylvania."

"So, this isn't a poison on a standard toxicology list?" Anissa asked.

"No. Far from it. I mean, it's not on anyone's list. This poison is as exotic as they come. Frankly, I'm still doing some research on it, but it's also a bit of a head-scratcher. Let me give you a little perspective on what I've been able to develop. I'm sure you've both heard of cyanide."

"Yeah. Wasn't that what Hitler took when he killed himself?" said Nowitzke as his foot pushed harder on the accelerator.

"Depending upon whose version of history you read, Chuck, but yeah. Anyway, batrachotoxin is a thousand times more deadly than cyanide. Two grains of this stuff is more than enough to kill an average-sized man." Wally paused, adding to the drama. "And there's no antidote."

"Okay, so when someone is poisoned with batrachotoxin, what happens?" asked Nowitzke.

"The poison blocks the transmission of nerve signals to the muscles, including the heart. Basically, it causes a sort of paralysis, resulting in an arrhythmia and cardiac failure. Someone who has been poisoned with batrachotoxin would look like they were having a massive heart attack to the average person. The victim would feel a crushing weight in their chest, and their eyes would bulge. Death takes place in minutes. Sound familiar?"

"No shit," said Nowitzke, nodding. "Wally, as an FYI, I think we've located all the numbered victims before Hecht, and in several of the cases, the ME or coroner ruled the cause of death as a heart attack."

"Well, even if a skilled ME noticed the puncture mark during the autopsy, they would still have difficulty pinpointing a cause of death because this is such an obscure poison, especially when everything else is screaming heart attack," Wally replied.

"I'll bet more than one detective was shocked by their ME's conclusion when their gut told them drugs but all the toxicology tests came back negative," added Anissa.

"Where do you get a poison like this, Wally?" Nowitzke asked.

"That's just it. You don't. At least not around here. It's certainly not something you can order on Amazon."

Nowitzke shook his head, trying to follow along. "I'm missing something. You've confirmed that you found batrachotoxin in

Senator Hecht's body. Then you're pretty much telling us that this isn't possible?"

"Let me give you some more background. The word 'batrachotoxin' in Greek breaks down to the words 'frog' and 'toxin.' Your best source to find this poison would be in the jungles of New Guinea or South America. You see, there are these small frogs about the size of a bottle cap. The one I've read about is called a dart frog. I'm sure you've seen documentaries on television about natives hunting with poison darts or arrows, right? Anyway, this dart frog is one of the species you get the poison from. By the way, it is also quite the process to extract the poison too. As I understand it, the natives nail the frog to a tree and burn it. When the frog's skin blisters, the poison bubbles to the surface and the natives dip their arrows. Fascinating stuff."

"Why couldn't someone just steal one of these frogs from a zoo and extract the poison?" asked Anissa.

"That wouldn't work," replied the ME. "The frogs don't produce the batrachotoxin on their own."

Anissa closed her eyes and scratched her head. "Okay, now I'm confused. How *do* the frogs produce the poison?"

"According to the literature, you can't raise these frogs in captivity to get the poison. The toxin comes from what the frogs eat . . . things indigenous to their jungle habitat. Based on what I read, the diet of the dart frog is typically plants and bugs."

There was a stunned silence in the car as Nowitzke looked at Anissa. "The hothouse?" he asked her. "We saw a small frog on the path there. Didn't Brad say he had beetles and plants from the jungle to keep it real?"

"Yes, he did," replied Anissa.

"Wally, question for you," said Nowitzke. "Do you think it would it be possible to build an artificial environment where these frogs could live? I mean, if you fed them the right stuff, could the frogs then make their own poison?"

The detectives heard nothing on the other end of the phone until

Wally cleared his voice. "Yeah, I suppose so. But it would take a lot of money to create the proper conditions to begin with. The other little complicating detail is that these types of frogs all seem to be on the endangered species list too, so getting them here would take some doing. Beyond the cash, it also requires real expertise to be able to make something like that work. However, I guess it's possible," he concluded. "Since I got the tox report back on the senator, I've been looking for more information on batrachotoxin. There isn't much in the way of documentation about it aside from it making one of those stupid top-ten lists on the internet about the world's deadliest poisons, and there are very few experts on the subject. Most of what I learned comes from an article written quite a while back. You'll never guess who wrote it."

"Lemme take a flyer. Brad Hawkins?" asked Nowitzke.

"What the . . . ?"

"Wally, we gotta go," interrupted the detective as he clicked off the call and gunned the Audi. "Shit. Looks like we need to have a serious conversation with Brad too," he said calmly. Anissa's phone rang again.

"Anissa, it's Chief Clark. Is Chuck with you?"

"Yeah," answered the senior detective.

"Good. We have a serious situation developing at Ivy House. Based on the early reports from security there, there was a home invasion, an assault, and what's brewing to be a potential hostage situation and standoff. Security reported seeing someone accost Elliott Gordon as he was going into the house for work. We're told that there is video of a young woman who was apparently jogging before she approached Elliott and pistol-whipped him. Then the suspect dragged him into the building. However, before she did, she took off her hat and smiled into the overhead camera."

Anissa and Nowitzke looked at each other, waiting for more detail. "What color hair does the woman have?" asked Anissa uneasily.

"Not sure why that matters . . ." After a long pause, Marcus replied. "Red. Red hair. Do you think there's any chance this might be the same woman from the fundraiser?"

"I think we were both wondering the same thing." Out of the corner of his eye, Nowitzke saw Anissa's head bobbing up and down.

"SWAT is on sight surrounding the building, along with pretty much every squad car in the field," advised Clark.

"Chief, can you keep everyone outside for the time being?" asked Nowitzke. "We've got a break in your cold case and were already on the way to Hawkins' place to speak to Elliott Gordon before the shit hit the fan. If the woman inside is who we think it is, Anissa and I want to call her and see if she'll let us into the house. We've got a better chance to resolve this if everyone keeps their cool."

"You got it. I'm on my way to the scene to assume on-site command," he replied before clicking off his phone.

As the detectives approached Ivy House, Nowitzke saw the cluster of emergency vehicles and first responders surrounding the residence, causing an eerie flashback to his first visit there, the major difference this time being the presence of a large, ominous black truck surrounded by several men wearing tactical gear. The Audi came to a stop halfway down the block as Anissa called Savanna on her cell phone.

"Hi, Nis, what's up?" the woman replied cheerfully as if she didn't have a care in the world.

"Savanna, are you in Ivy House with Elliott Gordon?"

"Yeah, I am. I guess posing for the camera on the way in must have given it away."

"Listen, I'm not sure if you've looked outside, but you've got a shitstorm brewing around you. The building is surrounded with cops. Is there anyone else with you?"

"Just Elliott and Brad. Oh, and I've also got this behemoth named Leonard zip-tied in the room with us. I was looking for a fourth to play bridge to pass the time. I told everyone else to get out of the house. And yes, I'm aware of what's going on outside. I'm watching the security cameras on the laptop in Brad's study."

Jesus, how did she subdue Leonard? "Will you let me and Chuck into the building so we can talk?" asked Anissa.

"No problem. I need you to be judge and jury. I can open the door from here," Savanna replied. "Just keep all your friends away from the building. I've got some serious business to take care of with these gentlemen."

"We've already got that figured out."

"See you in a few, girlfriend," she said before the phone line went dead.

CHAPTER 34

Nowitzke and Anissa walked up to the SWAT vehicle, finding Commander Derek Bonner in the eye of the developing chaos. Bonner, a bodybuilder and former Marine, had an intimidating presence and looked like a movie actor who had been specifically selected for his job. With intense green eyes, he maintained a mostly shaved scalp aside from a short tuft of brown hair on the top of his head. His appearance gave him a hawkish look, like he was aching to for an opportunity to flex his team's muscle. However, the commander's track record was stellar, having managed to diffuse most of the circumstances he had been involved in without his unit even firing a shot.

Although he was known as a stickler for details, for some reason Bonner had hit it off with Nowitzke, who had a decidedly different worldview for procedure. During an early conversation between the two, they had found a mutual passion. Beer. Bonner as a semi-professional home brewer, and Nowitzke as a semi-professional drinker.

"Anissa," greeted Bonner with a smile upon seeing the approaching detectives. "Chuck, I understand we've been instructed per Chief Clark to hold our position."

"Yeah, D. I think there's much more to the story beyond a hostage situation. Anissa and I have been working a cold case recently, and our impression is that the people inside have the answers we need."

"No problem. For the moment, we're good. The chief is still making his way here. What do you need from us?"

"Some time and a couple of tac vests," Nowitzke replied. He grabbed his pistol, briefly inspecting it to see that the magazine was full. "Also, one of your fine pilsners if you've got one in the truck. Something you should try, Nis."

"Tell you what . . ." said Bonner as he handed each detective a vest. "You close this matter without us getting involved and I'll give you a case."

"Nothing like being highly motivated, D."

The detectives tugged on their body armor, drawing the Velcro tabs tight. Then they parted the crowd of officers, making their way to the front door as Anissa called Savanna again.

"I see you on the camera, Anissa. I'm unlocking the door," said the redhead.

Upon hearing a buzz, Nowitzke turned and gave Bonner a hopeful look as he held the door open for his partner.

The lack of any sound within Ivy House immediately had both detectives on edge as they walked down the familiar hallway. Still, neither officer felt compelled to pull their weapon as they approached the door of Brad's study. Flanking the entrance to the room, Anissa took the lead and knocked while simultaneously pushing the heavy door open.

Inside, Savanna was sitting casually in Brad's office chair dressed in a jogging suit, her shoes resting on the massive desk. She presented a calm demeanor, and the only evidence that something was off was the snub-nosed .357 Magnum revolver she held in plain view pointed in the general direction of Brad and Elliott who were seated directly across from her. From what Nowitzke could tell, neither Brad nor Elliott was restrained in any way. Elliott had a perturbed look on his face as he slumped to one side of his chair holding a towel against the wound on the back of his head. And Brad looked like the picture of cool, almost relaxed, crossing his legs as he sat next to his security director. Leonard had been zip-tied, his hands in front of him. He dwarfed the upholstered chair where he was sitting, located off to the side of the other captives but still in Savanna's line of sight.

"What's going on?" Nowitzke asked quizzically as he and Anissa began moving toward Savanna. However, the woman rose to her feet, quickly stopping them, and motioned with her gun hand that each detective should sit in the leather chairs near the door.

"I need your weapons too," said Savanna. "Please put them on the credenza behind me. Oh, and Chuck, don't forget about the one around your ankle."

Nowitzke's shocked look mirrored that of Anissa. He reluctantly removed both weapons and scowled for what it was worth before the pair surrendered their guns.

"Now, take your chairs so we can get started. I've got a lot of questions."

"So do I," added Nowitzke to no one in particular.

Savanna winked at him as she circled the room. "I think all your questions will be answered today."

Brad cut in. "Before you get started, Miss . . ."

"Smythe."

"Why am I here?" he asked. "I employ Elliott, but that's it." He stood as if planning to leave the room.

"Park it, Brad." Savanna motioned him back to his seat with her weapon. "I've got my reasons. Personal ones that will become clear in a little while."

Brad nodded, seemingly resigned to being confined to the study for the time being. Yet he also maintained a confident look, in part because out of the corner of his eye, he could see Leonard quietly straining to break the zip tie around his wrists.

"Let me start with Mr. Gordon here," Savanna began. "A one-time cop who now serves at the beck and call of Brad Hawkins. Also, the asshole who sent Mr. Black to kill me on at least two occasions."

The bluntness of Savanna's statement made Brad's head snap toward Elliott. The former DA was now an interested spectator in the discussion.

"Here are the rules," continued Savanna. "I'll go through them once. If I ask you a question, give me a direct answer. No bullshit. No ignoring me. Understand that I already know much of the story that we're going to talk about. But each of you has information that will help fill in the gaps. If I get even a sense that you're lying to me or holding back, I'll give you one polite warning. The second time it happens, I'll shoot you in the kneecap. Capisce?"

Elliott's head dropped, and he avoided eye contact with Savanna. "Elliott, you're just making this harder on yourself than it needs to be," she said calmly from across the room. Then, she swooped down on him, stopping inches from his face before unleashing a menacing scream, "DO YOU UNDERSTAND?"

The intensity in her voice, backed up by the weapon, made Elliott stiffen in his chair.

"Tell me what happened on June 16, 1988," Savanna demanded, reverting to a more composed tone.

"What do you mean?" he croaked, a shocked and confused look on his face.

"Wrong answer," she replied evenly, sending the butt of her gun into his temple, drawing a loud yelp from him. She stepped back. "Now, let's try this again, knowing you've already used your first strike."

Taking a deep breath, Elliott tried to compose himself. "Listen, I don't know the whole story either. That's the honest-to-God truth."

Savanna assessed the look on his face. "Okay then, tell me what you know. Start with the Achievers Club and bring me up to June 16."

"The Achievers Club?" questioned Elliott. Savanna moved behind the desk, reached down, and tossed him a copy of the 1988 Neenah High School yearbook.

"Flip to page fifty-seven if you need to refresh your memory," she said. Nowitzke and Anissa again swapped looks. It was clear that Savanna had been well ahead of them.

Elliott never opened the book but began to tell his story slowly. "I was the advisor to the Achievers Club in 1988. A group from Neenah High School, just down the road. I served one year since I needed a mentoring credit to graduate from college. The club was exclusive, limited to graduating seniors who were at or near the top of their class, combining academics and extracurriculars like sports, drama, or service projects. It was highly involved in the community. Each of the kids was expected to work on a year-long project aimed at helping the less fortunate, and they had to raise their own funds. Upon graduation, the most exceptional member of the group was awarded a full college scholarship as determined by the advisor and two other outside community observers."

"How many students were in the club that year?" asked Savanna.

"Eight total. Seven guys and one remarkable young woman. If I remember correctly, it was eight students out of a graduating class of more than five hundred."

"Do you recall their names?"

"Yeah . . . even without the yearbook," he said, briefly glancing down at the annual in his lap. "Brock. Tucker. McClary. Devine. Henderson. Warren. Hecht. And Sandra Hawkins."

The names rang in Nowitzke's head for the second time in the last hour. Brad turned to look at Elliott upon the mention of his sister.

"Tell me about the club members," Savanna pressed.

"I guess I'd call it a mixed bag. A couple of nerds. Some others who had excellent credentials but were bored and on the verge of becoming slackers, like Frankie Brock, a dumbass set to go to the University of Minnesota but ended up getting involved with hard drugs. There were also one or two nice guys. Finally, a couple of real fucking pricks . . . Warren and Hecht. In my mind, Sandy was head and shoulders above the rest of the group. Interestingly, though, she had a relationship with Warren that I never understood. She could have done much better," offered Elliott. "Hecht was a total asshole. The kind of person who made others think they were friends, but only if it benefitted him. Even in high school, he was cut out to be a politician."

"You said the group worked on a community project of some sort?"

"Yeah, but I'll be damned if I can remember what it was. It's not important."

"How did the group get along?" asked Savanna.

"They were pretty competitive for the most part. At the beginning of the year, all of them were totally engaged. However, as senioritis set in, several were happy just to show up for the meetings and let others do the work. A few pitched in and did their part. At some point, though, Sandy ended up doing the lion's share of everything and brought the project over the goal line. By rights, she got most of the credit, even though she didn't want to be in the limelight. She was my favorite of the bunch." Elliott's eyes looked upward as if scanning his brain for more details. "God, she was so beautiful. Sandy had a magnetic personality and a brain. Very mature. Destined for great things. An amazing girl," he added, his voice trailing off. Brad tented his fingers under his nose and smiled as he listened to Elliott.

"How did the dynamics of the group play out?"

"I quickly figured out who the leaders were from the rest. What I didn't realize was that several of these guys really grew to hate Sandy because *everything* she did was stellar. She left them all in the dust. The negative feeling they had for her was something I didn't understand until it was too late." Elliott buried his head in his hands.

"When did you figure that out?"

"On graduation night. June 16, 1988."

"What happened?"

"My involvement with the group had ended a couple of weeks before the end of the school year. But I later learned the backstory, just so we're clear."

Savanna nodded for Elliott to continue.

"At the graduation ceremony, all the major awards for the school year were announced. It was no secret that Sandy ended up being named Achiever of the Year, earning a full ride to Wisconsin. Her dream. That evening, there were several celebrations. Some were officially sponsored by the school. Some not . . . meaning beer and booze were involved. From what I know, Sandy went to the school-sponsored party with her boyfriend, Danny Warren. Then Dan talked her into going to a house party with the other members of the Achievers Club. Sandy reluctantly agreed even though she wasn't a drinker. Anyway, as you can guess, everyone got shit-faced. And Sandy didn't know it, but her fucking boyfriend decided he had plans for her. When she was almost to the point of passing out, she asked Dan to take her home. However, Dan had already made up his mind that he was going to have sex with her. When he made his move, Sandy did her best to fight him off, but he beat her up before raping her."

The unease in the study was palpable as Brad and the others sat motionless in their chairs.

"Afterward, Dan realized what he'd done and, more importantly, what could happen to him. It was more than losing scholarship money. He was smart enough to know that going to prison was a real possibility. He somehow needed to cover his tracks. So, he stirred up the vitriol of the others in the Achievers Club. Each of them was now drunk, easy to manipulate, and pissed off all over again at Sandy. Dan told these guys to man up and fuck Sandy too." Elliott took a breath. "One by one, they took turns raping her," he said, his body now shuddering. He slammed his hand on the desk as tears streamed down his face. "Fucking Achievers!"

Brad shifted uncomfortably in his chair, holding an index finger of one hand parallel with his lips at the revelation. Nowitzke blinked hard at the admission but sat stoically. But Savanna's face was filled with resolve. "Continue," she urged.

Elliott looked down at the floor. "As the night wore on, the guys started sobering up, all knowing that they were in serious trouble. Somehow, they found my apartment and dumped Sandy on my doorstep, rang my doorbell, and disappeared. When I found her, I almost didn't recognize her. Her face was bruised, her eyes were blackened . . . almost swollen shut. Her clothes had been ripped to shreds, and she was naked from the waist down and covered in blood and jizz. One of the stupid fuckers even tried to rape her anally." Brad blanched in his chair upon hearing the description. "I'll bet it was Hecht," surmised Elliott.

"I wasn't sure what to do. Sandy was semiconscious and half-drunk. She begged me not to call the police. When I told her I was taking her to the hospital, she became hysterical and refused to go. I gently picked her up and got her to her feet. She was so weak. I helped her out of her clothes and into the shower so she could clean herself up. Then I made her some coffee and found something for her to wear before she crashed on my couch. She slept at my place for the better part of a week. Every day or so, she called you to tell you about what girlfriend she was staying with," he added, looking at Brad.

"Over the next several days, Sandy gradually felt better. The swelling in her face went down, but the bruises had mottled into a yellow and purple color. I was still pushing hard to take her to the hospital, but she flatly refused. Through her tears, Sandy told me the details of what happened, still trying to understand how her 'friends' could take advantage of her. She was sure that each had taken at least one turn. Then she started struggling with the idea that she had sent the wrong message to these guys. But I told her that was bullshit. No one deserves what happened to her. The worst of it, though, was at night. From my room, I could hear her cry out in her sleep as she relived her nightmare. By the end of the week, Sandy told me she needed to go home. I went to a store and bought her some clothes and makeup so she could cover what was left of the bruising. She thanked me for my kindness, gave me a peck on the cheek at my front door, and got into a cab. About a week later, I read in the local paper that she had disappeared."

Elliott took a deep breath. "I kept waiting for a news story about the police investigating the rape, but it never happened. Sandy never reported it." He hesitated, closing his eyes for a moment. "I also regret that I never told Sandy that I had feelings for her. Over the year I spent working with her, I had grown to love her. In theory, I knew that any relationship with her was a stretch anyway, me graduating from college while she was just starting school, all of eighteen years old. At that point in our lives, that four-year gap seemed insurmountable, so I never said anything. Eventually, I beat myself up for not having taken the risk. I never gave up hope of reconnecting with her, even though the rest of the world had pretty much written her off as dead.

"Months passed, and Sandy never turned up. By then, I was fixated on the assholes who had taken everything away from her. Her innocence. Her scholarship. The life she had planned. The more I thought about it, the more enraged I became. These so-called Achievers, their lives still intact with everything ahead of them. Each had gotten off scot-free. No prison or jail time, no trial, no punishment, no nothing. I told myself I would make each of them suffer for what they had done to Sandy. I decided to take matters into my own hands, starting with Frankie Brock.

"He seemed like a decent-enough kid when I knew him, but little Frankie spiraled out of control after graduation. He dropped off the grid and became a thief to finance his drug habit. My impression was that he was so consumed with guilt about Sandy that he didn't care about living anymore. By then, I had become a cop, with access to all the records I needed to find him. What's a more symbolic time to get each of the fuckers than their five-year anniversaries from graduation day?

"I still remember every detail of that night even after all these years. It was beastly hot. I had tracked Frankie down to a ripe-smelling alley where he lived in a cardboard box. In that heat, the smell of urine and shit was overpowering. When I found him, Frankie was almost unconscious, strung out from heroin but still struggling to inject himself. When I stood over him, he looked at me with a hint of recognition as I took the syringe from his hand. I drew back the plunger to add air to whatever was already in the tube, jammed it into the vein in his arm, and waited. A couple minutes went by. Then, little Frankie started to hyperventilate, and his eyes opened wide, bulging from the embolism moving toward his brain. He convulsed and writhed in pain for a few moments before I heard a loud exhale. As far as I was concerned, he had gotten off easy compared to what he had done. I left him to rot with the other human trash in the alley. Before I left, I took out a marker and wrote a big number one on his forehead.

"Afterwards, my brain was on fire. Part of me felt guilty, but then I felt the sweetness of revenge before paranoia set in. I kept wondering when the detectives would figure out what happened and come arrest me. But it turned out they really didn't give a shit. Frankie was just another fucking addict as far as they were concerned. Barely worth the paperwork they had to complete. No one ever came looking for me. A couple days later, I saw a small article in the paper about a local addict dying, and I realized how easy it was to kill someone that was supposed to die anyway."

Nowitzke sat back in his chair as Elliott's words echoed almost exactly what Wally Schmidt had told him earlier during the investigation.

"I was on my way," Elliott continued. "I began following the careers of the others. Then I figured out that killing them off and getting away with it might not be as simple as taking care of poor Frankie. The last thing I wanted was to spend time in prison. Cops don't do well in prison.

"I needed an alternative approach. As I searched for the perfect tool, it didn't take long to understand that *every* method leaves some sort of evidence behind. Bullets have signatures. Same as knives. It was a real problem until I had a conversation with a medical examiner at a law enforcement conference in New York. We were having drinks one night, and I asked this guy if it was possible for someone to get away with murder. He said it was not that hard to do, especially if you had no real connection to the victim. Half in the bag, he theorized that he would use a poison and explained that while most state crime labs tested for a decent list of toxins, they didn't test for all of them and the right one would easily slip through the cracks. He also said that the trick was getting the toxin without leaving a paper trail. But, if you could figure it out and administer the right poison, the effect on the victim could mimic a heart attack. Best of all, this guy said that by the time anyone even suspected a particular chemical, it would most likely disperse quickly in the deceased's body, becoming undetectable. When I got home, I researched several poisons before I stumbled onto something called batrachotoxin."

Anissa looked at Nowitzke.

"It's a poison from small frogs in South America that make the venom based on what they eat in their natural environment. Everything I needed to know about this mysterious poison was in an article written by Brad Hawkins."

Brad's head drooped at the mention of his name.

"The article gave me the recipe for exactly what I was looking for. Better yet, after Brad joined the DA's office, I searched him out to help him with his investigative work, trying to make an impression on him and forge a relationship. It was also an opportunity to stay close to the family if Sandy ever turned up. As Brad worked his way up the ladder at the DA's office, we became friends. One night after he successfully put away some scumbag, we were out celebrating. Maybe we each had one too many that night, but I brought up Sandy."

"You need to keep your mouth shut, Elliott," said Brad calmly.

"No, I have to tell the rest of the story," he replied. "I told Brad about me being an advisor to Sandy and her classmates before recounting the incident to him and explaining that it was my impression that it was what prompted her to disappear. For the first time in my life, I watched tears stream down Brad's face. After he collected himself, I admitted that I had fallen in love with Sandy, even though she never knew. I also said that I was determined to set things right. Then, I took a huge risk telling him what I had done to Frankie Brock and my plan for the other rapists. I asked him about batrachotoxin and the article he wrote. In Wisconsin, it seemed like the perfect solution if you could pull it off. An almost undetectable poison with no antidote that would kill almost instantaneously.

"When I finished telling him my plan, Brad sat in his chair . . . quiet . . . brooding . . . intense . . . calculating. Having seen that look on his face before, I thought my career and my life might have just ended. But then he sat forward and whispered, 'You know the statute of limitations has run on any rape charge involving Sandy. Even if I had the evidence, I couldn't prosecute these fuckers if I wanted to.' It was then I knew he was in."

Brad shifted in his chair to face the security officer. "Elliott, you need to be quiet right now. And Ms. Smythe, my counsel to you is that any confession you obtain from Elliott here has been coerced by you in the presence of police officers. Even a public defender would be able to have this case tossed from court."

"Do me a favor and shut the fuck up, Brad," replied Savanna, moving directly behind the man.

"I demand a lawyer," he continued. Instead, he earned the butt of a gun to the temple from Savanna, the blow making his eyes roll back into his head.

"Okay, Elliott, please continue," she calmly said.

Elliott nodded nervously. "Brad and I quickly moved from theory to tactics. We talked about the difficulty of getting the frogs in the first place and then the poison from frogs raised in captivity. He's a biologist by training, a highly motivated one with a lot of money. A dangerous combination. Brad built the hothouse on his property to specs he designed. He worked with some shady folks who needed a favor to import the frogs and another bunch to get the beetles and food. It was everything I needed to kill off the Achievers Club one by one.

"When we steamed the first batch of poison from a frog, I insisted on doing a test. Brad objected at first, but I told him I wasn't going to be holding the bag for leaving a puncture wound on one of the Achievers if the poison didn't work. When we finally agreed, I went back to the filthy alley where I had killed Brock and found another vagrant. I stuck him with a small injector I had built into a ring, careful not to get myself by accident. The old bastard was passed-out drunk.

When I poked him, he woke up, looking all pissed off at me until he grabbed his chest and died a minute later.

"I told Brad my plan to track down the rest of the assholes and take care of each one on the five-year anniversary of the rape. About a year in advance of the reunion date, I'd start researching the remaining Achievers, trying to cut one from the herd. Kind of like popping a bottle of champagne to celebrate each reunion.

"Brad turned a blind eye to what I was up to. He didn't want to know anything about what was taking place—who, where, or when. Kind of a plausible deniability thing, I guess. However, I remained on his staff. Ironically, in the meantime, Brad became a superstar in prosecuting rapes in the state. A national thought leader, no less. He handled justice his way while I tracked down each of the perps to hand out some of mine. Everything went to plan."

"But you messed up with Hecht?" asked Nowitzke, chiming in.

"Yeah. For some reason, the senator was different for me. A little intimidating. Larger than life. I had seen him at other fundraisers and wasn't sure if he would have any security people around him. I wanted his guard down when it came time to deliver the poison. Then, this little honey sidled up to Tony." He paused, looking at Savanna strangely as he cocked his head. "You knew the senator was going to die when you took him downstairs, didn't you?"

The expression on Savanna's face gave the answer to everyone in the room.

"How did you know?" asked Anissa.

"I had insider information," she replied. All eyes in the room now focused on her.

"Tell us," demanded Nowitzke.

"Like I said, Chuck, I knew much of the story from a reliable party. I even followed along as each of Sandy's 'friends' was murdered over time. I wasn't sure how it was done or exactly who was responsible for the homicides until Elliott here told us, but I did know they took place like clockwork. For the past five years, I've been biding my time, just waiting for June 16, 2023, and the senator's reunion with death. I wanted to be here for the big event. Even then, I didn't know what would take place until I heard Hecht scream like a little girl when Ernie Preston poked him. By the way, just to clarify for those in this room, Hecht had zero chance of having sex with me," offered the young woman. "Anyway, when the senator went into convulsions, I went looking for help to keep up any ruse, but I knew he would be dead in minutes."

Reliable party? thought Nowitzke. *How did Savanna "follow" along for years, let alone figure out when the attack on Hecht would take place?*

"So, that's your story, Elliott?" asked Savanna, strolling around the room like a lawyer who had just made her case to a jury. "You're basically saying you're a fucking hero, righting the big wrong with all these murders? Certainly not quid pro quo for the rapist Achievers. Definitely not for the homeless guy you experimented on. Even though you thought you'd get a medal when Hecht died, you still sent Black to kill Ernie and then me."

"Listen, I lost my way over the years," said Elliott, conceding the point. "Cover-ups are always worse than the crime itself. It wasn't personal."

"It was for me," Savanna replied. "And for Ernie's family. And Bob Edwards too."

"And me," added Anissa.

"The price of poker for me not doing time." Elliott's voice held no remorse. "I needed Black to clean up my messes and then take care of that other loose end when fat Bob figured out there was a video. Things escalated. I lost control of the situation. But I was determined not to go to prison."

"You will now," Savanna countered before turning her attention to his partner. "Or maybe not? Now, would you like to tell your story, Brad?"

"What story?"

"Remember the rules. Don't duck the issue. You're already an accomplice to multiple murders."

"You've got no real proof of anything aside from this psycho's little tale," he spat back at her. "No evidence of me being involved in any of the deaths. Only a coerced confession with no corroboration of any kind. Fuck you, Ms. Smythe."

"Such a witty reply. Are you going to tell your story, or do you want me to do it for you?"

Brad sat stone-faced.

"Okay, mister former DA, I'll cut you some slack on the rules. But I might require an answer to a question from time to time," said Savanna, not drawing a reaction from him. She sat back down behind the desk with the handgun still pointed at Brad and Elliott. "Now, we'll learn about the worst offender. This fairy tale begins with you offering your sister, Sandy, a graduation gift, n'est-ce pas?"

Brad glared at Savanna but still said nothing.

"Sandy chose Hawaii," she continued. "Her first big trip. She was so excited that she told all her friends. You flew first class with her to Oahu, stayed at a luxury resort, did some sightseeing, hung out by the palm trees and the pool, catching some rays. Beautiful."

"How could you possibly know that?"

"What got you, Brad?" asked Savanna, ignoring his question. "Seeing women in string bikinis flaunting their titties on the beach in front of you all day long? Did you have one too many mai tais? Please fill in the blanks for us," she demanded derisively. "C'mon, Mister 'Never Had Time for a Girlfriend' Brad. Give us some of that eloquent courtroom demeanor."

Brad gave her a dirty look before spewing, "You don't know jack shit!"

"Actually, I do. Last chance before I spill the beans." She stood again, still holding the gun, her arms folded. "Man up, for Chrissakes!" Savanna shouted. But he remained impassive. She crouched behind Elliott so they were at eye level. "Okay, Elliott. Let me introduce you to member number nine of the Achievers Club. This high-and-mighty son of a bitch Brad here took advantage of his sister, no less. At some point during the trip of her life, he sprung a boner and decided to rape Sandy in her hotel room. Caught her as she was coming out of the shower, threw her on her bed, and screwed her while she begged him to stop."

A hush returned to the room. Elliott turned to Brad, who was now staring at the floor, his body language answering the lingering question on everyone's mind.

"What were you thinking, Brad?" continued Savanna. "Incest? Couldn't find some horny bitch on the beach? No hooker at the hotel bar? Couldn't just jack off in the shower?" Her eyes pierced into his face, and she screamed, "My God, you fucked your own sister! She trusted you. Who could even imagine something so bad?"

The room went quiet again. Brad cleared his throat. "You don't know what you're talking about," he protested with a scowl. "You've got no proof."

"This isn't some court of law where having an attorney makes a difference. I think we all know you did it. We're your judge and jury," replied Savanna. "As for proof, I want you to know that I got the story directly from the source." She paused. "Sandy was my mother."

Brad's stony demeanor changed quickly, his head tilting as he stared at the young woman, studying her face, trying to determine if she was telling the truth. Nowitzke, who had closely observed the proceedings, could tell from the look in Savanna's eyes that she was. *Jesus!*

"She gave me all the gory details," said Savanna. "I don't know how you can even stand to look at yourself in a mirror. You fucked your little sister. Now having heard from Elliott about graduation night, I can understand Sandy's state of mind. Weeks later, after the Achievers put her over the top, she didn't know what else to do. She told me she had to get as far from here as she could . . . from everything she knew. The area. You. So, she just vanished. Left behind almost all of her most important possessions, knowing it would throw the police off her trail. Sandy went to Canada, changed her name, and decided to begin her life all over again. A fresh start. And then she had me."

"This is just bullshit," shot back Brad. "Who are you really? What the hell are you after? Money?"

"I guess nothing more than to let the world know what a wonderful mother she was in spite of what you did to her," replied Savanna in a subdued voice as she dropped back into her chair. "That she made a life for herself. That she was the success that everyone thought she would be." She looked at both detectives. "It's why I steered your inquiry to Banff so you could learn what people thought of her. And Chuck, your nudge came with a little help from my friend Rebecca Underwood, who mailed you the information about McClary.

"I needed to make sure you didn't get away with this, Brad. You've made a helluva life for yourself. If I'm not who I said I was, how else was I able to send Bobilly to you? Look at this high school yearbook, and you'll see her writing." She pointed to the book now on the desk in front of Brad. "This all had to come from someone very close to Sandy."

Brad's eyes narrowed angrily at Savanna. "I demand an attorney." He then made eye contact with Leonard, who was still working on his zip ties.

"But wait. I've got one other big piece of interesting news for you. Get a load of this," Savanna said, handing Brad an official-looking piece of paper from a folder on the desk.

The room was still as everyone watched Brad's eyes quickly scan the document. Then he peered up at Savanna, his head cocking with a look of shock on his face. He turned his attention back to the paper, studying it a second time in more detail. "This can't be right," he said, shaking his head. "There's no way."

"It is. The DNA proves it . . . Daddy!" Savanna exclaimed, sucking the air from the room. "I'm your spawn, Brad. Sandy knew you wouldn't accept this without the proper paperwork. You're a big-time lawyer. You should have figured out long ago that the biggest thief is the one who steals someone else's trust."

A convinced Elliott flew from his chair in a rage. His face red and his fists clenched, he tackled Brad in his chair, driving him to the floor. "You son of a bitch. How could you?" he shrieked as he rained punches on Brad before sliding behind him and putting him in a chokehold. Nowitzke sprang from his chair to separate the two men, arriving seconds before Anissa.

Brad, now turning blue as Elliott began to sap the life from him, implored Leonard with his eyes, managing to rasp, "Help! Help me!"

In an instant, Leonard flexed his elbows as far behind his back as possible like a pair of chicken wings before snapping them forward and breaking the zip tie. With lightning speed, he snatched a handgun hidden under his chair and approached the melee. He yanked Nowitzke off the pile, tossing him over the desk with ease. Then Leonard grabbed Anissa, flinging her like a rag doll into the wall before she landed on the floor with a heavy thud. Elliott was now on top of Brad with the advantage, intent on taking the man's life. Brad's face signaled that his time was quickly running out. Seeing what was taking place, Leonard calmly stepped back and pointed the gun at both men on the floor.

Savanna bolted toward the big man, trying to stop him, screaming, "No! No, Leonard. Don't . . ."

Six loud shots rang out, echoing off the study's walls as Savanna threw her body into Leonard, somehow managing to take him to the ground and kicking the gun away from him. "Goddammit, you weren't supposed to do that!" she yelled. But the damage was done. Elliott and Brad were both dead. Blood gushed across the floor as each man had taken multiple bullets. Nowitzke, who had the wind knocked out of him, regrouped and found his way back to Savanna, pulling her off the giant before handcuffing him behind his back.

"Please don't hurt him, Chuck. Please," begged Savanna. "He made a mistake. He wasn't supposed to kill them. My God, Leonard's my brother." The young woman was now quaking with emotion.

Nowitzke ignored her, reaching down and cuffing Savanna before moving her to a sitting position on the floor next to Leonard.

Having seen Leonard empty his weapon into Brad and Elliott, Nowitzke immediately called Bonner, knowing that the sound of gunfire would trigger a response from SWAT. "Derek, get in here now. No guns. Things are under control, but we need EMTs on the double," he said before moving to help Anissa. She groaned loudly as she tried to stand, then collapsed.

CHAPTER 35

M oments later, Brad's study was teeming with officers and first responders as the blue haze and the smell of gun powder dispersed into the hallway. The EMTs knew immediately that they were unable to help either Brad or Elliott and focused on assisting Anissa. When Chief Clark and Bonner entered the room, Nowitzke approached both men to give them a summary of what had taken place. His report included the unexpected findings about Brad, Elliott, Sandy, and Savanna in what amounted to the resolution of all the cold case deaths.

In the turmoil swirling around them, Savanna had calmed herself and began talking quietly to Leonard. "You weren't supposed to kill anyone," she said, shaking her head. "It's not what we talked about. These guys confessed, and we had all the evidence. Why did you do it?"

The big man appeared humbled by the questions from his sister. "I hated listening to the story. First Elliott, and then what we knew about Brad. They were bad men, and I was just pissed off. Brad wasn't my father, but Sandy was still my mother, and I loved her. And being around him, I knew he was a slippery asshole. I was worried that even if he went to trial for this, he and some lawyer would find a way to beat the system and he'd walk. Listening to his bullshit about coerced confessions convinced me. I wasn't going to take any chance of letting either one of them leave the room alive," he concluded. "When I pointed my gun at Brad, I just hoped he felt for a moment what it was like to have someone you trust betray you. Just like he betrayed Mom.

I saw a baffled look in his eyes when he realized I was going to kill him. Elliott deserved to die too. Even though he might have originally had the best of intentions, he was a serial killer. In my mind, his life was over when he sent people to kill you."

"I get it," Savanna replied. "But you're my brother, and you killed two men in what should have been an open-and-shut case. You have no defenses. My God, the thought of you going to prison makes me sick to my stomach."

"Don't worry about me." Leonard smiled, his eyes glistening. "When Mom died, you took her place. You raised me, took care of me, and were always there for me. I'm not sure if I ever said it, but I love you," he said. "There's no way I'm going to prison."

Savanna cocked her head and stared into her brother's eyes, hearing an unexpected tone of finality in his voice. Leonard blinked hard twice and flinched. Thirty seconds later, he gasped loudly and convulsed, his large body jerking wildly on the floor.

When reality hit, Savanna yelled. "Help! Chuck, Leonard needs help! Please," she screamed, trying to get someone's attention, knowing exactly what had happened. Nowitzke turned from Chief Clark and Bonner to Leonard. But by the time he knelt alongside the man, he was silent and still. "Check his hands. But be careful," implored Savanna.

After rolling Leonard onto his stomach, Nowitzke saw the gold ring on the man's pinky with the exposed pin and a trickle of blood coming from a puncture wound through the leg of his pants. The batrachotoxin had claimed its final victim.

****

The story about the dynamic former DA, who had once been considered a stalwart of the community, being involved in a decades-long string of murders was scandalous enough to bring unwanted national attention to the area. Adding in the death of a senator, a mysterious poison, the suggestion of incest, and the gang rape of a young woman was frosting on the cake for the buzzards from the TV networks who descended on Appleton. For a solid two weeks, the locals and the nation learned more salacious details about the case than they cared to. An inquiry by the current district attorney into Savanna's final confrontation of Brad and Elliott determined that no charges would be filed against her, particularly considering the favorable testimony given by Detectives Nowitzke and Taylor. Savanna Smythe was recognized as being instrumental in officially closing the longest-standing cold case in Appleton.

EPILOGUE

On a comfortable Sunday afternoon, Savanna received a police escort to the Appleton International Airport in Anissa's Audi, followed by Nowitzke in his new used car, a 2012 Dodge Avenger, which left a trailing cloud of black smoke. Both vehicles came to a stop in the white zone lined with "No Parking" signs, a calculated move mandated by Nowitzke, dictating that any goodbyes would be short. Savanna emerged from Anissa's vehicle, her hair in a ponytail, wearing oversized black sunglasses, a Green Bay Packers t-shirt, jeans, and sandals as Nowitzke lugged her bags from the trunk of the car. Anissa stepped delicately from her Audi, still nursing two sets of broken ribs from the various scrapes with Black and Leonard.

"I'm gonna miss you guys," said Savanna as she accepted a small cardboard box from Nowitzke. "Wow, I can't believe they got all of Leonard's ashes in this dinky carton. He's going home in first class today, even though he'll be in the overhead bin. He'll even have some company up there." She took Bobilly from her purse then paused, her gaze shifting to the detectives in front of her. "Listen, guys, I've always sucked at goodbyes. I'm sorry I didn't tell you about why I was here in the first place," she said earnestly. "You're both pros, and in the end, we helped each other finally get some justice for Sandy after so long. I hope you will remember me as a friend."

With that, Savanna turned toward the entrance of the airport, picked up her bags, and took a couple of steps before dropping them and running back to the detectives. "You're not getting off that easy,

Chuck," she said, planting a big kiss on his lips. She then looked at Anissa, smirked, and gave her a gentle hug. "You take care, Nis. Hey, maybe you can both come to Toronto next summer for a reunion?" Savanna jabbered nervously, turning back towards the terminal entrance door. "Canada's got lots of fun stuff. Cold beer. Fishing. Shopping. Great food. Hockey . . ." Her voice faded as she stepped into the building.

Once Savanna was gone, Nowitzke could only shake his head.

"She's incorrigible," offered Anissa, looking at her partner.

Nowitzke could only chuckle, nodding in agreement before taking on a more somber look. "What did you think of the funeral this morning?" he asked flatly, watching the sky as a plane came in for a landing.

At the question, Anissa closed her eyes and bit her lower lip. "Will was too young to die. It was a fitting send-off, but I hate going to them."

"We all do. Part of the job, I guess."

"The whole thing was a stark reminder that the lives of cops always hang in the balance at any given moment," she added, then after a pause, asked, "How are you doing, Chuck?"

He never took his eyes off the plane. "I'm struggling with this one," he said, shaking his head and letting out a deep sigh.

Anissa stepped closer to her boss and gave him a hug.

"Well, I've gotta run," said Nowitzke. "I'm having a drink with Natalie to get things sorted out with her. Any advice for me?"

"Yeah . . ." Anissa replied. "Wipe that fire-engine red lipstick off your face before you get there, or you might be dead on arrival. See you at Miss Alma's for dinner tonight?"

"Unless I get a better offer from Natalie."

****

Twenty minutes later, Nowitzke's car came to a stop on the street in front of Natalie's home. As he sat in his car, he felt his heart racing, unsure of what was going to happen. He finally got out of the vehicle and stepped onto the front walk, immediately smelling smoke, presumably from a wood fire smoldering in her backyard. *A good sign.* They had not seen each other in weeks since Nowitzke had to deal with the fallout from the investigation of Hawkins, Gordon, and the confrontation at Ivy House. In fact, they had only had a couple short phone calls since Natalie had been released from the hospital a week before. During their conversations, Nowitzke hadn't raised his discussion with Georg about the pending divorce, hoping rather to talk about it with Natalie in person. Approaching her front door, he felt those same nerves that he did the first time he had made that walk. However, any anxiety quickly melted away when he saw her smiling at him through the screen door. *A better sign.*

Natalie was wearing a red halter top and shorts, her feet bare and her grey hair tied back. She looked comfortable, even with her arm in a cast and sling. Pushing the door open, she greeted the detective with a deep kiss and gentle embrace. "Can I get you a beer?"

"Thought you'd never ask." Nowitzke trailed her into the kitchen where she grabbed two cans from the refrigerator. Moments later, they took up familiar positions near the fire pit in the secluded backyard. Each dropped gently into their chair with a respective tired groan. Natalie reached over and took Nowitzke's hand as they sat together in silence, the crackle of the fire the only sound. In minutes, Nowitzke finished his beer, crushed the can in his hands, and tossed it into the flame.

"Would you like another beer?" asked Natalie in her throaty voice. "Or would you rather come upstairs with me?"

"Is that a trick question?" he asked, surprised.

She rose and looked back at him, cocking her head, but said nothing.

"You sure you're up for it, with your injuries and all?"

Natalie grinned and began walking toward the back door, somehow managing to pull off her top along the way despite the cast. The chase up the stairs was on as they each littered the path with their clothes before falling together onto her bed.

A half hour later, they lay next to each other, now spent, but enjoying the touch of the cool breeze flowing through the window into the room over their sweaty bodies. Natalie's head rested on Nowitzke's chest as they pulled up the sheet. Drifting off, he took in her familiar scent once more. *How much better can life get?*

When he felt her stir, Nowitzke opened his eyes, looking into Natalie's dark-brown ones as she lay face-to-face with him.

"I heard you met Georg at the hospital," she said.

"Yeah. He told me he effed up big-time. I didn't say it, but I agreed with him. I figured that you were just about to tell me what was going on with his lawyer on the night Black shot at us."

Natalie blinked hard. "When I woke up from surgery, Georg was sitting in my hospital room. He said he was sorry for what he put me through, that he had no excuses for what he did but was still unable to explain why he left me. He called it the biggest mistake of his life, said he still loved me and that he wanted to stop the divorce, begging me to take him back."

"Jesus, Natalie. He caused you so much pain. You know, most of the time I'm not dialed in to what other people are feeling, but that day when we had our first lunch together, I could see in your face just how much you were hurting."

"Georg's priest told him that our divorce would be a sin against God," she added, starting to tear up.

Great, throw two more offenses onto my list, Nowitzke thought.

"I told Georg that I needed some time to think about what he had done and what was best for *me*."

Nowitzke took a deep breath. "Have you figured it out?"

"Yes, and I'm so sorry, Chuck," she said, now breaking down. "Georg and I have been married for twenty-two years. We were building a great life together, until . . ."

Until the asshole left you flat for no reason. The detective sensed the worst was coming.

"We had everything we needed. A house. A daughter.

Grandchildren. I don't know what else to say." She hesitated for a moment. "I can't throw that all away. I need to stay with Georg. To give it another try."

Nowitzke studied Natalie's curves for the final time, trying to make sense of her mixed message. "Are you sure that's best for you?"

She gave a noncommittal look but said nothing.

"Natalie, I don't get any of this," Nowitzke said, rising to lean on his elbow. "This guy crushed you for no reason even he can explain. I thought we had something special going." He tried to hold in his emotions, but his voice cracked.

"I love you, Chuck. Today, I did this for us, but mostly for me. A way to remember you that will always make me happy." She sounded remorseful yet wore an almost imperceptible smile as she sat up and gathered the blankets around her.

And now, through no fault of his own, Nowitzke's relationship with Natalie had ended. The detective collected his clothing from the stairwell in the most awkward goodbye he could have imagined. As they stood together on the porch, he drew her close and kissed her one final time before making the dead man's walk back to his car, a million unanswered questions still in his head.

****

Nowitzke rolled into Miss Alma's yard just as Anissa slowly climbed out of her Audi.

"Did you know sports cars suck when your body is all busted up?" she asked as he approached to help her.

"Wait until you get older."

Anissa stopped and studied him for a moment. "Smells like wood smoke and sex. I take it things went well with Natalie?"

"Hardly. My Spanish lessons are officially over. Natalie's going back to her husband," he replied blankly.

"Seriously? To the schmuck who dumped her?" Anissa replied, a perplexed look on her face. "I'm sorry, Chuck. I know you had feelings for Natalie."

"Well, at least I didn't fuck things up with her. It was a helluva parting gift though," he concluded. "How are you doing?" He took her arm to steady her as they walked toward the back door of Miss Alma's house.

"It's been a terrible day, starting with the memorial service this morning. I'm hurting, but I'll live. Don't worry about me."

"Sorry. You know that I will, no matter what you say," Nowitzke replied, then chuckled. "Jesus, you're moving as slow as I do."

"Stop that," Anissa said with a laugh that sent a jolt of electricity through her body. "My ribs are killing me. Doc says it'll take some time for them to heal."

"Next thing you know, you'll need to get your prostate checked too," the senior detective offered, making Anissa both laugh and cry again as they hobbled together into the house.

Even though Miss Alma had made an excellent meat and potatoes meal, dinner had taken on a gloomy tone. "Really, Natalie left you?" she asked, shaking her head as she sat at the kitchen table, stroking Sinker.

"Yeah." It was all Nowitzke could muster, his afternoon discussion with Natalie still playing in a loop in his head.

Miss Alma reached for his hand. "Well, this is one helluva Sunday dinner, if you'll excuse my French. First, Savanna goes home. Natalie's moved back in with that jerk of a husband. And Will's service," she said, hesitating as she mentioned the latter. "Would you tell me about that?" The elderly woman winced, part of her not wanting to hear the answer.

Nowitzke studied the table for a moment, then took a deep breath and a sip of the beer sitting in front of him. "Unfortunately, it's always quite the ceremony. Cops dressed in blue, showing up from everywhere. Long lines of police cars of all colors, shapes, and sizes. Headlights blinking, light bars engaged. A coffin draped with

an American flag. The eulogies, some of them real, some political or
tied to an agenda. A twenty-one-gun salute, followed by a lone bugle
playing 'Taps.' And then I always lose it when the bagpipes play
'Amazing Grace,'" added the detective as he stared off into space, his
eyes glistening. "I've seen it too many times. Sad husbands. Crying
wives and kids. Good men and women dying in the line of duty.
God, if I ever have to see it again, it will be too soon."

"But we all know there will be a next time," chimed in Anissa.

Miss Alma closed her eyes. "Chuck, based on what I saw on TV, it
could have easily been you."

"That's crossed my mind more than once. I just keep thinking
about Will," he said dully. "We never hit it off. We were never close. I
told him that he should think about getting into another line of work.
Thought he was in over his head. He had his issues, but he wasn't a bad
guy. All he wanted was to earn my respect. Then he goes and saves my
ass." He wiped his eyes with his fingers and pinched the bridge of his
nose. "Something I'm not sure I'd have the courage to do if I had to."

Anissa and Miss Alma sat quietly, listening as Nowitzke finished
his thoughts, their eyes following the man as he stood and stepped out
of the house. Moments later, he returned with an unopened bottle
of liquor. "Where I'm from, the tradition is to honor a fallen officer
with a toast and a new bottle of scotch. For me, this started when
my mentor was killed. Miss Alma, I know your feelings about hard
alcohol, but would you care to join Anissa and me?"

Miss Alma looked surprised by the invitation but sprang to her
feet to search her cupboards before returning with three juice glasses.
"They're all I have," she apologized, placing them on the table as she
sat down.

"They'll work." Nowitzke poured an inch of the brown alcohol
into each glass before pushing one to each of the ladies. "To Will. May
he rest in peace," he toasted.

Touching glasses, Anissa and Miss Alma repeated, "To Will."

Nowitzke's head bent back, taking one gulp before he snapped the empty glass back on the table. Anissa gasped as the alcohol double-clutched in her throat, but she survived the experience. Miss Alma took a moment to examine the liquor before calmly draining her glass without a peep. "That's very smooth. Twelve-year-old?" she asked.

"You're a sandbagger, Miss Alma," joked Nowitzke. "I thought your rules didn't allow for alcohol."

"The rules don't apply to me, Chuck." The old woman laughed, taking the bottle and refilling each glass. "I need to make one more toast," she said as she looked earnestly at Nowitzke and Anissa. "My life has changed for the better since I met you both. God bless you. You're my family." She closed her eyes briefly as if saying a silent prayer, then opened them wide. "To family!"

"To family," they repeated in unison.

ACKNOWLEDGMENTS

In writing each of my books, I have been fortunate to find subject matter experts that have helped the process. **Bill Larson** continues to be a go-to person regarding police matters, procedure, and in connecting me with other SMEs. In *Numbers Game*, a key contact from Bill was **Dr. Greg Schmunk**. In his role as a forensic pathologist, he has performed thousands of post-mortem examinations and testified in court hundreds of times. Even though his time is in great demand, he patiently answered all my questions that served to expand the depth of my book while adding to the breadth of my character, Dr. F. Walter Schmidt. I am also grateful to my friend, **Lilly Orozco**, for her help in translating several Spanish phrases and confirming their meaning for me.

If I've made any errors in translating fact to fiction in Numbers Game, the fault resides with me.

Finally, special thanks go out to **Shannon Ishizaki** and the team at **Ten16Press** for helping bring another one of my projects over the finish line. **Lauren Blue** did another stellar job in editing, polishing the rough edges, and improving the book. **Pam Parker** offered numerous suggestions and sage advice more than once. And **Kaeley Dunteman** and her team produced yet another attention-grabbing cover.

I thank you all for your help and support.

Also from J. P. Jordan:

MEN OF GOD

Having reluctantly accepted a job from family friend and CEO Emil Swenson, former pararescueman Nick Hayden quickly transitions from rescuing soldiers in Afghanistan to desk jockeying at Weston, a Wisconsin-based insurance company. He's tasked with closing a failing division responsible for insuring religious institutions, but recent investigations surrounding the murder of a formerly insured priest, a known pedophile, leave Nick feeling suspicious. Without any leads except a cryptic letter found at the crime scene, the case quickly goes cold, but another murder of a previously insured religious leader leads Nick to a chilling realization: a serial killer is on the hunt. When more obscure messages lead him to believe the next target has been chosen, the race to stop the ruthless killer begins.

Also from J. P. Jordan:

ALL IN

A professional crew of burglars has cracked several nearly impenetrable safes, stealing millions of dollars in diamonds and gold. Detectives Chuck Nowitzke and Anissa Taylor are called upon to investigate the highly sophisticated theft, but after they arrest one of the prime suspects, he is assassinated by an unknown boogeyman who is pulling the strings on a series of serious crimes against jewelers.

As the increasingly violent pattern of felonies continues, an insurance underwriter begins to receive messages from a mysterious texter making a connection between the crimes. Yet even with this information, law enforcement remains a step behind at every turn, until the unknown informant provides details about a nal heist that will rival all others. Nowitzke and Anissa are in a race against time to stop the dangerous boogeyman before he disappears forever.

www.ingramcontent.com/pod-product-compliance
Lightning Source LLC
Chambersburg PA
CBHW011422010726
47494CB00011B/2466